The Shadow of a Crime

Hall Caine

Complete & Unabridged

Tutis Digital Publishing Private Limited

First published in 1885 as *The Shadow of a Crime*.

This edition published by
Tutis Digital Publishing Pvt Ltd, 2008.

Preface

The central incident of this novel is that most extraordinary of all punishments known to English criminal law, the *peine forte et dure*. The story is not, however, in any sense historical. A sketchy background of stirring history is introduced solely in order to heighten the personal danger of a brave man. The interest is domestic, and, perhaps, in some degree psychological. Around a pathetic piece of old jurisprudence I have gathered a mass of Cumbrian folk-lore and folk-talk with which I have been familiar from earliest youth. To smelt and mould the chaotic memories into an organism such as may serve, among other uses, to give a view of Cumberland life in little, has been the work of one year.

The story, which is now first presented as a whole, has already had a career in the newspapers, and the interest it excited in those quarters has come upon me as a surprise. I was hardly prepared to find that my plain russet-coated dalesmen were in touch with popular sympathy; but they have made me many friends. To me they are very dear, for I have lived their life. It is with no affected regret that I am now parting with these companions to make way for a group of younger comrades.

There is one thing to say which will make it worth while to trouble the reader with this preface. A small portion of the dialogue is written in a much modified form of the Cumbrian dialect. There are four variations of dialect in Cumberland, and perhaps the dialect spoken on the West Coast differs more from the dialect spoken in the Thirlmere Valley than the latter differs from the dialect spoken in North Lancashire. The *patois* problem is not the least serious of the many difficulties the novelist encounters. I have chosen to give a broad outline of Cumbrian dialect, such as bears no more exact relation to the actual speech than a sketch bears to a finished picture. It is right as far as it goes.

A word as to the background of history. I shall look for the sympathy of the artist and the forgiveness of the historian in making two or three trifling legal anachronisms that do not interfere with the interest of the narrative. The year of the story is given, but the aim has been to reflect in these pages the black cloud of the whole period of the Restoration as it hung over England's remotest solitudes. In my rude sketch of the beginnings of the Quaker movement I must disclaim any intention of depicting the precise manners or indicating the exact doctrinal beliefs of the revivalists. If, however, I have described the Quakers as singing and praying with the fervor of the Methodists, it must not be forgotten that Quietism was no salient part of the Quakerism of Fox; and if I have hinted at Calvinism, it must be remembered that the "dividing of God's heritage" was one of the causes of the first schism in the Quaker Society.

H.C.

New Court, Lincoln's Inn.

CHAPTER I

The City of Wythburn

Tar-ry woo', tar-ry woo',
Tar-ry woo' is ill to spin:
Card it weel, card it weel,
Card it weel ere you begin.

Old Ballad.

The city of Wythburn stood in a narrow valley at the foot of Lauvellen, and at the head of Bracken Water. It was a little but populous village, inhabited chiefly by sheep farmers, whose flocks grazed on the neighboring hills. It contained rather less than a hundred houses, all deep thatched and thick walled. To the north lay the mere, a long and irregular water, which was belted across the middle by an old Roman bridge of bowlders. A bare pack-horse road wound its way on the west, and stretched out of sight to the north and to the south. On this road, about half a mile within the southernmost extremity of Bracken Water, two hillocks met, leaving a natural opening between them and a path that went up to where the city stood. The dalesmen called the cleft between the hillocks the city gates; but why the gates and why the city none could rightly say. Folks had always given them these names. The wiser heads shook gravely as they told you that city should be sarnty, meaning the house by the causeway. The historians of the plain could say no more.

They were rude sons and daughters of the hills who inhabited this mountain home two centuries ago. The country around them was alive with ghostly legend. They had seen the lights dance across Deer Garth Ghyll, and had heard the wail that came from Clark's Loup. They were not above trembling at the mention of these mysteries when the moon was flying across a darksome sky, when the wind moaned about the house, and they were gathered around the ingle nook. They had few channels of communication with the great world without. The pack-horse pedler was their swiftest newsman; the pedler on foot was their weekly budget. Five miles along the pack-horse road to the north stood their market town of Gaskarth, where they took their wool or the cloth they had woven from it. From the top of Lauvellen they could see the white sails of the ships that floated down the broad Solway. These were all but their only glimpses of the world beyond their mountains. It was

1

a mysterious and fearsome world.

There was, however, one link that connected the people of Wythburn with the world outside. To the north of the city and the mere there lived a family of sheep farmers who were known as the Rays of Shoulthwaite Moss. The family consisted of husband and wife and two sons. The head of the house, Angus Ray, came to the district early in life from the extreme Cumbrian border. He was hardly less than a giant in stature. He had limbs of great length, and muscles like the gnarled heads of a beech. Upon settling at Wythburn, he speedily acquired property of various kinds, and in the course of a few years he was the largest owner of sheep on the country side. Certainly, fortune favored Angus Ray, and not least noticeably when in due course he looked about him for a wife.

Mary Ray did not seem to have many qualities in common with her husband. She had neither the strength of limb nor the agile grace of the mountaineer. This was partly the result of the conditions under which her girlhood had been spent. She was the only child of a dalesman, who had so far accumulated estate in land as to be known in the vernacular as a statesman. Her mother had died at her birth, and before she had attained to young womanhood her father, who had married late in life, was feeble and unfit for labor. His hand was too nervous, his eye too uncertain, his breath too short for the constant risks of mountaineering; so he put away all further thought of adding store to store, and settled himself peaceably in his cottage under Castenand, content with the occasional pleasures afforded by his fiddle, an instrument upon which he had from his youth upward shown some skill. In this quiet life his daughter was his sole companion.

There was no sight in Wythburn more touching than to see this girl solacing her father's declining years, meeting his wishes with anticipatory devices, pampering him in his whims, soothing him in the imaginary sorrows sometimes incident to age, even indulging him with a sort of pathetic humor in his frequent hallucinations. To do this she had to put by a good many felicities dear to her age and condition, but there was no apparent consciousness of self-sacrifice. She had many lovers, for in these early years she was beautiful; and she had yet more suitors, for she was accounted rich. But neither flattery nor the fervor of genuine passion seemed to touch her, and those who sought her under the transparent guise of seeking her father usually went away as they came. She had a smile and the cheeriest word of welcome for all alike, and so the young dalesmen who wooed her from the ignoble motive came to think her a little of a coquette, while those who wooed her from the purer impulse despaired of ruffling with the gentlest gales of love the still atmosphere of her heart.

One day suddenly, however, the old statesman died, and his fiddle was heard no more across the valley in the quiet of the evening, but was left untouched for the dust to gather on it where he himself had hung it on the nail in the kitchen under his hat. Then when life seemed to the forlorn girl a wide blank, a world without a sun in it, Angus Ray went over for the first time as a suitor to the cottage under Castenand, and put his hand in hers and looked calmly into her eyes. He told her that a girl could not live long an unfriended life like hers – that she should not if she could; she could not if she would – would she not come to him?

It was the force of the magnet to the steel. With swimming eyes she looked up into his strong face, tender now with a tremor never before seen there; and as he drew her gently towards him her glistening tears fell hot and fast over her brightening and now radiant face, and, as though to hide them from him, she laid her head on his breast. This was all the wooing of Angus Ray.

They had two sons, and of these the younger more nearly resembled his mother. Willy Ray had not merely his mother's features; he had her disposition also. He had the rounded neck and lissom limbs of a woman; he had a woman's complexion, and the light of a woman's look in his soft blue eyes. When the years gave a thin curly beard to his cheek they took nothing from its delicate comeliness. It was as if nature had down to the last moment meant Willy for a girl. He had been an apt scholar at school, and was one of the few persons in Wythburn having claims to education. Willy's elder brother, Ralph, more nearly resembled his father. He had his father's stature and strength of limb, but some of his mother's qualities had also been inherited by him. In manner he was neither so austere and taciturn as his father, nor so gentle and amiable as his mother. He was by no means a scholar, and only the strong hand of his father had kept him as a boy in fear of the penalties incurred by the truant. Courage and resolution were his distinguishing characteristics.

On one occasion, when rambling over the fells with a company of schoolfellows, a poor blind lamb ran bleating past them, a black cloud of ravens, crows, and owl-eagles flying about it. The merciless birds had fallen upon the innocent creature as it lay sleeping under the shadow of a tree, had picked at its eyes and fed on them, and now, as the blood trickled in red beads down its nose, they croaked and cried and screamed to drive it to the edge of a precipice and then over to its death in the gulf beneath, there to feast on its carcass. It was no easy thing to fend off the cruel birds when in sight of their prey, but, running and capturing the poor lamb, Ralph snatched it up in his arms at the peril of his own eyes, and swung a staff about his head to beat off the birds as they darted and plunged and shrieked about him.

It was natural that a boy like this should develop into the finest shepherd on the hills. Ralph knew every path on the mountains, every shelter the sheep sought from wind and rain, every haunt of the fox. At the shearing, at the washing, at the marking, his hand was among the best; and when the flocks had to be numbered as they rushed in thousands through the gate, he could count them, not by ones and twos, but by fours and sixes. At the shearing feasts he was not above the pleasures of the country dance, the Ledder-te-spetch, as it was called, with its one, two, three – heel and toe – cut and shuffle. And his strong voice, that was answered oftenest by the echo of the mountain cavern, was sometimes heard to troll out a snatch of a song at the village inn. But Ralph, though having an inclination to convivial pleasures, was naturally of a serious, even of a solemn temperament. He was a rude son of a rude country, – rude of hand, often rude of tongue, untutored in the graces that give beauty to life.

By the time that Ralph had attained to the full maturity of his manhood, the struggles of King and Parliament were at their height. The rumor of these struggles was long in reaching the city of Wythburn, and longer in being discussed and understood there; but, to everybody's surprise, young Ralph Ray announced his intention of forthwith joining the Parliamentarian forces. The extraordinary proposal seemed incredible; but Ralph's mind was made up. His father said nothing about his son's intentions, good or bad. The lad was of age; he might think for himself. In his secret heart Angus liked the lad's courage. Ralph was "nane o' yer feckless fowk." Ralph's mother was sorely troubled; but just as she had yielded to his father's will in the days that were long gone by, so she yielded now to his. The intervening years had brought an added gentleness to her character; they had made mellower her dear face, now ruddy and round, though wrinkled. Folks said she had looked happier and happier, and had talked less and less, as the time wore on. It had become a saying in Wythburn that the dame of Shoulthwaite Moss was never seen without a smile, and never heard to say more than "God bless you!" The tears filled her eyes when her son came to kiss her on the morning when he left her home for the first time, but she wiped them away with her housewife's apron, and dismissed him with her accustomed blessing.

Ralph Ray joined Cromwell's army against the second Charles at Dunbar, in 1650. Between two and three years afterwards he returned to Wythburn city and resumed his old life on the fells. There was little more for the train-bands to do. Charles had fled, peace was restored, the Long Parliament was dissolved, Cromwell was Lord Protector. Outwardly the young Roundhead was not altered by the campaign. He had passed through it unscathed. He was somewhat graver in manner; there seemed to be a little less warmth and spontaneity in his greeting; his voice had lost one or two of its cheerier notes; his laughter was less hearty and more easily controlled. Perhaps this only meant that the world was doing its work with him. Otherwise he was the same man.

When Ralph returned to Wythburn he brought with him a companion much older than himself, who forthwith became an inmate of his father's home, taking part as a servant in the ordinary occupations of the male members of the household. This man had altogether a suspicious and sinister aspect which his manners did nothing to belie. His name was James Wilson, and he was undoubtedly a Scot, though he had neither the physical nor the moral characteristics of his race. His eyes were small, quick, and watchful, beneath heavy and jagged brows. He was slight of figure and low of stature, and limped on one leg. He spoke in a thin voice, half laugh, half whimper, and hardly ever looked into the face of the person with whom he was conversing. There was an air of mystery about him which the inmates of the house on the Moss did nothing to dissipate. Ralph offered no explanation to the gossips of Wythburn of Wilson's identity and belongings; indeed, as time wore on, it could be observed that he showed some uneasiness when questioned about the man.

At first Wilson contrived to ingratiate himself into a good deal of favor among the dalespeople. There was then an insinuating smoothness in his speech, a flattering, almost fawning glibness of tongue, which the simple folks knew no art to withstand. He seemed abundantly grateful for some unexplained benefits received from Ralph. "Atweel," Wilson would say, with his eyes on the ground, – "atweel I lo'e the braw chiel as 'twere my ain guid billie."

Ralph paid no heed to the brotherly protestations of his admirer, and exchanged only such words with him as their occupations required. Old Angus, however, was not so passive an observer of his new and unlooked-for housemate. "He's a good for nought sort of a fellow, slenken frae place to place wi' nowt but a sark to his back," Angus would say to his wife. Mr. Wilson's physical imperfections were an offence in the dalesman's eyes: "He's as widderful in his wizzent old skin as his own grandfather." Angus was not less severe on Wilson's sly smoothness of manner. "Yon sneaking old knave," he would say, "is as slape as an eel in the beck; he'd wammel himself into crookedest rabbit hole on the fell." Probably Angus entertained some of the antipathy to Scotchmen which was peculiar to his age. "I'll swear he's a taistrel," he said one day; "I dare not trust him with a mess of poddish until I'd had the first sup."

In spite of this determined disbelief on the part of the head of the family, old Wilson remained for a long time a member of the household at Shoulthwaite Moss, following his occupations with constancy, and always obsequious in the acknowledgment of his obligations. It was observed that he manifested a peculiar eagerness when through any stray channel intelligence was received in the valley of the sayings and doings in the world outside. Nothing was thought of this until one day the passing pedler brought the startling news that the Lord Protector was dead. The family were at breakfast in the kitchen of the old house when this tardy representative of the herald Mercury arrived, and, in reply to the customary inquiry as to the news he carried, announced the aforesaid fact. Wilson was alive to its significance with a curious wakefulness.

"It's braw tidings ye bring the day, man," he stammered with evident concern, and with an effort to hide his nervousness.

"Yes, the old man's dead," said the pedler, with an air of consequence commensurate with his message. "I reckon," he added, "Oliver's son Richard will be Protector now."

"A sairy carle, that same Richard," answered Wilson; "I wot th' young Charles 'ul soon come by his ain, and then ilka ane amang us 'ul see a bonnie war-day. We've playt at shinty lang eneugh. Braw news, man – braw news that the corbie's deid."

Wilson had never before been heard to say so much or to speak so vehemently. He got up from the table in his nervousness, and walked aimlessly across the floor.

"Why are you poapan about," asked Angus, in amazement; "snowkin like a pig at a sow?"

6

At this the sinister light in Wilson's eyes that had been held in check hitherto seemed at once to flash out, and he turned hotly upon his master, as though to retort sneer for sneer. But, checking himself, he took up his bonnet and made for the door.

"Don't look at me like that," Angus called after him, "or, maybe I'll clash the door in thy face."

Wilson had gone by this time, and turning to his sons, Angus continued, –

"Did you see how the waistrel snirpt up his nose when the pedler said Cromwell was dead?"

It was obvious that something more was soon to be made known relative to their farm servant. The pedler had no difficulty in coming to the conclusion that Wilson was some secret spy, some disguised enemy of the Commonwealth, and perhaps some Fifth Monarchy man, and a rank Papist to boot. Mrs. Ray's serene face was unruffled; she was sure the poor man meant no harm. Ralph was silent, as usual, but he looked troubled, and getting up from the table soon afterwards he followed the man whom he had brought under his father's roof, and who seemed likely to cause dissension there.

Not long after this eventful morning, Ralph overheard his father and Wilson in hot dispute at the other side of a hedge. He could learn nothing of a definite nature. Angus was at the full pitch of indignation. Wilson, he said, had threatened him; or, at least, his own flesh and blood. He had told the man never to come near Shoulthwaite Moss again.

"An' he does," said the dalesman, his eyes aflame, "I'll toitle him into the beck till he's as wankle as a wet sack."

He was not so old but that he could have kept his word. His great frame seemed closer knit at sixty than it had been at thirty. His face, with its long, square, gray beard, looked severer than ever under his cloth hood. Wilson returned no more, and the promise of a drenching was never fulfilled.

The ungainly little Scot did not leave the Wythburn district. He pitched his tent with the village tailor in a little house at Fornside, close by the Moss. The tailor himself, Simeon Stagg, was kept pitiably poor in that country, when one sack coat of homespun cloth lasted a shepherd half a lifetime. He would have lived a solitary as well as a miserable life but for his daughter Rotha, a girl of nineteen, who kept his little home together and shared his poverty when she might have enjoyed the comforts of easier homes elsewhere.

"Your father is nothing but an ache and a stound to you, lass," Sim would say in a whimper. "It'll be well for you, Rotha, when you give me my last top-sark and take me to the kirkyard yonder," the little man would snuffle audibly.

"Hush, father," the girl would say, putting the palm of her hand playfully over his mouth, "you'll be sonsie-looking yet."

Sim was heavily in debt, and this preyed on his mind. He had always been a grewsome body, sustaining none of the traditions of his craft for perky gossip. Hence he was no favorite in Wythburn, where few or none visited him. Latterly Sim's troubles seemed to drive him from his home for long walks in the night. While the daylight lasted his work gave occupation to his mind, but when the darkness came on he had no escape from haunting thoughts, and roamed about the lanes in an effort to banish them. It was to this man's home that Wilson turned when he was shut out of Shoulthwaite Moss. Naturally enough, the sinister Scot was a welcome if not an agreeable guest when he came as lodger, with money to pay, where poverty itself seemed host.

Old Wilson had not chosen the tailor's house as his home on account of any comforts it might be expected to afford him. He had his own reasons for not quitting Wythburn after he had received his very unequivocal "sneck posset." "Better a wee bush," he would say, "than na bield". Shelter certainly the tailor's home afforded him; and that was all that he required for the present. Wilson had not been long in the tailor's cottage before Sim seemed to grow uneasy under a fresh anxiety, of which his lodger was the subject. Wilson's manners had obviously undergone a change. His early smoothness, his slavering glibness, had disappeared. He was now as bitter of speech as he had formerly been conciliatory. With Sim and his troubles, real and imaginary, he was not at all careful to exhibit sympathy. "Weel, weel, ye must lie heids and thraws wi' poverty, like Jock an' his mither"; or, "If ye canna keep geese ye mun keep gezlins."

Sim was in debt to his landlord, and over the idea of ejectment from his little dwelling the tailor would brood day and night. Folks said he was going crazed about it. None the less was Sim's distress as poignant as if the grounds for it had been more real. "Haud thy bletherin' gab," Wilson said one day; "because ye have to be cannie wi' the cream ye think ye must surely be clemm'd." Salutary as some of the Scotsman's comments may have been, it was natural that the change in his manners should excite surprise among the dalespeople. The good people expressed themselves as "fairly maizelt" by the transformation. What did it all mean? There was surely something behind it.

The barbarity of Wilson's speech was especially malicious when directed against the poor folks with whom he lived, and who, being conscious of how essential he was to the stability of the household, were largely at his mercy. It happened on one occasion that when Wilson returned to the cottage after a day's absence, he found Sim's daughter weeping over the fire.

"What's now?" he asked. "Have ye nothing in the kail?"

Rotha signified that his supper was ready.

"Thou limmer," said Wilson, in his thin shriek, "how long 'ul thy dool last? It's na mair to see a woman greet than to see a goose gang barefit."

Ralph Ray called at the tailor's cottage the morning after this, and found Sim suffering under violent excitement, of which Wilson's behavior to Rotha had been the cause. The insults offered to himself he had taken with a wince, perhaps, but without a retort. Now that his daughter was made the subject of them, he was profoundly agitated.

"There I sat," he cried, as his breath came and went in gusts, – "there I sat, a poor barrow-back't creature, and heard that old savvorless loon spit his spite at my lass. I'm none of a brave man, Ralph: no, I must be a coward, but I went nigh to snatching up yon flail of his and striking him – aye, killing him! – but no, it must be that I'm a coward."

Ralph quieted him as well as he could, telling him to leave this thing to him. Ralph was perhaps Sim's only friend. He would often turn in like this at Sim's workroom as he passed up the fell in the morning. People said the tailor was indebted to Ralph for proofs of friendship more substantial than sympathy. And now, when Sim had the promise of a strong friend's shoulder to lean on, he was unmanned, and wept. Ralph was not unmoved as he stood by the forlorn little man, and clasped his hands in his own and felt the warm tears fall over them.

As the young dalesman was leaving the cottage that morning, he encountered in the porch the subject of the conversation, who was entering in. Taking him firmly but quietly by the shoulder, he led him back a few paces. Sim had leapt up from his bench, and was peering eagerly through the window. But Ralph did no violence to his lodger. He was saying something with marked emphasis, but the words escaped the tailor's ears. Wilson was answering nothing. Loosing his hold of him, Ralph walked quietly away. Wilson entered the cottage with a livid face, and murmuring, as though to himself, –

"Aiblins we may be quits yet, my chiel'. A great stour has begoon, my birkie. Your fire-flaucht e'e wull na fley me. Your Cromwell's gane, an' all traitors shall tryste wi' the hangman."

It was clear that whatever the mystery pertaining to the Scotchman, Simeon Stagg seemed to possess some knowledge of it. Not that he ever explained anything. His anxiety to avoid all questions about his lodger was sufficiently obvious. Yet that he had somehow obtained some hint of a dark side to Wilson's character, every one felt satisfied. No other person seemed to know with certainty what were Wilson's means of livelihood. The Scotchman was not employed by the farmers and shepherds around Wythburn, and he had neither land nor sheep of his own. He would set out early and return late, usually walking in the direction of Gaskarth. One day Wilson rose at daybreak, and putting a threshing-flail over his shoulder, said he would be away for a week. That week ensuing was a quiet one for the inmates of the cottage at Fornside.

Sim's daughter, Rotha, had about this time become a constant helper at Shoulthwaite Moss, where, indeed, she was treated with the cordiality proper to a member of the household. Old Angus had but little sympathy to spare for the girl's father, but he liked Rotha's own cheerfulness, her winsomeness, and, not least, her usefulness. She could milk and churn, and bake and brew. This was the sort of young woman that Angus liked best. "Rotha's a right heartsome lassie," he said, as he heard her in the dairy singing while she worked. The dame of Shoulthwaite loved every one, apparently, but there were special corners in her heart for her favorites, and Rotha was one of them.

"Cannot that lass's father earn aught without keeping yon sulking waistrel about him?" asked the old dalesman one day.

It was the first time he had spoken of Wilson since the threatened ducking. Being told of Wilson's violence to Rotha, he only said, "It's an old saying, 'A blate cat makes a proud mouse.'" Angus was never heard to speak of Wilson again.

Nature seemed to have meant Rotha for a blithe, bird-like soul, but there were darker threads woven into the woof of her natural brightness. She was tall, slight of figure, with a little head of almost elfish beauty. At milking, at churning, at baking, her voice could be heard, generally singing her favorite border song: –

> "Gae tak this bonnie neb o' mine,
> That pecks amang the corn,
> An' gi'e't to the Duke o' Hamilton
> To be a touting horn."

"Robin Redbreast has a blithe interpreter," said Willy Ray, as he leaned for a moment against the open door of the dairy in passing out. Rotha was there singing, while in a snow-white apron, and with arms bare above the elbows, she weighed the butter of the last churning into pats, and marked each pat with a rude old mark. The girl dropped her head and blushed as Willy spoke. Of late she had grown unable to look the young man in the face. Willy did not speak again. His face colored, and he went away. Rotha's manner towards Ralph was different. He spoke to her but rarely, and when he did so she looked frankly into his face. If she met him abroad, as she sometimes did when carrying water from the well, he would lift her pails in his stronger hands over the stile, and at such times the girl thought his voice seemed softer.

"I am thinking," said Mrs. Ray to her husband, as she was spinning in the kitchen at Shoulthwaite Moss, – "I am thinking," she said, stopping the wheel and running her fingers through the wool, "that Willy is partial to the little tailor's winsome lass."

"And what aboot Ralph?" asked Angus.

CHAPTER II

The Crime in the Night

On the evening of the day upon which old Wilson was expected back at Fornside, Ralph Ray turned in at the tailor's cottage. Sim's distress was, if possible, even greater than before. It seemed as if the gloomy forebodings of the villagers were actually about to be realized, and Sim's mind was really giving way. His staring eyes, his unconscious, preoccupied manner as he tramped to and fro in his little work-room, sitting at intervals, rising again and resuming his perambulations, now gathering up his tools and now opening them out afresh, talking meantime in fitful outbursts, sometimes wholly irrelevantly and occasionally with a startling pertinency, – all this, though no more than an excess of his customary habit, seemed to denote a mind unstrung. The landlord had called that morning for his rent, which was long in arrears. He must have it. Sim laughed when he told Ralph this, but it was a shocking laugh; there was no heart in it. Ralph would rather have heard him whimper and shuffle as he had done before.

"You shall not be homeless, Sim, if the worst comes to the worst," he said.

"Homeless, not I!" and the little man laughed again. Ralph felt unease. This change was not for the better. Rotha had been sitting at the window to catch the last glimmer of daylight as she spun. It was dusk, but not yet too dark for Ralph to see the tears standing in her eyes. Presently she rose and went out of the room.

"Never fear that I shall be clemm'd," said Sim. "No, no," he said, with a grin of satisfied assurance.

"God forbid!" said Ralph, "but things should be better soon. This is the back end, you know."

"Aye," answered the tailor, with a shrug that resembled a shiver.

"And they say," continued Ralph, "the back end is always the bare end."

"And they say, too," said Sim, "change is leetsome, if it's only out of bed into the beck!"

The tailor laughed loud, and then stopped himself with a suddenness quite startling. The jest sounded awful on his lips. "You say the back end's the bare end," he said, coming up to where Ralph sat in pain and amazement; "mine's all bare end. It's nothing but 'bare end' for some of us. Yesterday morning was wet and cold – you know how cold it was. Well, Rotha had hardly gone out when a tap came to the door, and what do you think it was? A woman, a woman thin and blear-eyed. Some one must have counted her face bonnie once. She was scarce older than my own lass, but she'd a poor weak barn at her breast and a wee lad that trudged at her side. She was wet and cold, and asked for rest and shelter for herself and the children-rest and shelter," repeated the tailor in a lower tone, as though muttering to himself, – "rest and shelter, and from me."

"Well?" inquired Ralph, not noticing Sim's self-reference.

"Well?" echoed Sim, as though Ralph should have divined the sequel.

"Had the poor creature been turned out of her home?"

"That and worse," said the little tailor, his frame quivering with emotion. "Do you know the king's come by his own again?" Sim was speaking in an accent of the bitterest mockery.

"Worse luck," said Ralph; "but what of that?"

"Why," said Sim, almost screaming, "that every man in the land who fought for the Commonwealth eight years ago is like to be shot as a traitor. Didn't you know that, my lad?" And the little man put his hands with a feverish clutch on Ralph's shoulders, and looked into his face.

For an instant there was a tremor on the young dalesman's features, but it lasted only long enough for Sim to recognize it, and then the old firmness returned.

"But what of the poor woman and her barns?" Ralph said, quietly.

"Her husband, an old Roundhead, had fled from a warrant for his arrest. She had been cast homeless into the road, she and all her household; her aged mother had died of exposure the first bitter night, and now for two long weeks she had walked on and on – on and on – her children with her – on and on – living Heaven knows how!"

A light now seemed to Ralph to be cast on the great change in his friend; but was it indeed fear for his (Ralph's) well-being that had goaded poor Sim to a despair so near allied to madness?

"What about Wilson?" he asked, after a pause.

The tailor started at the name.

"I don't know – I don't know at all," he answered, as though eager to assert the truth of a statement never called into dispute.

"Does he intend to come back to Fornside to-night, Sim?"

"So he said."

"What, think you, is his work at Gaskarth?"

"I don't know – I know nothing – at least – no, nothing."

Ralph was sure now. Sim was too eager to disclaim all knowledge of his lodger's doings. He would not recognize the connection between the former and present subjects of conversation.

The night had gathered in, and the room was dark except for the glimmer of a little fire on the open hearth. The young dalesman looked long into it: his breast heaved with emotion, and for the first time in his manhood big tears stood in his eyes. It must be so; it must be that this poor forlorn creature, who had passed through sufferings of his own, and borne them, was now shattered and undone at the prospect of disaster to his friend. Did he know more than he had said? It was vain to ask. Would he – do anything? Ralph glanced at the little man: barrow-backed he was, as he had himself said. No, the idea seemed monstrous. The young man rose to go; he could not speak, but he took Sim's hand in his and held it. Then he stooped and kissed him on the cheek.

Next morning, soon after daybreak, all Wythburn was astir. People were hurrying about from door to door and knocking up the few remaining sleepers. The voices of the men sounded hoarse in the mist of the early morning; the women held their heads together and talked in whispers. An hour or two later two or three horsemen drove up to the door of the village inn. There was a bustle within; groups of boys were congregated outside. Something terrible had happened in the night.

What was it?

Willie Ray, who had left home at early dawn, came back to Shoulthwaite Moss with flushed face and quick-coming breath. Ralph and his mother were at breakfast. His father, who had been at market the preceding day, had not risen.

"Dreadful, dreadful!" cried Willy. "Old Wilson is dead. Found dead in the dike between Smeathwaite and Fornside. Murdered, no doubt, for his wages; nothing left about him."

"Heaven bless us!" cried Mrs. Ray, "to kill a poor man for his week's wage!" And she sank back into the chair from which she had risen in her amazement.

"They've taken his body to the Red Lion, and the coroner is there from Gaskarth."

Willy was trembling in every limb.

Ralph rose as one stupefied. He said nothing, but taking down his hat he went out. Willy looked after him, and marked that he took the road to Fornside.

When he got there he found the little cottage besieged. Crowds of women and boys stood round the porch and peered in at the window. Ralph pushed his way through them and into the house. In the kitchen were the men from Gaskarth and many more. On a chair near the cold hearth, where no fire had been kindled since he last saw it, sat Sim with glassy eyes. His neck was bare and his clothes disordered. At his back stood Rotha, with her arms thrown round her father's neck. His long, thin fingers were clutching her clasped hands as with a vise.

"You must come with us," said one of the strangers, addressing the tailor. He was justice and coroner of the district.

Sim said nothing and did not stir. Then the young girl's voice broke the dreadful silence.

"Come, father; let us go."

Sim rose at this, and walked like one in a dream. Ralph took his arm, and as the people crowded upon them, he pushed them aside, and they passed out.

The direction of the company through the gray mist of that morning was towards the place where the body lay. Sim was to be accused of the crime. After the preliminaries of investigation were gone through, the witnesses were called. None had seen the murder. The body of the murdered man had been found by a laborer. There was a huge sharp stone under the head, and death seemed to have resulted from a fracture of the skull caused by a heavy fall. There was no appearance of a blow. As to Sim, the circumstantial evidence looked grave. Old Wilson had been seen to pass through Smeathwaite after dark; he must have done so to reach his lodgings at the tailor's house. Sim had been seen abroad about the same hour. This was not serious; but now came Sim's landlord. He had called on the tailor the previous morning for his rent and could not get it. Late the same night Sim had knocked at his door with the money.

"When I ax't him where he'd come from so late," said the man, "he glower't at me daiztlike, and said nought."

"What was his appearance?"

"His claes were a' awry, and he keep't looking ahint him."

At this there was a murmur among the bystanders. There could not be a doubt of Sim's guilt.

At a moment of silence Ralph stepped out. He seemed much moved. Might he ask the witnesses some questions? Certainly. It was against the rule, but still he might do so. Then he inquired exactly into the nature of the wound that had apparently caused death. He asked for precise information as to the stone on which the head of the deceased was found lying.

It lay fifty yards to the south of the bridge.

Then he argued that as there was no wound on the dead man other than the fracture of the skull, it was plain that death had resulted from a fall. How the deceased had come by that fall was now the question. Was it not presumable that he had slipped his foot and had fallen? He reminded them that Wilson was lame on one leg. If the fall were the result of a blow, was it not preposterous to suppose that a man of Sim's slight physique could have inflicted it? Under ordinary circumstances, only a more powerful man than Wilson himself could have killed him by a fall.

At this the murmur rose again among the bystanders, but it sounded to Ralph like the murmur of beasts being robbed of their prey.

As to the tailor having been seen abroad at night, was not that the commonest occurrence? With the evidence of Sim's landlord Ralph did not deal.

It was plain that Sim could not be held over for trial on evidence such as was before them. He was discharged, and an open verdict was returned. The spectators were not satisfied, however, to receive the tailor back again as an innocent man. Would he go upstairs and look at the body? There was a superstition among them that a dead body would bleed at a touch from the hand of the murderer. Sim said nothing, but stared wildly about him.

"Come, father," said Rotha, "do as they wish."

The little man permitted himself to be led into the room above. Ralph followed with a reluctant step. He had cleared his friend, but looked more troubled than before. When the company reached the bedside, Ralph stood at its head while one of the men took a cloth off the dead man's face.

There was a stain of earth on it.

Then they drew Sim up in front of it. When his eyes fell on the white, upturned face, he uttered a wild cry and fell senseless to the floor. Ha! The murmur rose afresh. Then there was a dead silence. Rotha was the first to break the awful stillness. She knelt over her father's prostrate form, and said amid stifling sobs, –

"Tell them it is not true; tell them so, father."

The murmur came again. She understood it, and rose up with flashing eyes.

"*I* tell them it is not true," she said. Then stepping firmly to the bedside, she cried, "Look you all! I, his daughter, touch here this dead man's hand, and call on God to give a sign if my father did this thing."

So saying, she took the hand of the murdered man, and held it convulsively in her own.

The murmur died to a hush of suspense and horror. The body remained unchanged. Loosing her grip, she turned on the bystanders with a look of mingled pride and scorn.

"Take this from heaven for a witness that my father is innocent."

The tension was too much for the spectators, and one by one they left the room. Ralph only remained, and when Sim returned to consciousness he raised him up, and took him back to Fornside.

CHAPTER III

In the Red Lion

What hempen homespuns have we swaggering here?
                              Midsummer Night's Dream.

Time out of mind there had stood on the high street of Wythburn a modest house of entertainment, known by the sign of the Red Lion. Occasionally it accommodated the casual traveller who took the valley road to the north, but it was intended for the dalesmen, who came there after the darkness had gathered in, and drank a pot of home-brewed ale as they sat above the red turf fire.

This was the house to which Wilson's body had been carried on the morning it was found on the road. That was about Martinmas. One night, early in the ensuing winter, a larger company than usual was seated in the parlor of the little inn. It was a quaint old room, twice as long as it was broad, and with a roof so low that the taller shepherds stooped as they walked under its open beams.

From straps fixed to the rafters hung a gun, a whip, and a horn. Two square windows, that looked out over the narrow causeway, were covered by curtains of red cloth. An oak bench stood in each window recess. The walls throughout were panelled in oak, which was carved here and there in curious archaic devices. The panelling had for the most part grown black with age; the rosier spots, that were polished to the smoothness and brightness of glass, denoted the positions of cupboards. Strong settles and broad chairs stood in irregular places about the floor, which was of the bare earth, grown hard as stone, and now sanded. The chimney nook spanned the width of one end of the room. It was an open ingle with seats in the wall at each end, and the fire on the ground between them. A goat's head and the horns of an ox were the only ornaments of the chimney-breast, which was white-washed.

On this night of 1660 the wind was loud and wild without. The snowstorm that had hung over the head of Castenand in the morning had come down the valley as the day wore on. The heavy sleet rattled at the windows. In its fiercer gusts it drowned the ring of the lusty voices. The little parlor looked warm and snug with its great cobs of old peat glowing red as they burnt away sleepily on the broad hearth. At intervals the door would open and a shepherd would enter. He had housed his sheep for the night, and now, seated as the newest comer on the warmest bench near the fire, with a pipe in one hand and a pot of hot ale in the other, he was troubled by the tempest no more.

"At Michaelmas a good fat goose, at Christmas stannen' pie, and good yal awt year roond," said an old man in the chimney corner. This was Matthew Branthwaite, the wit and sage of Wythburn, once a weaver, but living now on the husbandings of earlier life. He was tall and slight, and somewhat bent with age. He was dressed in a long brown sack coat, belted at the waist, below which were pockets cut perpendicular at the side. Ribbed worsted stockings and heavy shoes made up, with the greater garment, the sum of his visible attire. Old Matthew had a vast reputation for wise saws and proverbs; his speech seemed to be made of little else; and though the dalespeople had heard the old sayings a thousand times, these seemed never to lose anything of their piquancy and rude force.

"It's a bad night, Mattha Branthet," said a new-comer.

"Dost tak me for a born idiot?" asked the old man. "Dost think I duddent known that afore I saw thee, that thou must be blodderen oot,' It's a bad neet, Mattha Branthet?'" There was a dash of rustic spite in the old man's humor which gave it an additional relish.

"Ye munnet think to win through the world on a feather bed, lad," he added.

The man addressed was one Robbie Anderson, a young fellow who had for a long time indulged somewhat freely in the good ale which the sage had just recommended for use all the year round. Every one had said he was going fast to his ruin, making beggars of himself and of all about him. It was, nevertheless, whispered that Robbie was the favored sweetheart among many of Matthew Branthwaite's young daughter Liza; but the old man, who had never been remarkable for sensibility, had said over and over again, "She'll lick a lean poddish stick, Bobbie, that weds the like of thee." Latterly the young man had in a silent way shown some signs of reform. He had not, indeed, given up the good ale to which his downfall had been attributed; but when he came to the Red Lion he seemed to sleep more of his time there than he drank. So the village philosopher had begun to pat him on the back, and say, encouragingly, "There's nowt so far aslew, Bobbie, but good manishment may set it straight."

Robbie accepted his rebuff on this occasion with undisturbed equanimity, and, taking a seat on a bench at the back, seemed soon to be lost in slumber.

The dalesmen are here in strength to-night. Thomas Fell, the miller of Legberthwaite, is here, with rubicund complexion and fully developed nose. Here, too, is Thomas's cousin, Adam Rutledge, fresh from an adventure at Carlisle, where he has tasted the luxury of Doomsdale, a noisome dungeon reserved for witches and murderers, but sometimes tenanted by obstreperous drunkards. Of a more reputable class here is Job Leathes, of Dale Head, a tall, gaunt dalesman, with pale gray eyes. Here is Luke Cockrigg, too, of Aboonbeck Bank; and stout John Jackson, of Armboth, a large and living refutation of the popular fallacy that the companionship of a ghost must necessarily induce such appalling effects as are said to have attended the apparitions which presented themselves to the prophets and seers of the Hebrews. John has slept for twenty years in the room at Armboth in which the spiritual presence is said to walk, and has never yet seen anything more terrible than his own shadow. Here, too, at Matthew Branthwaite's side, sits little blink-eyed Reuben Thwaite, who *has* seen the Armboth bogle. He saw it one night when he was returning home from the Red Lion. It took the peculiar form of a lime-and-mould heap, and, though in Reuben's case the visitation was not attended by convulsions or idiocy, the effect of it was unmistakable. When Reuben awoke next morning he found himself at the bottom of a ditch.

"A wild neet onyways, Mattha," says Reuben, on Robbie Anderson's retirement. "As I com alang I saw yan of Angus Ray haystacks blown flat on to the field – doon it went in a bash – in ya bash frae top to bottom."

"That minds me of Mother Garth and auld Wilson haycocks," said Matthew.

"Why, what was that?" said Reuben.

"Deary me, what thoo minds it weel eneuf. It was the day Wilson was cocking Angus hay in the low meedow. Mistress Garth came by in the evening, and stood in the road opposite to look at the north leets. 'Come, Sarah,' says auld Wilson, 'show us yan of thy cantrips; I divn't care for thee.' But he'd scarce said it when a whirlblast came frae the fell and owerturn't iv'ry cock. Then Sarah she laughed oot loud, and she said, 'Ye'll want na mair cantrips, I reckon.' She was reet theer."

"Like eneuf," said several voices amid a laugh.

"He was hard on Mother Garth was Wilson," continued Matthew; "I nivver could mak ought on it. He called her a witch, and seurly she is a laal bit uncanny."

"Maybe she wasn't always such like," said Mr. Jackson.

"Maybe not, John," said Matthew; "but she was olas a cross-grained yan sin the day she came first to Wy'burn."

"I thought her a harmless young body with her babby,' said Mr. Jackson.

"Let me see," said Reuben Thwaite; "that must be a matter of six-and-twenty year agone."

"Mair ner that," said Matthew. "It was long afore I bought my new loom, and that's six-and-twenty year come Christmas."

"Ey, I mind they said she'd run away frae the man she'd wedded somewhere in the north," observed Adam Rutledge through the pewter which he had raised to his lips. "Ower fond of his pot for Sarah."

"Nowt o' t' sort," said Matthew. "He used to pommel and thresh her up and doon, and that's why she cut away frae him, and that's why she's sic a sour yan."

"Ey, that's reets on it," said Reuben.

"But auld Wilson's spite on her olas did cap me a laal bit," said Matthew again. "He wanted her burnt for a witch. 'It's all stuff and bodderment aboot the witches,' says I to him ya day; 'there be none. God's aboon the devil!' 'Nay, nay,' says Wilson, 'it'll be past jookin' when the heed's off. She'll do something for some of us yit.'"

"Hush," whispered Reuben, as at that moment the door opened and a tall, ungainly young dalesman, with red hair and with a dogged expression of face, entered the inn.

A little later, amid a whirl of piercing wind, Ralph Ray entered, shaking the frozen snow from his cloak with long skirts, wet and cold, his staff in his hand, and his dog at his heels. Old Matthew gave him a cheery welcome.

"It's like ye'd as lief be in this snug room as on the fell to-neet, Ralph?" There was a twinkle in the old man's eye; he had meant more than he said.

"I'd full as soon be here as in Sim's cave, Matthew, if that's what you mean," said Ralph, as he held the palms of his hands to the fire and then rubbed them on his knees.

"Thou wert nivver much of a fool, Ralph," Matthew answered. And with a shovel that facetious occupant of the hearth lifted another cob of turf on to the fire.

"It's lang sin' Sim sat aboon sic a lowe as that," he added, with a motion of his head downwards.

"Worse luck," said Ralph in a low tone, as though trying to avoid the subject.

"Whear the pot's brocken, there let the sherds lie, lad," said the old man; "keep thy breath to cool thy poddish, forby thy mug of yal, and here't comes."

As he spoke the hostess brought up a pot of ale, smoking hot, and put it in Ralph's hand.

"Let every man stand his awn rackups, Ralph. Sim's a bad lot, and reet serv'd."

"You have him there, Mattha Branthet," said the others with a laugh, "a feckless fool." The young dalesman leaned back on the bench, took a draught of his liquor, rested the pot on his knee, and looked into the fire with the steady gaze of one just out of the darkness. After a pause he said quietly, –

"I'll wager there's never a man among you dare go up to Sim's cave to-night. Yet you drive him up there every night of the year."

"Bad dreams, lad; bad dreams," said the old man, shaking his head with portentous gravity, "forby the boggle of auld Wilson – that's maybe what maks Sim ga rakin aboot the fell o' neets without ony eerand."

"Ay, ay, that's aboot it," said the others, removing their pipes together and speaking with the gravity and earnestness of men who had got a grip of the key to some knotty problem. "The ghost of auld Wilson."

"The ghost of some of your stout sticks, I reckon," said Ralph, turning upon them with a shadow of a sneer on his frank face.

His companions laughed. Just then the wind rose higher than before, and came in a gust down the open chimney. The dogs that had been sleeping on the sanded floor got up, walked across the room with drooping heads, and growled. Then they lay down again and addressed themselves afresh to sleep. The young dalesman looked into the mouth of his pewter and muttered, as if to himself, –

"Because there was no evidence to convict the poor soul, suspicion, that is worse than conviction, must so fix upon him that he's afraid to sleep his nights in his bed at home, but must go where never a braggart loon of Wythburn dare follow him."

"Aye, lad," said the old man, with a wink of profound import, "foxes hev holes."

The sally was followed by a general laugh.

Not noticing it, Ralph said, –

"A hole, indeed! a cleft in the bare rock, open to nigh every wind, deluged by every rain, desolate, unsheltered by bush or bough – a hole no fox would house in."

Ralph was not unmoved, but the sage in the chimney corner caught little of the contagion of his emotion. Taking his pipe out of his mouth, and with the shank of it marking time to the doggerel, he said, –

> "Wheariver there's screes
> There's mair stones nor trees."

The further sally provoked a louder laugh. Just then another gust came down the chimney and sent a wave of mingled heat and cold through the room. The windows rattled louder with the wind and crackled sharper with the pelting sleet. The dogs rose and growled.

"Be quiet there," cried Ralph. "Down, Laddie, down." Laddie, a large-limbed collie, with long shaggy coat still wet and matted and glistening with the hard unmelted snow, had walked to the door and put his nose to the bottom of it.

"Some one coming," said Ralph, turning to look at the dog, and speaking almost under his breath.

Robbie Anderson, who had throughout been lounging in silence on the bench near the door, got up sleepily, and put his great hand on the wooden latch. The door flew open by the force of the storm outside. He peered for a moment into the darkness through the blinding sleet. He could see nothing.

"No one here!" he said moodily.

And, putting his broad shoulder to the stout oak door, he forced it back. The wind moaned and hissed through the closing aperture. It was like the ebb of a broken wave to those who had heard the sea. Turning about, as the candles on the table blinked, the young man lazily dashed the rain and sleet from his beard and breast, and lay down again on the settle, with something between a shiver and a yawn. "Cruel night, this," he muttered, and so saying, he returned to his normal condition of somnolence.

The opening and the closing of the door, together with the draught of cold air, had awakened a little man who occupied that corner of the chimney nook which faced old Matthew. Coiled up with his legs under him on the warm stone seat, his head resting against one of the two walls that bolstered him up on either hand, beneath a great flitch of bacon that hung there to dry, he had lain asleep throughout the preceding conversation, only punctuating its periods at intervals with somewhat too audible indications of slumber. In an instant he was on his feet. He was a diminutive creature, with something infinitely amusing in his curious physical proportions. His head was large and well formed; his body was large and ill formed; his legs were short and shrunken. He was the schoolmaster of Wythburn, and his name Monsey Laman. The dalesmen found the little schoolmaster the merriest comrade that ever sat with them over a glass. He had a crack for each of them, a song, a joke, a lively touch that cut and meant no harm. They called him "the little limber Frenchman," in allusion to a peculiarity of gait which in the minds of the heavy-limbed mountaineers was somehow associated with the idea of a French dancing master.

With the schoolmaster's awakening the conversation in the inn seemed likely to take a livelier turn. Even the whistling sleet appeared to become less fierce and terrible. True, the stalwart dalesman on the door bench yawned and slept as before; but even Ralph's firm lower lip began to relax, and he was never a gay and sportive elf. The rest of the company charged their pipes afresh and called on the hostess for more spiced ale.

"'Blessing on your heart,' says the proverb, 'you brew good ale.' It's a Christian virtue, eh, Father?" said Monsey, addressing Matthew in the opposite corner.

"Praise the ford as ye find it," said that sage; "I've found good yal maks good yarn. Folks that wad put doon good yal ought to be theirselves putten doon."

"Then you must have been hanged this many a long year, Father Matthew," said Monsey, "for you've put down more good ale than any man in Wythburn."

Old Matthew had to stand the laugh against himself this time. In the midst of it he leaned over to Ralph, and, as though to cover his discomfiture, whispered, "He's gat a lad's heart, the laal man has."

Then, with the air of one about to communicate a novel idea, –

"And sic as ye gie, sic will ye get, frae him."

"Well, well," he added aloud, "ye munnet think I cannot stand my rackups."

The old man, despite this unexpected fall, was just beginning to show his mettle. The sententious graybeard was never quite so happy, never looked quite so wise, never shook his head with such an air of good-humored consequence, never winked with such profundity of facetiousness, as when "the laal limber Frenchman" was giving a "merry touch." Wouldn't Monsey sing summat and fiddle to it too; aye, that he would, Mattha knew reet weel.

"Sing!" cried the little man, – "sing! Monsieur, the dog shall try me this conclusion. If he wag his tail, then will I sing; if he do not wag his tail, then – then will I not be silent. What say you Laddie?" The dog responded to the appeal with an opportune if not an intelligent wag of that member on which so momentous an issue hung. From one of the rosy closets in the wall a fiddle was forthwith brought out, and soon the noise of the tempest was drowned in the preliminary tuning of strings and running of scales.

"You shall beat the time, my patriarch," said Monsey.

"Nay, man; it's thy place to kill it," answered Matthew.

"Then you shall mark the beat, or beat the mark, or make your mark. You could never write, you know."

It was a sight not to be forgotten to see the little schoolmaster brandishing his fiddlestick, beating time with his foot, and breaking out into a wild shout when he hit upon some happy idea, for he rejoiced in a gift of improvisation. A burst of laughter greeted the climax of his song, which turned on an unheroic adventure of old Matthew's. The laughter had not yet died away when a loud knocking came to the door. Ralph jumped to his feet.

"I said some one was coming; and he's been here before, whoever he is."

At that he walked to the door and opened it. Laddie was there before him.

"Is Ralph Ray here?"

It was the voice of a woman, charged with feeling.

Ralph's back had been to the light, and hence his face had not been recognized. But the light fell on the face of the new-comer.

"Rotha!" he said. He drew her in, and was about to shut out the storm behind her.

"No," she said almost nervously. "Come with me; some one waits outside to see you; some one who won't – can't come in."

She was wet; her hair was matted over her forehead, the sleet lying in beads upon it. A hood that had been pulled hurriedly over her head was blown partly aside. Ralph would have drawn her to the fire.

"Not yet," she said again. Her eyes looked troubled, startled, denoting pain.

"Then I will go with you at once," he said.

They turned; Laddie darted out before them, and in a moment they were in the blackness of the night.

CHAPTER IV

The Outcast

The storm had abated. The sleet and rain had ceased, but the wind still blew fierce and strong, driving black continents of cloud across a crescent moon. It was bitingly cold. Rotha walked fast and spoke little. Ralph understood their mission. "Is he far away?" he said.

"Not far."

Her voice had a tremor of emotion, and as the wind carried it to him it seemed freighted with sadness. But the girl would have hidden her fears.

"Perhaps he's better now," she said.

Ralph quickened his steps. The dog had gone on in front, and was lost in the darkness.

"Give me your hand, Rotha; the sleet is hard and slape."

"Don't heed me, Ralph; go faster; I'll follow."

Just then a sharp bark was heard close at hand, followed by another and another, but in a different key. Laddie had met a friend.

"He's coming," Rotha said, catching her breath.

"He's here."

With the shrill cry of a hunted creature that has got back, wounded, to its brethren, Sim seemed to leap upon them out of the darkness.

"Ralph, take me with you – take me with you; do not let me go back to the fell to-night. I cannot go – no, believe me, I cannot – I dare not. Take me, Ralph; have mercy on me; do not despise me for the coward that I am; it's enough to make me curse the great God – no, no; not that neither. But, Ralph, Ralph – "

The poor fellow would have fallen breathless and exhausted at Ralph's feet, but he held him up and spoke firmly but kindly to him, –

"Bravely, Sim; bravely, man; there," he said, as the tailor regained some composure.

"You sha'n't go back to-night. How wet you are, though! There's not a dry rag to your body, man. You must first return with me to the fire at the Red Lion, and then we'll go – "

"No, no, no!" cried Sim; "not there either – never there; better the wind and rain, aye, better anything, than that."

And he turned his head over his shoulder as though peering into the darkness behind. Ralph understood him. There were wilder companions for this poor hunted creature than any that lived on the mountains.

"But you'll never live through the night in clothes like these."

Sim shivered with the cold; his teeth chattered; his lank hands shook as with ague.

"Never live? Oh, but I must not die, Ralph; no not yet – not yet."

Was there, then, something still left in life that a poor outcast like this should cling to it?

"I'll go back with you," he said more calmly. They turned, and with Sim between them Ralph and Rotha began to retrace their steps. They had not far to go, when Sim reeled like a drunken man, and when they were within a few paces he stopped.

"No," he said, "I can't." His breath was coming quick and fast.

"Come, man, they shall give you the ingle bench; I'll see to that. Come now," said Ralph soothingly.

"I've walked in front of this house for an hour to-night, I have," said Sim, "to and fro, to and fro, waiting for you; waiting, waiting; starting at my own shadow cast from the dim lowe of the windows, and then flying to hide when the door did at last – at long last – open or shut."

Ralph shuddered. It had been as he thought. Then he said, –

"Yes, yes; but you'll come now, like a brave fellow – 'a braw chiel,' you know."

Sim started at the pleasantry with which Ralph had tried to soothe his spirits. It struck a painful memory. Ralph felt it too.

"Come," he said, in an altered tone.

"No," cried Sim, clasping his hands over his head. "They're worse than wild beasts, they are. To-night I went up to the cave as usual. The wind was blowing strong and keen in the valley; it had risen to a tempest on the screes. I went in and turned up the bracken for my bed. Then the rain began to fall; and the rain became hail, and the hail became sleet, and pelted in upon me, it did. The wind soughed about my lone home – my home!"

Again Sim reeled in the agony of his soul.

"This is peace to that wind," he continued; "yes, peace. Then the stones began to rumble down the rocks, and the rain to pour in through the great chinks in the roof of the cave. Yet I stayed there – I stayed. Well, the ghyll roared louder and louder. It seemed to overflow the gullock, it did. I heard the big bowders shifted from their beds by the tumbling waters. They rolled with heavy thuds down the brant sides of the fell – down, down, down. But I kept closer, closer. Presently I heard the howl of the wolves – "

"No, Sim; not that, old friend." "Yes, the pack from Lauvellen. They'd been driven out of their caves – not even they could live in their caves tonight." The delirium of Sim's spirit seemed to overcome him.

"No more now, man," said Ralph, putting his arm about him. "You're safe, at least, and all will be well with you."

"Wait. Nearer and nearer they came, nearer and nearer, till I knew they were above me, around me. Yet I kept close, I did, I almost felt their breath. Well, well, at last I saw two red eyes gleaming at me through the darkness – "

"You're feverish to-night, Sim," interrupted Ralph.

"Then a great flash of lightning came. It licked the ground afore me – ay, licked. Then a burst of thunder – it must have been a thunderbolt – I couldn't hear the wind and sleet and water. I fainted, that must have been it. When I came round I groped about me where I lay – "

"A dream, Sim."

"No, it was no dream! What was it I touched? I was delivered! Thank heaven, *that* death was not mine. I rose, staggered out, and fled."

By the glimmering light from the windows of the inn – there came the sound of laughter from within – Ralph could see that hysterical tears coursed down the poor tailor's cheeks. Rotha stood aside, her hands covering her face.

"And, at last, when you could not meet me here, you went to Fornside for Rotha to seek me?" asked Ralph.

"Yes, I did. Don't despise me – don't do that." Then in a supplicating tone he added, –

"I couldn't bear it from you, Ralph."

The tears came again. The direful agony of Sim's soul seemed at length to conquer him, and he fell to the ground insensible. In an instant Rotha was on her knees in the hardening road at her father's side; but she did not weep.

"We have no choice now," she said in a broken voice.

"None," answered Ralph. "Let me carry him in."

When the door of the inn had closed behind Ralph as he went out with Rotha, old Matthew Branthwaite, who had recovered his composure after Monsey's song, and who had sat for a moment with his elbow on his knee, his pipe in his hand and his mouth still open, from which the shaft had just been drawn, gave a knowing twitch to his wrinkled face as he said, –

"So, so, that's the fell the wind blows frae!"

"Blow low, my black feutt," answered Monsey, "and don't blab."

"When the whins is oot of blossom, kissing's oot o' fashion – nowt will come of it," replied the sage on reflection.

"Wrong again, great Solomon!" said Monsey. "Ralph is not the man to put away the girl because her father is in disgrace."

"Do ye know he trystes with the lass?"

"Not I."

"Maybe ye'r like the rest on us: ye can make nowt on him, back ner edge."

"Right now, great sage; the sun doesn't shine through him."

"He's a great lounderan fellow," said one of the dalesmen, speaking into the pewter at his mouth. He was the blacksmith of Wythburn.

"What do you say?" asked Monsey.

"Nowt!" the man growled sulkily.

"So ye said nowt?" inquired Matthew.

"Nowt to you, or any of you."

"Then didst a nivver hear it said, 'He that talks to himsel' clatters to a fool'?"

The company laughed.

"No," resumed Matthew, turning to the schoolmaster, "Ralph will nivver tryste with the lass of yon hang-gallows of a tailor. The gallows rope's all but roond his neck already. It's awesome to see him in his barramouth in the fell side. He's dwinnelt away to a atomy.

"It baffles me where he got the brass frae to pay his rent," said one of the shepherds. "Where did he get it, schoolmaster?"

Monsey answered nothing. The topic was evidently a fearsome thing to him. His quips and cracks were already gone.

"Where did he get it, *I* say?" repeated the man; with the air of one who was propounding a trying problem.

Old Matthew removed his pipe.

"A fool may ask mair questions ner a doctor can answer."

The shepherd shifted in his seat.

"That Wilson was na shaks nowther," continued Matthew quietly. "He was accustomed to 'tummel' his neighbors, and never paused to inquire into their bruises. He'd olas the black dog on his back – leastways latterly. Ey, the braizzant taistrel med have done something for Ralph an he lived langer. He was swearing what he'd do, the ungratefu' fool; auld Wilson was a beadless body."

"They say he threatened Ralph's father, Angus," said Monsey, with a perceptible shiver.

"Ay, but Angus is bad to bang. I mind his dingin' ower a bull on its back. A girt man, Angus, and varra dreadfu' when he's angert."

"Dus'ta mind the fratch thoo telt me aboot atween Angus and auld Wilson?" said Reuben Thwaite to Matthew Branthwaite.

"What quarrel was that?" asked Monsey.

"Why, the last fratch of all, when Wilson gat the sneck posset frae Shoulthwaite," said Matthew.

"I never heard of it," said the schoolmaster.

"There's nowt much to hear. Ralph and mysel' we were walking up to the Moss together ya day, when we heard Angus and Wilson at a bout of words. Wilson he said to Angus with a gay, bitter sneer, 'Ye'll fain swappit wi' me yet,' said he. 'He'll yoke wi' an unco weird. Thy braw chiel 'ul tryste wi' th' hangman soon, I wat.' And Angus he was fair mad, I can tell ye, and he said to Wilson, 'Thoo stammerin' and yammerin' taistrel, thoo; I'll pluck a lock of thy threep. Bring the warrant, wilt thoo? Thoo savvorless and sodden clod-heed! I'll whip thee with the taws. Slipe, I say, while thoo's weel – slipe!'"

"And Angus would have done it, too, and not the first time nowther," said little Reuben, with a knowing shake of the head.

"Well, Matthew, what then?" said Monsey.

"Weel, with that Angus he lifted up his staff, and Wilson shrieked oot afore he gat the blow. But Angus lowered his hand and said to him, says he, 'Time eneuf to shriek when ye're strucken.'"

"And when the auld one did get strucken, he could not shriek," added Reuben.

"We know nowt of that reetly," said Matthew, "and maybe nivver will."

"What was that about a warrant?" said Monsey.

"Nay, nay, laal man, that's mair ner ony on us knows for certain." "But ye have a notion on it, have ye not?" said Reuben, with a twinkle which was intended to flatter Matthew into a communicative spirit.

"I reckon I hev," said the weaver, with a look of self-satisfaction.

"Did Ralph understand it?" asked Monsey.

"Not he, schoolmaister. If he did, I could mak' nowt on him, for I asked him theer and then."

"But ye knows yersel' what the warrant meant, don't ye?" said Reuben significantly.

"Weel, man, it's all as I telt ye; the country's going to the dogs, and young Charles he's cutting the heed off nigh a'most iv'ry man as fought for Oliver agen him. And it's as I telt ye aboot the spies of the government, there's a spy ivrywhear – maybe theer's yan here now – and auld Wilson he was nowt ner mair ner less ner a spy, and he meant to get a warrant for Ralph Ray, and that's the lang and short on it."

"I reckon Sim made *the* short on it," said Reuben with a smirk. "He scarce knew what a good turn he was doing for young Ralph yon neet in Martinmas."

"But don't they say Ralph saved Wilson's life away at the wars?" said

Monsey. "Why could he want to inform against him and have him hanged?"

"A dog winnet yowl an ye hit him with a bone, but a spy is worse ner ony dog," answered Matthew sententiously.

"But *why* could he wish to do it?"

"His fratch with Angus, that was all."

"There must have been more than that, Matthew, there must."

"I never heeard on it, then."

"Old Wilson must have had money on him that night," said Monsey, who had been looking gravely into the fire, his hands clasped about his knees. Encouraged by this support of the sapient idea he had hinted at, the shepherd who had spoken before broke in with, "Where else did he get it *I* say?"

"Ye breed of the cuckoo," said Matthew, "ye've gat no rhyme but yan."

Amid the derisive laughter that followed, the door of the inn was again opened, and in a moment more Ralph Ray stood in the middle of the floor with Simeon Stagg in his arms. Rotha was behind, pale but composed. Every man in the room rose to his feet. The landlord stepped forward, with no pleasant expression on his face; and from an inner room his wife came bustling up. Little Monsey stood clutching and twitching his fingers. Old Matthew had let the pipe drop out of his mouth, and it lay broken on the hearth.

"He has fainted," said Ralph, still holding his burden; "turn that bench to the fire."

No one stirred. Every one stood for the moment as if stupefied. Sim's head hung over Ralph's arm: his face was as pale as death.

"Out of the way," said Ralph, brushing past a great lumbering fellow, with his mouth agape.

The company found their tongues at last. Were they to sit with "this hang-gallows of a tailor"? The landlord, thinking himself appealed to, replied that he "couldn't hev na brulliment" in his house.

"There need be no broil," said Ralph, laying the insensible form on a seat and proceeding to strip off the wet outer garments. Then turning to the hostess, he said, –

"Martha, bring me water, quick."

Martha turned about and obeyed him without a word.

"He'll be better soon," said Ralph to Robbie Anderson. He was sprinkling water on the white face that lay before him. Robbie had recovered his wakefulness, and was kneeling at Sim's feet, chafing his hands.

Rotha stood at her father's side, motionless.

"There, he's coming to. Martha," said Ralph, "hadn't you better take Rotha to the kitchen fire?"

The two women left the room.

Sim's eyes opened; there was a watery humor in them which was not tears. The color came back to his cheeks, but with the return of consciousness his face grew thinner and more haggard. He heaved a heavy sigh, and seemed to realize his surroundings. With the only hand disengaged (Robbie held one of them) he clutched at Ralph's belt.

"I'm better – let me go," he said in a hoarse voice, trying to rise.

"No!" said Ralph, – "no!" and he gently pushed him back into his recumbent position.

"You had best let the snuffling waistrel go," said one of the men in a surly tone. "Maybe he never fainted at all."

It was the blacksmith who had growled at the mention of Ralph's name in Ralph's absence. They called him Joe Garth.

"Be silent, you loon," answered Robbie Anderson, turning upon the last speaker.

Ralph seemed not to have heard him.

"Here," he said, tossing Sim's coat to Matthew, who had returned with a new pipe to his seat in the chimney corner, "dry that at the fire." The coat had been growing hard with the frost.

"This wants the batling stone ower it," said the old weaver, spreading it out before him.

"See to this, schoolmaster," said Ralph, throwing Sim's cap into his lap.

Monsey jumped, with a scream, out of his seat as though stung by an adder.

Ralph looked at him for a moment with an expression of pity.

"I might have known you were timid at heart, schoolmaster. Perhaps you're gallant over a glass."

There could be no doubt of little Monsey's timidity. All his jests had forsaken him.

Sim had seen the gesture that expressed horror at contact even with his clothes. He was awake to every passing incident with a feverish alertness.

"Let me go," he said again, with a look of supplicatory appeal.

Old Matthew got up and opened the door.

"Sista, there's some betterment in the weather, now; it teem't awhile ago."

"What of that?" asked Ralph; but he understood the observation.

"For God's sake let me go," cried Sim in agony, looking first at one face and then at another.

"No," said Ralph, and sat down beside him. Robbie had gone back to his bench.

"Ye'll want the bull-grips to keep *him* quiet," said old Matthew to Ralph, with a sneer.

"And the ass's barnicles to keep your tongue in your mouth," added Ralph sternly.

"For fault of wise men fools sit on the bench, or we should hev none of this," continued Matthew. "I reckon some one that's here is nigh ax't oot by Auld Nick in the kirk of the nether world."

"Then take care you're not there yourself to give something at the bridewain."

Old Mathew grumbled something under his breath.

There was a long silence. Ralph had rarely been heard to speak so bitterly. It was clear that opposition had gone far enough. Sim's watery eyes were never for an instant still. Full of a sickening apprehension, they cast furtive glances into every face. The poor creature seemed determined to gather up into his wretched breast the scorn that was blasting it. The turf on the hearth gave out a great heat, but the tailor shivered as with cold. Then Ralph reached the coat and cap, and, after satisfying himself that they were dry, he handed them back to Sim, who put them on. Perhaps he had mistaken the act, for, rising to his feet, Sim looked into Ralph's face inquiringly, as though to ask if he might go.

"Not yet, Sim," said Ralph. "You shall go when I go. You lodge with me to-night."

Monsey in the corner looked aghast, and crept closer under the flitch of bacon that hung above him.

"Men," said Ralph, "hearken here. You call it a foul thing to kill a man, and so it is."

Monsey turned livid; every one held his breath. Ralph went on, –

"Did you ever reflect that there are other ways of taking a man's life besides killing him?"

There was no response. Ralph did not seem to expect one, for he continued, –

"You loathe the man who takes the blood of his fellow-man, and you're right so to do. It matters nothing to you that the murdered man may have been a worse man than the murderer. You're right there too. You look to the motive that inspired the crime. Is it greed or revenge? Then you say, 'This man must die.' God grant that such horror of murder may survive among us." There was a murmur of assent.

"But it is possible to kill without drawing blood. We may be murderers and never suspect the awfulness of our crime. To wither with suspicion, to blast with scorn, to dog with cruel hints, to torture with hard looks', – this is to kill without blood. Did you ever think of it? There are worse hangmen than ever stood on the gallows."

"Ay, but *he's* shappin' to hang hissel'," muttered Matthew Branthwaite. And there was some inaudible muttering among the others.

"I know what you mean," Ralph continued. "That the guilty man whom the law cannot touch is rightly brought under the ban of his fellows. Yes, it is Heaven's justice."

Sim crept closer to Ralph, and trembled perceptibly.

"Men, hearken again," said Ralph. "You know I've spoken up for Sim," and he put his great arm about the tailor's shoulders; "but you don't know that I have never asked him, and he has never said whether he is innocent or not. The guilty man may be in this room, and he may not be Simeon Stagg. But if he were my own brother – my own father – "

Old Matthew's pipe had gone out; he was puffing at the dead shaft. Sim rose up; his look of abject misery had given place to a look of defiance; he stamped on the floor.

"Let me go; let me go," he cried.

Robbie Anderson came up and took him by the hand; but Sim's brain seemed rent in twain, and in a burst of hysterical passion he fell back into his seat, and buried his head in his breast.

"He'll be hanged with the foulest collier yet," growled one of the men. It was Joe Garth again. He was silenced once more. The others had begun to relent.

"I've not yet asked him if he is innocent," continued Ralph; "but this persecution drives me to it, and I ask him now."

"Yes, yes," cried Sim, raising his head, and revealing an awful countenance. A direful memory seemed to haunt every feature.

"Do you know the murderer?"

"I do – that is – what am I saying? – let me go."

Sim had got up, and was tramping across the floor. Ralph got up too, and faced him.

"It is your duty, in the sight of Heaven, to give that man's name."

"No, no; heaven forbid," cried Sim.

"It is your duty to yourself and to – "

"I care nothing for myself."

"And to your daughter – think of that. Would you tarnish the child's name with the sin laid on the father's – "

"God in heaven help me!" cried Sim, tremulous with emotion. "Ralph, Ralph, ask me no more – you don't know what you ask."

"It is your duty to Heaven, I say."

He put his hand on Sim's shoulder, and looked steadily in his eyes. With a fearful cry Sim broke from his grasp, sprung to the door, and in an instant was lost in the darkness without. Ralph stood where Sim had left him, transfixed by some horrible consciousness. A slow paralysis seemed to possess all his senses. What had he read in those eyes that seemed to live before him still?

"Good neet," said old Matthew as he got up and trudged out. Most of the company rose to go. "Good night," said more than one, but Ralph answered nothing. Robbie Anderson was last.

"Good night, Ralph," he said. His gruff voice was thick in his throat.

"Aye, good night, lad," Ralph answered vacantly.

Robbie had got to the door, and was leaning with one hand on the door-frame. Coming back, he said, –

"Ralph, where may your father be to-night?"

"At Gaskarth – it's market day – he took the last shearing."

He spoke like one in a sleep. Then Robbie left him.

"Is Rotha ready to go?" he asked.

CHAPTER V

The Empty Saddle

The night has been unruly:...
Lamentings heard i' the air; strange screams of death.

Macbeth.

The storm was now all but over. The moon shone clear, and the clouds that scudded across its face were few. Lauvellen, to the east, was visible to the summit; and Raven Craig, to the west, loomed black before the moon. A cutting wind still blew, and a frost had set in sharp and keen. Already the sleet that had fallen was frozen in sheets along the road, which was thereby made almost impassable even to the sure footsteps of the mountaineer. The trees no longer sighed and moaned with the wind; on the stiffening firs lay beads of frozen snow, and the wind as it passed through them soughed. The ghylls were fuller and louder, and seemed to come from every hill; the gullocks overflowed, but silence was stealing over the streams, and the deeper rivers seemed scarcely to flow.

Ralph and Rotha walked side by side to Shoulthwaite Moss. It was useless for the girl to return to Fornside, Ralph had said. Her father would not be there, and the desolate house was no place for her on a night like this. She must spend the night under his mother's charge.

They had exchanged but few words on setting out. The tragedy of her father's life was settling on the girl's heart with a nameless misery. It is the first instinct of the child's nature to look up to the parent as its refuge, its tower of strength. That bulwark may be shattered before the world, and yet to the child's intuitive feeling it may remain the same. Proudly, steadfastly the child heart continues to look up to the wreck that is no wreck in the eyes of its love. Ah! how well it is if the undeceiving never comes! But when all that seemed strong, when all that seemed true, becomes to the unveiled vision weak and false, what word is there that can represent the sadness of the revealment?

"Do you think, Ralph, that I could bear a terrible answer if I were to ask you a terrible question?"

Rotha broke the silence between them with these words. Ralph replied promptly, –

"Yes, I do. What would you ask?"

The girl appeared powerless to proceed. She tried to speak and stopped, withdrawing her words and framing them afresh, as though fearful of the bluntness of her own inquiry. Her companion perceived her distress, and coming to her relief with a cheerier tone, he said, –

"Don't fear to ask, Rotha. I think I can guess your question. You want to know if – "

"Ralph," the girl broke in hurriedly – she could better bear to say the word herself than to hear him say it – "Ralph, he is my father, and that has been enough. I could not love him the less whatever might happen. I have never asked him – anything. He is my father, and though he be – whatever he may be – he is my father *still*, you know. But, Ralph, tell me – you say I can bear it – and I can – I feel I can now – tell me, Ralph, *was* it poor father after all?"

Rotha had stopped and covered up her face in her hands. Ralph stopped too. His voice was deep and thick as he answered slowly, –

"No, Rotha, it was not."

"*Not* father?" cried the girl; "you know it was not?"

"I *know* it was not."

The voice again was not the voice of one who brings glad tidings, but the words were themselves full of gladness for the ear on which they fell, and Rotha seemed almost overcome by her joy. She clutched Ralph's arm with both hands.

"Heaven be praised!" she said; "now I can brave anything – poor, poor father!"

After this the girl almost leapt over the frozen road in the ecstasy of her new-found delight. The weight of weary months of gathering suspense seemed in one moment to have fallen from her forever. Half laughing, half weeping, she bounded along, the dog sporting beside her. Her quick words rippled on the frosty air. Occasionally she encountered a flood that swept across the way from the hills above to the lake beneath, but her light foot tripped over it before a hand could be offered her. Their path lay along the pack-horse road by the side of the mere, and time after time she would scud down to the water's edge to pluck the bracken that grew there, or to test the thin ice with her foot. She would laugh and then be silent, and then break out into laughter again. She would prattle to herself unconsciously and then laugh once more. All the world seemed made anew to this happy girl to-night.

True enough, nature meant her for a heartsome lass. Her hair was dark, and had a tangled look, as though lately caught in brambles or still thick with burrs. Her dark eyebrows and long lashes shaded the darkest of black-brown eyes. Her mouth was alive with sensibility. Every shade of feeling could play upon her face. Her dress was loose, and somewhat negligently worn; one never felt its presence or knew whether it were poor or fine. Her voice, though soft, was generally high-pitched, not like the whirl of wind through the trees, but like its sigh through the long grass, and came, perhaps, to the mountain girl from the effort to converse above the sound of these natural voices. There was a tremor in her voice sometimes, and, when she was taken unawares, a sidelong look in her eyes. There was something about her in these serious moods that laid hold of the imagination. She had surely a well of strength which had been given for her own support and the solace of others at some future moment, only too terrible. But not to-night, as she tripped along under the moonlight, did the consciousness of that moment overshadow her.

And what of Ralph, who strode solemnly by her side? A change had come over him of late. He spoke little, and never at all of the scenes he had witnessed in his long campaign – never of his own share in them. He had become at once an active and a brooding man. The shadow of a supernatural presence seemed to hang over everything. Tonight that shadow was blacker than before.

In the fulness of her joy Rotha had not marked the tone in which Ralph spoke when he gave her in a word all the new life that bounded in her veins. But that tone was one of sadness, and that word had seemed to drain away from veins of his some of the glad life that now pulsated in hers. Was it nothing that the outcast among men whom he alone, save this brave girl, had championed, had convinced him of his innocence? Nothing that the light of a glad morning had broken on the long night of the blithe creature by his side, and brightened her young life with the promise of a happier future?

"Look, Ralph, look at the withered sedge, all frost-covered!" said Rotha in her happiness, tripping up to his side, with a sprig newly plucked in her hand. Ralph answered her absently, and she rattled on to herself, "Rotha shall keep you, beautiful sedge! How you glisten in the moonlight!" Then the girl broke out with a snatch of an old Border ballad, –

> Dacre's gane to the war, Willy,
> Dacre's gane to the war;
> Dacre's lord has crossed the ford,
> And left us for the war.

"Poor father," she said more soberly, "poor father; but he'll come back home now – come back to our *own* home again"; and then, unconscious of the burden of her song, she sang, –

> Naworth's halls are dead, Willy,
> Naworth's halls are dead;
> One lonely foot sounds on the keep,
> And that's the warder's tread.

The moon shone clearly; the tempest had lulled, and the silvery voice of the girl was all that could be heard above the distant rumble of the ghylls and the beat of Ralph's heavy footsteps. In a moment Rotha seemed to become conscious that her companion was sad as well as silent. How had this escaped her so long? she thought.

"But you don't seem quite so glad, Ralph," she said in an altered tone, half of inquiry, half of gentle reproach, as of one who felt that her joy would have been the more if another had shared it.

"Don't I? Ah, but I *am* glad – that is, I'm glad your father won't need old Mattha's bull-grips," he said, with an attempt to laugh at his own pleasantry.

How hollow the laugh sounded on his own ears! It was not what his father would have called heartsome. What was this sadness that was stealing over him and stiffening every sense? Had he yet realized it in all its fulness? Ralph shook himself and struck his hand on his breast, as though driving out the cold. He could not drive out the foreboding that had taken a seat there since Sim looked last in his eyes and cried, "Let me go."

Laddie frisked about them, and barked back at the echo of his own voice, that resounded through the clear air from the hollow places in the hills. They had not far to go now. The light of the kitchen window at Shoulthwaite would be seen from the turn of the road. Only through yonder belt of trees that overhung the "lonnin," and they would be in the court of Angus Ray's homestead.

"Ralph," said Rotha – she had walked in silence for some little time – "all the sorrow of my life seems gone. You have driven it all away." Her tremulous voice belied the light laugh that followed.

He looked down at her tear-dimmed eyes. Was her great sorrow indeed gone? Had he driven it away from her? If so, was it not all, and more, being gathered up into his own heart instead? Was it not so?

"You have borne it bravely, Rotha – very bravely," he answered. "Do you think, now, that I could have borne it as you have done?"

There was a tremor in his tone and a tenderness of expression in his face that Rotha had never before seen there.

"Bear it as I have done?" she repeated. "There is nothing you could not bear." And her radiant face was lit up in that white moonlight with a perfect sunshine of beauty.

"I don't know, Rotha, my girl," he answered falteringly; "I don't know – yet." The last words were spoken with his head dropped on to his breast.

Rotha stepped in front of him, and, putting her hand on his shoulder, stopped him and looked searchingly in his face.

"What is this sadness, Ralph? Is there something you have not told me – something behind, which, when it comes, will take the joy out of this glad news you give me?"

"I could not be so cruel as that, Rotha; do you think I could?"

A smile was playing upon his features as he smoothed her hair over her forehead and drew forward the loose hood that had fallen from it.

"And there is nothing to come after – nothing?"

"Nothing that need mar your happiness, my girl, or disturb your love.

47

You love your father, do you not?"

"Better than all the world!" Rotha answered impulsively. "Poor father!"

"Better than all the world," echoed Ralph vacantly, and with something like a sigh. Her impetuous words seemed to touch him deeply, and he repeated them once more, but they died away on his lips. "Better than all the – " Then they walked on.

They had almost reached the belt of trees that overhung the road.

"Ralph," said Rotha, pausing, "may I – kiss you?"

He stooped and kissed her on the forehead. Then the weight about his heart seemed heavier than before. By that kiss he felt that between him and the girl at his side there was a chasm that might never be bridged. Had he loved her? He hardly knew; he had never put it to himself so. Did she not love him? He could not doubt it. And her kiss! yes, it was the kiss of love; but *what* love? The frank, upturned face answered him but too well.

They were within the shadow of the trees now, and could see the lights at Shoulthwaite. In two minutes more their journey would be done.

"Take my hand, Rotha; you might slip on the frosty road in darkness like this."

The words were scarcely spoken, when Rotha gave a little cry and stumbled. "In an instant Ralph's arm was about her, and she had regained her feet.

"What is that?" she said, trembling with fear, and turning backwards.

"A drift of frozen sleet, no doubt," Ralph said, kicking with his foot at the spot where Rotha slipped.

"No, no," she answered, trembling now with some horrible apprehension.

Ralph had stepped back, and was leaning over something that lay across the road. The dog was snuffling at it.

"What is it?" said Rotha nervously.

He did not answer. He was on his knees beside it; his hands were on it. There was a moment of agonizing suspense.

"What is it?" Rotha repeated.

Still there came no reply. Ralph had risen, but he knelt again. His breath was coming fast. Rotha thought she could hear the beating of his heart.

"Oh, but I must know!" cried the girl. And she stepped backward as though to touch for herself the thing that lay there.

"Nothing," said Ralph, rising and taking her firmly by the hand that she had outstretched, – "nothing – a sack of corn has fallen from the wagon, nothing more." He spoke in a hoarse whisper.

He drew her forward a few paces, but she stopped. The dog was standing where Ralph had knelt, and was howling wofully.

"Laddie, come here," Ralph said; "Rotha, come away."

"I could bear the truth, Ralph – I think I could," she answered.

He put his arm about her, and drew her along without a word. She felt his powerful frame quiver and his strong voice die within him. She guessed the truth. She knew this man as few had known him, as none other could know him.

"Go back, Ralph," she said; "I'll hurry on." And still the dog howled behind them.

Ralph seemed not to hear her, but continued to walk by her side. Her heart sank, and she looked piteously into his face.

And now the noise reached them of hurrying footsteps in front. People were coming towards them from the house. Lanterns were approaching them. In another moment they were in the court. All was astir. The whole household seemed gathered there, and in the middle of the yard stood the mare Betsy, saddled but riderless, her empty wool-creels strapped to her sides.

"Thank Heaven, here is Ralph," said Willy. He was standing bareheaded, with the bridle in his hand.

"Bless thee!" cried Mrs. Ray as her son came up to her. "Here is the mare back home, my lad, but where is thy father?"

"The roads are bad to-night, mother," Ralph said, with a violent effort to control the emotion that was surging up to his throat.

"God help us, Ralph; you can't mean that!" said Willy, catching his brother's drift.

"Give me the lantern, boy," said Ralph to a young cowherd that stood near. "Rotha, my lass, take mother into the house." Then he stepped up to where his mother stood petrified with dismay, and kissed her tenderly. He had rarely done so before. The good dame understood him and wept. Rotha put her arms about the mother's neck and kissed her too, and helped her in.

Willy was unmanned. "You don't mean that you know that father – "

He could say no more. Ralph had raised the lantern to the level of the mare's creels to remove the strap that bound them, and the light had fallen on his face.

"Ralph, is he hurt – much hurt?"

"He is – dead!"

Willy fell back as one that had been dealt a blow.

"God help me! O God, help me!" he cried.

"Give me the reins," said Ralph, "and be here when I come back. I can't be long. Keep the door of the kitchen shut – mother is there. Go into his room, and see that all is ready."

"No, no, I can't do that." Willy was shuddering visibly.

"Remain here, at least, and give no warning when I return."

"Take me with you, Ralph; I can't stay here alone."

"Take the lantern, then," said Ralph.

And the brothers walked, with the mare between them, to where the path was, under the shadow of the trees. What shadow had fallen that night on their life's path, which Time might never raise? Again and again the horse slipped its foot on the frozen road. Again and again Willy would have stopped and turned back; but he went on-he dared not to leave his brother's side. The dog howled in front of them. They reached the spot at last.

Angus Ray lay there, his face downwards. The mighty frame was still and cold and stiff as the ice beneath it. The strong man had fallen from the saddle on to his head, and, dislocating his neck, had met with instant death. Close at hand were the marks of the horse's sliding hoofs. She had cast one of her shoes in the fall, and there it lay. Her knees, too, were still bleeding.

"Give me the lantern, Willy," said Ralph, going down on his knees to feel the heart. He had laid his hand on it before, and knew too well it did not beat. But he opened the cloak and tried once more. Willy was walking to and fro across the road, not daring to look down. And in the desolation of that moment the great heart of his brother failed him too, and he dropped his head over the cold breast beside which he knelt, and from eyes unused to weep the tears fell hot upon it.

"Take the lantern again, Willy," Ralph said, getting up. Then he lifted the body on to the back of the mare that stood quietly by their side.

As he did so a paper slipped away from the breast of the dead man.

Willy picked it up, and seeing "Ralph Ray" written on the back of it, he handed it to his brother, who thrust it into a pocket unread.

Then the two walked back, their dread burden between them.

CHAPTER VI

The House on the Moss

When the dawn of another day rose over Shoulthwaite, a great silence had fallen on the old house on the moss. The man who had made it what it was – the man who had been its vital spirit – slept his last deep sleep in the bedroom known as the kitchen loft. Throughout forty years his had been the voice first heard in that mountain home when the earliest gleams of morning struggled through the deep recesses of the low mullioned windows. Perhaps on the day following market day he sometimes lay an hour longer; but his stern rule of life spared none, and himself least of all. If at sixty his powerful limbs were less supple than of old, if his Jove-like head with its flowing beard had become tipped with the hoar frost, he had relaxed nothing of his rigid self-government on that account. When the clock in the kitchen had struck ten at night, Angus had risen up, whatever his occupation, whatever his company, and retired to rest. And the day had hardly dawned when he was astir in the morning, rousing first the men and next the women of his household. Every one had waited for his call. There had been no sound more familiar than that of his firm footstep, followed by the occasional creak of the old timbers, breaking the early stillness. That footstep would be heard no more.

Dame Ray sat in a chair before the kitchen fire. She had sat there the whole night through, moaning sometimes, but speaking hardly at all. Sleep had not come near her, yet she scarcely seemed to be awake. Last night's shock had more than half shattered her senses, but it had flashed upon her mind a vision of her whole life. Only half conscious of what was going on about her, she saw vividly as in a glass the incidents of those bygone years, that had lain so long unremembered. The little cottage under Castenand; her old father playing his fiddle in the quiet of a summer evening; herself, a fresh young maiden, busied about him with a hundred tender cares; then a great sorrow and a dead waste of silence, – all this appeared to belong to some earlier existence. And then the sun had seemed to rise on a fuller life that came later. A holy change had come over her, and to her transfigured feeling the world looked different. But that bright sun had set now, and all around was gloom. Slowly she swayed herself to and fro hour after hour in her chair, as one by one these memories came back to her – came, and went, and came again.

On Rotha the care of the household had fallen. The young girl had sat long by the old dame overnight, holding her hand and speaking softly to her between the outbursts of her own grief. She had whispered something about brave sons who would yet be her great stay, and then the comforter herself had needed comfort and her voice of solace had been stilled. When the daylight came in at the covered windows, Rotha rose up unrefreshed; but with a resolute heart she set herself to the duties that had dropped so unexpectedly upon her. She put the spinning-wheel into the neuk window-stand and the woo-wheel against the wall. They would not be wanted now. She cleared the sconce and took down the flitches that hung from the rannel-tree to dry. Then she cooked the early breakfast of oatmeal porridge, and took the milk that the boy brought from the cow shed and put it into the dishes that she had placed on the long oak table which stretched across the kitchen.

Willy Ray had been coming and going most of the night from the kitchen to his own room – a little carpeted closet of a bedroom that went out from the first landing on the stairs, and looked up to the ghyll at the back. The wee place was more than his sleeping-room; he had his books there, but he had neither slept nor read that night. He wandered about aimlessly, with the eyes of one walking in his sleep, breaking out sometimes into a little hysterical scream, followed by a shudder, and then a sudden disappearance. Death had come to him for the first time, and in a fearful guise. Its visible presence appalled him. He was as feeble as a child now. He was ready to lean on the first strong human arm that offered; and though Rotha understood but vaguely the troubles that beset his mind, her quick instinct found a sure way to those that lay heavy at his heart. She comforted him with what good words she could summon, and he came again and again to her with his odd fancies and his recollections of the poor feeble philosophy which he had gleaned from books. The look in the eyes of this simple girl and the touch of her hand made death less fearsome than anything besides. Willy seemed to lean on Rotha, and she on her part appeared to grow stronger as she felt this.

Ralph had gone to bed much as usual the night before – after he had borne upstairs what lay there. He was not seen again until morning, and when he came down and stood for a moment over his mother's chair as she sat gazing steadfastly into the fire, Rotha was stooping over the pan, with the porridge thivle in her hand. She looked up into his face, while his hand rested with a speechless sympathy on his mother's arm, and she thought that, mingled with a softened sorrow, there was something like hope there. The sadness of last night was neither in his face nor in his voice. He was even quieter than usual, but he appeared to have grown older in the few hours that had intervened. Nevertheless, he went through his ordinary morning's work about the homestead with the air of one whose mind was with him in what he did. After breakfast he took his staff out of the corner and set out for the hills, his dog beside him.

During the day, Rotha, with such neighborly help as it was the custom to tender, did all the little offices incident to the situation. She went in and out of the chamber of the dead, not without awe, but without fear. She had only once before looked on death, or, if she had seen it twice before this day, her first sight of it was long ago, in that old time of which memory scarcely held a record, when she was carried in her father's arms into a darkened room like this and held for a moment over the white face that she knew to be the face of her mother. But, unused as she had been to scenes made solemn by death, she appeared to know her part in this one.

Intelligence of the disaster that had fallen on the household at Shoulthwaite Moss was not long in circulating through Wythburn. One after another, the shepherds and their wives called in, and were taken to the silent room upstairs. Some offered such rude comfort as their sympathetic hearts but not too fecund intellects could devise, and as often as not it was sorry comfort enough. Some stood all but speechless, only gasping out at intervals, "Deary me." Others, again, seemed afflicted with what old Matthew Branthwaite called "doddering" and a fit of the "gapes."

It was towards nightfall when Matthew himself came to Shoulthwaite. "I'm the dame's auldest neighbor," he had said at the Red Lion that afternoon, when the event of the night previous had been discussed. "It's nobbut reet 'at I should gang alang to her this awesome day. She'll be glad of the neighborhood of an auld friend's crack." They were at their evening meal of sweet broth when Matthew's knock came to the door, followed, without much interval, by his somewhat gaunt figure on the threshold.

"Come your ways in," said Mrs. Ray. "And how fend you, Mattha?"

"For mysel', I's gayly. Are ye middlin' weel?" the old man said.

"I'm a lang way better, but I'm going yon way too. It's far away the bainer way for me now." And Mrs. Ray put her apron to her eyes.

"Ye'll na boune yit, Mary," said Matthew. "Ye'll na boune yon way for mony a lang year yit. So dunnet ye beurt, Mary."

Mattha's blubbering tones somewhat discredited his stoical advice.

Rotha had taken down a cup, and put the old man to sit between herself and Willy, facing Mrs. Ray.

"I met Ralph in the morning part," said Matthew; "he telt me all the ins and outs aboot it. I reckon he were going to the kirk garth aboot the berryin'."

Mrs. Ray raised her apron to her eyes again. Willy got up and left the room. He at least was tortured by this kind of comfort.

"He's of the bettermer sort, *he* is," said Matthew with a motion of his head towards the door at which Willy had gone out. "He taks it bad, does Willy. Ralph was chapfallen a laal bit, but not ower much. Deary me, but ye've gat all sorts of sons though you've nobbut two. Weel, weel," he added, as though reconciling himself to Willy's tenderness and Ralph's hardness of heart, "if there were na fells there wad be na dales."

Matthew had turned over his cup to denote that his meal was finished. The dame rose and resumed her seat by the fire. During the day she had been more cheerful, but with the return of the night she grew again silent, and rocked herself in her chair.

"It's just t'edge o' dark, lass," said Matthew to Rotha while filling his pipe. "Wilt thoo fetch the cannels?"

The candles were brought, and the old man lit his pipe from one of them and sat down with Mrs. Ray before the fire.

"Dus'ta mind when Angus coomt first to these parts?" he said. "*I* do reet weel. I can a' but fancy I see him now at the manor'al court at Deer Garth Bottom. What a man he was, to be sure! Ralph's nobbut a bit boy to what his father was then. Folks say father and son are as like as peas, but nowt of the sort. Ye could nivver hev matched Angus in yon days for limb and wind. Na, nor sin' nowther. And there was yan o' the lasses frae Castenand had set een on Angus, but she nivver let wit. As bonny a lass as there was in the country side, she was. They say beauty withoot bounty's but bauch, but she was good a' roond. She was greetly thought on. Dus'ta mind I was amang the lads that went ahint her – I was, mysel'. But she wad hev nowt wi' me; she trysted wid Angus; so I went back home and broke the click reel of my new loom straight away. And it's parlish odd I've not lived marraless iver sin'."

This reminiscence of his early and all but only love adventure seemed to touch a sensitive place in the old man's nature, and he pulled for a time more vigorously at his pipe.

Mrs. Ray Still sat gazing into the fire, hardly heeding the old weaver's garrulity, and letting him chatter on as he pleased. Occasionally she would look anxiously over her shoulder to ask Rotha if Ralph had got back, and on receiving answer that he had not yet been seen she would resume her position, and, with an absent look in her eyes, gaze back into the fire. When a dog's bark would be heard in the distance above the sound of the wind, she would break into consciousness afresh, and bid Rotha prepare the supper. But still Ralph did not come. Where could he be?

It was growing late when Matthew got up to go. He had tried his best to comfort his old neighbor in her sorrow. He had used up all his saws and proverbs that were in the remotest degree appropriate to the occasion, and he had thrown in a few that were not remarkable for appositeness or compatibility. All alike had passed by unheeded. The dame had taken the good will for the good deed, and had not looked the gift-horses too closely in the mouth.

"Good night, Mattha Branthet," she said, in answer to his good by; "good night, and God bless thee."

Matthew had opened the door, and was looking out preparatory to his final leavetaking.

"The sky's over-kessen to-neet," he said. "There's na moon yit, and t'wind's high as iver. Good neet, Mary; it's like ye'll be a' thrang eneuf to-morrow wi' the feast for the berryin', and it's like eneuf ma mistress and laal Liza will be ower at the windin'.'"

The dame sighed audibly.

"And keep up a blithe heart, Mary. Remember, he that has gude crops may thole some thistles."

When the door had closed behind the weaver, Willy came back to the kitchen from his little room.

"Ralph not home yet?" he said, addressing Rotha.

"Not yet," the girl answered, trying vainly to conceal some uneasiness.

"I wonder what Robbie Anderson wanted with him? He was here twice, you know, in the morning. And the schoolmaster – what could little Monsey have to say that he looked so eager? It is not his way."

"Be sure it was nothing out of the common," said Rotha. "What happened last night makes us all so nervous."

"True; but there was a strange look about both of them – at least I thought so, though I didn't heed it then. They say misfortunes never come singly. I wish Ralph were home."

Mrs. Ray had risen from her seat at the fire, and was placing one of the candles upon a small table that stood before the neuk window.

With her back to the old dame, Rotha put her finger on her lip as a motion to Willy to say no more.

CHAPTER VII

Sim's Cave

When Ralph retired to his own room on the night of his father's death there lay a heavier burden at his heart than even that dread occurrence could lodge there. To such a man as he was, death itself was not so terrible but that many passions could conquer the fear of it. As for his father, he had not tasted death; he had not seen it; his death was but a word; and the grave was not deep. No, the grave was not deep. Ah, what sting lay in that thought! – what fresh sting lay there!

Ralph called up again the expression on the face of Simeon Stagg as he asked him in the inn that night (how long ago it seemed!) to give the name of the man who had murdered Wilson. "It's your duty in the sight of Heaven," he had said; "would you tarnish the child's name with the guilt laid on the father's?" Then there had come into Sim's eyes something that gave a meaning to his earlier words, "Ralph, you don't know what you ask." Ah, did he not know now but too well? Ralph walked across the room with a sense as of a great burden of guilt weighing him down. The grave was not deep – oh, would it were, would it were! Would that the grave were the end of all! But no, it was as the old book said: when one dies, those who survive ask what he has left behind; the angel who bends above him asks what he has sent before. And the father who had borne him in his arms – whom he had borne – what had he sent before?

Ralph tramped heavily to and fro. His dog slept on the mat outside his door, and, unused to such continued sounds within, began to scrape and growl.

After all, there was no certain evidence yet. To-morrow morning he would go up the fell and see Sim alone. He must know the truth. If it concerned him as closely as he divined, the occasion to conceal it was surely gone by with this night's event. Then Robbie Anderson, – what did he mean? Ralph recalled some dim memory of the young dalesman asking about his father. Robbie was kind to Sim, too, when the others shunned him. What did it all mean?

With a heavy heart Ralph began to undress. He had unbelted himself and thrown off his jerkin, when he thought of the paper that had fallen from his father's open breast as he lifted him on to the mare. What was it? Yes, there it was in his pocket, and with a feverish anxiety Ralph opened it.

Had he clung to any hope that the black cloud that appeared to be hanging over him would not, after all, envelop him? Alas! that last vestige of hope must leave him. The paper was a warrant for his own arrest on a charge of treason. It had been issued at the court of the high constable at Carlisle, and set forth that Ralph Ray had conspired to subvert the government of his sovereign while a captain in the trained bands of the rebel army of the "late usurper." It was signed and countersigned, and was marked for the service of James Wilson, King's agent. It was dated too; yes, two days before Wilson's death.

All was over now; this was the beginning of the end; the shadow had fallen. By that paradox of nature which makes disaster itself less hard to bear than the apprehension of disaster, Ralph felt relieved when he knew the worst. There was much of the mystery still unexplained, but the morrow would reveal it; and Ralph lay down to sleep, and rose at daybreak, not with a lighter, but with an easier heart.

When he took up his shepherd's staff that morning, he turned towards Fornside Fell. Rising out of the Vale of Wanthwaite, the fell half faced the purple heights of Blencathra. It was brant from side to side, and as rugged as steep. Ralph did not ascend the screes, out went up by Castle Rock, and walked northwards among the huge bowlders. The frost lay on the loose fragments of rock, and made a firm but perilous causeway. The sun was shining feebly and glinting over the frost. It had sparkled among the icicles that hung in Styx Ghyll as he passed, and the ravine had been hard to cross. The hardy black sheep of the mountains bleated in the cold from unseen places, and the wind carried their call away until it died off into a moan.

When Ralph got well within the shadow cast on to the fell from the protruding head of the Castle Rock, he paused and looked about him. Yes, he was somewhat too high. He began to descend. The rock's head sheltered him from the wind now, and in the silence he could hear the thud of a pick or hammer, and then the indistinct murmur of a man's voice singing. It was Sim's voice; and here was Sim's cave. It was a cleft in the side of the mountain, high enough and broad enough for a man to pass in. Great bowlders stood above and about it.

The sun could never shine into it. A huge rock stood alone and apparently unsupported near its mouth, as though aeons long gone by an iceberg had perched it there. The dog would have bounded in upon Sim where he sat and sang at his work, but Ralph checked him with a look. Inexpressibly eerie sounded the half-buried voice of the singer in that Solitary place. The weird ditty suited well with both.

She lean'd her head against a thorn,
The sun shines fair on Carlisle wa';
And there she has her young babe born,
And the lyon shall be lord of a'.

She's howket a grave by the light o' the moon,
The sun shines fair on Carlisle wa';
And there she's buried her sweet babe in,
And the lyon shall be lord of a'.

The singer stopped, as though conscious of the presence of a listener, and looking up from where he sat on a round block of timber, cutting up a similar block into firewood, he saw Ralph Ray leaning on his staff near the cave's mouth. He had already heard of the sorrow that had fallen on the household at Shoulthwaite. With an unspeakable look of sympathy in his wild, timid eyes, as though some impulse of affection urged him to throw his arms about Ralph and embrace him, while some sense of shame impelled him to kneel at his feet, Sim approached him, and appeared to make an effort to speak. But he could say nothing. Ralph understood his silence and was grateful for it. They went into the cave, and sat down in the dusk.

"You can tell me all about it, now," Ralph said, without preamble of any sort, for each knew well what lay closest at the other's heart. "He is gone now, and we are here together, with none but ourselves to hear."

"I knew you must know it one day," Sim said, "but I tried hard to hide it from you – I did, believe me, I tried hard – I tried, but it was not to be."

"It is best so," Ralph answered; "you must not bear the burden of guilt that is not your own."

"I'm no better than guilty myself," said Sim. "I don't reckon myself innocent; not I. No, I don't reckon myself innocent."

"I think I understand you, Sim; but you were not guilty of the deed?"

"No, but I might have been – I might but for an accident – the accident of a moment; but I've thought sometimes that the crime is not in the deed, but the intention. No, Ralph, I *am* the guilty man, after all: your father had never thought of the crime, not he, but I had brooded over it."

"Did you go out that night intending to do it?" Ralph said.

"Yes; at least I think I did, but I don't feel sure; my mind was in a broil; I hardly knew what I meant to do. If Wilson had told me as I met him in the road – as I intended to meet him – that he had come back to do what he had threatened to do so often – then – yes, *then*, I must have done it – I *must*."

"What had he threatened?" Ralph asked, but there was no note of inquiry in his voice. "Whom did it concern?"

"It concerned yourself, Ralph," said Sim, turning his head aside. "But no matter about that," he added. "It's over now, it is."

Ralph drew out of his pocket the paper that had fallen from his father's breast.

"Is this what you mean?" he said, handing it to Sim.

Sim carried it to the light to read it. Returning to where Ralph sat, he cried in a shrill voice, –

"Then he *had* come back to do it. O God, why should it be murder to kill a scoundrel?"

"Did you know nothing of this until now?"

"Nothing. Wilson threatened it, as I say; he told me he'd hang you on the nearest gibbet, he did – you who'd saved his life – leastways, so they say – the barren-hearted monster!"

"It's ill-luck to serve a bad man, Sim. Well?"

"I never quite thought he'd do it; no, I never did quite think it. Why is it not a good deed to kill a bad man?"

"How did it happen, Sim?" said Ralph.

"I hardly know – that's the truth. You mind well enough it was the day that Abraham Coward, my landlord, called for his rent. It was the day the poor woman and her two wee barns took shelter with me. You looked in on me that night, you remember. Well, when you left me – do you recollect *how*?"

"Yes, Sim."

"My heart was fair maizlet before, but that – that – kiss infected my brain. I must have been mad, Ralph, that's the fact, when I thought of what the man meant to do to the only friend I had left in the world – my own friend and my poor little girl's. I went out to the lanes and wandered about. It was very dark. Suddenly the awful thought came back upon me, it did. I was standing at the crossways, where the road goes off to Gaskarth. I knew Wilson must come by that road. Something commanded me to walk on. I had been halting, but now a dreadful force compelled me to go – ay, compelled me. I don't know what it was, but it seemed as if I'd no power against it, none. It stifled all my scruples, all of them, and I ran – yes, ran. But I was weak, and had to stop for breath. My heart was beating loud, and I pressed my hand hard upon it as I leaned against the wall of the old bridge yonder. It went thump, thump. Then I could hear him coming. I knew his step. He was not far off, but I couldn't stir; no, not stir. My breath seemed all to leave me when I moved. He was coming closer, he was, and in the distance beyont him I could hear the clatter of a horse's feet on the road. The man on the horse was far off, but he galloped, he galloped. It must be done now, I thought; now or not at all. I – I picked up a stone that lay near, I did, and tried to go forward, but fell back, back. I was powerless. That weakness was agony, it was. Wilson had not reached the spot where I stood when the man on the horse had overtaken him. I heard him speak as the man rode past. Then I saw it was your father, and that he turned back. There were high words on his side, and I could hear Wilson's bitter laugh – you recollect that laugh?"

"Yes, yes; well?"

"In a moment Angus had jumped from the horse's back – and then I heard a thud – and that's all."

"Is that all you know?"

"Not all; no, not all, neither. Your father had got up into the saddle in an instant, and I labored out into the middle of the road. He saw me and stopped. 'Ye've earned nowt of late,' he said; 'tak this, my man, and gae off and pay your rent.' Then he put some money into my hand from his purse and galloped on. I thought he'd killed Wilson, and I crept along to look at the dead man. I couldn't find him at first, and groped about in the darkness till my hand touched his face. Then I thought he was alive, I did. The touch flayt me, and I fled away – I don't know how. Ralph, I saw the mark of my hand on his face when they drew me up to it next day in the bedroom of the inn. That night I paid my rent with your father's money, and then I went home."

"It was my father's money, then – not Wilson's?" said Ralph.

"It was as I say," Sim answered, as though hurt by the implication.

Ralph put his hand on Sim's shoulder. Self-condemned, this poor man's conscience was already a whirlpool that drew everything to itself.

"Tell me, Sim – that is, if you can – tell me how you came to suspect Wilson of these dealings."

As he said this Ralph tapped with his fingers the warrant which Sim had returned to him.

"By finding that James Wilson was not his name."

"So you found that, did you; how?"

"It was Mother Garth's doings, not mine," said Sim.

"What did she tell you?"

"Nothing; that is, nothing about Wilson going by a false name. No; I found that out for myself, though it was all through her that I found it."

"You knew it all that bad night in Martinmas, did you not?"

"That's true enough, Ralph. The old woman, she came one night and broke open Wilson's trunk, and carried off some papers – leastways one paper."

"You don't know what it was?"

"No. It was in one of Wilson's bouts away at – at Gaskarth, so he said. Rotha was at the Moss: she hadn't come home for the night. I had worked till the darknin', and my eyes were heavy, they were, and then I had gone into the lanes. The night came on fast, and when I turned back I heard men singing and laughing as they came along towards me."

"Some topers from the Red Lion, that was all?"

"Yes, that was all. I jumped the dike and crossed the fields instead of taking the road. As I came by Fornside I saw that there was a light in the little room looking to the back. It was Wilson's room; he would have no other. I thought he had got back, and I crept up – I don't know why – I crept up to the window and looked in. It was not Wilson who was there. It was Mrs. Garth. She had the old man's trunk open, and was rummaging among some papers at the bottom of it."

"Did you go in to her?"

"I was afeart of the woman, Ralph; but I did go in, dotherin' and stammerin'."

"What did she say?"

"She was looking close at a paper as I came upon her. She started a little, but when she saw who it was she bashed down the lid of the trunk and brushed past me, with the paper in her hand. 'You can tell him, if you like, that I have been here.' That was all she said, and before I had turned about she had gone, she had. What was that paper, Ralph; do you know?"

"Perhaps time will tell, perhaps not."

"There was something afoot atween those two; what was it?"

"Can't you guess? You discovered his name."

"Wilson Garth, that was it. That was the name I found on his papers. Yes, I opened the trunk and looked at them when the woman had gone; yes, I did that."

"You remember how she came to these parts? That was before my time of remembrance, but not before yours, Sim."

"I think they said she'd wedded a waistrel on the Borders."

"Did they ever say the man was dead?"

"No, I can't mind that they ever did. I can't mind it. He had beaten her and soured her into the witch that she is now, and then she had run away frae him with her little one, Joe that now is. That was what they said, as I mind it."

"Two and two are easily put together, Sim. Wilson Garth, not James Wilson, was the man's name."

"And he was Mrs. Garth's husband and the father of Joe?"

"The same, I think."

Sim seemed to stagger under the shock of a discovery that had been slow to dawn upon him.

"How did it come, Ralph, that you brought him here when you came home from the wars? Everything seems, someways, to hang on that."

"Everything; perhaps even this last disaster of all." Ralph passed his fingers through his hair, and then his palm across his brow. Sim observed a change in his friend's manner.

"It was wrong of me to say that, it was," he said. "I don't know that it's true, either. But tell me how it came about."

"It's a short story, old friend, and easily told, though it has never been told till now. I had done the man some service at Carlisle."

"Saved his life, so they say."

"It was a good turn, truly, but I had done it – at least, the first part of it – unawares. But that's *not* a short story."

"Tell me, Ralph."

"It's dead and done with, like the man himself. What remains is not dead, and cannot soon be done with. Some of us must meet it face to face even yet. Wilson – that was his name in those days – was a Royalist when I encountered him. What he had been before, God knows. At a moment of peril he took his life at the hands of a Roundhead. He had been guilty of treachery to the Royalists, and he was afraid to return to his friends. I understood his position and sheltered him. When Carlisle fell to us he clung closer to me, and when the campaign was over he prayed to be permitted to follow me to these parts. I yielded to him reluctantly. I distrusted him, but I took his anxiety to be with me for gratitude, as he said it was. It was not that, Sim."

"Was it fear? Was he afeart of being hanged by friends or foes? Hadn't he been a taistrel to both?"

"Partly fear, but partly greed, and partly revenge. He was hardly a week at Shoulthwaite before I guessed his secret – I couldn't be blind to that. When he married his young wife on the Borders, folks didn't use to call her a witch. She had a little fortune coming to her one day, and when she fled the prospect of it was lost to her husband. Wilson was in no hurry to recover her while she was poor-a vagrant woman with his child at her breast. The sense of his rights as a husband became keener a little later. Do you remember the time when young Joe Garth set himself up in the smithy yonder?"

"I do," said Sim; "it was the time of the war. The neighbors told of some maiden aunt, an old crone like herself, who had left Joe's mother aboon a hundred pound."

"Wilson knew that much better than our neighbors. He knew, too, where his wife had hidden herself, as she thought, though it had served his turn to seem ignorant of it until then. Sim, he used *me* to get to Wythburn."

"Teush!"

"Once here, it was not long before he had made his wife aware of his coming. I had kept an eye on him, and I knew his movements. I saw that he meant to ruin the Garths, mother and son, to strip them and leave them destitute. I determined that he should not do it. I felt that mine was the blame that he was here to molest them. 'Tamper with them,' I said, 'show once more by word or look that you know anything of them, and I'll hand you over as a traitor to the nearest sheriff.'"

"Why didn't you do it anyhow, why didn't you?" said Sim eagerly.

"That would have been unwise. He now hated me for defeating his designs."

"You had saved his life."

"He hated me none the less for that. There was only one way now to serve either the Garths or myself, and that was to keep the man in hand. I neither sent him away nor let him go."

"You were more than a match for him to the last," said Sim, "and you saved me and my lass from him too. But what about Joe Garth and his old mother? They don't look over-thankful to you, they don't."

"They think that I brought Wilson back to torment them. No words of mine would upset the notion. I'm sorry for that, but leave such mistakes for time to set right. And when the truth comes in such a case it comes to some purpose."

"Aye, when it comes – *when* it comes."

Sim spoke in an undertone, and as though to himself.

"It's long in the coming sometimes, it is."

"It seems long, truly." The dalesman had caught Sim's drift, and with his old trick of manner, more expressive than his words, he had put his hand on Sim's arm.

"And now there is but one chance that has made it quite worth the while that we should have talked frankly on the subject, you and I, and that is the chance that others may come to do what Wilson tried to do. The authorities who issued this warrant will hardly forget that they issued it. There was a stranger here the day after the inquest. I think I know what he was."

Sim shuddered perceptibly.

"He went away then, but we'll see him once more, depend upon it."

"Is it true, as Wilson said, that Oliver's men are like to be taken?"

"There's a spy in every village, so they say, and blank warrants, duly signed, in every sheriff's court, ready to be filled in with any name that malice may suggest. These men mean that Puritanism shall be rooted out of England. We cannot be too well prepared."

"I wish I could save you, Ralph; leastways, I wish it were myself instead, I do."

"You thought to save me, old friend, when you went out to meet Wilson that night three months ago. My father, too, he thought to save me when he did what he did. You were both rash, both wrong. You could not have helped me at all in that way. Poor father! How little he has helped me, Heaven knows – Heaven alone knows – yet."

Ralph drew his hand across his eyes.

CHAPTER VIII

Robbie's Redemption

Sim accompanied Ralph half-way down the hill when he rose to go. Robbie Anderson could be seen hastening towards them. His mission must be with Ralph, so Sim went back.

"I've been to Shoulthwaite to look for you," said Robbie. "They told me you'd taken the hills for it, so I followed on."

"You look troubled, my lad," said Ralph; "has anything happened to you?"

"No, Ralph, but something may happen to you if you don't heed me what I say."

"Nothing that will trouble me much, Robbie – nothing of that kind can happen now."

"Yon gommarel of a Joe Garth, the blacksmith, has never forgotten the thrashing you gave him years ago for killing your dog – Laddie's mother that was."

"No, he'll never forgive me; but what of that? I've not looked for his forgiveness."

"But, I'm afeared, Ralph, he means to pay you back more than four to the quarter. Do you know he has spies lodging with him? They've come down here to take you off. Joe has been at the Red Lion this morning – drunk, early as it is. He blurted it out about the spies, so I ran off to find you."

"It isn't Joe that has done the mischief, my lad, though the spies, or whatever they are, may pay him to play underspy while it serves their turn."

"Joe or not Joe, they mean to take you the first chance. Folks say everything has got upside down with the laws and the country now that the great man himself is dead. Hadn't you best get off somewhere?

"It was good of you, Robbie, to warn me; but I can't leave home yet; my father must be buried, you know."

"Ah!" said Robbie in an altered tone, "poor Angus!"

Ralph looked closely at his companion, and thought of Robbie's question last night in the inn.

"Tell me," he said, glancing searchingly into Robbie's eyes, "did you know anything about old Wilson's death?"

The young dalesman seemed abashed. He dropped his head, and appeared unable to look up.

"Tell me, Robbie; I know much already."

"I took the money," said the young man; "I took it, but I threw it into the beck the minute after."

"How was it, lad? Let me know."

Robbie was still standing, with his head down, pawing the ground as he said, –

"I'd been drinking hard – you know that. I was drunk yon night, and I hadn't a penny in my pouch. On my way home from the inn I lay down in the dike and fell asleep. I was awakened by the voices of two men quarrelling. You know who they were. Old Wilson was waving a paper over his head and laughing and sneering. Then the other snatched it away. At that Wilson swore a dreadful oath, and flung himself on – the other. It was all over in a moment. He'd given the little waistrel the cross-buttock, and felled him on his head. I saw the other ride off, and I saw Simeon Stagg. When all was still, I crept out and took Wilson's money – yes, I took it; but I flung it into the next beck. For the moment, when I touched him I thought he was alive. I've not been drinking hard since then, Ralph; no, nor never will again."

"Ey, you'll do better than that, Robbie."

Ralph said no more. There was a long silence between the two men, until Robbie, unable to support it any longer, broke in again with, "I took it, but I flung it into the next beck."

The poor fellow seemed determined to dwell upon the latter fact as in some measure an extenuation of his offence. In his silent hours of remorse he had cherished it as one atoning circumstance. It had been the first fruits of a sudden resolution of reform. Sobered by the sense of what part he had played in crime, the money that had lain in his hand was a witness against him; and when he had flung it away he had only the haunting memory left of what he would have done in effect, but had, in fact, done only in name.

"Why did you not say this at the inquest?" asked Ralph. "You might have cleared Simeon Stagg. Was it because you must have accused my father?"

"I can't say it was that. I felt guilty myself. I felt as if half the crime had been mine."

There was another pause.

"Robbie," Ralph said at length, "would you, if I wished it, say no more about all this?"

"I've said nothing till now, and I need say nothing more."

"Sim will be as silent – if I ask him. There is my poor mother, my lad; she can't live long, and why should she be stricken down? Her dear old head is bowed low enough already."

"I promise you, Ralph," said Robbie. He had turned half aside, and was speaking falteringly. He remembered one whose head had been bowed lower still – one whose heart had been sick for his own misdeeds, and now the grass was over her.

"Then that is agreed."

"Ralph, there's something I should have said before, but I was afeared to say it. Who would have believed the word of a drunkard? That's what I was, God forgive me! Besides, it would have done no good to say it, that I can see, and most likely some harm."

"What was it?"

"Didn't they say they found Wilson lying fifty yards below the river?"

"They did; fifty yards to the south of the bridge."

"It was as far to the north that I left him. I'm sure of it. I was sobered by what happened. I could swear it in heaven, Ralph. It was full fifty yards on the down side of the bridge from the smithy."

"Think again, my lad; it's a serious thing that you say."

"I've thought of it too much. It has tormented me day and night. There's no use in trying to persuade myself I must be wrong. Fifty yards on the down side of the beck from the smithy – that was the place, Ralph."

The dalesman looked grave. Then a light crossed his face as if a wave of hope had passed through him. Sim had said he was leaning against the bridge. All that Angus could have done must have been done to the north of it. Was it possible, after all, that Angus had not killed Wilson by that fall?

"You say that for the moment, when you touched him, you thought Wilson was not dead?"

"It's true, I thought so."

Sim had thought the same.

"Did you see any one else that night?"

"No."

"Nor hear other footsteps?"

"No, none but my own at last – none."

It was no clew. Unconsciously Ralph put his hand to his breast and touched the paper that he had placed there. No, there was no hope. The shadow that had fallen had fallen forever.

"Perhaps the man recovered enough to walk a hundred yards, and then fell dead. Perhaps he had struggled to reach home?"

"He would be going the wrong way for that, Ralph."

"True, true; it's very strange, very, if it is as you say. He was fifty yards beyond the smithy – north of it?"

"He was."

The dalesmen walked on. They had got down into the road, when the little schoolmaster ran up against them almost before he had been seen.

"Oh, here you are, are you?" he gasped.

"Are they coming?" said Robbie Anderson, jumping on to the turf hedge to get a wider view.

"That they are."

The little man had dropped down on to a stone, and was mopping his forehead. When he had recovered his breath, he said, –

"I say, Monsieur the Gladiator, why didn't you kill when you were about it? I say, why didn't you kill?" and Monsey held his thumbs down, as he looked in Ralph's face.

"Kill whom?" said Ralph. He could not help laughing at the schoolmaster's ludicrous figure and gesture.

"Why, that Garth – a bad garth – a kirk-garth – a kirk-warner's garth-a devil's garth – *Joe* Garth?"

"I can't see them," said Robbie, and he jumped down again into the road.

"Oh, but you will, you will," said Monsey; and stretching his arm out towards Ralph with a frantic gesture, he cried, "You fly, fly, fly, fly!"

"Allow me to point out to you," observed Ralph, smiling, "that I do not at all fly, nor shall I know why I should not remain where I am until you tell me."

"Then know that your life's not worth a pin's fee if you remain here to be taken. Oh, that Garth – that devil's garth – that – that – *Joe* Garth!"

There was clearly no epithet that suited better with Monsey's mood than the said monster's proper name.

"Friends," said Ralph, more seriously, "it's clear I can't leave before I see my father buried, and it's just as clear I can't see him buried if I stay. With your help I may do both – that is, seem to do both."

"How? how? unfold – I can interpret you no conundrums," said Monsey. "To go, and yet not to go, that is the question."

"Can I help you?" said Robbie with the simplicity of earnestness.

"Go back, schoolmaster, to the Lion."

"I know it – I've been there before – well?"

"Say, if your conscience will let you – I know how tender it is – say you saw me go over Lauvellen in the direction of Fairfield. Say this quietly – say it to old Matthew in a whisper and as a secret; that will be enough."

"I've shared with that patriarch some secrets before now, and they've been common property in an hour – common as the mushrooms on the common – common as his common saws – common – "

"Robbie, the burial will take place the day after to-morrow, at three in the afternoon, at the kirk-garth – "

"Oh, that Garth, – that devil's garth – that Joe – "

"At the kirk-garth at Gosforth," continued Ralph. "Go round the city and the dale, and bid every master and mistress within the warning to Shoulthwaite Moss at nine o'clock in the morning. Be there yourself as the representative of the family, and see all our old customs observed. The kirk-garth is twenty miles away, across rugged mountain country, and you must follow the public pass."

"Styehead Pass?"

Ralph nodded assent. "Start away at eleven o'clock; take the old mare to bear the body; let the boy ride the young horse, and chain him to the mare at the bottom of the big pass. These men, these spies, these constables, whatever they may be, will lie in wait for me about the house that morning. If they don't find me at my father's funeral they'll then believe that I must have gone. Do *you* hold the mare's head, Robbie – mind that. When you get to the top of the pass, perhaps some one will relieve you – perhaps so, perhaps not. You understand?"

"I do."

"Let nothing interfere with this plan as I give it you. If you fail in any single particular, all may be lost."

"I'll let nothing interfere. But what of Willy? What if he object?

"Tell him these are my wishes – he'll yield to that."

There was a moment's silence.

"Robbie, that was a noble resolve you told me of; and you can keep it, can you not?"

"I can – God help me."

"Keep it the day after to-morrow – you remember our customs, sometimes more honored, you know, in the breach than the observance – you can hold to your resolve that day; you *must* hold to it, for everything hangs on it. It is a terrible hazard."

Robbie put his hand in Ralph's, and the two stalwart dalesmen looked steadily each into the other's face. There was a dauntless spirit of resolution in the eyes of the younger man. His resolve was irrevocable. His crime had saved him.

"That's enough," said Ralph. He was satisfied.

"Why, you sleep – you sleep," cried the little schoolmaster. During the preceding conversation he had been capering to and fro in the road, leaping on to the hedge, leaping back again, and putting his hands to the sides of his eyes to shut away the wind that came from behind him, while he looked out for the expected enemy.

"You sleep – you sleep – that Garth – that devil's garth – that worse than kirk-garth – that – that – !"

"And now we part," said Ralph, "for the present. Good by, both!" And he turned to go back the way he came.

Monsey and Robbie had gone a few paces in the other direction, when the little schoolmaster stopped, and, turning round, cried in a loud voice, "O yes, I know it – the Lion. I've been there before. I'll whisper Father Matthew that you've gone – "

Robbie had put his arm on Monsey's shoulder and swung him round, and Ralph heard no more.

CHAPTER IX

The Shadow of the Crime

But yester-night I prayed aloud
In anguish and in agony.

Coleridge.

The night was far advanced, and yet Ralph had not returned to Shoulthwaite. It was three hours since Matthew Branthwaite had left the Moss. Mrs. Ray still sat before the turf fire and gazed into it in silence. Rotha was by her side, and Willy lay on the settle drawn up to the hearth. All listened for the sound of footsteps that did not come.

The old clock ticked out louder and more loud; the cricket's measured chirp seemed to grow more painfully audible; the wind whistled through the leafless boughs without, and in the lulls of the abating storm the low rumble of the ghyll could be heard within. What kept Ralph away? It was no unusual thing for him to be abroad from dawn to dusk, but the fingers of the clock were approaching eleven, and still he did not come. On this night, of all others, he must have wished to be at home.

Earlier in the evening Rotha had found occasion to go on some errand to the neighboring farm, and there she had heard that towards noon Ralph had been seen on horseback crossing Stye Head towards Wastdale. Upon reporting this at the Moss, the old dame had seemed to be relieved.

"He thinks of everything," she had said. All that day she had cherished the hope that it would be possible to bury Angus over the hills, at Gosforth. It was in the old churchyard there that her father lay-her father, her mother, and all her kindred. It was twenty miles to those plains and uplands, that lay beyond the bleak shores of Wastdale. It was a full five hours' journey there and back. But when twice five hours had been counted, and still Ralph had not returned, the anxiety of the inmates of the old house could no longer be concealed. In the eagerness of their expectation the clock ticked louder than ever, the cricket chirped with more jubilant activity, the wind whistled shriller, the ghylls rumbled longer, but no welcomer sound broke the stillness.

At length Willy got up and put on his hat. He would go down the lonnin to where it joined the road, and meet Ralph on the way. He would have done so before, but the horror of walking under the shadow of the trees where last night his father fell had restrained him. Conquering his fear, he sallied out.

The late moon had risen, and was shining at full. With a beating heart he passed the dreaded spot, and reached the highway beyond. He could hear nothing of a horse's canter. There were steps approaching, and he went on towards whence they came. Two men passed close beside him, but neither of them was Ralph. They did not respond to his greeting when, in accordance with the custom of the country, he bade them "Good night." They were strangers, and they looked closely – he thought suspiciously – at him as they went by.

Willy walked a little farther, and then returned. As he got back to the lane that led to the house, the two men passed him again. Once more they looked closely into his face. His fear prompted him to speak, but again they went on in silence. As Willy turned up towards home, the truth flashed upon him that these men were the cause of Ralph's absence. He knew enough of what was going on in the world to realize the bare possibility that his brother's early Parliamentarian campaign might bring him into difficulties even yet. It seemed certain that the lord of Wythburn Manor would be executed. Only Ralph's obscurity could save him.

When Willy got back into the kitchen, the impression that Ralph was being pursued and dogged was written on his face. His mother understood no more of his trouble than that his brother had not returned; she looked from his face back to the fire, that now died slowly on the hearth. Rotha was quicker to catch the significance of Willy's nervous expression and fitful words. To her the situation now appeared hardly less than tragic. With the old father lying dead in the loft above, what would come to this household if the one strong hand in it was removed? Then she thought of her own father. What would become of him? Where was he this night? The sense of impending disaster gave strength to her, however. She rose and put her hand on Willy's arm as he walked to and fro across the earthen floor. She was the more drawn to him from some scarce explicable sense of his weakness.

"Some one coming now," he said in eager tones – his ears were awake with a feverish sensitiveness – "some one at the back." It was Ralph at last. He had come down the side of the ghyll, and had entered the house from behind. All breathed freely.

"God bless thee!" said Mrs. Ray.

"You've been anxious. It was bad to keep you so," he said, with an obvious effort to assume his ordinary manner.

"I reckon thou couldst not have helped it, my lad," said Mrs. Ray. Relieved and cheerful, she was bustling about to get Ralph's supper on the table.

"Well, no," he answered. "You know, I've been over to Gosforth – it's a long ride – I borrowed Jackson's pony from Armboth; and what a wild country it is, to be sure! It blew a gale on Stye Head. It's bleak enough up there on a day like this, mother. I could scarce hold the horse."

"I don't wonder, Ralph; but see, here's thy poddish – thou must be fair clemm'd."

"No, no; I called at Broom Hill."

"How did you come in at the back, lad? Do you not come up the lonnin?"

"I thought I'd go round by the low meadow and see all safe, and then the nearest way home was on the hill side, you know."

Willy and Rotha glanced simultaneously at Ralph as he said this, but they found nothing in his face, voice, or manner to indicate that his words were intended to conceal the truth.

"But look how late it is!" he said as the clock struck twelve; "hadn't we better go off to bed, all of us?"

"I think I must surely go off," said Mrs. Ray, and with Rotha she left the kitchen. Willy soon followed them, leaving Ralph to eat his supper alone. Laddie, who had entered with his master, was lying by the smouldering fire, and after the one had finished eating, the other came in for his liberal share of the plain meal. Then Ralph rose, and, lifting up his hat and staff, walked quietly to his brother's room. Willy was already in bed, but his candle was still burning. Sitting on an old oak chest that stood near the door of the little room, Ralph said, –

"I shall perhaps be off again before you are awake in the morning, but all will be done in good time. The funeral will be on the day after to-morrow. Robbie Anderson will see to everything."

"Robbie Anderson?" said Willy in an accent of surprise.

"You know it's the custom in the dale for a friend of the family to attend to these offices."

"Yes; but Robbie Anderson of all men!"

"You may depend upon him," said Ralph.

"This is the first time I've heard that he can depend upon himself, said Willy.

"True – true – but I'm satisfied about Robbie. No, you need fear nothing. Robbie's a changed man, I think."

"Changed he must be, Ralph, if you would commit to his care what could not be too well discharged by the most trustworthy friend of the family."

"Yes, but Robbie will do as well as another – better. You know, Willy, I have an old weakness for a sheep that strays. When I get it back I fancy, somehow, it's the best of the flock."

"May your straggler justify your odd fancy this time, brother!"

"Rotha will see to what has to be done at home," said Ralph, rising and turning to go.

"Ralph," said Willy, "do you know I – " He faltered and began again, obviously changing the subject. "Have you been in there to-night?" with a motion of the head towards the room wherein lay all that remained of their father.

"No; have you?"

"No; I dare not go. I would not if I could. I wish to remember him as he lived, and one, glance at his dead face would blot out the memory forever."

Ralph could not understand this. There was no chord in his nature that responded to such feelings; but he said nothing in reply.

"Ralph," continued Willy, "do you know I think Rotha – I almost thin – do you not think that Rotha rather cares for me?"

A perceptible tremor passed over Ralph's face. Then he said, with something like a smile, "Do you think she does, my lad?"

"I do – I almost do think so."

Ralph had resumed his seat on the oak chest. The simple, faltering words just spoken had shaken him to the core. Hidden there – hidden even from himself – had lain inert for months a mighty passion such as only a great heart can know. In one moment he had seen it and known it for what it was. Yes, he had indeed loved this girl; he loved her still. When he spoke again his voice seemed to have died inwards; he appeared to be speaking out of his breast.

"And what of yourself, Willy?" he asked.

"I think I care for her, too, – I think so."

How sure was the other of a more absolute affection than the most positive words could express! Ralph sat silent for a moment, as was his wont when under the influence of strong feeling. His head inclined downwards, and his eyes were fixed on the floor. A great struggle was going on within him. Should he forthwith make declaration of his own passion? Love said, Yes! love should be above all ties of kindred, all claims of blood. But the many tongues of an unselfish nature said, No! If this thing were wrong, it would of itself come to nought; if right, it would be useless to oppose it. The struggle was soon over, and the impulse of self-sacrifice had conquered. But at what a cost – at what a cost!

"Yet there is her father, you know," Willy added. "One dreads the thought of such a match. There may be something in the blood – at least, one fears – "

"You need have no fear of Rotha that comes of her relation to Simeon Stagg. Sim is an innocent man."

"So you say – so you say. Let us hope so. It's a terrible thought-that of marriage with the flesh and blood of – of a murderer."

"Rotha is as free from taint of crime as – you are. She is a noble girl, and worthy of you, worthy of any man, whatever her father may be," said Ralph.

"Yes, yes, I know; I thought you'd say so. I'm glad, Ralph – I can't tell you how glad I am – to hear you say so. And if I'm right – if Rotha really loves me – I know you'll be as glad as I am."

Ralph's face trembled slightly at this, but he nodded his head and smiled.

"Not that I could think of it for a long time," Willy continued. "This dreadful occurrence must banish all such thoughts for a very long time."

Willy seemed to find happiness in the prospect, remote as it might be. Ralph's breast heaved as he looked upon his brother's brightening face. That secret of his own heart must lie forever buried there. Yes, he had already resolved upon that. He should never darken the future that lay pictured in those radiant eyes. But this was a moment of agony nevertheless. Ralph was following the funeral of the mightiest passion of his soul. He got up and opened the door.

"Good night, and God bless you!" he said huskily.

"One moment, Ralph. Did you see two men, strangers, on the road to-night? Ah, I remember, you came in at the back."

"Two friends of Joe Garth's," said Ralph, closing the door behind him.

When he reached his own room he sat for some minutes on the bed. What were the feelings that preyed upon him? He hardly knew. His heart was desolate. His life seemed to be losing its hope, or his hope its object. And not yet had he reached the worst. Some dread forewarning of a sterner fate seemed to hang above him.

Rising, Ralph threw off his shoes, and drew on a pair of stouter ones. Then he laced up a pair of leathern leggings, and, taking down a heavy cloak from behind the door, he put it across his arm. He had no light but the light of the moon.

Stepping quietly along the creaky old corridor to the room where his father lay, Ralph opened the door and entered. A clod of red turf smouldered on the hearth, and the warm glow from it mingled with the cold blue of the moonlight. How full of the odor of a dead age the room now seemed to be! The roof was opened through the rude timbers to the whitened thatch. Sheepskins were scattered about the black oaken floor. Ralph walked to the chimney-breast, and stood on one of the skins as he leaned on the rannel-tree shelf. How still and cheerless it all was!

The room stretched from the front to the back of the house, and had a window at each end. The moon that shone through the window at the front cast its light across the foot of the bed. Ralph had come to bid his last good-night to him who lay thereon. It was in this room that he himself had been born. He might never enter it again.

How the strong man was laid low! All his pride of strength had shrunk to this! "The lofty looks of men shall be humbled, and the haughtiness of men shall be bowed down." What indeed was man, whose breath was in his nostrils!

The light was creeping up the bed. Silent was he who lay there as the secret which he had never discharged even to his deaf pillow. Had that secret mutinied in the heart that knew its purple war no more? Ah! how true it was that conscience was a thousand swords. With no witness against him except himself, whither could he have fled from the accusation that burned within him as a fire! Not chains nor cells could have spoken to this strong man like the awful voice of his solitary heart. How remorse must have corroded that heart! How he must have numbered the hours of that remorse! How one sanguinary deed must have trampled away all joyous memories! But the secret agony was over at last: it was over now.

The moonlight had crept up to the head. It was silvering the gray hairs that rested there. Ralph stepped up to the bedside and uncovered the face. Was it changed since he looked on it last? Last night it was his father's face: was it laden with iniquity now? How the visible phantom of one horrible moment must have stood up again and again before these eyes! How sternly fortune must have frowned on these features! Yet it was his father's face still.

And what of that father's great account? Who could say what the final arbitrament would be? Had he who lay there, the father, taken up all this load of guilt and remorse for love of him, the son? Was he gone to a dreadful audit, too, and all for love of him? And to know nothing of it until now – until it was too late to take him by the hand or to look into his eyes! Nay, to have tortured him unwittingly with a hundred cruel words! Ralph remembered how in days past he had spoken bitterly in his father's presence of the man who allowed Simeon Stagg to rest under an imputation of murder not his own. That murder had been done to save his own life – however unwisely, however rashly, still to save his (Ralph's) own life.

Ralph dropped to his knees at the bedside. What barrier had stood between the dead man and himself that in life the one had never revealed himself to the other? They were beyond that revealment now, yet here was everything as in a glass. "Oh, my father," cried Ralph as his head fell between his hands, "would that tears of mine could scald away your offence!"

Then there came back the whisper of the old words, "The lofty looks of men shall be humbled, and the haughtiness of men shall be bowed down."

Ralph knelt long at his father's side, and when he rose from his knees it was with a calmer but a heavier heart.

"Surely God's hand is upon me," he murmured. The mystery would yield no other meaning. "Gone to his account with the burden, not of my guilt, but of my fate, upon him."

Ralph walked to the fire and turned over the expiring peat. It gave a fitful flicker. He took from his pocket the paper that had fallen from his father's breast, and looked long at it in the feeble light. It was all but the only evidence of the crime, and it must be destroyed. He put the paper to the light. Drawing it away, he paused and reflected. He thought of his stricken mother, and his resolve seemed fixed. He must burn this witness against his father; he must crush the black shadow of it in his hand. Could he but crush as easily the black shadow of impending doom! Could he but obliterate as completely the dread reckoning of another world!

The paper that hung in his hand had touched the flickering peat. It was already ignited, but he drew it once more away, and crushed the burning corner to ashes in his palm.

No, it must not be destroyed. He thought of how Rotha had stood over her father's prostrate form in the room of the village inn, and cried in her agony, "Tell them it is not true." Who could say what this paper might yet do for him and her?

Ralph put the warrant back, charred and crumbled, into the breast pocket of the jerkin he wore.

The burning of the paper had for a moment filled the chamber with light. After the last gleam of it had died away, and the ash of the burnt portion lay in his palm, Ralph walked to the front window and looked out. All was still. Only the wind whistled. How black against the moon loomed the brant walls of the Castle Rock across the vale!

Turning about, Ralph re-covered the face and said, "Death is kindest; how could I look into this face alive?"

And the whisper of the old words came back once more: "The lofty looks of men shall be humbled, and the haughtiness of men shall be bowed down."

Ralph walked to the window at the back and gently pushed it open. It overlooked the fell and the Shoulthwaite Ghyll. A low roof went down from it almost to the ground. He stepped out on to this, and stood for a moment in the shadow that lay upon it.

He must take his last look now. He must bid his last good-night. The moon through the opposite window still shone on the silvery hair. The wind was high. It found its way through the open casement. It fluttered the face-cloth above the face. Ralph pushed back the sash, and in a moment he was gone.

CHAPTER X

Mattha Branth'et "Flytes" the Parson

The household on the Moss were early astir on the morning appointed for the funeral of Angus Ray. Matthew Branthwaite's wife and daughter were bustling about the kitchen of the old house soon after daybreak.

Mrs. Branthwaite was a fragile little body, long past her best, with the crow's feet deeply indented about her eyes, which had the timid look of those of a rabbit, and were peculiarly appropriate to a good old creature who seemed to be constantly laboring against the idea that everything she did was done wrongly. Her daughter Liza was a neat little thing of eighteen, with the bluest of blue eyes, the plumpest of plump cheeks, and the merriest of merry voices. They had walked from their home in the gray dawn in order to assist at the preliminaries to the breakfast which had to be eaten by a large company of the dalesmen before certain of them set out on the long journey across the fells.

The previous day had been the day of the "winding," a name that pointed to the last offices of Abraham Strong, the Wythburn carpenter. In the afternoon of the winding day the mistresses of the houses within the "warning" had met to offer liberal doses of solace and to take equally liberal doses of sweet broth, a soup sweetened with raisins and sugar, which was reserved for such melancholy occasions.

According to ancient custom, the "maister men" of the dale were to assemble at nine o'clock on the morning following the winding, and it was to meet their needs that old Mrs. Branthwaite and her daughter had walked over to assist Rotha. The long oak table had to be removed from the wall before the window, and made to stand down the middle of the floor. Robbie Anderson had arrived early at the Moss in order to effect this removal. After his muscles had exercised themselves upon the ponderous article of furniture, and had placed the benches called skemmels down each side and chairs at each end, he went into the stable to dress down the mare and sharpen her shoes preparatory to her long journey.

The preliminaries in the kitchen occupied a couple of hours, and during this time Mrs. Ray and Willy sat together in a room above. The reason of Ralph's absence had been explained to his mother by Rotha, who had received her information from Robbie Anderson. The old dame had accepted the necessity with characteristic resignation. What Ralph thought well to do she knew would be best. She did not foresee evil consequences.

Willy had exhibited more perturbation. Going into his brother's room on the morning after their conversation, he saw clearly enough that the bed had not been slept upon. The two friends of Joe Garth's, of whom Ralph had spoken with so much apparent unconcern, had obviously driven him away from home in the depth of the night. Then came Rotha's explanation.

His worst fears were verified. Was it conceivable that Ralph could escape the machinations of those who had lain a web that had already entangled the lord of Wythburn himself? Every one who had served in the trained bands of the Parliament was at the mercy of any man, who, for the gratification of personal spite, chose to become informer against him.

The two strangers had been seen in the city during the preceding day. It was obviously their purpose to remain until time itself verified the rumor that Ralph had left these parts to escape them. The blacksmith had bragged in his cups at the Red Lion that Wilfrey Lawson of the constable's court at Carlisle would have Ralph Ray in less than a week. Robbie Anderson had overheard this, and had reported it at the Moss. Robbie professed to know better, and to be able to laugh at such pretensions. Willy was more doubtful. He thought his better education, and consequently more intimate acquaintance with the history of such conflicts with the ruling powers, justified him in his apprehensions. He sat with his mother while the business was going on downstairs, apparently struggling with an idea that it was his duty to comfort her, but offering such curious comfort that the old dame looked up again and again with wide eyes, which showed that her son was suggesting to her slower intellect a hundred dangers and a hundred moods of sorrow that she could neither discover for herself nor cope with.

Towards nine the "maister men" of Wythburn began to arrive at Shoulthwaite. Such of them as intended to accompany the remains of their fellow-dalesman to their resting place at Gosforth came on mountain ponies, which they dismounted in the court and led into a spare barn. Many came on foot, and of these by much the larger part meant to accompany the *cortège* only to the top of the Armboth Fell, and, having "sett" it so far, to face no more of the more than twenty miles of rough country that lay between the valley and the churchyard on the plains by the sea.

Matthew Branthwaite was among the first to arrive. The old weaver was resplendent in the apparel usually reserved for "Cheppel Sunday." The external elevation of his appearance from the worn and sober brown of his daily "top-sark" seemed to produce a corresponding elevation of the weaver's spirit. Despite the solemnity of the occasion, he seemed tempted to let fall a sapient proverb of anything but a funereal tone. On stepping into the kitchen and seeing the provision that had been made for a repast, he did indeed intimate his intention of assisting at the ceremony in the language of the time-honored wren who cried "I helps" as she let a drop of water fall into the sea. At this moment the clergyman from the chapel-of-ease on the Raise arrived at the Moss, and Matthew prepared to put his precept into practice.

The priest, Nicholas Stevens by name, was not a Cumbrian. He had kept his office through three administrations, and to their several forms of legislation he had proved equally tractable. His spirit of accommodation had not been quite so conspicuous in his dealings with those whom he conceived to be beneath him. But in truth he had left his parishioners very largely to their own devices. When he was moved to come among them, it was with the preoccupied air not so much of the student or visionary as of a man who was isolated from those about him by combined authority, influence, and perhaps superior blood. He now took his seat at the head of the table with the bearing of one to whom it had never occurred to take a lower place. He said little at first, and when addressed he turned his face slowly round to him who spoke with an air of mingled abstraction and self-satisfaction, through which a feeble smile of condescension struggled and seemed to say in a mild voice, "Did you speak?"

Matthew sat at the foot of the table, and down each side were seated the dalesmen, to the number of twenty-four. There were Thomas Fell and Adam Rutledge, Job Leathes and Luke Cockrigg, John Jackson of Armboth, and little Reuben Thwaite.

His reverence cut up the ham into slices as formal as his creed, while old Matthew poured out the contents of two huge black jacks. Robbie Anderson carried the plates to and fro; Mrs. Branthwaite and Liza served out the barley and oaten bread.

The breakfast was hardly more than begun when the kitchen door was partially opened, and the big head of a little man became visible on the inner side of it, the body and legs of the new-comer not having yet arrived in the apartment.

"Am I late?" the head said in a hoarse whisper from its place low down on the door-jamb. It was Monsey Laman, red and puffing after a sharp run.

"It's the laal Frenchman. Come thy ways in," said Matthew. Rotha, who was coming and going from the kitchen to the larder, found a chair for the schoolmaster, and he slid into it with the air of one who was persuading himself that his late advent was unobserved.

"I met that Garth – that – Joe Garth on the road, and he kept me," whispered Monsey apologetically to Matthew across the table. The presence of Death somewhere in the vicinity had banished the schoolmaster's spirit of fun.

While this was going on at one end of the table, Rotha had made her way to the other end, with the ostensible purpose of cutting up the cheese, but with the actual purpose of listening to a conversation in which his reverence Nicholas Stevens was beginning to bear an unusually animated part. Some one had made allusion to the sudden and, as was alleged, the unseemly departure of Ralph Ray on the eve of his father's funeral. Some one else had deplored the necessity for that departure, and had spoken of it as a cruel outrage on the liberties of a good man. From this generous if somewhat disloyal sentiment his reverence was expressing dissent. He thought it nothing but just that the law should take its course.

This might involve the mortification of our private feelings; it would certainly be a grief to him, loving, as he did, the souls committed to his care; but individual affections must be sacrificed to the general weal. The young man, Ralph Ray, had outraged the laws of his country in fighting and conspiring against his anointed King. It was hard, but it was right, that he should be punished for his treason.

His reverence was speaking in cold metallic tones, that fell like the clank of chains on Rotha's ears.

"Moreover, we should all do our best for the King," said the clergyman, "to bring such delinquents to justice."

"Shaf!" cried Matthew Branthwaite from the other end of the table. The little knots of talkers had suddenly become silent.

"Shaf!" repeated Matthew; "what did ye do yersel for the King in Oliver's days? Wilt thoo mak me tell thee? Didst thoo not tak what thoo called the oath of abjuration agen the King five years agone? Didst thoo not? Ey? And didst thoo not come round and ask ivery man on us to do the same?"

The clergyman looked confounded. He dropped his knife and, unable to make a rejoinder, turned to those about him and said, in a tone of amazement, "Did you ever hear the like?"

"Nay," cried Matthew, following up his advantage, "ye may hear it agen, an ye will."

Poor Mrs. Branthwaite seemed sorely distressed. Standing by her husband's chair, she appeared to be struggling between impulse and fear in an attempt to put her hand on the mouth of her loquacious husband, in order to avert the uncertain catastrophe which she was sure must ensue from this unexpected and uncompromising defiance of the representative in Wythburn of the powers that be.

Rotha gave Matthew a look of unmistakable gratitude, which, however, was wasted on that infuriated iconoclast. Fixing his eyes steadily on the priest, the weaver forthwith gave his reverence more than one opportunity of hearing the unwelcome outburst again, telling him by only too palpable hints that the depth of his loyalty was his stipend of £300 a year, and the secret of his willingness to see Ralph in the hands of the constable of Carlisle was the fact that the young man had made no secret of his unwillingness to put off his hat to a priest who had thrice put off his own hat to a money-bag.

"Gang yer gate back to yer steeple-house, Nicholas Stevens," said Matthew, "and mortify yer fatherly bosom for the good of the only soul the Almighty has geàn to yer charge, and mind the auld saying, 'Nivver use the taws when a gloom will do the turn.'"

"You deserve the taws about your back, sirrah, to forget my sacred office so far as to speak so," said the minister.

"And ye hev forgat yer sacred office to call me nicknames," answered Matthew, nothing abashed.

"I see you are no better than those blaspheming Quakers whom Justice Rawlinson has wisely committed to the common gaol – poor famished seducers that deserve the stocks!"

"Rich folk hev rowth of friends," rejoined Matthew, "an' olas will hev while the mak of thyself are aboot."

His reverence was not slow to perceive that the pulpit had been no match for the Red Lion as a place of preparation for an encounter like the present. Gathering up with what grace he could the tattered and besmeared skirts of his priestly dignity, he affected contempt for the weaver by ignoring his remarks; and, turning to those immediately around him, he proceeded with quite unusual warmth to deliver a homily on duty. Reverting to the subject of Ralph Ray's flight from Wythburn, he said that it was well that the young man had withdrawn himself, for had he remained longer in these parts, and had the high sheriff at Carlisle not proceeded against him, he himself, though much against his inclination, might have felt it his duty as a servant of God and the King to put the oath of allegiance to him.

"I do not say positively that I should have done so," he said, in a confidential parenthesis, "but I fear I could not have resisted that duty."

"Dree out the inch when ye've tholed the span," cried Matthew; "I'd nivver strain lang at sic a wee gnat as that."

Without condescending to notice the interruption, his reverence proceeded to say he had recently learned that it had been the intention of the judges on the circuit to recommend Angus Ray, the lamented departed, as a justice for the district. This step had been in contemplation since the direful tragedy which had recently been perpetrated in their midst, and of which the facts remained still unexplained, though circumstantial evidence pointed to a solution of the mystery.

When saying this the speaker turned, as though with an involuntary and unconscious gaze, towards the spot where Rotha stood. He had pushed past the girl on coming through the porch without acknowledging her salutation.

"And if Angus Ray had lived to become a justice," continued the Reverend Nicholas, "it very likely must have been his duty before God and the King to apprehend his son Ralph on a charge of treason."

Robbie Anderson, who was standing by, felt at that moment that it would very likely be *his* duty before long to take the priest by certain appendages of his priestly apparel, and carry him less than tenderly to a bed more soft than odorous.

"It must have been his duty, I repeat," said his reverence, speaking with measured emphasis, "before God and the King."

"Leave God oot on't," shouted Matthew. "Ye may put that in when ye get intil yer pulpit, and then ye'll deceive none but them that lippen till ye. Don't gud yersel wi' God's name."

"It is written," said his reverence, "'It is an abomination to kings to commit wickedness; for the throne is established by righteousness.'"

"Dus'ta think to knock me doon wi' the Bible?" said Matthew with a touch of irreverence. "I reckon ony cock may crouse on his own middenheed. Ye mind me of the clerk at Tickell, who could argify none at all agen the greet Geordie Fox, so he up and broke his nose wi' a bash of his family Bible."

This final rejoinder proved too much for the minister, who rose, the repast being over, and stalked past Rotha into the adjoining chamber, where the widow and Willy sat in their sorrow. The dalesmen looked after his retreating figure, and as the door of the inner room closed, they heard his metallic voice ask if the deceased had judiciously arranged his temporal affairs.

During the encounter between the weaver and the clergyman the company had outwardly observed a rigid neutrality. Little Liza, it is true, had obviously thought it all the best of good fun, and had enjoyed it accordingly. She had grinned and giggled just as she had done on the preceding Sunday when a companion, the only surviving child of Baptist parents now dead, had had the water sprinkled on her face at her christening in the chapel on the Raise. But Luke Cockrigg, Reuben Thwaite, and the rest had remained silent and somewhat appalled. The schoolmaster had felt himself called upon to participate in the strife, but being in the anomalous position of owing his official obligations to the minister and his convictions to the side championed by the weaver, he had contented him with sundry grave shakes of his big head, which shakes, being subject to diverse interpretations, were the least compromising expressions of opinion which his genius could suggest to him. No sooner, however, had the door closed on the clergyman than a titter went round the table. Matthew was still at a white heat. Accustomed as he was to "tum'le" his neighbors at the Red Lion, he was now profoundly agitated. It was not frequently that he brought down such rare game in his sport.

"Mattha Branthet," said Reuben Thwaite, "what, man, thoo didst flyte the minister! What it is to hev the gift o' gob and gumption!"

"Shaf! It's kittle shootin' at crows and clergy," replied Matthew.

The breakfast being over, the benches were turned towards the big peat fire that glowed red on the hearth and warmed the large kitchen on this wintry day. The ale jars were refilled, pipes and tobacco were brought in, and the weaver relinquished his office of potman to his daughter.

"I'd be nobbut a clot-heed," he said when abdicating, "and leave nane for mysel if I sarrad it oot."

Robbie Anderson now put on his great cloak, and took down a whip from a strap against the rafters.

"What's this?" said little Reuben to Robbie. "Are you going without a glass?"

Robbie signified his intention of doing just that and nothing else. At this there was a general laugh, after which Reuben, with numerous blinkings of his little eyes, bantered Robbie about the great drought not long before, when a universal fast had been proclaimed, and Robbie had asked why, if folks could not get water, they would not content themselves with ale.

"Liza, teem a short pint intil this lang Robbie," said Matthew.

Liza brought up a foaming pot, but the young man put it aside with a bashful smile at the girl, who laughed and blushed as she pressed it back upon him.

"Not yet, Liza; when we come back, perhaps."

"Will you not take it from me?" said the girl, turning her pretty head aside, and giving a sly dig of emphasis to the pronouns.

"Not even from you, Liza, yet awhile."

The mischievous little minx was piqued at his refusal, and determined that he should drink it, or decline to do so at the peril of losing her smiles.

"Come, Robbie, you shall drink it off – you must."

"No, my girl, no."

"I think I know those that would do it if I asked them," said Liza, with an arch elevation of her dimpled chin and a shadow of a pout.

"Who wouldn't do it, save Robbie Anderson?" he said, laughing for the first time that morning as he walked out of the kitchen.

In a few minutes he returned, saying all was ready, and it was time to start away. Every man rose and went to the front of the house. The old mare Betsy was there, with the coffin strapped on her broad back. Her bruised knees had healed; the frost had disappeared, her shoes were sharpened, and she could not slip. When the mourners had assembled and ranged themselves around the horse, the Reverend Nicholas Stevens came out with the relatives, the weeping mother and son, with Rotha Stagg, and the "Old Hundredth" was sung.

Then the procession of men on foot and men on horseback set off, Robbie Anderson in front leading the mare that bore the coffin, and a boy riding a young horse by his side. Last of all rode Willy Ray, and as they passed beneath the trees that overhung the lane, he turned in the saddle and waved his arm to the two women, who, through the blinding mist of tears, watched their departure from the porch.

CHAPTER XI

Liza's Wiles

The procession had just emerged from the lane, and had turned into the old road that hugged the margin of the mere, when two men walked slowly by in the opposite direction. Dark as it had been when Willy encountered these men before, he had not an instant's doubt as to their identity.

The reports of Ralph's disappearance, which Matthew had so assiduously promulgated in whispers, had reached the destination which Ralph had designed for them. The representatives of the Carlisle high constable were conscious that they had labored under serious disadvantages in their efforts to capture a dalesman in his own stronghold of the mountains. Moreover, their zeal was not so ardent as to make them eager to risk the dangers of an arrest that was likely to be full of peril. They were willing enough to accept the story of Ralph's flight, but they could not reasonably neglect this opportunity to assure themselves of its credibility. So they had beaten about the house during the morning under the pioneering of the villager whom they had injudiciously chosen as their guide, and now they scanned the faces of the mourners who set out on the long mountain journey.

Old Matthew's risibility was evidently much tickled by the sense of their thwarted purpose. Despite the mournful conditions under which he was at that moment abroad, he could not forbear to wish them, from his place in the procession, "a gay canny mornin'"; and failing to satisfy himself with the effect produced by this insinuating salutation, he could not resist the further temptation of reminding them that they had frightened and not caught their game.

"Fleyin' a bird's not the way to grip it," he cried, to the obvious horror of the clergyman, whose first impulse was to remonstrate with the weaver on his levity, but whose maturer reflections induced the more passive protest of a lifted head and a suddenly elevated nose.

This form of contempt might have escaped the observation of the person for whom it was intended had not Reuben Thwaite, who walked beside Matthew, gently emphasized it with a jerk of the elbow and a motion of the thumb.

"He'll glower at the moon till he falls in the midden," said Matthew with a grunt of amused interest.

The two strangers had now gone by, and Willy Ray breathed freely, as he thought that with this encounter the threatened danger had probably been averted.

Then the procession wound its way slowly along the breast of Bracken Water. When Robbie Anderson, in front, had reached a point at which a path went up from the pack-horse road to the top of the Armboth Fell, he paused for a moment, as though uncertain whether to pursue it.

"Keep to the auld corpse road," cried Matthew; and then, in explanation of his advice, he explained the ancient Cumbrian land law, by which a path becomes public property if a dead body is carried over it.

Before long the procession had reached the mountain path across Cockrigg Bank, and this path it was intended to follow as far as Watendlath.

Here the Reverend Nicholas Stevens left the mourners. In accordance with an old custom, he might have required that they should pass through his chapel yard on the Raise before leaving the parish, but he had waived his right to this tribute to episcopacy. After offering a suitable blessing, he turned away, not without a withering glance at the weaver, who was muttering rather too audibly an adaptation of the rhyme, –

> I'll set him up on yon crab-tree,
> It's sour and dour, and so is he.

"I reckon," continued Matthew to little Reuben Thwaite, by his side, as the procession started afresh, – "I reckon yon auld Nick," with a lurch of his thumb over his shoulder, "likes Ash Wednesday better ner this Wednesday – better ner ony Wednesday – for that's the day he curses every yan all roond, and asks the folks to say Amen tul him."

The schoolmaster had walked demurely enough thus far; nor did the departure of the clergyman effect a sensible elevation of his spirits. Of all the mourners, the "laal limber Frenchman" was the most mournful.

It was a cheerless winter morning when they set out from Shoulthwaite. The wind had never fallen since the terrible night of the death of Angus.

As they ascended the fell, however, it was full noon. The sun had broken languidly through the mists that had rolled midway across the mountains, and were now being driven by the wind in a long white continent towards the south, there to gather between more sheltered headlands to the strength of rain. When they reached the top of the Armboth Fell the sky was clear, the sun shone brightly and bathed the gorse that stretched for miles around in varied shades of soft blue, brightening in some places to purple, and in other places deepening to black. The wind was stronger here than it had been in the valley, and blew in gusts of all but overpowering fierceness from High Seat towards Glaramara.

"This caps owte," said Matthew, as he lurched to the wind. "Yan waddent hev a crowful of flesh on yan's bones an yan lived up here."

When the procession reached the village of Watendlath a pause was made. From this point onward the journey through Borrowdale towards the foot of Stye Head Pass must necessarily be a hard and tiresome one, there being scarcely a traceable path through the huge bowlders. Here it was agreed that the mourners on foot should turn back, leaving the more arduous part of the journey to those only who were mounted on sure-footed ponies. Matthew Branthwaite, Monsey Laman, and Reuben Thwaite were among the dozen or more dalesmen who left the procession at this point.

When, on their return journey, they had regained the summit of the Armboth Fell, and were about to descend past Blea Tarn towards Wythburn, they stood for a moment at that highest point and took a last glimpse of the mournful little company, with the one riderless horse in front, that wended its way slowly beyond Rosthwaite, along the banks of the winding Derwent, which looked to them now like a thin streak of blue in the deep valley below.

Soon after the procession left the house on the Moss, arrangements were put in progress for the meal that had to be prepared for the mourners upon their return in the evening.

Some preliminary investigations into the quantity of food that would have to be cooked in the hours intervening disclosed the fact that the wheaten flour had run short, and that some one would need to go across to the mill at Legberthwaite at once if hot currant cake were to be among the luxuries provided for the evening table.

So Liza took down her cloak, tied the ribbons of her bonnet about her plump cheeks, and set out over the dale almost immediately the funeral party turned the end of the lonnin. The little creature tripped along jauntily enough, with a large sense of her personal consequence to the enterprises afoot, but without an absorbing sentiment of the gravity of the occurrences that gave rise to them. She had scarcely crossed the old bridge that led into the Legberthwaite highway when she saw the blacksmith coming hastily from the opposite direction.

Now, Liza was not insensible of her attractions in the eyes of that son of Vulcan, and at a proper moment she was not indisposed to accept the tribute of his admiration. Usually, however, she either felt or affected a measure of annoyance at the importunity with which he prosecuted his suit, and when she saw him coming towards her on this occasion her first feeling was a little touched with irritation. "Here's this great tiresome fellow again," she thought; "he can never let a girl go by without speaking to her. I've a great mind to leap the fence and cross the fields to the mill."

Liza did not carry into effect the scarcely feminine athletic exercise she had proposed to herself; and this change of intention on her part opens up a more curious problem in psychology than the little creature herself had any notion of. The fact is that just as Liza had resolved that she would let nothing in the world interfere with her fixed determination not to let the young blacksmith speak to her, she observed, to her amazement, that the gentleman in question had clearly no desire to do so, but was walking past her hurriedly, and with so preoccupied an air as actually seemed to suggest that he was not so much as conscious of her presence.

It was true that Liza did not want to speak to Mr. Joseph. It was also true that she had intended to ignore him. But that *he* should not want to speak to *her*, and that *he* should seem to ignore *her*, was much more than could be borne by her stubborn little bit of coquettish pride, distended at that moment, too, by the splendors of her best attire. In short, Liza was piqued into a desire to investigate the portentous business which had obviously shut her out of the consciousness of the blacksmith.

"Mr. Garth," she said, stopping as he drew up to her.

"Liza, is that you?" he replied; "I'm in a hurry, lass – good morning."

"Mr. Garth," repeated Liza, "and maybe you'll tell me what's all your hurry about. Has some one's horse dropped a shoe, or is this your hooping day, or what, that you don't know a body now when you meet one in the road?"

"No, no, my lass – good morning, Liza, I must be off."

"Very well, Mr. Garth, and if you must, you must. *I'm* not the one to keep any one 'at doesn't want to stop; not I, indeed," said Liza, tossing up her head with an air as of supreme indifference, and turning half on her heel. "Next time you speak to me, you – you – you *will* speak to me – mind that." And with an expression denoting the triumph of arms achieved by that little outburst of irony and sarcasm combined, Liza tossed the ribbons aside that were pattering her face in the wind, and seemed about to continue her journey.

Her parting shot had proved too much for Mr. Garth. That young man had stopped a few paces down the road, and between two purposes seemed for a moment uncertain which to adopt; but the impulse of what he thought his love triumphed over the impulse of what proved to be his hate. Retracing the few steps that lay between him and the girl, he said, –

"Don't take it cross, Liza, my lass; if I thought you really wanted to speak to me, I'd stop anywhere for nowt – that I would. I'd stop anywhere for nowt; but you always seemed to me over throng with yon Robbie, that you did; but if for certain you really did want me – that's to say, want to speak to me – I'd stop anywhere for nowt."

The liberal nature of the blacksmith's offer did not so much impress the acute intelligence of the girl as the fact that Mr. Garth was probably at that moment abroad upon an errand which he had not undertaken from equally disinterested motives. Concerning the nature of this errand she felt no particular curiosity, but that it was unknown to her, and was being withheld from her, was of itself a sufficient provocation to investigation.

Liza was a simple country wench, but it would be an error to suppose that because she had been bred up in a city more diminutive than anything that ever before gave itself the name, and because she had lived among hand-looms and milking-pails, and had never seen a ball or an opera, worn a mask or a domino, she was destitute of the instinct for intrigue which in the gayer and busier world seems to be the heritage of half her sex. Putting her head aside demurely, as with eyes cast, down she ran her fingers through one of her loose ribbons, she said softly, –

"And who says I'm so very partial to Robbie? *I* never said so, did I? Not that I say I'm partial to anybody else either – not that I *ay* so – Joseph!"

The sly emphasis which was put upon the word that expressed Liza's unwillingness to commit herself to a declaration of her affection for some mysterious entity unknown seemed to Mr. Garth to be proof beyond contempt of question that the girl before him implied an affection for an entity no more mysterious than himself. The blacksmith's face brightened, and his manner changed. What had before been almost a supplicating tone, gave place to a tone of secure triumph.

"Liza," he said, "I'm going to bring that Robbie down a peg or two. He's been a perching himself up alongside of Ralph Ray this last back end, but I'm going to feckle him this turn."

"No, Joseph; are you going to do that, though?" said Liza, with a brightening face that seemed to Mr. Garth to say, "Do it by all means."

"Mayhap I am," said the blacksmith, significantly shaking his head. He was snared as neatly by this simple face as ever was a swallow by a linnet hidden in a cage among the grass.

"And that Ralph, too, the great lounderan fellow, he treats me like dirt, that he does."

"But you'll pay him out now, won't you, Joseph?" said Liza, as though glorying in the blacksmith's forthcoming glory.

"Liza, my lass, shall I tell you something?" Under the fire of a pair of coquettish little eyes, his head as well as his heart seemed to melt, and he became eagerly communicative. Dropping his voice, he said, –

"That Ralph's not gone away at all. He'll be at his father's berrying, that he will."

"Nay!" cried Liza, without a prolonged accent of surprise; and, indeed, this fact had come upon her with so much unexpectedness that her curiosity was now actually as well as ostensibly aroused.

"Yes," said Mr. Garth; "and there's those as knows where to lay hands on him this very day – that there is."

"I shouldn't be surprised, now, if yon Robbie Anderson has been up to something with him," said Liza, with a curl of the lip intended to convey an idea of overpowering disgust at the conduct of the absent Robbie.

"And maybe he has," said Mr. Garth, with a ponderous shake of the head, denoting the extent of his reverse. Evidently "he could an' he would."

"But you'll go to them, won't you, Joseph? That is them as wants them – leastways one of them – them as wants *him* will go and take him, won't they?"

"That they will," said Joseph emphatically. "But I must be off, lass; for I've the horses to get ready, forby the shortness of the time."

"So you're going on horseback, eh, Joey? Will it take you long?"

"A matter of two hours, for we must go by the Black Sail and come back to Wastdale Head, and that's round-about, thou knows." "So you'll take them on Wastdale Head, then, eh?" said Liza, turning her head aside as though in the abundance of her maidenly modesty, but really glancing slyly under the corner of her bonnet in the direction taken by the mourners, and wondering if they could be overtaken.

Joseph was a little disturbed to find that he had unintentionally disclosed so much of the design. The potency of the bright blue eyes that looked up so admiringly into his face at the revelation of the subtlety with which he had seen through a mystery impenetrable to less powerful vision, had betrayed him into unexpected depths of confidence.

Having gone so far, however, Mr. Garth evidently concluded that the best course was to make a clean breast of it – an expedient which he conceived to be insusceptible of danger, for he could see that the funeral party were already on the brow of the hill. So, with one foot stretched forward as if in the preliminary stage of a hurried leave-taking, the blacksmith told Liza that he had met the schoolmaster that morning, and had gathered enough from a word the little man had dropped without thought to put him upon the trace of the old garrulous body with whom the schoolmaster lodged; that his mother, Mistress

Garth, had undertaken the office of sounding this person, and had learned that Ralph had hinted that he would relieve Robbie Anderson of his duty at the top of the Stye Head Pass.

Having heard this, Liza had heard enough, and she was not unwilling that the blacksmith should make what speed he could out of her sight, so that she in turn might make what speed she could out of his sight, and, returning to the Moss without delay, communicate her fearful burden of intelligence to Rotha.

CHAPTER XII

The Flight on the Fells

I

After going a few paces in order to sustain the appearance of continuing the journey on which she had set out, Liza waited until the blacksmith was far enough away to admit of retracing her steps to the bridge. There she climbed the wooden fence, and ran with all speed across the fields to Shoulthwaite. She entered the house in a fever of excitement, but was drawn back to the porch by Rotha, who experienced serious difficulty in restraining her from a more public exposition of the facts with which she was full to the throat than seemed well for the tranquillity of the household. With quick-coming breath she blurted out the main part of her revelations, and then paused, as much from physical exhaustion as from an overwhelming sense of the threatened calamity.

Rotha was quick to catch the significance of the message communicated in Liza's disjointed words. Her pale face became paler, the sidelong look that haunted her eyes came back to them at this moment, her tremulous lips trembled visibly, and for a few minutes she stood apparently powerless and irresolute.

Then the light of determination returned to the young girl's face. Leaving Liza in the porch, she went into the house for her cloak and hood. When she rejoined her companion her mind was made up to a daring enterprise.

"The men of Wythburn, such of them as we can trust," she said, "are in the funeral train. We must go ourselves; at least I must go."

"Do let me go, too," said Liza; "but where are you going?"

"To cross the fell to Stye Head."

"We can't go there, Rotha – two girls."

"What of that? But you need not go. It's eight miles across, and I may run most of the way. They've been gone nearly an hour; they are out of sight. I must make the short cut through the heather."

The prospect of the inevitable excitement of the adventure, amounting, in Liza's mind, to a sensation equivalent to sport, prevailed over her dread of the difficulties and dangers of a perilous mountain journey, and she again begged to be permitted to go.

"Are you quite sure you wish it?" said Rotha, not without an underlying reluctance to accept of her companionship. "It's a rugged journey. We must walk under Glaramara." She spoke as though she had the right of maturity of years to warn her friend against a hazardous project.

Liza protested that nothing would please her but to go. She accepted without a twinge the implication of superiority of will and physique which the young daleswoman arrogated. If social advantages had counted for anything, they must have been all in Liza's favor; but they were less than nothing in the person of this ruddy girl against the natural strength of the pale-faced young woman, the days of whose years scarcely numbered more than her own.

"We must set off at once," said Rotha; "but first I must go to Fornside."

To go round by the tailor's desolate cottage did not sensibly impede their progress. Rotha had paid hurried visits daily to her forlorn little home since the terrible night of the death of the master of Shoulthwaite. She had done what she could to make the cheerless house less cheerless. She had built a fire on the hearth and spread out her father's tools on the table before the window at which he worked. Nothing had tempted him to return. Each morning she found everything exactly as she had left it the morning before.

When the girls reached the cottage, Liza instinctively dropped back. Rotha's susceptible spirit perceived the restraint, and suffered from the sentiment of dread which it implied.

"Stay here, then," she said, in reply to her companion's unspoken reluctance to go farther. In less than a minute Rotha had returned. Her eyes were wet.

"He is not here," she said, without other explanation. "Could we not go up the fell?"

The girls turned towards the Fornside Fell on an errand which both understood and neither needed to explain.

"Do the words of a song ever torment you, Liza, rising up in your mind again and again, and refusing to go away?"

"No – why?" said Liza, simply.

"Nothing – only I can't get a song out of my head today. It comes back and back –

> One lonely foot sounds on the keep,
> And that's the warder's tread."

The girls had not gone far when they saw the object of their search leaning over a low wall, and holding his hands to his eyes as though straining his sight to catch a view of some object in the distance. Simeon Stagg was already acquiring the abandoned look of the man who is outlawed from his fellows. His hair and beard were growing long, shaggy, and unkempt. They were beginning to be frosted with gray. His dress was loose; he wore no belt. The haggard expression, natural to his thin face, had become more marked.

Sim had not seen the girls, and in the prevailing wind his quick ear had not caught the sound of their footsteps until they were nearly abreast of him. When he became fully conscious of their presence, Rotha was standing by his side, with her hand on his arm. Liza was a pace or two behind.

"Father," said Rotha, "are you strong enough to make a long journey?"

Sim had turned his face full on his daughter's with an expression of mingled shame, contrition, and pride. It was as though his heart yearned for that love which he thought he had forfeited the right to claim.

In a few words Rotha explained the turn of events. Sim's agitation overpowered him. He walked to and fro in short, fitful steps, crying that there was no help, no help.

"I thought I saw three men leading three horses up High Seat from behind the smithy. It must have been those very taistrels, it must. I was looking at them the minute you came up. See, there they are – there beyond the ghyll on the mere side of yon big bowder. But they'll be at the top in a crack, that they will – and the best man in Wythburn will be taken – and there's no help, no help."

The little man strode up and down, his long, nervous fingers twitching at his beard.

"Yes, but there *is* help," said Rotha; "there *must* be."

"How? How? Tell me – you're like your mother, you are – that was the very look she had."

"Tell *me*, first, if Ralph intended to be on Stye Head or Wastdale Head."

"He did – Stye Head – he left me to go there at daybreak this morning."

"Then he can be saved," said the girl firmly. "The mourners must follow the path. They have the body and they will go slowly. It will take them an hour and a half more to reach the foot of the pass. In that time Liza and I can cross the fell by Harrop Tarn and Glaramara and reach the foot, or perhaps the head, of the pass. But this is not enough. The constables will not follow the road taken by the funeral. They know that if Ralph is at the top of Stye Head he will be on the lookout for the procession, and must see them as well as it."

"It's true, it is," said Sim.

"They will, as the blacksmith said, go through Honister and Scarf Gap and over the Black Sail to Wastdale. They will ride fast, and, returning to Stye Head, hope to come upon Ralph from behind and capture him unawares. Father," continued Rotha, – and the girl spoke with the determination of a strong man, – "if you go over High Seat, cross the dale, walk past Dale Head, and keep on the far side of the Great Gable, you will cut off half the journey and be there as soon as the constables, and you may keep them in sight most of the way. Can you do this? Have you the strength? You look worn and weak."

"I can – I have – I'll go at once. It's life or death to the best man in the world, that it is."

"There's not a moment to be lost. Liza, we must not delay an instant longer."

II

Long before the funeral train had reached the top of the altitude. Ralph had walked over the more rugged parts of the pass, and had satisfied himself that there was no danger to be apprehended on this score. The ghyll was swollen by the thaw. The waters fell heavily over the great stones, and sent up clouds of spray, which were quickly dissipated by the wind. Huge hillocks of yellow foam gathered in every sheltered covelet. The roar of the cataract in the ravine silenced the voice of the tempest that raged above it.

From the heights of the Great Gable the wind came in all but overpowering gusts across the top of the pass. Ralph had been thrown off his feet at one moment by the fierceness of a terrific blast. It was the same terrible storm that began on the night of his father's death. Ralph had at first been anxious for the safety of the procession that was coming, but he had found a more sheltered pathway under a deep line of furze bushes, and through this he meant to pioneer the procession when it arrived. There was one gap in the furze at the mouth of a tributary ghyll. The wind was strong in this gap, which seemed like a natural channel to carry it southward; but the gap was narrow, it would soon be crossed.

From the desultory labor of such investigations Ralph returned again and again to the head of the great cleft and looked out into the distance of hills and dales. The long coat he wore fell below his knees, and was strapped tightly with a girdle. He wore a close-fitting cap, from beneath which his thick hair fell in short wavelets that were tossed by the wind. His dog, Laddie, was with him.

Ralph took up a position within the shelter of a bowlder, and waited long, his eyes fixed on the fell six miles down the dale.

The procession emerged at length. The chill and cheerless morning seemed at once to break into a spring brightness – there at least, if not here. Through the leaden wintry sky the sun broke down the hilltop at that instant in a shaft of bright light. It fell like an oasis over the solemn company walking there. Then the shaft widened and stretched into the dale, and then the mists that rolled midway between him and it passed away, and a blue sky was over all.

III

"Which way now?"

"Well, I reckon there be two roads; maybe you'd like – "

"Which way now? Quick, and no clatter!"

"Then gang your gate down between Dale Head and Grey Knotts as far as Honister."

"Let's hope you're a better guide than constable, young man, or, as that old fellow said in the road this morning, we'll fley the bird and not grip him. Your clattering tongue had served us a scurvy trick, my man; let your head serve us in better stead, or mayhap you'll lose both – who knows?"

The three men rode as fast as the uncertain pathway between the mountains would allow. Mr. Garth mumbled something beneath his breath. He was beginning to wish himself well out of an ungracious business. Not even revenge sweetened by profit could sustain his spirits under the battery of the combined ridicule and contempt of the men he had undertaken to serve.

"A fine wild-goose chase this," said one of the constables. He had not spoken before, but had toiled along on his horse at the obvious expenditure of much physical energy and more temper.

"Grumbling again, Jonathan; when will you be content?" The speaker was a little man with keen eyes, a supercilious smile, a shrill sharp voice, and peevish manners.

"Not while I'm in danger of breaking my neck every step, or being lost on a moor nearly as trackless as an ocean, or swallowed up in mists like the clouds of steam in a century of washing days, or drowned in the soapsuds of ugly, gaping pits, – tarns you call them, I believe. And all for nothing, too, – not so much as the glint of a bad guinea will we get out of this fine job."

"Don't be too sure of that," said the little man. "If this blockhead here," with a lurch of the head backwards to where the blacksmith rode behind, "hasn't blundered in his 'reckonings,' we'll bag the game yet."

"That you never will, mark my words. I've taken the measure of our man before to-day. He's enough for fifty such as our precious guide. I knew what I was doing when I went back last time and left him."

"Ah, they rather laughed at you then, didn't they? – hinted you were a bit afraid," said the little man, with a cynical smile.

"They may laugh again, David, if they like; and the man that laughs loudest, let him be the first to come in my place next bout; he'll be welcome."

"Well, I must say, this is strange language. I never talked like that, never. It's in contempt of duty, nothing less," said Constable David.

"Oh, you're the sort of man that sticks the thing you call duty above everything else – above wife, life, and all the rest of it – and when duty's done with you it generally sticks you below everything else. I've been a fool in my time, David, but I was never a fool of that sort. I've never been the dog to drop a good jawful of solids to snap at its shadow. When I've been that dog I've quietly put my meat down on the plank, and then – There's another break-neck paving-stone – 'bowders' you call them. No horse alive could keep its feet in such country."

The three men rode some distance in silence. Then the little man, who kept a few yards in front, drew up and said, –

"You say the warrant was not on Wilson's body when you searched it. Is it likely that some of these dalesmen removed it before you came down?"

"Yes, one dalesman. But that job must have been done when another bigger job was done. It wasn't done afterwards. I was down next morning. I was sent after the old Scotchman."

"Didn't it occur to you that the man to whose interest it was to have that warrant had probably got hold of it?"

"Yes; and that he'd burnt it, too. A man doesn't from choice carry a death-warrant next his heart. It would make a bad poultice."

"What now," cried the little man to the blacksmith, who had been listening to the conversation, and in his amazement and confusion had unconsciously pulled at the reins of his horse, and brought it to a stand.

"What are you gaping at now? Come, go along in front. Is this your Scarf Gap?"

IV

Simeon Stagg had followed the three men closely enough to keep them in view, and yet had kept far enough away to escape identification. Ascending the Bleaberry Fell, he had descended into Watendlath, and crossed under the "Bowder" stone as the men passed the village of Rosthwaite. He had lost sight of them for a while as they went up towards Honister, but when he had gained the breast of Grey Knotts he could clearly descry them two miles away ascending the Scarf Gap. If he could but pass Brandreth before they reached the foot of the Black Sail he would have no fear of being seen, and, what was of more consequence, he would have no doubt of being at Stye Head before them. He could then get in between the Kirk Fell and the Great Gable long before they could round the Wastdale Head and return to the pass.

But how weak he felt! How jaded these few miles had made him! Sim remembered that he had eaten little for three days. Would his strength outlast the task before him? It should; it must do so. Injured by tyranny, the affections of this worn-out outcast among men had, like wind-tossed trees, wound their roots about a rock from which no tempest could tear them.

Sim's step sometimes quickened to a run and sometimes dropped to a labored slouch. The deep declivities, the precipitous ascents, the broad chasm-like basins, the running streams, the soft turf, had tried sorely the little strength that remained to him. Sometimes he would sit for a minute with his long thin hand pressed hard upon his heart; then he would start away afresh, but rather by the impulse of apprehension than by that of renewed strength.

Yes, he was now at the foot of Brandreth, and the horses and their riders had not emerged above the Scarf. How hot and thirsty he felt!

Here stood a shepherd's cottage, the first human habitation he had passed since he left Watendlath. Should he ask for some milk? It would refresh and sustain him. As Sim stood near the gate of the cottage, doubtful whether to go in or go on, the shepherd's wife came out. Would she give him a drink of milk? Yes, and welcome. The woman looked closely at him, and Sim shrank under her steady gaze. He was too far from Wythburn to be dogged by the suspicion of crime, yet his conscience tormented him. Did all the world, then, know that Simeon Stagg would have been a murderer if he could – that in fact he had committed murder in his heart? Could he never escape from the unspoken reproach? No; not even on the heights of these solitary hills!

The woman turned about and went into the house for the milk. While she was gone, Sim stood at the gate. In an instant the thought of his own necessities, his own distresses, gave place to the thought of Ralph Ray's. At that instant he turned his eyes again to the Scarf Gap. The three men had covered the top, and were on the more level side of the hill, riding hard down towards Ennerdale. They would be upon him in ten minutes more.

The woman was coming from her house with a cup of milk in her hand; but, without waiting to accept of it, Sim started away and ran at his utmost speed over the fell. The woman stood with the cup in her hand, watching the thin figure vanishing in the distance, and wondering if it had been an apparition.

V

"You can't understand why Mr. Wilfrey Lawson is so keen to lay hands on this man Ray?" said Constable David.

"That I cannot," said Constable Jonathan.

"Why, isn't it enough that he was in the trained bands of the Parliament?"

"Enough for the King – and this new law of Puritan extermination – yes; for Master Wilfrey – no. Besides, the people can't stand this hanging of the old Puritan soldiers much longer. The country had been worried and flurried by the Parliament, and cried out like a wearied man for rest – any sort of rest – and it has got it – got it with a vengeance. But there's no rest more restless than that of an active man except that of an active country, and England won't put up with this butchering of men to-day for doing what was their duty yesterday – yes, their duty, for that's what you call it."

"So you think Master Wilfrey means to set a double trap for Ray?"

"I don't know what he means; but he doesn't hunt down a common Roundhead out of thousands with nothing but 'duty' in his head; that's not Master Wilfrey Lawson's way."

"But this man was a captain of the trained bands latterly," said the little constable. "Fellow," he cried to Mr. Garth, who rode along moodily enough in front of them, "did this Ray ever brag to you of what he did as captain in the army?"

"What was he? Capt'n? I never heard on't," growled the blacksmith.

"Brag – pshaw! He's hardly the man for that," said Constable Jonathan.

"I mind they crack't of his saving the life of old Wilson," said Mr. Garth, growling again.

"And if he took it afterwards, what matter?" said Constable Jonathan, with an expression of contempt. "Push on, there. Here we're at the top. Is it down now? What's that below? A house, truly – a house at last. Who's that running from it? We must be near our trysting place. Is that our man? Come, if we are to do this thing, let us do it."

"It's the fellow Ray, to a certainty," said the little man, pricking his horse into a canter as soon as he reached the first fields of Ennerdale.

In a few minutes the three men had drawn up at the cottage on the breast of Brandreth where Sim had asked for a drink.

"Mistress! Hegh! hegh! Who was the man that left you just now?"

"I dunnet know wha't war – some feckless body, I'm afeart. He was a' wizzent and savvorless. He begged ma a drink o' milk, but lang ere a cud cum tul him he was gane his gate like yan dazt-like."

"Who could this be? It's not our man clearly. Who could it be, blacksmith?"

The gentleman addressed had turned alternately white and red at the woman's description. There had flashed upon his brain the idea that little Lizzie Branthwaite had betrayed him.

"I reckon it must have been that hang-gallows of a tailor – that Sim," he said, perspiring from head to foot.

"And he's here to carry tidings of our coming. Push on – follow the man – heed this blockhead no longer."

VI

The procession of mourners, with Robbie Anderson and the mare at its head, had walked slowly down Borrowdale after the men on foot had turned back towards Withburn. Following the course of the winding Derwent, they had passed the villages of Stonethwaite and Seathwaite, and in two hours from the time they set out from Shoulthwaite they had reached the foot of Stye Head Pass. The brightness of noon had now given place to the chill leaden atmosphere of a Cumbrian December.

In the bed of the dale they were sheltered from the wind, but they saw the mists torn into long streaks overhead, and knew that the storm had not abated. When they came within easy range of the top of the great gap between the mountains over which they were to pass, they saw for a moment a man's figure clearly outlined against the sky.

"He's yonder," thought Robbie, and urged on the mare with her burden. He remembered that Ralph had said, "Chain the young horse to the mare at the bottom of the pass," and he did so. Before going far, however, he found this new arrangement impeded rather than accelerated their progress.

"The pass has too many ins and outs for this," he thought, and he unchained the horses. Then they went up the ravine with the loud ghyll boiling into foam at one side of them.

VII

"I cannot go farther, Rotha. I must sit down. My foot is swelling. The bandage is bursting it."

"Try, my girl; only try a little longer: only hold out five minutes more; only five short minutes, and we may be there."

"It's of no use trying," said Liza with a whimper; "I've tried and tried; I must sit down or I shall faint." The girl dropped down on to the grass and began to untie a linen bandage that was about her ankle.

"O dear! O dear! There they are, more than half-way up the pass. They'll be at the top in ten minutes! And there's Ralph; yes, I can see him and the dog. What shall we do? What *can* we do?"

"Go and leave me and come back – no, no, not that either; don't leave me in this place," said Liza, crying piteously and moaning with the pain of a sprained foot.

"Impossible," said Rotha. "I might never find you again on this pathless fell."

"Oh, that unlucky stone!" whimpered Liza, "I'm bewitched, surely. It's that Mother Garth – "

"Ah, he sees us," said Rotha. She was standing on a piece of rock and waving a scarf in the wind. "Yes, he sees us and answers. But what will he understand by that? O dear! O dear! Would that I could make Willy see, or Robbie – perhaps *they* would know. Where can father be? O where?"

A terrible sense of powerlessness came upon Rotha as she stood beside her prostrate companion within sight of the goal she had labored to gain, and the strong-hearted girl burst into a flood of tears.

VIII

Yes, from the head of the pass Ralph Ray saw the scarf that was waved by Rotha, but he was too far away to recognize the girls.

"Two women, and one of them lying," he thought; "there has been an accident."

Where he stood the leaden sky had broken into a drizzling rain, which was being driven before the wind in clouds like mist. It was soaking the soft turf, and lying heavy on the thick moss that coated every sheltered stone.

"Slipt a foot, no doubt," thought Ralph. "I must ride over to them when the horses come up and have crossed the pass; I cannot go before."

The funeral train was now in sight. In a few minutes more it would be at his side. Yes, there was Robbie Anderson leading the mare. He had not chained the young horse, but that could be done at this point. It should have been done at the bottom, however. How had Robbie forgotten it?

Ralph's grave face became yet more grave as he looked down at the solemn company approaching him. Willy had recognized him. See, his head drooped as he sat in the saddle. At this instant Ralph thought no longer of the terrible incidents and the more terrible revelations of the past few days. He thought not at all of the untoward fortune that had placed him where he stood. He saw only the white burden that was strapped to the mare, and thought only of him with whom his earliest memories were entwined.

Raising his head, and dashing the gathering tears from his eyes, he saw one of the women on the hill opposite running towards him and crying loudly, as if in fear; but the wind carried away her voice, and he could not catch her words.

From her gestures, however, he gathered that something had occurred behind him. No harm to the funeral train could come of their following on a few paces, and Ralph turned about and walked rapidly upwards. Then the woman's voice seemed louder and shriller than ever, and appeared to cry in an agony of distress.

Ralph turned again and stood. Had he mistaken the gesture? Had something happened to the mourners? No, the mare walked calmly up the pass. What could it mean? Still the shrill cry came to him, and still the words of it were borne away by the wind. Something was wrong – something serious. He must go farther and see.

Then in an instant he became conscious that Simeon Stagg was running towards him with a look of terror. Close behind him were two men, mounted, and a third man rode behind them. Sim was being pursued. His frantic manner denoted it. Ralph did not ask himself why. He ran towards Sim. Quicker than speech, and before Sim had recovered breath, Ralph had swung himself about, caught the bridles of both horses, and by the violent lurch had thrown both riders from their seats. But neither seemed hurt. Leaping to their feet together, they bounded down upon Ralph, and laying firm hold upon him tried to manacle him.

Then, with the first moment of reflection, the truth flashed upon him. It was he who had been pursued, and he had thrown himself into the arms of his pursuers.

They were standing by the gap in the furze bushes. The mourners were at the top of the pass, and they saw what had happened. Robbie Anderson was coming along faster with the mare. The two men saw that help for their prisoner was at hand. They dropped the manacles, and tried to throw Ralph on to the back of one of their horses. Sim was dragging their horse away. The dog was barking furiously and tearing at their legs. But they were succeeding: they were overpowering him; they had him on the ground.

Now, they were all in the gap of the furze bushes, struggling in the shallow stream. Robbie dropped the reins of the mare, and ran to Ralph's aid. At that moment a mighty gust of wind came down from the fell, and swept through the channel. It caught the mare, and startled by the loud cries of the men and the barking of the dog, and affrighted by the tempest, she started away at a terrific gallop over the mountains, with the coffin on her back.

"The mare, the mare!" cried Ralph, who had seen the accident as Robbie dropped the reins; "for God's sake, after her!"

The strength of ten men came into his limbs at this. He rose from where the men held him down, and threw them from him as if they had been green withes that he snapped asunder. They fell on either side, and lay where they fell. Then he ran to where the young horse stood a few paces away, and lifting the boy from the saddle leapt into it himself. In a moment he was galloping after the mare.

But she had already gone far. She was flying before the wind towards the great dark pikes in the distance. Already the mists were obscuring her. Ralph followed on and on, until the company that stood as though paralyzed on the pass could see him no mere.

CHAPTER XIII

A 'Batable Point

When Constable David tried to rise after that fall, he discovered too many reasons to believe that his leg had been broken. Constable Jonathan had fared better as to wind and limb, but upon regaining his feet he found the voice of duty silent within him as to the necessity of any further action such as might expose him to more serious disabilities. With the spirit of the professional combatant, he rather admired the prowess of their adversary, and certainly bore him no ill-will because he had vanquished them.

"The man's six foot high if he's an inch, and has the strength of an ox," he said, as he bent over his coadjutor and inquired into the nature of his bruises.

Constable David seemed disposed to exhibit less of the resignation of a brave humility that can find solace and even food for self-flattery in defeat, than of the vexation of a cowardly pride that cannot reconcile itself to a stumble and a fall.

"It all comes of that waistrel Mister Burn-the-wind," he said, meaning to indicate the blacksmith by this contemptuous allusion to that gentleman's profession.

Constable Jonathan could not forbear a laugh at the name, and at the idea it suggested.

"Ay, but if he'd burned the wind this time instead of blowing it," he said, "we might have raised it between us. Come, let me raise you into this saddle instead. Hegh, hegh, though," he continued, as the horse lurched from him with every gust, "no need to raise the wind up here. Easy – there – you're right now, I think. You'll need to ride on one stirrup."

It was perhaps natural that the constabulary view of the disaster should be limited to the purely legal aspect of the loss of a prisoner; but the subject of the constable's reproaches was not so far dominated by official ardor as to be insensible to the terrible accident of the flight of the horse with the corpse. Mr. Garth had brought his own horse to a stand at some twenty paces from the spot where Ralph Ray had thrown his companions from their saddles, and in the combat ensuing he had not experienced any unconquerable impulse to participate on the side of what stood to him for united revenge and profit, if not for justice also. When, in the result, the mare fled over the fells, he sat as one petrified until Robbie Anderson, who had earlier recovered from his own feeling of stupefaction, and in the first moment of returning consciousness had recognized the blacksmith and guessed the sequel of the rencontre, brought him up to a very lively sense of the situation by bringing him down to his full length on the ground with the timely administration of a well-planted blow. Mr. Garth was probably too much taken by surprise to repay the obligation in kind, but he rapped out a volley of vigorous oaths that fell about his adversary as fast as a hen could peck. Then he remounted his horse, and, with such show of valorous reluctance as could still be assumed after so unequivocal an overthrow, he made the best of haste away.

He was not yet, however, entirely rewarded for his share in the day's proceedings. He had almost reached Wythburn on his return home when he had the singular ill-fortune to encounter Liza. That young damsel was huddled, rather than seated, on the back of a horse, the property of one of the mourners whom Rotha had succeeded in hailing to their rescue. With Rhoda walking by her side, she was now plodding along towards the city in a temper primed by the accidents of the day to a condition of the highest irascibility. As a matter of fact, Liza, in her secret heart, was chiefly angry with herself for the reckless leap over a big stone that had given the sprained ankle, under the pains of which she now groaned; but it was due to the illogical instincts of her sex that she could not consciously take so Spartan a view of her position as to blame herself for what had happened.

It was at this scarcely promising juncture of accident and temper that she came upon the blacksmith, and at the first sight of him all the bitterness of feeling that had been brewing and fermenting within her, and in default of a proper object had been discharged on the horse, on the saddle, on the roads, and even on Rotha, found a full and magnificent outlet on the person of Mr. Joseph Garth.

While that gentleman had been jogging along homewards he had been fostering uncomfortable sentiments of spite respecting the "laal hussy" who had betrayed him. He had been mentally rehearsing the withering reproaches and yet more withering glances which he meant to launch forth upon her when next it should be her misfortune to cross his path. Such disloyalty, such an underhand way of playing double, seemed to

Mr. Garth deserving of any punishment short of that physical one which it would be most enjoyable to inflict, but which it might not, with that Robbie in the way, be quite so pleasant to stand responsible for. Perhaps it was due to an illogical instinct of the blacksmith's sex that his conscience did not trouble him when he was concocting these pains and penalties for duplicity. Certainly, when the two persons in question came face to face at the turning of the pack-horse road towards the city, logic played an infinitesimal part in their animated intercourse.

Mr. Garth meant to direct a scorching sneer as silent preamble to his discourse; but owing to the fact that Robbie's blow had fallen about the blacksmith's eyes, and that those organs had since become sensibly eclipsed by a prodigious and discolored swelling, what was meant for a withering glance looked more like a meaningless grin. At this apparent levity under her many distresses, Liza's wrath rose to boiling point, and she burst out upon Mr. Joseph with more of the home-spun of the country-side than ever fell from her lips in calmer moments.

"Thoo dummel-head, thoo," she said, "thoo'rt as daft as a besom. Thoo *hes* made a botch on't, thoo blatherskite. Stick that in thy gizzern, and don't thoo go bumman aboot like a bee in a bottle – thoo Judas, thoo."

Mr. Garth was undoubtedly taken by surprise this time. To be attacked in such a way by the very person he meant to attack, to be accounted the injurer by the very person who, he thought, had injured him, sufficed to stagger the blacksmith's dull brains.

"Nay, nay," he said, when he had recovered his breath; "who's the Judas? – that's a 'batable point, I reckon."

"Giss!" cried Liza, without waiting to comprehend the significance of the insinuation, and – like a true woman – not dreaming that a charge of disloyalty could be advanced against her, – "giss! giss!" – the call to swine – "thoo'rt thy mother's awn son – the witch."

Utterly deprived of speech by this maidenly outburst of vituperation, Mr. Garth lost all that self-control which his quieter judgment had recognized as probably necessary to the safety of his own person. White with anger, he raised his hand to strike Liza, who thereupon drew up, and, giving him a vigorous slap on each cheek, said, "Keep thy neb oot of that, thoo bummeller, and go fratch with Robbie Anderson – I hear he dinged thee ower, thoo sow-faced 'un."

The mention of this name served as a timely reminder to Mr. Garth, who dropped his arm and rode away, muttering savagely under his breath.

"Don't come hankerin' after me again," cried Liza (rather unnecessarily) after his vanishing figure.

This outburst was at least serviceable in discharging all the

ill-nature from the girl's breast; and when she had watched the blacksmith until he had disappeared, she replied to Rotha's remonstrances as so much scarcely girl-like abuse by a burst of the heartiest girlish laughter.

There was much commotion at the Red Lion that night. The "maister men" who had left the funeral procession at Watendlath made their way first to the village inn, intending to spend there the hours that must intervene before the return of the mourners to Shoulthwaite. They had not been long seated over their pots when the premature arrival of John Jackson and some of the other dalesmen who had been "sett" on the way to Gosforth led to an explanation of the disaster that had occurred on the pass. The consternation of the frequenters of the Red Lion, as of the citizens of Wythburn generally, was as great as their surprise. Nothing so terrible had happened within their experience. They had the old Cumbrian horror of an accident to the dead. No prospect was dearer to their hope than that of a happy death, and no reflection was more comforting than that one day they would have a suitable burial. Neither of these had Angus had. A violent end, and no grave at all; nothing but this wild ride across the fells that might last for days or months. There was surely something of Fate in it.

The dalesmen gathered about the fire at the Red Lion with the silence that comes of awe.

"A sad hap, this," said Reuben Thwaite, lifting both hands.

"I reckon we must all turn out at the edge of the dawn to-morrow, and see what we can do to find old Betsy," said Mr. Jackson.

Matthew Branthwaite's sagest saws had failed him. Such a contingency as this had never been foreseen by that dispenser of proverbs. It had lifted him out of himself. Matthew's sturdy individualism might have taken the form of liberalism, or perhaps materialism, if it had appeared two centuries later; but in the period in which his years were cast, the art of keeping close to the ground had not been fully learned. Matthew was filled with a sentiment which he neither knew nor attempted to define. At least he was sure that the mare was not to be caught. It was to be a dispensation somehow and someway that the horse should gallop over the hills with its dead burden to its back from year's end to year's end. When Mr. Jackson suggested that they should start out in search of it, Matthew said, –

"Nay, John, nowt of the sort. Ye may gang ower the fell, but ye'll git na Betsy. It's as I telt thee; it's a Fate. It'll be a tale for iv'ry mother to flyte childer with."

"The wind did come with a great bouze," said John. "It must have been the helm-wind, for sure; yet I cannot mind that I saw the helm-bar. Never in my born days did I see a horse go off with such a burr."

"And you could not catch hold on it, any of you, ey?" asked one of the company with a shadow of a sneer.

"Shaf! dost thoo think yon fell's like a blind lonnin?" said Matthew.

"Nay, but it's a bent place," continued Mr. Jackson. "How it dizzied and dozzled, too! And what a fratch yon was! My word! but Ralph did ding them over, both of them!"

"He favors his father, does Ralph," said Matthew.

"Ey! he's his father's awn git," chimed Reuben. "But that Joe Garth is a merry-begot, I'll swear."

"Shaf! he hesn't a bit of nater intil him, nowther back nor end. He's now't but riffraff," said Matthew. Ralph Ray's peril and escape were incidents too unimportant to break the spell of the accident to the body of his father.

Robbie Anderson turned in late in the evening.

"Here's a sorry home coming," he said as he entered.

It was easy to see that Robbie was profoundly agitated. His eyes were aflame; he rose and sat, walked a pace or two and stood, passed his fingers repeatedly through his short curly beard, slapped his knee, and called again and again for ale. When he spoke of the accident on the fell, he laughed with a wild effort at a forced and unnatural gayety.

"It's all along of my being dintless, so it is," he muttered, after little Reuben Thwaite had repeated for some fresh batch of inquirers the story, so often told, of how the mare took to flight, and of how Ralph leaped on to the young horse in pursuit of it.

"All along of you, Robbie; how's that, man?"

"If I'd chained the young horse at the bottom of the hill there would have been no mare to run away, none."

"It's like that were thy orders, then, Robbie?"

"It were that, damn me, it were – the schoolmaster there, he knows it."

"Ralph told him to do it; I heard him myself," said Monsey, from his place in the chimney-nook, where he sat bereft of his sportive spirit, yet quite oblivious of the important part which his own loquacity had unwittingly played in the direful tragedy.

"But never bother now. Bring me more ale, mistress: quick now, my lass."

Robbie had risen once more, and was tramping across the floor in his excitement. "What's come over Robbie?" whispered Reuben to Matthew. "What fettle's he in – doldrums, I reckon."

"Tak na note on him. Robbie's going off agen I'm afeart. He's broken loose. This awesome thing is like to turn the lad's heed, for he'd the say ower it all."

"Come, lass, quick with the ale."

"Ye've had eneuf, Robbie," said the hostess. "Go thy ways home. Thou findst the beer very heady, lad. Thou shalt have more in the morning."

"To-night, lass; I must have some to-night, that I must."

"Robbie *is* going off agen, surely," whispered Reuben. "It's a sorry sight when yon lad takes to the drink. He'll be deed drunk soon."

"Say nowt to him," answered Matthew. "He's fair daft to-neet."

The evening was far advanced when the dalesmen rose to go.

"Our work's cut out for us in the morning, men." said John Jackson. "Let's off to our beds."

CHAPTER XIV

Until the Day Break

Until the day break, and the shadows flee away.

It was not at first that Ralph was a prey to sentiments of horror. His physical energy dominated all emotion, and left no room for terrible imaginings – no room for a full realization of what had occurred. That which appeared to paralyze the others – that which by its ghastly reality appeared to fix them to the earth with the rigidity of stone – endowed him with a power that seemed all but superhuman, and inspired him with an impulse that leapt to its fulfilment.

Mounted on the young horse, he galloped after the mare along the long range of the pikes, in and out of their deep cavernous alcoves, up and down their hillocks and hollows, over bowlders, over streams, across ghylls, through sinking sloughs and with a drizzling rain overhead. At one moment he caught sight of the mare and her burden as they passed swiftly over a protruding headland which was capped from his point of view by nothing but the mist and the sky. Then he followed on the harder; but faster than his horse could gallop over the pathless mountains galloped the horse of which he was in pursuit. He could see the mare no more. Yet he rode on and on.

When he reached the extremity of the dark range and stood at that point where Great Howe fringes downward to the plain, he turned about and rode back on the opposite side of the pikes. Once more he rode in and out of cavernous alcoves, up and down hillocks and hollows, over bowlders, over streams, across rivers, through sinking sloughs, and still with a drizzling rain overhead. The mare was nowhere to be seen.

Then he rode on to where the three ranges of mountains meet at Angle Tarn and taking first the range nearest the pikes he rode under the Bow Fell, past the Crinkle Crags to the Three-Shire Stones at the foot of Greyfriars, where the mountains slope downward to the Duddon valley. Still the mare was nowhere to be seen.

Returning then to the Angle Tarn, he followed the only remaining range past the Pike of Stickle until he looked into the black depths of the Dungeon Ghyll. And still the mare was nowhere to be seen. Fear was behind her, and only by fear could she be overtaken. It was at about two o'clock in the afternoon that the disaster had occurred. It was now fully three hours later, and the horse Ralph rode, fatigued and wellnigh spent, was slipping its feet in the gathering darkness. He turned its head towards Wythburn, and rode down to the city by Harrop Tarn.

At the first house – it was Luke Cockrigg's, and it stood on the bank above the burn – he left the horse, and borrowed a lantern. The family would have dissuaded him from an attempt to return to the fells, but he was resolved. There was no reasoning against the resolution pictured on his rigid and cadaverous countenance.

The drizzling rain still fell and the night had closed in when Ralph set his face afresh towards the mountains.

And now the sickening horrors of sentiment overtook him, for now he had time to reflect upon what had occurred. The figure of the riderless horse flying with its dead burden before the wind had fixed itself on his imagination; and while the darkness was concealing the physical surroundings, it was revealing the phantasm in the glimmering outlines of every rock and tree. Look where he would, peering long and deep into the blackness of a night without moon or stars, without cloud or sky, with only a blank density around and about, Ralph seemed to see in fitful flashes that came and went – now on the right and now on the left of him, now in front and now behind, now on the earth at his feet and now in the dumb vapor floating above him – the spectre of that riderless horse. Sometimes he would stop and listen, thinking he heard a horse canter close past him; but no, it was the noise of a hidden river as its waters leapt over the stones. Sometimes he thought he heard the neigh of a horse in the distance; but no, it was only the whinny of the wind. His dog had followed close behind him when he fled from the pass, and it was still at his heels. Sometimes Laddie would dart away and be lost for a few minutes in the darkness. Then the dog's muffled bark would be heard, and Ralph's blood would seem to stand still with a dread apprehension that dared not to take the name of hope. No; it was only a sheep that had strayed from its fold, and had taken shelter from wind and rain beneath a stone in a narrow cleft, and was now sending up into the night the pitiful cry of a lost and desolate creature.

No, no, no; nowhere would the hills give up the object of his search; and Ralph walked on and on with a heart that sank and still sank.

He knew these trackless uplands as few knew them, and not even the abstraction of mind that came with these solitary hours caused him an uncertain step. On and on, through the long dark night, to the Stye Head once more, and again along the range of the rugged pikes, calling the mare by the half-articulate cry she knew so well, and listening for her answering neigh, but hearing only the surging of the wind or the rumble of the falling ghyll; then on and on, and still on.

When the earliest gleams of light flecked the east, Ralph was standing at the head of the Screes. Slowly the gray bars stretched across the sky, wider and more wide, brighter and more bright, now changed to yellow and now to pink, chasing the black walls of darkness that died away on every side. In the basin below, at the foot of the steep Screes, whose sides rumbled with rolling stones, lay the black mere, half veiled by the morning mist. Still veiled, too, were the dales of Ireton, but far away, across the undulating plains through which the river rambled, flowed the wide Western Sea, touched at its utmost bar by the silvery light of the now risen sun.

Ralph turned about and walked back, with the flush of the sky reflected on his pale and stony face. His lantern, not yet extinguished, burned small and feeble in his hand. Another night was breaking to another day; another and another would yet break, and all the desolation of a heart, the ruin of many hearts – what was it before Nature's unswerving and unalterable course! The phantasms of a night that had answered to his hallucinations were as nothing to the realities of a morning whose cruel light showed him only more plainly the blackness of his despair.

The sentiments of horror which now possessed him were more terrible because more spiritual than before. To know no sepulture! The idea was horrible in itself, horrible in its association with an old Hebrew curse more remorseless than the curse of Cain, most horrible of all because to Ralph's heightened imagination it seemed to be a symbol – a symbol of retribution past and to come.

Yes, it was as he had thought, as he had half thought; God's hand was on him – on him of all others, and on others only through him. Having once conceived this idea in its grim totality, having once fully received the impress of it from the violence and suddenness of a ghastly occurrence, Ralph seemed to watch with complete self-consciousness the action of the morbid fancy on his mind. He traced it back to the moment when the truth (or what seemed to him the truth) touching the murder of Wilson had been flashed upon him by a look from Simeon Stagg. He traced it yet farther back to that night at Dunbar, when, at the prompting of what he mistook for mercy, he had saved the life of the enemy that was to wreck his own life and the lives of all that were near and dear to him. To his tortured soul guilt seemed everywhere about him, whether his own guilt or the guilt of others, was still the same; and now God had given this dread disaster for a sign that vengeance was His, that retribution had come and would come.

Was it the dream of an overpowered imagination – the nightmare of a distempered fancy? Yet it would not be shaken off. It had bathed the whole world in another light – a lurid light.

Ralph walked fast over the fells, snatching at sprigs of heather, plucking the slim boughs from the bushes, pausing sometimes to look long at a stone, or a river, or a path that last night appeared to be as familiar to him as the palm of his hand, and had suddenly become strange and a mystery. The shadow of a supernatural presence hung over all.

Throughout that day he walked about the fells, looking for the riderless horse, and calling to it, but neither expecting to see nor to hear it. He saw once and again the people of Wythburn abroad on the errand that kept him abroad, but they never came within hail, and a stifling sense of shame kept him apart, none the less that he knew not wherefore such shame should fall on him, all the same that they knew not that it had fallen.

The day would come when all men would see that God's hand was on him.

Yes, Ralph; but when that day does indeed come, then all men shall also see that whom God's hand rests on has God at his right hand.

When the darkness was closing in upon a second night, Ralph was descending High Seat towards Shoulthwaite Moss. Behind him lagged the jaded dog, walking a few paces with drooping head and tail; then lying for a minute, and rising to walk languidly again.

CHAPTER XV

Ralph's Sacrifice

When he reached the old house, Ralph was prepared for the results of any further disaster, for disaster had few further results for which it was needful to prepare. A light burned in the kitchen, and another in that room above it where lately his father had lain. When Ralph entered, Willy Ray was seated before the fire, his hand in the hand of Rotha, who sat by his side. On every feature of his pallid face were traces of suffering.

"What of mother?" said Ralph huskily, his eyes traversing the kitchen.

Willy rose and put his hand on Ralph's shoulder. "We will go together," he said, and they walked towards the stair that led to the floor above.

There she lay, the mother of these stricken sons, unconscious of their sufferings, unconscious of her own. Yet she lived. Since the terrible intelligence had reached her of what had happened on the pass she had remained in this state of insensibility, being stricken into such torpidity by the shock of the occurrence. Willy's tears fell fast as he stood by the bed, and his anguish was subdued thereby to a quieter mood. Ralph's sufferings were not so easily fathomable. He stooped and kissed the unconscious face without relaxing a muscle in the settled fixity of his own face. Leaving his brother in the room, he returned to the kitchen. How strange the old place looked to him now! Had everything grown strange? There were the tall clock in the corner, the big black worm-eaten oak cabinet, half-cupboard, half-drawers; there was the long table like a rock of granite; there was the spinning wheel in the neuk window; and there were the whips and the horns on the rafters overhead – yet how unfamiliar it all seemed to be!

Rotha was hastily preparing supper for him. He sat on the settle that was drawn up before the fire, and threw off his heavy and sodden shoes. His clothes, which had been saturated by the rain of the preceding night, had dried upon his back. He was hungry; he had hot eaten since yesterday at midday; and when food was put upon the table he ate with the voracious appetite that so often follows upon a long period of mental distress.

As he sat at his supper, his eyes followed constantly the movements of the girl, who was busied about him in the duties of the household. It were not easy to say with what passion or sentiment his heart was struggling with respect to her. He saw her as a hope gone from him, a joy not to be grasped, a possible fulfilment of that part of his nature which was never to be fulfilled. And she? Was she conscious of any sentiment peculiar to herself respecting this brave rude man, whose heart was tender enough to be drawn towards her and yet strong enough to be held apart at the awful bidding of an iron fate? Perhaps not. She in turn felt drawn towards him; she knew the force of a feeling that made him a centre of her thoughts, a point round which her deeper emotions insensibly radiated. But this was associated in her mind with no idea of love. If affection touched her at all, perhaps at this moment it went out where her pity – rather, her pride – first found play. Perhaps Ralph seemed too high above her to inspire her love. His brother's weaker, more womanly nature came closer within her range.

There was now a long silence between them.

"Rotha," said Ralph at length, "this will be my last night at the Moss; the last for a long time, at least – I didn't expect to be here to-night. Can you promise one thing, my girl? It won't be hard for you now – not very hard *now*." He paused.

"What is it, Ralph?" said Rotha, in a voice of apprehension.

"Only that you won't leave the old house while my mother lives."

Rotha dropped her head. She thought of the lonely cottage at Fornside, and of him who should live there. Ralph divined the thought that was written in her face.

"Get him to come here if you can," he said. "He could help Willy with the farm."

"He would not come," she said. "I'm afraid he would not."

"Then neither will he return to Fornside. Promise me that while she lives – it can't be long, Rotha, it may be but too short – promise me that you'll make this house your home."

"My first duty is to him," said Rotha with her hand to her eyes.

"True – that's true," said Ralph; and the sense that two homes were made desolate silenced him with something that stole upon him like stifling shame. There was only one way out of the difficulty, and that was to make two homes one. If she loved his brother, as he knew that his brother loved her, then –

"Rotha," said Ralph, with a perceptible tremulousness of voice," I will ask you another question, and, perhaps – who knows rightly? – perhaps it is harder for me to ask than for you to answer; but you will answer me – will you not? – for I ask you solemnly and with the light of Heaven on my words – on the most earnest words, I think, that ever came out of my heart."

He paused again. Rotha sat on the end of the settle, and with fingers intertwined, with eyelids quivering and lips trembling, she gazed in silence into the fire.

"This is no time for idle vanities," he said; "it's no time to indulge unreal modesties; and you have none of either if it were. God has laid His hand on us all, Rotha; yes, and our hearts are open without disguise before Him – and before each other, too, I think."

"Yes," said Rotha. She scarcely knew what to say, or whither Ralph's words tended. She only knew that he was speaking as she had never heard him speak before. "Yes, Ralph," she repeated.

"Perhaps, as I say, it's harder for me to ask than for you to answer, Rotha," he continued, and the strong man looked into the girl's eyes with a world of tenderness. "Do you think you have any feeling for Willy – that is, more than the common? I saw how you sat together as I came in to you. I've marked you before, when he has been by. I've marked him, too. You've been strength and solace to him in this trouble. Do you think if he loved you, Rotha – do you think, then, you could love him? Wait," he added, as she raised her eyes, and with parted lips seemed prepared to speak. "It is not for him I ask. God knows it is as much for you as for him, and perhaps – perhaps, I say, most of all – for myself."

With a frank voice and face, with luminous eyes in which there was neither fear nor shame, Rotha answered, –

"Yes, I could love him; I think I do so now."

She spoke to Ralph as she might have spoken to a father whom she reverenced, and from whom no secret of her soul should be hid. He heard her in silence. Not until now, not until he had heard her last word, had he realized what it would cost him to hear it. The agony of a lifetime seemed crushed into that short moment. But he had made it for himself, and now at length it was over. To yield her up – perhaps it was a link in the chain of retribution. To say nothing of his own love – perhaps it would be accepted as a dumb atonement. To see her win the love and be won by the love of his brother – perhaps it would soften his exile with thoughts of recompense for a wrong that it had been his fate to do to her and hers, though she knew it not. There was something like the white heat of subdued passion in his voice when he spoke again.

"He *does* love you, Rotha," he said quietly, "and he will ask you to be his wife. But he cannot do so yet, and, meantime, while my mother lives – while I am gone – God knows where – while I am away from the old home – I ask you now once more to stay."

The great clock in the corner ticked out loud in the silence of the next minute; only that and the slow breathing of the dog sleeping on the hearth fell on the ear.

"Yes, I will stay," said the girl; and while she spoke Willy Ray walked into the kitchen.

Then they talked together long and earnestly, these three, under the shadow of the terrible mystery that hung above them all, of life and death. Ralph spoke as one overawed by a sense of fatality. The world and its vicissitudes had left behind engraven on his heart a message and lesson, and it was not altogether a hopeful one. He saw that fate hung by a thread; that our lives are turned on the pivot of some mere chance; that, traced back to their source, all our joys and all our sorrows appear to come of some accident no more momentous than a word or a look. In solemn tones he seemed to say that there is a plague-spot of evil at the core of this world and this life, and that it infects everything. We may do our best – we should do our best – but we are not therefore to expect reward. Perhaps that reward will come to us while we live. More likely it will be the crown laid on our grave. Happy are we if our loves find fulfilment – if no curse rests upon them. Should we hope on? He hardly knew. Destiny works her own way!

Thus they talked in that solitary house among the mountains. They sat far into the night, these rude sons and this daughter of the hills, groping in their own uncertain, unlearned way after solutions of life's problems that wiser heads than theirs ages on ages before and since have never compassed, shouting for echoes into the voiceless caverns of the world's great and awful mysteries.

CHAPTER XVI

At Sunrise on the Raise

The friends thou hast, and their adoption tried,
Grapple them to thy soul with hooks of steel.

At sunrise the following morning two men walked through Wythburn towards the hillock known as the Raise, down the long road that led to the south. The younger man had attained to the maturity of full manhood. Brawny and stalwart, with limbs that strode firmly over the ground; with an air of quiet and reposeful power; with a steadily poised head; with a full bass voice, soft, yet deep; with a face that had for its utmost beauty the beauty of virile strength and resolution, softened, perhaps, into tenderness of expression by washing in the waters of sorrow, – such, now, was Ralph Ray. Over a jerkin he wore the long sack coat, belted and buckled, of the dalesmen of his country. Beneath a close-fitting goatskin cap his short, wavy hair lay thick and black. A pack was strapped about him from shoulder to waist. He carried the long staff of a mountaineer.

Were there in the wide world of varying forms and faces a form and a face so much unlike his own as were those of the man who walked, nay, jerked along, in short, fitful paces, by his side? Little and slight, with long thin gray hair and dishevelled beard, with the startled eyes of a frighted fawn, and with its short, fearful glances, with a sharp face, worn into deep ridges that changed their shape with every step and every word, with nervous, twitching fingers, with a shrill voice and quick speech, – it was Simeon Stagg, the outcast, the castaway.

These two were to part company soon. Not more devoted to its master was the dog that ran about them than was Sim to Ralph. He was now to lose the only friend who had the; will and the strength to shield him against the cruel world that was all the world to him.

They were walking along the pack-horse road on the breast of the fell, and they walked long in silence. Each was busy with his thoughts – the one too weak, the other too strong, to give them utterance.

"There," said Ralph as they reached the top of the Raise, "we must part now, old friend." He tried to give a cheery tone to his voice. "You'll go on to the fell every day and look around – an idle task, I fear, but still you'll go, as I would have gone if I might have stayed in the old country."

Sim nodded assent.

"And now you'll go back to the Mess, as I told you. Rotha will want you there, and Willy too. You'll fill my place till I return, you know."

Sim shook his head.

"I'd be nothing but an ache and a stound to the lass, as I've olas been – nothing but an ache and a stound to them all."

"No, not that; a comfort, if only you will try to have it so. Be a man, Sim – look men in the face – things will mend with you now. Go back and live with them at the old home; they'll want you there."

"Since you will not let me come with you, Ralph, tell me when will you come back? I'm afeart – I don't know why – but some'at tells me you'll not come back – tell me, Ralph, that you *will*."

"These troublous times will soon be past," said Ralph. "There'll be a great reckoning day soon, I fear. Then we'll meet again – never doubt it. And now good bye – good bye once more, old friend, and God be with you."

Ralph turned about and walked a few paces southward. The dog followed him.

"Go back, Laddie," said Ralph. Laddie stood and looked into his face with something of the supplicatory appeal that was on the countenance of the man he had just left. The faithful creature had followed Ralph throughout life; he had been to his master a companion more constant than his shadow; he had never before been driven away.

"Go back, Laddie," said Ralph again, and not without a tremor in his deep voice. The dog dropped his head and slunk towards Sim.

Then Ralph walked on.

The sun had risen over Lauvellen, and the white wings of a fair morning lay on the hamlet in the vale below. Sim stood long on the Raise, straining dim eyes into the south, where the diminishing figure of his friend was passing out of his ken.

It was gone at length; the encircling hills had hidden it. Then the unfriended outcast turned slowly away.

CHAPTER XVII

The Garths: Mother and Son

The smoke was rising lazily in blue coils from many a chimney as Sim turned his back on the Raise and retraced his steps to Wythburn.

In the cottage by the smithy – they stood together near the bridge – the fire had been newly kindled. Beneath a huge kettle, swung from an unseen iron hook, the boughs crackled and puffed and gave out the odor of green wood.

Bared up to the armpits and down to the breast, the blacksmith was washing himself in a bowl of water placed on a chair. His mother sat on a low stool, with a pair of iron tongs in her hands, feeding the fire from a bundle of gorse that lay at one side of the hearth. She was a big, brawny, elderly woman with large bony hands, and a face that had hard and heavy features, which were dotted here and there with discolored warts. Her dress was slatternly and somewhat dirty. A soiled linen cap covered a mop of streaky hair, mouse-colored and unkempt.

"He's backset and foreset," she said in a low tone. "Ey, eye; he's made a sad mull on't."

Mrs. Garth purred to herself as she lifted another pile of gorse on to the crackling fire.

Joe answered with a grating laugh, and then with a burr he applied a towel to his face.

"Nay, nay, mother. He has a gay bit of gumption in him, has Ray. It'll be no kitten play to catch hold on him, and *they* know that *they* do."

The emphasis was accompanied by a lowered tone, and a sidelong motion of the head towards a doorway that led out of the kitchen.

"Kitten play or cat play, it's dicky with him; nought so sure, Joey," said Mrs. Garth; and her cold eyes sparkled as she purred again with satisfaction.

"That's what you're always saying," said Joe testily; "but it never comes to anything and never will."

"Weel, weel, there's nought so queer as folk," mumbled Mrs. Garth.

Joe seemed to understand his mother's implication.

"I'm moider'd to death," he said, "what with yourself and them. I'm right glad they're going off this morning, that's the truth."

This declaration of Mr. Garth's veracity was not conducive to amiability.

He looked as black as his sanguine complexion would allow.

Mrs. Garth glanced up at him. "Why, laddie, what ails thee? Thou'rt as crook't as a tiphorn this morning," she said, in a tone that was meant to coax her son out of a cantankerous temper.

"I'm like to be," grumbled Mr. Garth.

"Why, laddie?" asked his mother, purring, now in other fashion.

"Why?" said Joe, – "why? – because I can never sleep at night now, no, nor work in the day neither – that's *why*."

"Hush!" said Mrs. Garth, turning a quick eye towards the aforementioned door. Then quietly resuming her attentions to the gorse, she added, in another tone, "That's nowther nowt nor summat, lad."

"It'll take a thicker skin nor mine, mother, to hold out much longer," said Joe huskily, but struggling to speak beneath his breath.

"Yer skin's as thin as a cat-lug," said Mrs. Garth in a bitter whisper.

"I've told you I cannot hold out much longer," said Joe, "and I cannot."

"Hod thy tongue, then," growled Mrs. Garth over the kettle.

There was a minute's silence between them.

The blacksmith donned his upper garments. His mother listened for the simmer and bubble of the water on the fire.

"How far did ye bargain to tak them?"

"To Gaskarth – the little lame fellow will make for the Carlisle coach once they're there?"

"When was t'horse and car to be ready?"

"Nine o'clock forenoon."

"Then it's full time they were gitten roused."

Mrs. Garth rose from the stool, hobbled to the door which had been previously indicated by sundry nods and jerks, and gave it two or three sharp raps.

A voice from within answered sleepily, "Right – right as a trivet, old lady," and yawned.

Mrs. Garth put her head close to the door-jamb.

"Ye'd best be putten the better leg afore, gentlemen," she said with becoming amiability; "yer breakfast is nigh about ready, gentlemen."

"The better leg, David, eh? Ha! ha! ha!" came from another muffled voice within.

Mrs. Garth turned about, oblivious of her own conceit. In a voice and manner that had undergone a complete and sudden change, she whispered to Joe, –

"Thou'rt a great bledderen fool."

The blacksmith had been wrapped in his thoughts. His reply was startlingly irrelevant.

"Fool or none, I'll not do it," said Joe emphatically.

"Do what?" asked his mother in a tone of genuine inquiry.

"What I told you."

"Tut, what's it to thee?"

"Ay, but it *is* something to me, say I."

"Tush, thou'rt yan of the wise asses."

"If these constables," lurching his head, "if they come back, as they say, to take Ralph, I'll have no hand in't."

"And why did ye help them this turn?" said Mrs. Garth, with an elevation of her heavy eyebrows.

"Because I knew nowt of what they were after. If I'd but known that it were for – for – *him* – "

"Hod thy tongue. Thou wad mak a priest sweer," said Mrs. Garth. The words rolled within her teeth.

"*I* heard what they said of the warrant, mother," said Joe; "it were the same warrant, I reckon, as old Mattha's always preaching aboot, and it's missing, and it seems to me that they want to make out as Ray – as Ralph – "

"Wilt ye *never* hod yer bletheren tongue?" said Mrs. Garth in a husky whisper. Then in a mollified temper she added, –

"An what an they do, laddie; what an they do? Did ye not hear yersel that it were yan o' the Rays – yan o' them; and what's the odds which – what's the odds, I say – father and son, they were both of a swatch."

At this moment there came from the inner room some slight noise of motion, and the old woman lifted her finger to her lip.

"And who knows it were *not* yan on 'em – who?" added Mrs. Garth, after a moment's silence.

"Nay, mother," said Joe, and his gruff voice was husky in his throat, – "nay, mother, but there *is* them that knows."

The woman gave a short forced titter.

"Ye wad mak a swine laugh, ye wad," she said.

Then, coming closer to where her son now stood with a "lash" comb in his hand before a scratched and faded mirror, she said under her breath, –

"There'll be no rest for *him* till summat's done, none; tak my word for that. But yance they hang some riff-raff for him it will soon be forgotten. Then all will be as dead as hissel', back and end. What's it to thee, man, who they tak for't? Nowt, *Theer's nea sel' like awn sel', Joey.*"

Mrs. Garth emphasized her sentiment with a gentle prod of her son's breast.

"That's what you told me long ago," said the blacksmith, "when you set me to work to help hang the tailor. I cannot bear the sight of him, I cannot."

Mrs. Garth took her son roughly by the shoulder.

"Ye'd best git off and see to t' horse and car. Stand blubbering here and ye'll gang na farther in two days nor yan."

There was a step on the road in front.

"Who's that gone by?" asked Mrs. Garth.

Joe stepped to the window.

"Little Sim," he said, and dropped his head.

CHAPTER XVIII

The Dawn of Love

Though she lost the best of her faculties, Mrs. Ray did not succumb to the paralytic seizure occasioned by the twofold shock which she had experienced. On the morning after Ralph's departure from Wythburn she seemed to awake from the torpor in which she had lain throughout the two preceding days. She opened her eyes and looked up into the faces that were bent above her.

There were evidences of intelligence surviving the wreck of physical strength. Speech had gone, but her eyes remained full of meaning. When they spoke to her she seemed to hear. At some moments she, appeared to struggle with the impulse to answer, but the momentary effort subsided into an inarticulate gurgle, and then it was noticed that for an instant the tears stood in her eyes.

"She wants to say, 'God bless you,'" said Rotha when she observed these impotent manifestations, and at such times the girl would stoop and put her lips to the forehead of the poor dear soul.

There grew to be a kind of commerce in kind between these two, destitute as the one was of nearly every channel of communication. The hundred tricks of dumb show, the glance, the lifted brow, the touch of the hand, the smile, the kiss, – all these acquired their several meanings, and somehow they seemed to speak to the silent sufferer in a language as definite as words. It came to be realized that this was a condition in which Mrs. Ray might live for years.

After a week, or less, they made a bed for her in a room adjoining the kitchen, and once a day they put her in a great arm-chair and wheeled her into her place by the neuk window.

"It will be more heartsome for her," said Rotha when she suggested the change; "she'll like for us to talk to her all the same that she can't answer us, poor soul."

So it came about that every morning the invalid spent an hour or two in her familiar seat by the great ingle, the chair she had sat in day after day in the bygone times, before these terrible disasters had come like the breath of a plague-wind and bereft her of her powers.

"I wonder if she remembers what happened," said Willy; "do you think she has missed them – father and Ralph?"

"Why, surely," said Rotha. "But her ears are better than her eyes. Don't you mark how quick her breath comes sometimes when she has heard your voice outside, and how bright her eyes are, and how she tries to say, 'God bless you!' as you come up to her?"

"Yes, I think I've marked it," said Willy, "and I've seen that light in her eyes die away into a blank stare or puzzled look, as if she wanted to ask some question while she lifted them to my face."

"And Laddie there, when he barks down the lonnin – haven't you seen her then – her breast heaving, the fingers of that hand of hers twitching, and the mumble of her poor lost voice, as though she'd say, 'Come, Rotha, my lass, be quick with the supper – he's here, my lass, he's back?'"

"I think you must be right in that, Rotha – that she misses Ralph," said Willy.

"She's nobbut a laal bit quieter, that's all," said Matthew Branthwaite one morning when he turned in at Shoulthwaite. "The dame nivver were much of a talker – not to say a *talker*, thoo knows; but mark me, she loves a crack all the same."

Matthew acted pretty fully upon his own diagnosis of his old neighbor's seizure. He came to see her frequently, stayed long, rehearsed for her benefit all the gossip of the village, fired off his sapient proverbs, and generally conducted himself in his intercourse with the invalid precisely as he had done before. In answer to any inquiries put to him at the Red Lion he invariably contented himself with his single explanation of Mrs. Ray's condition, "She's nobbut a laal bit quieter, and the dame nivver were much of a talker, thoo knows."

Rotha Stagg remained at Shoulthwaite in accordance with her promise given to Ralph. It was well for the household that she did so. Young as the girl was, she alone seemed to possess either the self-command or the requisite energy and foresight to keep the affairs of the home and of the farm in motion. It was not until many days after the disasters that had befallen the family that Willy Ray recovered enough self-possession to engage once more in his ordinary occupations. He had spent the first few days in the room with his stricken mother, almost as unconscious as herself of what was going on about him; and indeed his nature had experienced a shock only less serious.

Meantime, Rotha undertook the management of the home-stead. None ever disputed her authority. The tailor's daughter had stepped into her place as head of the household at the Moss, and ruled it by that force of will which inferior natures usually obey without question, and almost without consciousness of servitude. She alone knew rightly what had to be done.

As for the tailor himself, he had also submitted – at least partially – to his daughter's passive government. A day or two after Ralph Ray's departure, Rotha had gone in search of her father, and had brought him back with her. She had given him his work to do, and had tried to interest him in his occupations. But a sense of dependence seemed to cling to him, and at times he had the look of some wild creature of the hills which had been captured indeed, but was watching his opportunity of escape.

Sim rose at daybreak, and, wet or dry, he first went up on to the hills. In an hour or two he was back again. Rotha understood his purpose, but no word of explanation passed between them. She looked into his face inquiringly day' after day, but nothing she saw there gave hint of hope. The mare was lost. She would never be recovered.

Sometimes a fit of peculiar despondency would come upon Sim. At such times he would go off without warning, and be seen no more for days. Rotha knew that he had gone to his old haunts on the hill, for nothing induced him to return to his cottage at Fornside. No one went in pursuit of him. In a day or two he would come back and take up his occupation as if he had never been away. Walking leisurely into the court-yard, he would lift a besom and sweep, or step into the stable and set to work at stitching up a rent in the old harness.

Willy Ray can hardly be said to have avoided Sim; he ignored him. There was a more potent relation between these two than any of which Willy had an idea. Satisfied as he had professed himself to be that Sim was an innocent man, he was nevertheless unable to shake off an uneasy sentiment of repulsion experienced in his presence. He struggled to hold this in check, for Rotha's sake. But there was only one way in which to avoid the palpable manifestation of his distrust, and that was to conduct himself in such a manner as to appear unconscious of Sim's presence in the house.

"The girl is not to blame," he said to himself again and again. "Rotha is innocent, whoever may be guilty."

He put the case to himself so frequently in this way, he tried so hard to explain to his own mind that Rotha at least was free of all taint, that the very effort made him conscious of a latent suspicion respecting Sim.

As to Sim's bearing towards Willy, it was the same as he had adopted towards almost the whole of the little world in which he lived; he took up the position of the guilty man, the man to be shunned, the man from whose contaminating touch all other men might fairly shrink. It never occurred to Sim that there lay buried at his own heart a secret that could change the relations in which he stood towards this younger and more self-righteous son of Angus Ray.

Perhaps, if it had once been borne in upon him that another than himself was involved in the suspicion which had settled upon his name – if he had even come to realize that Rotha might suffer the stigma of a fatal reproach for no worse offence than that she was her father's daughter – perhaps, if he had once felt this as a possible contingency, he would have shaken off the black cloud that seemed to justify the odium in which he was held by those about him, and lifted up his head for her sake if not for his own.

But Sim lacked virile strength. The disease of melancholy had long kept its seat at his heart, and that any shadow of doubt could rest on Rotha as a result of a misdeed, or supposed misdeed, of his had never yet occurred to Sim's mind.

And truly Rotha was above the blight of withering doubt. Rude daughter of a rude age, in a rude country and without the refinements of education, still how pure and sweet she was; how strong, and yet how tender; how unconscious in her instinct of self-sacrifice; how devoted in her loyalty; how absolute in her trust!

But deep and rich as was Rotha's simple nature, it was yet incomplete. She herself was made aware that a great change was even now coming to pass. She understood the transformation little, if at all; but it seemed as though, somehow, a new sense were taking hold of her. And, indeed, a new light had floated into her little orbit. Was it too bright as yet for her to see it for what it was? It flooded everything about her, and bathed the world in other hues than the old time. Disaster had followed on disaster in the days that had just gone by, but nevertheless – she knew not how – it was not all gloom in her heart. In the waking hours of the night there was more than the memory of the late events in her mind; her dreams were not all nightmares; and in the morning, when the swift recoil of sad thoughts rushed in at her first awakening, a sentiment of indefinite solace came close behind it. What was it that was coming to pass?

It was love that was now dawning upon her, though still vague and indeterminate; it hardly knew its object.

Willy Ray took note of this change in the girl, and thought he understood it. He accepted it as the one remaining gleam of hope and happiness for both of them amid the prevailing gloom. Rotha avoided the searching light of his glances. When the work of the household was in hand she shook off the glamour of the new-found emotion.

In the morning when the men came down for breakfast, and again in the evening when they came in for supper, the girl busied herself in her duties with the ardor of one having no thought behind them and no feeling in which they did not share. But when the quieter hours of the day left her free for other thoughts, she would stand and look long into the face of the poor invalid to whom she had become nurse and foster-child in one; or walk, without knowing why, to the window neuk, and put her hand on the old wheel, that now rested quiet and unused beneath it, while she looked towards the south through eyes that saw nothing that was there.

She was standing so one morning a fortnight or more after Ralph's departure from Wythburn, when Willy came into the kitchen, and, before she was conscious of his presence, sat in the seat of the little alcove within which she stood.

He took the hand that lay disengaged by her side and told her in a word or two of his love. He had loved her long in silence. He had loved her before she became the blessing she now was to him and to his; to-day he loved her more than ever before.

It was a simple story, and it came with the accent of sincerity in every word.

He thought perhaps she loved him in return – he had sometimes thought so – was he wrong?

There was a pause between them. Regaining some momentary composure, the girl turned her eyes once more aside and looked through the neuk window towards the south. She felt the color mounting to her cheeks, and knew that the young man had risen to his feet beside her. He, on his part, saw only the fair face before him, and felt only the little hand that lay passively in his own.

"It's a sad sort of home to bring you to. It would be idle to ask if you have been happy here – it would be a mockery; but – but – "

"I *have* been happy; that is, happy to do as Ralph wished me."

"And as *I* wished?"

"As you wished too, Willy."

"You've been a blessing to us, Rotha. I sometimes think, though, that it was hardly fair to bring you into the middle of this trouble."

"He did it for the best," said Rotha.

"Who?"

There was a little start of recovering consciousness.

"Ralph," she answered, and dropped her head.

"True – he did it for the best," repeated Willy, and relapsed into silence.

"Besides, I had no home then, you know."

How steadfastly the girl's eyes were fixed oh the distant south!

"You had your father's home, Rotha."

"Ah, no! When it ceased to be poor father's home, how could it be mine any longer? No, I was homeless."

There was another pause.

"Then let me ask you to make this house your home forever. Can you not do so?"

"I think so – I can scarcely tell – he said it might be best – "

Willy let loose her hand. Had he dreamed? Was it a wild hallucination – the bright gleam of happiness that had penetrated the darkness that lay about him at every step?

How yearningly the girl's eyes still inclined to yonder distant south.

"Let us say no more about it now, Rotha," he said huskily. "If you wish it, we'll talk again on this matter – that is, I say, if you *wish* it; if not, no matter."

The young man was turning away. Without moving the fixed determination of her gaze, Rotha said quietly, –

"Willy, I think perhaps I *do* love you – perhaps – I don't know. I remember he said that our hearts lay open before each other – "

"Who said so, Rotha?"

There was another start of recovering consciousness. Then the wide eyes looked full into his, and the tongue that would have spoken refused that instant to speak. The name that trembled in a half-articulate whisper on the parted lips came upwards from the heart.

But the girl was ignorant of her own secret even yet.

"We'll say no more about it now, Rotha," repeated Willy in a broken voice. "If you wish it, we'll talk again; give me a sign, and perhaps we'll talk on this matter again."

In another moment the young man was gone.

CHAPTER XIX

The Betrothal

It was not till she was alone that the girl realized the situation. She put her hand over her eyes – the hand that still tingled with the light pressure of his touch.

What had happened? Had Willy asked her to become his wife? And had she seemed to say No?

The sound of his voice was still lingering on her ears; it was a low broken murmur, such as might have fallen to a sob.

Had she, then, refused? That could not be. She was but a poor homeless girl, with nothing to recommend her to such a man as he was. Yet she knew – she had heard – that he loved her, and would one day ask her to be his wife. She had thought that day was far distant. She had never realized that it would be now. Why had he not given her time to think? If Ralph knew what she had done!

For an hour or two Rotha went about the house with a look of bewilderment in her eyes.

Willy came back soon afterwards, and helped her to wheel his mother in her chair to her place by the hearth. He had regained his wonted composure, and spoke to her as if nothing unusual had occurred. Perhaps it had been something like a dream, all this that haunted her. Willy was speaking cheerfully enough. Just then her father came into the kitchen, and slunk away silently to a seat in the remotest corner of the wide ingle. Willy went out almost immediately. Everything was in a maze. Could it be that she had seemed to say No?

Rotha was rudely awakened from her trance by the entrance at this moment of the parson of the chapel on the Raise. The present was the first visit the Reverend Nicholas Stevens had paid since the day of the funeral. He had heard of the latest disaster which had befallen the family at the Moss. He had also learned something of the paralytic seizure which the disaster had occasioned. He could not any longer put away the solemn duty of visitation. To take the comfort of his presence, to give the light of his countenance to the smitten, was a part of his sacred function. These accidents were among the sore trials incident to a cure of souls. The Reverend Nicholas had brushed himself spick-and-span that morning, and, taking up his gold-headed cane, had walked the two miles to Shoulthwaite.

Rotha was tying the ribbons of Mrs. Ray's white cap under her chin as the vicar entered. She took up a chair for him, and placed it near the invalid. But he did not sit immediately. His eye traversed the kitchen at a glance. He saw Mrs. Ray propped up with her pillows, and looking vacantly about her, but his attention seemed to be riveted on Sim, who sat uneasily on the bench, apparently trying to escape the concentrated gaze.

"What have we here?" he said in a cold and strident voice. "The man Simeon Stagg? Is he here too?"

The moment before Rotha had gone into the dairy adjoining, and, coming back, she was handing a bowl of milk to her father. Sim clutched at the dish with nervous fingers.

The Reverend Nicholas walked with measured paces towards where he sat. Then he paused, and stood a yard or two behind Sim, whose eyes were still averted.

"I was told you had made your habitation on the hillside; a fitting home, no doubt, for one unfit to house with his fellows."

Sim's hand trembled violently, and he set the bowl of milk on the floor beside him. Rotha was standing a yard or two apart, her breast heaving.

"Have you left it for good, pray?" There was the suspicion of a sneer in the tone with which the question was asked.

"Yes, he *has* left it for good," said Rotha, catching her breath.

Sim had dropped his head on his hand, his elbow resting on his knee.

"More's the shame, perhaps; who knows but it may have been the best place for shame to hide in!"

Sim got up, and turning about, with his eyes still fixed on the ground, he hurried out of the house.

"You've driven him away again – do you know that?" said Rotha, regaining her voice, and looking fall into the vicar's face, her eyes aflame.

"If so, I have done well, young woman." Then surveying her with a look of lofty condescension, he added, "And what is your business here?"

"To nurse Mrs. Ray; that is part of it."

"Even so? And were you asked to come?"

"Surely."

"By whom?"

"Ralph, her son."

"Small respect he could have had for you, young woman."

"Tell me what you mean, sir," said the girl, with a glance of mingled pride and defiance.

"Tell you what I mean, young woman! Have you, then, no modesty? Has that followed the shame of the hang-dog vagrant who has just left us?"

"Not another word about him! If you have anything to say about me, say it, sir."

"What! – the father dead! the mother stricken into unconsciousness – two sons – and you a young woman – was there no matron in the parish, that a young woman must come here?"

Rotha's color, that had tinged her cheeks, mounted to her eyes and descended to her neck. The prudery that was itself a sin had penetrated the armor of her innocence. Without another word, she turned and left the kitchen.

"Well, Widow Ray," she heard his reverence say, in an altered tone, as he faced the invalid. She listened for no more.

Her trance was over now, and rude indeed had been the awakening.

Perhaps, after all, she had no business in this house – perhaps the vicar was right. Yet that could not be. She thought of Mrs. Ray smitten down and dependent upon those about her for help in every simple office of life, and she thought of the promise she had made to Ralph. "Promise me," he had said, "that you will stay in the old home as long as mother lives." And she had promised; her pledged word was registered in heaven.

But then, again, perhaps Ralph had not foreseen that his mother might live for years in her present state. No doubt he thought her near to death. He could not have intended that she should live long in his brother's house.

Yet he *had* so intended. "He will ask you to be his wife, Rotha," Ralph had said, "but he can't do so yet."

This brought her memory back to the earlier events of the morning. Willy Ray had already asked her to become his wife. And what had she done on her part? Had she not seemed to say No?

Willy was far above her. It was true enough that she was a poor homeless girl, without lands, without anything but the hands she worked with. Willy was now a statesman, and he was something of a scholar too. Yes, he was in every way far above her. Were there not others who might love him? Yet Ralph had seemed to wish her to become his brother's wife, and what Ralph had said would be best, must of course be so.

She could not bring herself to leave Shoulthwaite – that was clear enough to her bewildered sense. Nor could she remain on the present terms of relation – that, also, was but too clear. If Ralph were at home, how different everything would be! He would lead her with a word out of this distressing maze.

When Willy Ray parted from Rotha after he had told her of his love, he felt that the sunshine had gone out of his life forever. He had been living for weeks and months in a paradise that was not his own. Why he had loved this girl he could hardly say. She was – every one knew it – the daughter of a poor tailor, and he was the poorest and meanest creature in the country round about.

The young man could not help telling himself that he might have looked to marry the daughter of the largest statesman in a radius of miles.

But then, the girl herself was a noble creature – none could question it. Rude, perhaps, in some ways, without other learning than the hard usage of life had given her; yet she was a fine soul, as deep as the tarn on the mountain-top, and as pure and clear.

And he had fancied she loved him. No disaster had quite overshadowed the bright hope of that surmise. Yet had she not loved Ralph instead? Perhaps the girl herself did not realize that in reality the love of his brother had taken hold of her. Did Ralph himself love the girl? That could not be, or he should have guessed the truth the night they spoke together. Still, it *might* be that Ralph loved her after all.

By the following morning Rotha had decided that her duty at this crisis lay one way only, and that way she must take. Ralph had said it would be well for her to become Willy's wife, and she had promised him never to leave the Moss while his mother lived. She would do as he had said.

Willy had asked her for a sign, and she must give hint, one – a sign that she was willing to say "Yes" if he spoke again to-day as he had spoken yesterday.

Having once settled this point, her spirits experienced a complete elevation. What should the sign be? Rotha walked to the neuk window and stood to think, her hand on the wheel and her eyes towards the south. What, then, should the sign be?

It was by no means easy to hit on a sign that would show him at a glance that her mind was made up; that, however she may have wavered in her purpose yesterday, her resolve was fixed to-day. She stood long and thought of many plans, but none harmonized with her mood.

"Why should I not tell him – just in a word?" Often as she put if to herself so, she shrank from the ordeal involved.

No, she must hit on a sign, but she began to despair of lighting on a fitting one. Then she shifted her gaze from the landscape through the window, and turned to where Mrs. Ray sat in her chair close by. How vague and vacant was the look in those dear eyes! how mute hung the lips that were wont to say, "God bless you!" how motionless lay the fingers that once spun with the old wheel so deftly!

The old spinning-wheel – here it was, and Rotha's right hand still rested upon it. Ah! the wheel – surely *that* was, the sign she wanted.

She would sit and spin – yes, she could spin, too, though it was long since she had done so – she would sit in his mother's chair – the one his mother used to sit in when she spun – and perhaps he would understand from that sign that she would try to take his mother's place if he wished her so to do.

Quick, let it be done at once. He usually came up to the house at this time of the morning.

She looked at the clock. He would be here soon, she thought; he might be coming now.

And Willy Ray was, in truth, only a few yards from the house at the moment. He had been up on to the hills that morning. He had been there on a similar errand several mornings before, and had never told himself frankly what that errand really was. Returning homewards on this occasion, he had revolved afresh the subject that lay nearest to his heart.

If Ralph really loved the girl – but how should he know the truth as to that, unless Rotha knew it? If the girl loved his brother, he could relinquish her. He was conscious of no pang of what was called jealousy in this matter. An idol that he had worshipped seemed to be shattered – that was all.

If he saw that Rotha loved Ralph, he must give up forever his one dream of happiness – and there an end.

It was in this mood that he opened the kitchen door, just as Rotha had put her foot on the treadle and taken the flax in her hand.

There the girl sat, side by side with his mother, spinning at the wheel which within his recollection no hand but one had touched. How fresh and fair the young face looked, tinged, as it was at this moment, too, with a conscious blush!

Rotha had tried to lift her eyes as Willy entered. She intended to meet his glance with a smile. She wished to catch the significance of his expression. But the lids were heavier than lead that kept her gaze fixed on the "rock" and flax below her.

She felt that after a step or two he had stood still in front of her. She knew that her face was crimson. Her eyes, too, were growing dim.

"Rotha, my darling!" She heard no more.

The spinning-wheel had been pushed hastily aside. She was on her feet, and Willy's arms were about her.

CHAPTER XX

"Fool, of Thyself Speak Well"

As the parson left Shoulthwaite that morning he encountered Joe Garth at the turning of the lonnin. The; blacksmith was swinging along the road, with a hoop over his shoulder. He lifted his cap as the Reverend Nicholas came abreast of him. That worthy was usually too much absorbed to return such salutations, but he stopped on this occasion.

"Would any mortal think it?" he said; "the man Simeon Stagg is here housed at the home of my old friend and esteemed parishioner, Angus Ray!"

Mr. Garth appeared to be puzzled to catch the relevancy of the remark. He made no reply.

"The audacity of the man is past belief," continued the parson. "Think of his effrontery! Does he imagine that God or man has forgotten the mystery of that night in Martinmas?"

The blacksmith realized that some response was expected from him. With eyes bent on the ground, he muttered, "He's getting above with himself, sir."

"Getting above himself! I should think so, forsooth. But verily a reckoning day is at hand. Woe to him who carries a load of guilt at his heart and thinks that no man knows of it. Better a millstone were about his neck, and he were swallowed up in the great deep."

The parson turned away. Garth stood for a moment without perceiving that he was alone, his eyes still bent on the ground. Then he walked moodily in the other direction.

When he reached his home, Joe threw down the hoop in the smithy and went into the house. His mother was there.

"Sim, he's at Shoulthwaite," he said. "It's like enough his daughter is there, too."

A sneer crossed Mrs. Garth's face.

"Tut, she's yan as wad wed the midden for sake of the muck."

"You mean she's setting herself at one of the Rays?"

Mrs. Garth snorted, but gave no more explicit reply.

"Ey, she's none so daft, is yon lass," observed the blacksmith.

This was not quite the trace he had meant to follow. After a pause he said, "What came of his papers – in the trunk?"

"Whose?"

"*Thou* knows."

Mrs. Garth gave her son a quick glance.

"It's like they're still at Fornside. I must see to 'em again."

The blacksmith responded eagerly, –

"Do, mother, do."

There was another pause. Joe made some pretence of scraping a file which he had picked up from a bench.

"Thou hasn't found out if old Angus made a will?" said Mrs. Garth.

"No."

"No, of course not," said Mrs. Garth, with a curl of the lip. "What I want doing I must do myself. Always has been so, and always will be."

"I wish it were true, mother," muttered Joe in a voice scarcely audible.

"What's that?"

"Nowt."

"I'll go over to Shoulth'et to-morrow," purred Mrs. Garth. "If the old man made no will, I'll maybe have summat to say as may startle them a gay bit."

The woman grunted to herself at the prospect. "Ey, ey," she mumbled, "it'll stop their match-makin'. Ey, ey, and what's mair, what's mair, it'll bring yon Ralph back helter-skelter."

"Mother, mother," cried the blacksmith, "can you never leave that ugly thing alone?"

CHAPTER XXI

Mrs. Garth at Shoulthwaite

The next day or two passed by with Rotha like a dream. Her manners had become even gentler and her voice even softer than before, and the light of self-consciousness had stolen into her eyes. Towards the evening of the following day Liza Branthwaite ran up to the Moss to visit her. Rotha was in the dairy at the churn, and when Liza pushed open the door and came unexpectedly upon her she experienced a momentary sense of confusion which was both painful and unaccountable. The little lady was herself flushed with a sharp walk, and muffled up to the throat from a cutting wind.

"Why, Rotha, my girl, what ever may be the matter with you?" said Liza, coming to a pause in the middle of the floor, and, without removing the hands that had been stuffed up her sleeves from the cold, looking fixedly in her face.

"I don't know, Liza; I wish you could tell me, lass," said Rotha, recovering enough self-possession to simulate a subterfuge.

"Here I've been churning and churning since morning, and don't seem much nigher the butter yet."

"It's more than the butter that pests you," said Liza, with a wise shake of the head.

"Yes; it must be the churn. I can make nothing of it."

"Shaf on the churn, girl! You just look like Bessie MacNab when they said Jamie o' the Glen had coddled her at the durdum yon night at Robin Forbes's."

"Hush, Liza," said Rotha, stooping unnecessarily low to investigate the progress of her labors, and then adding, from the depths of the churn, "why, and how did Bessie look?"

"Look? look?" cried Liza, with a tip of the chin upwards, as though the word itself ought to have been sufficiently explicit, – "look, you say? Why," continued Liza, condescending at length to be more definite as to the aforesaid young lady's appearance after a kiss at a country dance, "why, she looked just for the world like you, Rotha."

Then throwing off her thick outer garment without waiting for any kind of formal invitation, Liza proceeded to make herself at home in a very practical way.

"Come, let me have a turn at the churn," she said, "and let us see if it is the churn that ails you – giving you two great eyes staring wide as if you were sickening for a fever, and two cheeks as red as the jowls of 'Becca Rudd's turkey."

In another moment Liza was rolling up the sleeves of her gown, preparatory to the experimental exercise she had proposed to herself; but this was not a task that had the disadvantage of interrupting the flow of her gossip.

"But I say, lass," she rattled on, "have you heard what that great gammerstang of a Mother Garth has been telling 'Becca Rudd about *you*? 'Becca told me herself, and I says to 'Becca, says I, 'Don't you believe it; it's all a lie, for that old wizzent ninny bangs them all at lying; and that's saying a deal, you know. Besides,' I says, 'what does it matter to her or to you, 'Becca, or to me, if so be that it *is* true, which I'm not for believing that it is, not I,' I says."

"But what was it, Liza? You've not told me what it was, lass, that Mrs. Garth had said about me."

Rotha had stopped churning, and was standing, with the color rising even closer round her eyes. Luckily, Liza had no time to observe the minor manifestations of her friend's uneasiness; she had taken hold of the "plunger," and was squaring herself to her work.

"Say!" she cried; "why the old carlin will say aught in the world but her prayers – she says that you're settin' your cap at one of these Rays boys; that's about what she says the old witchwife, for she's no better. But it's as I said to 'Becca Rudd, says I, 'If it *is* true what traffic is it of anybody's; but it isn't true,' I says, 'and if it *is*, where's the girl that has more right? It can't be Ralph that she's settin' her cap at, 'Becca,' I says, 'for Ralph's gone, and mayhap never to come to these parts again the longest day he lives.'"

"Don't say that, Liza," interrupted Rotha in a hoarse voice.

"Why not? Those redcoats are after him from Carlisle, arn't they?"

"Don't say he'll not come back. We scarce know what may happen."

"Well, that's what father says, anyway. But, back or not back, it can't be Ralph, I says to 'Becca."

"There's not a girl worthy of him, Liza; not a girl on the country side. But we'll not repeat their old wife's gossip, eh, lass?"

"Not if you're minded not to, Rotha. But as to there being no girl worthy of Ralph," said Liza, pausing in her work and lifting herself into an erect position with an air of as much dignity as a lady of her stature could assume, "I'm none so sure of that, you know. He has a fine genty air, I will say; and someways you don't feel the same to him when he comes by you as you do to other men, and he certainly is a great traveller; but to say that there isn't a girl worthy of him, that's like Nabob Johnny tellin' Tibby Fowler that he never met the girl that wasn't partial to him."

Rotha did not quite realize the parallel that had commended itself to Liza's quick perception, but she raised no objection to the sentiment, and would have shifted the subject.

"What about Robbie, my lass?" she said.

"'And as to Willy Ray,' says I to 'Becca," continued the loquacious churner, without noticing the question, "'it isn't true as Rotha would put herself in his way; but she's full his match, and you can't show me one that is nigher his equal.'"

Rotha's confusion was increasing every minute.

"'What if her father can't leave her much gear, she has a head that's worth all the gold in Willy's pocket, and more.' Then says 'Becca, 'What about Kitty Jackson?' 'Shaf,' says I, 'she's always curlin' her hair before her bit of a looking-glass.' 'And what about Maggie of Armboth?' says 'Becca. 'She hasn't got such a head as Rotha,' says I, 'forby that she's spending a fortune on starch, what with her caps, and her capes, and her frills, and what not.'"

Liza had by this time rattled away, until by the combined exertion of arms and tongue she had brought herself to a pause for lack of breath.

Resting one hand on the churn, she lifted the other to her head to push back the hair that had tumbled over her forehead. As she tossed up her head to facilitate the latter process, her eyes caught a glimpse of Rotha's crimsoning face. "Well," she said, "I must say this churn's a funny one; it seems to make you as red as 'Becca's turkey, whether you're working at it or lookin' at some one else."

"Do you think I could listen to all that praise of myself and not blush?" said Rotha, turning aside.

"I could – just try me and see," responded Liza, with a laugh. "That's nothing to what Nabob Johnny said to me once, and I gave him a slap over the lug for it, the strutting and smirking old peacock. Why, he's all lace – lace at his neck and at his wrists, and on his – "

"You didn't favor *him* much, Liza."

"No, but Daddie did; and he said" (the wicked little witch imitated her father's voice and manner), "'Hark ye, lass, ye must hev him and then ye'll be yan o' his heirs!' He wants one or two, I says, 'for the old carle would be bald but for the three that are left on his crown.'"

"Well, but what about Robbie Anderson?" said Rotha, regaining her composure, with a laugh.

At this question Liza's manner underwent a change. The perky chirpness that had a dash of wickedness, not to say of spite, in it, entirely disappeared. Dropping her head and her voice together, she answered, –

"I don't know what's come over the lad. He's maunderin' about all day long except when he's at the Lion, and then, I reckon, he's maunderin' in another fashion."

"Can't you get him to bide by his work?"

"No; it's first a day for John Jackson at Armboth, and then two days for Sammy Robson at the Lion, and what comes one way goes the other. When he's sober – and that's not often in these days – he's as sour as Mother Garth's plums, and when he's tipsy his head's as soft as poddish."

"It was a sad day for Robbie when his old mother died," said Rotha.

"And that was in one of his bouts" said Liza; "but I thought it had sobered him forever. He loved the old soul, did Robbie, though he didn't always do well by her. And now he's broken loose again."

It was clearly as much as Liza could do to control her tears, and, being conscious of this, she forthwith made a determined effort to simulate the sternest anger.

"I hate to see a man behave as if his head were as soft as poddish. Not that *I* care," she added, as if by an afterthought, and as though to conceal the extent to which she felt compromised; "it's nothing to *me*, that I can see. Only Wythburn's a hard-spoken place, and they're sure to make a scandal of it."

"It's a pity about Robbie," said Rotha sympathetically.

Liza could scarcely control her tears. After she had dashed a drop or two from her eyes, she said: "I cannot tell what it's all about. He's always in a ponder, ponder, with his mouth open – except when he's grindin' his teeth. I hate to see a man walking about like a haystack. And Robbie used to have so much fun once on a time."

The tears were stealing up to Liza's eyes again.

"He can't forget what happened on the fell with the mare – that was a fearful thing, Liza."

"Father says it's 'cause Robbie had the say over it all; but Joe Garth says it comes of Robbie sticking himself up alongside of Ralph Ray. What a genty one Robbie used to be!"

Liza's face began to brighten at some amusing memories.

"Do you mind Reuben Thwaite's merry night last winter at Aboon Beck?"

"I wasn't there, Liza," said Rotha.

"Robbie was actin' like a play-actor, just the same as he'd seen at Carlisle. He was a captain, and he murdered a king, and then he was made king himself, and the ghost came and sat in his chair at a great feast he gave. Lord o' me! but it was queer. First he came on when he was going to do the murder and let wit he saw a dagger floating before him. He started and jumped same as our big tom cat when Mouser comes round about him. You'd have died of laughing. Then he comes on for the bank'et, and stamps his foot and tells the ghost to be off; and then he trembles and dodders from head to foot like Mouser when he's had his wash on Saturday nights. You'd have dropt, it was so queer."

Liza's enjoyment of the tragedy had not been exhausted with the occasion, for now she laughed at the humors of her own narrative.

"But those days are gone," she continued. "I met Robbie last night, and I says, says I, 'Have you pawned your dancing shoes, Robbie, as you're so glum?' And that's what he is, save when he's tipsy, and then what do ye think the maizelt creature does?"

"What?" said Rotha.

"Why," answered Liza, with a big tear near to toppling over the corner of her eye, "why, the crack't 'un goes and gathers up all the maimed dogs in Wythburn; 'Becca Rudd's 'Dash,' and that's lame on a hind leg, and Nancy Grey's 'Meg,' and you know she's blind of one eye, and Grace M'Nippen's 'King Dick,' and he's been broken back't this many a long year, and they all up and follow Robbie when he's nigh almost drunk, and then he's right – away he goes with his cap a' one side, and all the folks laughin' – the big poddish-head!"

There was a great sob for Liza in the heart of the humor of that situation; and trying no longer to conceal her sorrow at her lover's relapse into drinking habits, she laid her head on Rotha's breast and wept outright.

"We must go to Mrs. Ray; she'll be lonely, poor old thing," said Rotha, drying Liza's eyes; "besides, she hasn't had her supper, you know."

The girls left the dairy, where the churning had made small progress as yet, and went through the kitchen towards the room where the Dame of Shoulthwaite lay in that long silence which had begun sooner with her than with others.

As they passed towards the invalid's room, Mrs. Garth came in at the porch. It was that lady's first visit for years, and her advent on this occasion seemed to the girls to forebode some ill. But her manner had undergone an extraordinary transformation. Her spiteful tone was gone, and the look of sourness, which had often suggested to Liza her affinity to the plums that grew in her own garden, had given place to what seemed to be a look of extreme benevolence.

"It's slashy and cold, but I've come to see my old neighbor," she said. "I'm sure I've suffered lang and sair ower her affliction, poor body."

Without much show of welcome from Rotha, the three women went into Mrs. Ray's room and sat down.

"Poor body, who wad have thought it?" said Mrs. Garth, putting her apron to her eye as she looked up at the vacant gaze in the eyes of the sufferer. "I care not now how soon my awn glass may run out. I've so fret myself ower this mischance that the wrinkles'll soon come."

"She needn't wait much for them if she's anxious to be off," whispered Liza to Rotha.

"Yes," continues Mrs. Garth, in her melancholy soliloquy, "I fret mysel' the lee-lang day."

"She's a deal over slape and smooth," whispered Liza again. "What's it all about? There's something in the wind, mind me."

"The good dear old creatur; and there's no knowin' now if she's provided for; there's no knowin' it, I say, is there?"

To this appeal neither of the girls showed any disposition to respond. Mrs. Garth thereupon applied the apron once more to her eye, and continued: "Who wad have thought she could have been brought down so low, she as held her head so high."

"So she did, did she! Never heard on it," Liza broke in.

Not noticing the interruption, Mrs. Garth continued: "And now, who knows but she may come down lower yet – who knows but she may?"

Still failing to gain a response to her gloomy prognostications, Mrs. Garth replied to her own inquiry.

"None on us knows, I reckon! And what a down-come it wad be for her, poor creatur!"

"She's sticking to that subject like a cockelty burr," said Liza, not troubling this time to speak beneath her breath. "What ever does she mean by it?"

Rotha was beginning to feel concerned on the same score, so she said: "Mrs. Ray, poor soul, is not likely to come to a worse pass while she has two sons to take care of her."

"No good to her, nowther on 'em – no good, I reckon; mair's the pity," murmured Mrs. Garth, calling her apron once more into active service.

"How so?" Rotha could not resist the temptation to probe these mysterious deliverances.

"Leastways, not 'xcept the good dear man as is gone, Angus hissel', made a will for her; and, as I say to my Joey, there's no knowin' as ever he did; and nowther is there."

Rotha replied that it was not usual for a statesman to make a will. The law was clear enough as to inheritance. There could be no question of Mrs. Ray's share of what had been left. Besides, if there were, it would not matter much in her case, where everything that was the property of her sons was hers, and everything that was hers was theirs.

Mrs. Garth pricked up her ears at this. She could not conceal her interest in what Rotha had said, and throwing aside her languor, she asked, in anything but a melancholy tone, "So he's left all hugger-mugger, has he?"

"I know nothing of that," replied Rotha; "but if he has not made a will it cannot concern us at all. It's all very well for the lords of the manor and such sort of folk to make their wills, for, what with one thing and another, their property runs cross and cross, and there's scarce any knowing what way it lies; but for a statesman owning maybe a hundred or two of acres and a thousand or two of sheep, forby a house and the like, it's not needful at all. The willing is all done by the law."

"So it is, so it is, lass," said Mrs. Garth. The girls thought there was a cruel and sinister light in the old woman's eyes as she spoke. "Ey, the willin's all done by t' law; but, as I says to my Joey, 'It isn't always done to our likin', Joey'; and nowther is it."

Liza could bear no longer Mrs. Garth's insinuating manner. Coming forward with a defiant air, the little woman said: "Look you, don't you snurl so; but if you've anything to say, just open your mouth and tell us what it's about."

The challenge was decidedly unequivocal.

"'Od bliss the lass!" cried Mrs. Garth with an air of profound astonishment "What ails the bit thing?"

"Look here, you've got a deal too much talk to be jannic, *you* have," cried Liza, with an emphasis intended to convey a sense of profound contempt of loquaciousness in general and of Mrs. Garth's loquaciousness in particular.

Mrs. Garth's first impulse was to shame her adversary out of her warlike attitude with a little biting banter. Curling her lip, she said not very relevantly to the topic in hand, "They've telt me yer a famous sweethearter, Liza."

"That's mair nor iver *you* could have been," retorted the girl, who always dropt into the homespun of the country side in degree as she became excited.

"Yer gitten ower slape, a deal ower slippery," said Mrs. Garth. "I always told my Joey as he'd have to throw ye up, and I'm fair pleased to see he's taken me at my word."

"Oh, he has, has he?" said Liza, rising near to boiling point at the imputation of being the abandoned sweetheart of the blacksmith. "I always said as ye could bang them all at leein. I would not have your Joey if his lips were droppin' honey and his pockets droppin' gold. Nothing would hire me to do it. Joey indeed!" added Liza, with a vision of the blacksmith's sanguine head rising before her, "why, you might light a candle at his poll."

Mrs. Garth's banter was not calculated to outlast this kind of assault. Rising to her feet, she said: "Weel, thou'rt a rare yan, I *will* say. Yer ower fond o' red ribbons, laal thing. It's aff with her apron and on with her bonnet, iv'ry chance. I reckon ye'd like a silk gown, ye wad."

"Never mind my clothes," said Liza. Mrs. Garth gave her no time to say more, for, at the full pitch of indignation, she turned to Rotha, and added: "And ye're a rare pauchtie damsel. Ye might have been bred at

Court, you as can't muck a byre."

"Go home to bed, old Cuddy Garth," said Liza, "and sup more poddish, and take some of the wrinkles out of your wizzent skin."

"Setting yer cap at the Rays boys," continued Mrs. Garth, "but it'll be all of no use to ye, mark my word. Old Angus never made a will, and the law'll do all the willin', ye'll see."

"Don't proddle up yon matter again, woman," said Liza.

"And dunnet ye threep me down. I'll serve ye all out, and soon too."

Mrs. Garth had now reached the porch. She had by this time forgotten her visit of consolation and the poor invalid, who lay on the bed gazing vacantly at her angry countenance.

"Good evening, Sarah," cried Liza, with an air of provoking familiarity. "May you live all the days o' your life!"

Mrs. Garth was gone by this time.

Rotha stood perplexed, and looked after her as she disappeared down the lonnin. Liza burst into a prolonged fit of uproarious laughter.

"Hush, Liza; I'm afraid she means mischief."

"The old witch-wife!" cried Liza. "If tempers were up at the Lion for sale, what a fortune yon woman's would fetch!"

CHAPTER XXII

The Threatened Outlawry

Rotha's apprehension of mischief, either as a result of Mrs. Garth's menace or as having occasioned it, was speedily to find realization.

A day or two after the rencontre, three strangers arrived at Shoulthwaite, who, without much ceremony, entered the house, and took seats on the long settle in the kitchen.

Rotha and Willy were there at the moment, the one baking oaten cake, and the other tying a piece of cord about a whip which was falling to pieces. The men wore plain attire, but a glance was enough to satisfy Willy that one of them was the taller of the two constables who had tried to capture Ralph on Stye Head.

"What do you want?" he asked abruptly.

"A little courtesy," answered the stalwart constable, who apparently constituted himself spokesman to his party.

"From whom do you come?"

"*From* whom and *for* whom! – you shall know both, young man. We come from the High Sheriff of Carlisle, and we come for – so please you – Ralph Ray."

"He's not here."

"So we thought." The constables exchanged glances and broad smiles.

"He's not here, I tell you," said Willy, obviously losing his self-command as he became excited.

"Then go and fetch him."

"I would not if I could; I could not if I would. So be off."

"We might ask you for the welcome that is due to the commissioners of a sheriff."

"You *take* it. But you'll be better welcome to take yourselves after it."

"Listen, young master, and let it be to your profit. We want Ralph Ray, sometime captain in the rebel army of the late usurper in possession. We hold a warrant for his arrest. Here it is." And the man tapped with his fingers a paper which he drew from his belt.

"I tell you once more he is not here," said Willy.

"And we tell you again, Go and fetch him, and God send you may find him! It will be better for all of you," added the constable, glancing about the room.

Willy was now almost beyond speech with excitement. He walked nervously across the kitchen, while the constable, with the utmost calmness of voice and manner, opened his warrant and read: –

"These are to will and require you forthwith to receive into your charge the body of Ralph Ray, and him detain under secure imprisonment – "

"You've had the warrant a long while to no purpose, I believe," Willy broke in. "You may keep it still longer."

The constable took no further note of the interruption than to pause in his reading, and begin again in the same measured tones: –

"We do therefore command, publish, and declare that the said Ralph Ray, having hitherto withheld himself from judgment, shall within fourteen days next after personally deliver himself to the High Sheriff of Carlisle, under pain of being excepted from any pardon or indemnity both for his life and estate."

Then the constable calmly folded up his paper, and returned it to its place in his belt. Willy now stood as one transfixed.

"So you see, young man, it will be best for you all to go and fetch him."

"And what if I cannot?" asked Willy. "What then will happen?"

"Outlawry; and God send that that be all!"

"And what then?"

"The confiscation to the Crown of these goods and chattels."

"How so?" said Rotha, coming forward. "Mrs. Ray is still alive, and this is a brother."

"They must go elsewhere, young mistress."

"You don't mean that you can turn the poor dame into the road?" said Rotha eagerly.

The man shrugged his shoulders. His companions grinned, and shifted in their seats.

"You can't do it; you cannot do it," said Willy emphatically, stamping his foot on the floor.

"And why not?" The constable was unmoved. "Angus Ray is dead. Ralph Ray is his eldest son."

"It's against the law, I tell you," said Willy.

"You seem learned in the law, young farmer; enlighten us, pray."

"My mother, as relict of my father, has her dower, as well as her own goods and chattels, which came from her own father, and revert to her now on her husband's death."

"True; a learned doctor of the law, indeed!" said the constable, turning to his fellows.

"I have also my share," continued Willy, "of all except the freehold. These apportionments the law cannot touch, however it may confiscate the property of my brother."

"Look you, young man," said the constable, facing about and lifting his voice; "every commissioner must feel that the law had the ill-luck to lose an acute exponent when you gave up your days and nights to feeding sheep; but there is one point which so learned a doctor ought not to have passed over in silence. When you said the wife of the deceased had a right to her dower, and his younger son to his portion, you forgot that the wife and children of a traitor are in the same case with a traitor himself."

"Be plain, sir; what do you mean?" said Willy.

"That wise brain of yours should have jumped my meaning; it is that Angus Ray was as much a traitor as his son Ralph Ray, and that if the body of the latter is not delivered to judgment within fourteen days, the *whole* estate of Shoulthwaite will be forfeited to the Crown as the property of a felon and of the outlawed son of a felon."

"It's a quibble – a base, dishonorable quibble," said Willy; "my father cared nothing for your politics, your kings, or your commonwealths."

The constables shifted once more in their seats.

"He feels it when it comes nigh abreast of himself," said one of them, and the others laughed.

Rotha was in an agony of suspense. This, then, was what the woman had meant by her forebodings of further disaster to the semiconscious sufferer in the adjoining room. The men rose to go. Wrapping his cloak about him, the constable who had been spokesman said, –

"You see it will be wisest to do as we say. Find him for us, and he *may* have the benefit of pardon and indemnity for his life and estate."

"It's a trick, a mean trick," cried Willy, tramping the floor; "your pardon is a mockery, and your indemnity a lie."

"Take care, young man; keep your strong words for better service, and do you profit by what we say."

"*That* for what you say," cried Willy, losing all self-control and snapping his fingers before their faces. "Do your worst; and be sure of this, that nothing would prevail with me to disclose my brother's whereabouts even if I knew it, which I do not."

The constables laughed. "We know all about it, you see. Ha! ha! You want a touch of your brother's temper, young master. He could hardly fizz over like this. We should have less trouble with him if he could. But he's a vast deal cooler than that – worse luck!"

Willy's anger was not appeased by this invidious parallel. "That's enough," he cried at all but the full pitch of his voice, pointing at the same time to the door.

The men smiled grimly and turned about.

"Remember, a fortnight to-day, and we'll be with you again."

Rotha clung to the rannel-tree rafter to support herself. Willy thrust out his arm again, trembling with excitement.

"A fortnight to-day," repeated the constable calmly, and pulled the door after him.

CHAPTER XXIII

She Never Told her Love

When the door had closed behind the constables, Willy Ray sank exhausted into a chair. The tension of excitement had been too much for his high-strung temperament, and the relapse was swift and painful.

"Pardon and indemnity!" he muttered, "a mockery and a lie – that's what it is, as I told them. Once in their clutches, and there would be no pardon and no indemnity. I know enough for that. It's a trick to catch us, but, thank God, we cannot be caught."

"Yet I think Ralph ought to know; that is, if we can tell him," said Rotha. She was still clinging to the rannel-tree over the ingle. Her face, which had been flushed, was now ashy pale, and her lips were compressed.

"He would deliver himself up. I know him too well; I cannot doubt what he would do," said Willy.

"Still, I think he ought to know," said Rotha. The girl was speaking in a low tone, but with every accent of resolution.

"He would be denied the pardon if he obtained the indemnity. He would be banished perhaps for years."

"Still, I think he ought to know." Rotha spoke calmly and slowly, but with every evidence of suppressed emotion.

"My dear Rotha," said Willy in a peevish tone, "I understand this matter better than you think for, and I know my brother better than you can know him. There would be no pardon, I tell you. Ralph would be banished."

"Let us not drive them to worse destruction," said Rotha.

"And what *could* be worse?" said Willy, rising and walking aimlessly across the room. "They might turn us from this shelter, true; they might leave us nothing but charity or beggary, that is sure enough. Is this worse than banishment? Worse! Nothing can be worse – "

"Yes, but something *can* be worse," said the girl firmly, never shifting the fixed determination of her gaze from the spot whence the constables had disappeared. "Willy, there *is* worse to come of this business, and Ralph should be told of it if we can tell him."

"You don't know my brother," repeated Willy in a high tone of extreme vexation. "He would be banished, I say."

"And if so – " said Rotha.

"If so!" cried Willy, catching at her unfinished words, – "if so we should purchase our privilege of not being kicked out of this place at the price of my brother's liberty. Can you be so mean of soul, Rotha?"

"Your resolve is a noble one, but you do me much wrong," said Rotha with more spirit than before.

"Nay, then," said Willy, assuming a tone of some anger, not unmixed with a trace of reproach, "I see how it is. I know now what you'd have me to do. You'd keep me from exasperating these bloodhounds to further destruction in the hope of saving these pitiful properties to us, and perchance to our children. But with what relish could I enjoy them if bought at such a price? Do you think of that? And do you think of the curse that would hang on them – every stone and every coin – for us and for our children, and our children's children? Heaven forgive me, but I was beginning to doubt if one who could feel so concerning these things were worthy to bear the name that goes along with them."

"Nay, sir, but if it's a rue-bargain it is easily mended," said the girl, her eyes aflame and her figure quivering and erect.

Willy scarcely waited for her response. Turning hurriedly about, he hastened out of the house.

"It is a noble resolve," Rotha said to herself when left alone; "and it makes up for a worse offence. Yes, such self-sacrifice merits a deeper forgiveness than it is mine to offer. He deserves my pardon. And he shall have it, such as it is. But what he said was cruel indeed – indeed it was."

The girl walked to the neuk window and put her hand on the old wheel. The tears were creeping up into the eyes that looked vacantly towards the south.

"Very, very cruel; but then he was angry. The men had angered him. He was sore put about. Poor Willy, he suffers much. Yet it was cruel; it *was* cruel, indeed it was."

Rotha walked across the kitchen and again took hold of the rannel-tree. It was as though her tempest-tossed soul were traversing afresh every incident of the scenes that had just before been enacted on that spot where now she stood alone.

Alone! the burden of a new grief was with her. To be suspected of selfish motives when nothing but sacrifice had been in her heart, that was hard to bear. To be suspected of such motives by that man, of all others, who should have looked into her heart and seen what lay there, that was yet harder. "Willy's sore put about, poor lad," she told herself again; but close behind this soothing reflection crept the biting memory, "It was cruel, what he said; indeed it was."

The girl tried to shake off the distress which the last incident had perhaps chiefly occasioned. It was natural that her own little sorrow should be uppermost, but the heart that held it was too deep to hold her personal sorrow only.

Rotha stepped into the room adjoining, which for her convenience, as well as that of the invalid, had been made the bedroom of Mrs. Ray. Placid and even radiant in its peacefulness lay the face of Ralph's mother. There was not even visible at this moment the troubled expression which, to Rotha's mind, denoted the baffled effort to say, "God bless you!" Thank God, she at least was unconscious of what had happened and was still happening! It was with the thought of her alone – the weak, unconscious sufferer, near to death – that Rotha had said that worse might occur. Such an eviction from house and home might bring death yet nearer. To be turned into the road, without shelter – whether justly or unjustly, what could it matter? – this would be death itself to the poor creature that lay here.

No, it could not, it should not happen, if she had power to prevent it.

Rotha reached over the bed and put her arms about the head of the invalid and fervently kissed the placid face. Then the girl's fair head, with its own young face already ploughed deep with labor and sorrow, fell on to the pillow, and rested there, while the silent tears coursed down her cheeks.

"Not if I can prevent it," she whispered to the deaf ears. But in the midst of her thought for another, and that other Willy's mother as well as Ralph's, like a poisonous serpent crept up the memory of Willy's bitter reproach. "It was cruel, very cruel."

In the agony of her heart the girl's soul turned one way only, and that was towards him whose absence had occasioned this latest trouble. "Ralph! Ralph!" she cried, and the tears that had left her eyes came again in her voice.

But perhaps, after all, Willy was right. To be turned into the road would not mean that this poor sufferer should die of the cold of the hard winter. There were tender hearts round about, and shelter would be found for her. Yet, no! it was Ralph's concernment, and what right had they to take charity for his mother without his knowledge? Ralph ought to be told, if they could tell him. Yes, he *must* be told.

Having come to a settled resolution on this point, Rotha rose up from the bed, and, brushing her tangled hair from her forehead, walked back into the kitchen. Standing where she had stood while the constables were there, she enacted every incident and heard every syllable afresh.

There could be no longer any doubt that Ralph should know what had already happened and what further was threatened. Yet who was to tell him, and how was he to be told? It was useless to approach Willy in his present determination rather to suffer eviction than to do Ralph the injury of leading, or seeming to lead, to his apprehension.

"That was a noble purpose, but it was wrong," thought Rotha, and it never occurred to her to make terms with a mistake. "It was a noble purpose," she thought again; and when the memory of her own personal grief crept up once more, she suppressed it with the reflection, "Willy was sore tried, poor lad."

Who was to tell Ralph, and how was he to be told? Who knew where he had gone, or, knowing this, could go in search of him? Would that she herself had been born a man; then she would have travelled the kingdom over, but she would have found him. She was only a woman, however, and her duty lay here – here in the little circle with Ralph's mother, and in his house and his brother's. Who could go in search of Ralph?

At this moment of doubt, Sim walked into the courtyard of the homestead. He had not been seen since the day of the parson's visit, but, without giving sign of any consciousness that he had been away, he now took up a spade and began to remove a drift of sleet that had fallen during the previous night. Rotha's eyes brightened, and she hastened to the door and hailed him.

"Father," she said, when Sim had followed her into the house, "you made a great journey for Ralph awhile ago; could you make another now?"

"What has happened? Do they rype the country with yon warrant still?" asked Sim.

"Worse than that," said Rotha. "If that were all, we could leave Ralph to settle with them; they would never serve their warrant, never."

"Worse; what's worse, lass?" said Sim, changing color.

"Outlawry," said Rotha.

"What's that, girl? – what's outlawry? – nothing to do with – with – with Wilson, has it?" said Sim, speaking beneath his breath, and in quick and nervous accents.

"No, no: not that. It means that unless Ralph is delivered up within fourteen days this place will be taken by the bailiffs of the Sheriff."

"And what of that?" said Sim. "Let them take it – better let them have it than Ralph fall into their hands."

"Father, poor Mistress Ray would be turned into the roads – they'd have no pity, none."

"I'll uphod thee that's true," said Sim. "It staggers me."

"We must find Ralph, and at once too," said Rotha.

"Find him? He's gone, but Heaven knows where."

"Father, if I were a man, I'd find him, God knows I would."

"It's nigh about the worst as could have happened, it is," said Sim.

"The worst will be to come if we do not find him."

"But how? where? Following him will be the rule o' thumb," said Sim.

"You said he took the road over the Raise," said Rotha. "He'll not go far, depend upon that. The horse has not been caught. Ralph is among the mountains yet, take my word for it, father."

"It's bad weather to trapes the fells, Rotha. The ground is all slush and sladderment."

"So it is, so it is; and you're grown weak, father. I'll go myself. Liza Branthwaite will come here and fill my place."

"No, no, I'll go; yes, that I will," said Sim. Rotha's ardor of soul had conquered her father's apprehension of failure.

"It's only for a fortnight at most, that's all," added Sim.

"No more than that. If Ralph is not found in a fortnight, make your way home."

"But he shall be found, God helping me, he shall," said Sim.

"He *will* help you, father," said Rotha, her eyes glistening with tears.

"When should I start away?"

"To-morrow, at daybreak; that's as I could wish you," said Rotha.

"To-morrow – Sunday? Let it be to-night. It will rain to-morrow, for it rained on Friday. Let it be to-night, Rotha."

"To-night, then," said the girl, yielding to her father's superstitious fears. Thrusting her hand deep into a pocket, she added, "I have some money, not much, but it will find you lodgings for a fortnight."

"Never mind the money, girl," said Sim; "give me the horse-wallet on my back, with a bit of barley bread – and that will do."

"You must take the money as well. These are cold, hard nights. Promise me you'll lodge at the inns on the road; remember to keep yourself strong, for it's your only chance of finding Ralph – promise me!"

"I give you my word, Rotha."

"And now promise to say nothing of this to Willy," said Rotha.

Sim did not reply, but a quick glance expressed more than words of the certainty of secrecy in that regard.

"When you've crossed the Raise, follow on to Kendal," said Rotha, "and ask everywhere as you go. A fortnight to-day the men return; remember that, and tell Ralph when you meet."

"I fear he'll give himself up, I do," said Sim ruefully, and still half doubting his errand.

"That's for him to decide, and he knows best," answered Rotha. "To-night, after supper, be you at the end of the lonnin, and I'll meet you there."

Then Sim went out of the house.

When Willy Ray left Rotha an hour ago it was with an overwhelming sense of disappointment. Catching at an unfinished phrase, he had jumped to a false conclusion as to her motives. He thought that he had mistaken her character, and painful as it had been to him some days ago to think that perhaps the girl had not loved him, the distress of that moment was as nothing to the agony of this one, when he began to suspect that perhaps he did not love her. Or if, indeed, he loved her, how terrible it was to realize, as he thought he did but too vividly, that she was unworthy of his love! Had she not wished to save the old home at the cost of his brother's liberty? True, Ralph was *his* brother, not *hers*, and perhaps it was too much to expect that she should feel his present situation as deeply as he did. Yet he had thought her a rich, large soul, as unselfish as pure. It was terrible to feel that this had been an idle dream, a mere mockery of the poor reality, and that his had been a vain fool's paradise.

Then to think that he was forever to be haunted by this idle dream; to think that the shattered idol which he could no longer worship was to live with him to the end, to get up and lie down with him, and stand forever beside him!

Perhaps, after all, he had been too hard on the girl. Willy told himself it had been wrong to expect so much of her. She was – he must look the stern fact in the face – she was a country girl, and no more. Then was she not also the daughter of Simeon Stagg?

Yes, the sunshine had been over her when he looked at her before, and it had bathed her in a beauty that was not her own. That had not been her fault, poor girl. He had been too hard on her. He would go and make amends.

As Willy entered the house, Sim was coming out of it. They passed without a word.

"Forgive me, Rotha," said Willy, walking up to her and taking her hand. "I spoke in haste and too harshly."

Rotha let her hand lie in his, but made no reply. After his apology, Willy would have extenuated his fault.

"You see, Rotha, you don't know my brother as well as I do, and hence you could not foresee what would have happened if we had done what you proposed."

Still there was no response. Willy's words came more slowly as he continued: "And it was wrong to suppose that whether Ralph were given up or not they would leave us in this place, but it was natural that you should think it a good thing to save this shelter."

"I was thinking of your mother, Willy," said Rotha, with her eyes on the ground.

"My mother – true." Willy had not thought of this before; that Rotha's mind had been running on the possible dangers to his mother of the threatened eviction had never occurred to him until now. He had been wrong – entirely so. His impulse was to take the girl in his arms and confess the injustice of his reflections; but he shrank from this at the instant, and then his mind wriggled with apologies for his error.

"To spare mother the peril of being turned into the roads – that would have been something; yes, much. Ralph himself must have chosen to do that. But once in the clutches of those bloodhounds, and it might have meant banishment for years, for life perhaps – aye, perhaps even death itself."

"And even so," said Rotha, stepping back a pace and throwing up her head, while her hands were clinched convulsively, – "and even so," she repeated. "Death comes to all; it will come to him among the rest, and how could he die better? If he were a thousand times my brother, I could give him up to such a death."

"Rotha, my darling," cried Willy, throwing his arms about her, "I am ashamed. Forgive me if I said you were thinking of yourself. Look up, my darling; give me but one look, and say you have pardoned me."

Rotha had dropped her eyes, and the tears were now blinding them.

"I was a monster to think of it, Rotha; look in my face, my girl, and say you forgive me."

"I could have followed you over the world, Willy, and looked for no better fortune. I could have trusted to you, and loved you, though we had no covering but the skies above us."

"Don't kill me with remorse, Rotha; don't heap coals of fire on my head. Look up and smile but once, my darling."

Rotha lifted her tear-dimmed eyes to the eyes of her lover, and Willy stooped to kiss her trembling lips. At that instant an impulse took hold of him which he was unable to resist, and words that he struggled to suppress forced their own utterance.

"Great God!" he cried, and drew back his head with a quick recoil, "how like your father you are!"

CHAPTER XXIV

Treason or Murder

The night was dark that followed. It had been a true Cumbrian day in winter. The leaden sky that hung low and dense had been relieved only by the white rolling mists that capped the fells and swept at intervals down their brant and rugged sides. The air had not cleared as the darkness came on. There was no moon. The stars could not struggle through the vapor that lay beneath them. There was no wind. It was a cold and silent night.

Rotha stood at the end of the lonnin, where the lane to Shoulthwaite joined the pack-horse road. She was wrapped in a long woollen cloak having a hood that fell deep over her face. Her father had parted from her half an hour ago, and though the darkness had in a moment hidden him from her sight, she had continued to stand on the spot at which he had left her.

She was slight of figure and stronger of will than physique, but she did not feel the cold. She was revolving the step she had taken, and thinking how great an issue hung on the event. Sometimes she mistrusted her judgment, and felt an impulse to run after her father and bring him back. Then a more potent influence would prompt her to start away and overtake him, yet only in order to bear his message the quicker for her fleeter footsteps.

But no; Fate was in it: a power above herself seemed to dominate her will. She must yield and obey. The thing was done.

The girl was turning about towards the house, when she heard footsteps approaching her from the direction which her father had taken. She could not help but pause, hardly knowing why, when the gaunt figure of Mrs. Garth loomed large in the road beside her. Rotha would now have hastened home, but the woman had recognized her in the darkness.

"How's all at Shoulth'et?" said Mrs. Garth in her blandest tones; "rubbin' on as usual?"

Rotha answered with a civil commonplace, and turned to go. But Mrs. Garth had stood, and the girl felt compelled to stand also.

"It's odd to see ye not at work, lass," said the woman in a conciliatory way; "ye're nigh almost always as thrang as Thorp wife, tittyvating the house and what not."

Again some commonplace from Rotha, and another step homewards.

"I've just been takin' a sup o' tea with laal 'Becca Rudd. It's early to go home, but, as I says to my Joey, there's no place like it; and nowther is there. It's like ye've found that yersel', lass, afore this."

There was an insinuating sneer in the tone in which Mrs. Garth uttered her last words. Getting no response, she added, –

"And yer fadder, I reckon *he's* found it out too, bein' so lang beholden to others. I met the poor man on the road awhile ago."

"It's cold and sappy, Mrs. Garth. Good night," said Rotha.

"Poor man, he has to scrat now," said Mrs. Garth, regardless of Rotha's adieu. "I reckon he's none gone off for a spoag; he's none gone for a jaunt."

The woman was angry at Rotha's silence, and, failing to conciliate the girl, she was determined to hold her by other means. Rotha perceived the purpose, and wondered within herself why she did not go.

"But he's gone on a bootless errand, I tell ye," continued Mrs. Garth.

"What errand?" It was impossible to resist the impulse to probe the woman's meaning.

Mrs. Garth laughed. It was a cruel laugh, with a crow of triumph in it.

"Yer waxin' apace, lass; I reckon ye think ye'll be amang the next batch of weddiners," said Mrs. Garth.

Rotha was not slow to see the connection of this scarcely relevant observation. Did the woman know on what errand her father had set out? Had she guessed it? And if so, what matter?

"I wish the errand had been mine instead," said Rotha calmly. But it was an unlucky remark.

"Like enough. Now, that's very like," said Mrs. Garth with affected sincerity. "Ye'll want to see him badly, lass; he's been lang away. Weel, it's nought but nature. He's a very personable young man. There's no sayin' aught against it. Yes, he's of the bettermer sort, that way."

Of what use was it to continue this idle gossip? Rotha was again turning about, when Mrs. Garth added, half as comment and half as question, –

"And likely ye've never had the scribe of a line from him sin' he left. But he's no wanter; he'll never marry ye, lass, so ye need never set heart on him."

Rotha stepped close to the woman and looked into her face. What wickedness was now brewing?

"Nay, saucer een," said Mrs. Garth with a snirt, "art tryin' to skiander me like yon saucy baggish, laal Liza?"

"Come, Mrs. Garth, let us understand one another," said Rotha solemnly. "What is it you wish to tell me? You said my father had gone on a bootless errand. What do you know about it? Tell me, and don't torment me, woman."

"Nay, then, I've naught to say. Naught but that Ralph Ray is on the stormy side of the hedge *this* time."

Mrs. Garth laughed again.

"He is in trouble, that is true; but what has he done to you that you should be glad at his misfortunes?"

"Done? done?" said Mrs. Garth; "why – but we'll not talk of that, my lass. Ask *him* if ye'd know. Or mayhap ye'll ask yon shaffles, yer father."

What could the woman mean?

"Tak my word for it; never set heart on yon Ralph: he's a doomed man. It's not for what he did at the wars that the redcoats trapes after him. It's worse nor that – a lang way war' nor that."

"What is it, woman, that you would tell me? Be fair and plain with me," cried the girl; and the words were scarcely spoken when she despised herself for regarding the matter so seriously.

But Mrs. Garth leaned over to her with an ominous countenance, and whispered, "There's murder in it, and that's war' nor war. May war' never come among us, say I!" Rotha put her hands over her face, and the next moment the woman shuffled on.

It was out at length.

Rotha staggered back to the house. The farm people had taken supper, and were lounging in various attitudes of repose on the skemmel in the kitchen.

The girl's duties were finished for the day, and she went up to her own room. She had no light, and, without undressing, she threw herself on the bed. But no rest came to her. Hour after hour she tossed about, devising reason on reason for disbelieving the woman's word. But apprehension compelled conviction.

Mrs. Garth had forewarned them of the earlier danger, and she might be but too well informed concerning this later one.

Rotha rejected from the first all idea of Ralph being guilty of the crime in question. She knew nothing of the facts, but her heart instantly repudiated the allegation. Perhaps the crime was something that had occurred at the wars six years ago. It could hardly be the same that still hung over their own Wythburn. That last dread mystery was as mysterious as ever. Ralph had said that her father was innocent of it, and she knew in her heart that he must be so. But what was it that he had said? "Do you *know* it was not father?" she had asked; and he had answered, "I *know* it was not." Did he mean that he himself –

The air of her room felt stifling on that winter's night. Her brow was hot and throbbing, and her lips were parched and feverish. Rising, she threw open the window, and waves of the cold mountain vapor rolled in upon her.

That was a lie which had tried a moment ago to steal into her mind – a cruel, shameless lie. Ralph was as innocent of murder as she was. No purer soul ever lived on earth; God knew it was the truth.

Hark! what cry was that which was borne to her through the silent night? Was it not a horse's neigh?

Rotha shuddered, and leaned out of the window. It was gone. The reign of silence was unbroken. Perhaps it had been a fancy. Yet she thought it was the whinny of a horse she knew.

Rotha pulled back the sash and returned to her bed. How long and heavy were the hours till morning! Would the daylight never dawn? or was the blackness that rested in her own heart to lie forever over all the earth?

But it came at last – the fair and gracious morning of another day came to Rotha even as it always has come to the weary watcher, even as it always will come to the heartsore and heavy-laden, however long and black the night.

The girl rose at daybreak, and then she began to review the late turn of events from a practical standpoint.

Assuming the woman's word to be true, in what respect was the prospect different for Mrs. Garth's disclosure? Rotha had to confess to herself that it was widely different. When she told Willy that she could give up Ralph, were he a thousand times her brother, to such a death of sacrifice as he had pictured, she had not conceived of a death that would be the penalty of murder. That Ralph would be innocent of the crime could not lessen the horror of such an end. Then there was the certainty that conviction on such a charge would include the seizure of the property. Rotha dwelt but little on the chances of an innocent man's acquittal. The law was to her uninformed mind not an agent of justice, but an instrument of punishment, and to be apprehended was to be condemned.

Ralph must be kept out of the grip of the law. Yes, that was beyond question. Whether the woman's words were true or false, the issues were now too serious to be played with.

She had sent her father in pursuit of Ralph, and the effect of what he would tell of the forthcoming eviction might influence Ralph to adopt a course that would be imprudent, even dangerous – nay, even fatal, in the light of the more recent disclosure.

What had she done? God alone could say what would come of it.

But perhaps her father could still be overtaken and brought back. Yet who was to do it? She herself was a woman, doomed as such to sit at her poor little wheel, to lie here like an old mastiff or its weak tottering whelp, while Ralph was walking – perhaps at her bidding – to his death.

She would tell Willy, and urge him to go in pursuit of Sim. Yet, no, that was not possible. She would have to confess that she had acted against his wish, and that he had been right while she had been wrong. Even that humiliation was as nothing in the face of the disaster that she foresaw: but Willy and Sim! – Rotha shuddered as she reflected how little the two names even could go together.

The morning was growing apace, and still Rotha's perplexity increased. She went downstairs and made breakfast with an absent mind.

The farm people came and went; they spoke, and she answered; but all was as a dream, except only the one grim reality that lay on her mind.

She was being driven to despair. It was far on towards midday, and she was alone; still no answer came to her question. She threw herself on the settle, and buried her face in her hands. She was in too much agony to weep. What had she done? What could she do?

When she lifted her eyes, Liza Branthwaite was beside her, looking amazed and even frightened.

"What has happened, lass?" said Liza fearfully.

Then Rotha, having no other heart to trust with her haunting secret, confided it to this simple girl.

"And what can I do?" she added in a last word.

During the narration, Liza had been kneeling, with her arms in her friend's lap. Jumping up when Rotha had ceased, she cried, in reply to the last inquiry, "I know. I'll just slip away to Robbie. He shall be off and fetch your father back."

"Robbie?" said Rotha, looking astonished.

"Never fear, *I'll* manage *him*. And now, cheer up, my lass; cheer up."

In another moment Liza was running at her utmost speed down the lonnin.

CHAPTER XXV

Liza's Device

When she reached the road, the little woman turned towards Wythburn. Never pausing for an instant, she ran on and on, passing sundry groups of the country folks, and rarely waiting to exchange more than the scant civilities of a hasty greeting.

It was Sunday morning, and through the dense atmosphere that preceded rain came the sound of the bells of the chapel on the Raise, which rang for morning service.

"What's come over little Liza?" said a young dalesman, who, in the solemnity of Sunday apparel, was wending his way thither, as the little woman flew past him, "tearing," as he said, "like a crazy thing."

"Some barn to be christened afore the service, Liza?" called another young dalesman after her, with the memory of the girl's enjoyment of a similar ceremony not long before.

Liza heeded neither the questions nor the banter. Her destination was certainly not the church, but she ran with greater speed in that direction than the love of the Reverend Nicholas's ministrations had yet prompted her to compass.

The village was reached at length, and her father's house was near at hand; but the girl ran on, without stopping to exchange a word with her sententious parent, who stood in the porch, pipe in hand, and clad in those "Cheppel Sunday" garments with which, we fear, the sanctuary was rarely graced.

"Why, theer's Liza," said Matthew, turning his head into the house to speak to his wife, who sat within; "flying ower the road like a mad greyhound."

Mrs. Branthwaite had been peeling apples towards the family's one great dinner in the week. Putting down the bowl which contained them, she stepped to the door and looked after her daughter's vanishing figure.

"Sure enough, it is," she said. "Whatever's amiss? The lass went over to the Moss. Why, she stopping, isn't she?" "Ey, at the Lion," answered Mattha. "I reckon there's summat wrang agen with that Robbie. I'll just slip away and see."

Panting and heated on this winter's day, red up to the roots of the hair and down to the nape of the neck, Liza had come to a full pause at the door of the village inn. It was not a false instinct that had led the girl to choose this destination. Sunday as it was, the young man whom she sought was there, and, morning though it might be, he was already in that condition of partial inebriation which Liza had recognized as the sign of a facetious mood.

Opening the door with a disdainful push, compounded partly of her contempt for the place and partly of the irritation occasioned by the events that had brought her to the degradation of calling there, Liza cried out, as well as she could in her present breathless condition, –

"Robbie, come your ways out of this."

The gentleman addressed was at the moment lying in a somewhat undignified position on the floor. Half sprawling, half resting on one knee, Robbie was surprised in the midst of an amusement of which the perky little body whom he claimed as his sweetheart had previously expressed her high disdain. This consisted of a hopeless endeavor to make a lame dog dance. The animal in question was no other than 'Becca Rudd's Dash, a piece of nomenclature which can only be described as the wildest and most satirical misnomer. Liza had not been too severe on Dash's physical infirmities when she described him as lame on one of his hind legs, for both those members were so effectually out of joint as to render locomotion of the simplest kind a difficulty attended by violent oscillation. This was probably the circumstance that had recommended Dash as the object of Robbie's half-drunken pastime; and after a fruitless half-hour's exercise the tractable little creature, with a woeful expression of face, was at length poised on its hindmost parts just as Liza pushed open the door and called to its instructor.

The new arrival interrupted the course of tuition, and Dash availed himself of his opportunity to resume the normal functions of his front paws. At this the reclining tutor looked up from his place on the floor with a countenance more of sorrow than of anger, and said, in a tone that told how deeply he was grieved, "*There*, lass, see how you've spoilt it!"

"Get up, you daft-head! Whatever are you mufflin' about, you silly one, lying down there with the dogs and the fleas?"

Liza still stood in the doorway with an august severity of pose that would have befitted Cassandra at the porch. Her unsparing tirade had provoked an outburst of laughter, but not from Robbie. There were two other occupants of the parlor – Reuben Thwaite, who had never been numbered among the regenerate, and had always spent his Sunday mornings in this place and fashion; and little Monsey Laman, whose duty as schoolmaster usually embraced that of sexton, bell-ringer, and pew-opener combined, but who had escaped his clerical offices on this Sabbath morning by some plea of indisposition which, as was eventually perceived, would only give way before liberal doses of the medicine kept at the sign of the Red Lion.

The laughter of these worthies did not commend itself to Liza's sympathies, for, turning hotly upon them, she said, "And you're worse nor he is, you old sypers."

"Liza, Liza," cried Robbie, raising his forefinger in an attitude of remonstrance, which he had just previously been practising on the unhappy Dash, – "Liza, think what it is to call this reverend clerk and sexton and curate a *toper!*"

"And so he is; he's like yourself, he's only half-baked, the half thick."

"Now – now – now, Liza!" cried Robbie, raising himself on his haunches the better to give effect to his purpose of playing the part of peacemaker and restraining the ardor of his outspoken little friend.

"Come your ways out, I say," said Liza, not waiting for the admonition that was hanging large on the lips of the blear-eyed philosopher on the floor.

"Come your ways," she repeated; "I would be solid and solemn with you."

Robbie was at this instant struggling to regain possession of the itinerant Dash, who, perceiving a means of escape, was hobbling his way to the door.

"Wait a minute," said Robbie, having captured the runaway, – "wait a minute, Liza, and Dash will show you how to dance like Mother Garth."

"Shaf on Dash!" said Liza, taking a step or two into the room and securing to that animal his emancipation by giving him a smack that knocked him out of Robbie's hands. "Do you think I've come here to see your tipsy games?"

Robbie responded to this inquiry by asking with provoking good nature if she had not rather come to give him a token of her love.

"Give us a kiss, lass," he said, getting up to his feet and extending his arms to help himself.

Liza gave him something instead, but it produced a somewhat louder and smarter percussion.

"What a whang over the lug she brong him!" said Reuben, turning to the schoolmaster.

"I reckon it's mair wind ner wool, like clippin' a swine," said Matthew Branthwaite, who entered the inn at this juncture.

Robbie's good humor was as radiant as ever. "A kiss for a blow," he said, laughing and struggling with the little woman. "It's a Christian virtue, eh, father?"

"Ye'll not get many of them, at that rate," answered Mattha, less than half pleased at an event which he could not comprehend. "It's slow wark suppin' buttermilk with a pitchfork."

"Will you *never* be solid with me?" cried Liza, with extreme vexation pictured on every feature as her scapegrace sweetheart tried to imprison her hands in order to kiss her. "I tell you – " and then there was some momentary whispering between them, which seemed to have the effect of sobering Robbie in an instant. His exuberant vivacity gave place to a look of the utmost solemnity, not unmixed with a painful expression as of one who was struggling hard to gather together his scattered wits.

"They'll only have another to take once they catch *him*," said Robbie in an altered tone, as he drew his hand hard across his eyes.

There was some further whispering, and then the two went outside. Returning to the door, Liza hailed her father, who joined them on the causeway in front of the inn.

Robbie was another man. Of his reckless abandonment of spirit no trace was left.

Mattha was told of the visit of the constables to Shoulthwaite, and of Sim's despatch in search of Ralph.

"He'll be off for Carlisle," said Robbie, standing square on his legs, and tugging with his cap off at the hair at the back of his head.

"Like eneuf," answered Mattha, "and likely that's the safest place for him. It's best to sit near the fire when the chimney smokes, thoo knows."

"He'll none go for safety, father," answered Robbie; and turning to Liza, he added, "But what was it you said about Mother Garth?"

"The old witch-wife said that Ralph was wanted for murder," replied the girl.

"It's a lie," said Robbie vehemently.

"I'll uphod thee there," said Mattha; "but whatever's to be done?"

"Why, Robbie must go and fetch Sim back," said Liza eagerly.

"The lass is right," said Robbie; "I'll be off." And the young man swung on his heel as though about to carry out his purpose on the instant.

"Stop, stop," said Mattha; "I reckon the laal tailor's got farther ner the next cause'y post. You must come and tak a bite of dinner and set away with summat in yer pocket."

"Hang the pocket! I must be off," said Robbie. But the old man took him too firmly by the arm to allow of his escape without deliberate rudeness. They turned and walked towards the weaver's cottage.

"What a maizelt fool I've been to spend my days and nights in this hole!" said Robbie, tipping his finger over his shoulder towards the Red Lion, from which they were walking.

"I've oft telt thee so," said Mattha, not fearing the character of a Job's comforter.

"And while this bad work has been afoot too," added Robbie, with a penitent drop of the head.

They had a tributary of the Wyth River to pass on the way to Mattha's house. When they came up to it, Robbie cried, "Hold a minute!" Then running to the bank of the stream, he dropt on to his knees, and before his companions could prevent him he had pulled off his cap and plunged his head twice or thrice in the water.

"What, man!" said Mattha, "ye'd want mair ner the strength of men and pitchforks to stand again the like of that. Why, the water is as biting as a stepmother welcome on a winter's mornin' same as this."

"It's done me a power of good though," said Robbie shaking his wet hair, and then drying it with a handkerchief which Liza had handed him for the purpose. "I'm a stone for strength," added Robbie, but rising to his feet he slipped and fell.

"Then didsta nivver hear that a tum'lan stone gedders na moss," said Mattha.

The jest was untimely, and the three walked on in silence. Once at the house the dinner was soon over, and not even Mrs. Branthwaite's homely, if hesitating, importunity could prevail with Robbie to make a substantial meal.

"Come, lad," said Matthew, "you've had but a stepmother bit."

"I've had more than I've eaten at one meal for nigh a month – more than I've taken since that thing happened on the fell," answered Robbie, rising from the table, strapping his long coat tightly about him with his belt, and tying cords about the wide flanges of his big boots.

"Mattha will sett thee on the road, Robbie," said Mrs. Branthwaite.

"Nay, nay; I reckon, I'd be scarce welcome. Mayhap the lad has welcomer company."

This was said in an insinuating tone, and with a knowing inclination of the head towards Liza, whose back was turned while she stole away to the door.

"Nay, now, but nobody shall sett me," said Robbie, "for I must fly over the dikes like a racehorse."

"Ye've certainly got a lang stroke o' the grund, Robbie."

Robbie laughed, waved his hand to the old people, who still sat at dinner, and made his way outside.

Liza was there, looking curiously abashed, as though she felt at the moment prompted to an impulse of generosity of which she had cause to be ashamed.

"Gi'e us a kiss, now, my lass," whispered Robbie, who came behind her and put his arm about her waist.

There was a hearty smacking sound.

"What's that?" cried Mattha from within; "I thought it might be the sneck of a gate."

CHAPTER XXVI

"Fool, Do not Flatter"

When Mrs. Garth reached home, after her interview with Rotha in the road, there was a velvety softness in her manner as of one who had a sense of smooth satisfaction with herself and her surroundings.

The blacksmith, who was working at a little bench which he had set up in the kitchen, was also in a mood of more than usual cheerfulness.

"Ey, he's caught – as good as caught," said Mrs. Garth.

Her son laughed, but there was the note of forced merriment in his voice.

"Where do they say he is – Lancaster?"

"That's it, not a doubt on't."

"Were they sure of him – the man at Lancaster?"

"No, but *I* were when they telt me what mak of man it was."

The blacksmith laughed again over a chisel which he was tempering.

"It's nothing to me, is it, mother?"

"Nowt in the warld, Joey, ma lad."

"They are after him for a traitor, but I cannot see as it's anything to me what they do with him when they catch hod on him; it's nothing to me, is it, mother?"

"Nowt."

Garth chuckled audibly. Then in a low tone he added, –

"Nor nothing to me what comes of his kin afterwards."

He paused in his work; his manner changed; he turned to where

Mrs. Garth was coiled up before the fire.

"Had *he* any kin, mother?"

Mrs. Garth glanced quickly up at her son.

"A brother, na mair."

"What sort of a man, mother?"

"The spit of hissel'."

"Seen anything of him?"

"Not for twenty year."

"Nor want to neither?"

Mrs. Garth curled her lip.

CHAPTER XXVII

Ralph at Lancaster

The night of the day on which the officers of the Sheriff's court of Carlisle visited Shoulthwaite, the night of Simeon Stagg's departure from Wythburn in pursuit of Ralph, the night of Rotha's sorrow and her soul's travail in that solitary house among the mountains, was a night of gayety and festival in the illuminated streets of old Lancaster. The morning had been wet and chill, but the rain-clouds swept northward as the day wore on, and at sundown the red bars belted the leaden sky that lay to the west of the towers of the gray castle on the hill.

A proclamation by the King had to be read that day, and the ancient city had done all that could be done under many depressing conditions to receive the royal message with fitting honors. Flags that had lain long furled, floated from parapet and pediment, from window and balcony, from tower and turret. Doors were thrown open that had not always swung wide on their hinges, and open house was kept in many quarters.

Towards noon a man mounted the steps in the Market Place, and read this first of the King's proclamations and nailed it to the Cross.

A company of red-coated soldiers were marched from the Castle Hill to the hill on the southwest, which had been thrown up six years before by the russet-coated soldiery who had attacked and seized the castle. Then they were marched back and disbanded for the night.

When darkness fell over highway and byway, fires were lit down the middle of the narrow streets, and they sent up wide flakes of light that brightened the fronts of the half-timbered houses on either side, and shot a red glow into the sky, where the square walls of the Dungeon Tower stood out against dark rolling clouds. Little knots of people were at every corner, and groups of the baser sort were gathered about every fire. Gossip and laughter and the click of the drinking-horn fell everywhere on the ear. But the night was still young, and order as yet prevailed.

The Market Place was the scene of highest activity. Numbers of men and boys sat and stood on the steps of the Cross, discussing the proclamation that had been read there. Now and again some youth of more scholarship than the rest held a link to the paper, and lisped and stammered through its bewildering sentences for the benefit of a circle of listeners who craned their necks to hear.

The proclamation was against public vice and immorality of various sorts which were unpunishable by law. It set forth that there were many persons who had no method of expressing their allegiance to their Sovereign but that of drinking his health, and others who had so little regard for morality and religion as to have no respect for the virtue of the female sex.

The loyalty of the Lancasterians might be unimpeachable, but their amusement at the proclamation was equally beyond question.

"That from Charles Stuart!" said one, with a laugh; and he added, with more familiarity of affection for his King than reverence for his august state, "What a sly dog he is, to be sure!"

"Who is that big man in the long coat?" said another, who had not participated in the banter of his companions on the Puritanical devices of Charles and his cronies. He was jerking his head aside to where a man whom we have known in other scenes was pushing his way through the crowd.

"Don't know; no one knows, seemingly," answered the politician whose penetration had solved the mystery of the proclamation against vice and all loose livers.

"He's been in Lancaster this more nor a week, hasn't he?"

"Believe he has; and so has the little withered fellow that haunts him like his shadow. Don't seem over-welcome company, so far as I can see."

"Where's the little one now?"

"I reckon he's nigh about somewhere."

Ralph Ray borrowed a link from a boy who was near, and stood before the paper that was posted upon the Cross. Just then a short, pale-faced, elderly man, with quick eyes beneath shaggy brows, elbowed his way between the people and came up close at Ray's side.

It was clearly not his object to read the proclamation, for after a glance at it his eyes were turned towards Ralph's face. If he had hoped to catch the light of an expression there he was disappointed. Ralph read the proclamation without changing a muscle of his countenance. He was returning the link to its owner, when the little man reached out his long finger, and, touching the paper as it hung on the Cross, looked up into Ralph's eyes with a cunning leer, and said, "Unco' gude, eh?"

Ralph made no reply. As though determined to draw him into converse, the little man shrugged his shoulders, and added, "Clarendon's work that, eh?"

There was still no response, so the speaker continued: "It'll deceive none. It's lang sin' the like of it stood true in England – worse luck!"

The dialect in which this was spoken was of that mongrel sort which in these troublous days was sometimes adopted by degenerate Scotchmen who, living in England, had reasons of their own for desiring to conceal their nationality.

"I'll wager it's all a joke," added the speaker, dropping his voice, but still addressing Ralph, and ignoring the people that stood around them.

Ralph turned about, and, giving but a glance to his interlocutor, passed out of the crowd without a word.

The little man remained a moment or two behind, and then slunk down the street in the direction which Ralph had taken.

There was to be a performance at the theatre that night, and already the people had begun to troop towards St. Leonard's Gate. Chairs were being carried down the causeway, with link-boys walking in front of them, and coaches were winding their way among the fires in the streets. Scarlet cloaks were mingling with the gray jerkins of the townspeople, and swords were here and there clanking on the pavement.

The theatre was a rude wooden structure that stood near the banks of the river, on a vacant plot of ground that bordered the city on the east and skirted the fields. It had a gallery that sloped upwards from the pit, and the more conspicuous seats in it were draped in crimson cloth. The stage, which went out as a square chamber from one side of the circular auditorium, was lighted by lamps that hung above the heads of the actors.

Before the performance began every seat was filled. The men hailed their friends from opposite sides of the house, and laughed and chaffed, and sang snatches of Royalist and other ballads. The women, who for the most part wore veils or masks, whispered together, flirted their fans, and returned without reserve the salutations that were offered them.

Ralph Ray, who was there, stood at the back of the pit, and close at his left was the sinister little man who had earlier in the evening been described as his shadow. Their bearing towards each other was the same as had been observed at the Cross: the one constantly interrogating in a low voice; the other answering with a steadfast glance or not at all.

When the curtain rose, a little butterfly creature, in the blue-and-scarlet costume of a man, – all frills and fluffs and lace and linen, – came forward, with many trips and skips and grimaces, and pronounced a prologue, which consisted of a panegyric on the King and his government in their relations to the stage.

It was not very pointed, conclusive, or emphatic, but it was rewarded with applause, which rose to a general outburst of delighted approval when the rigor of the "late usurpers" was gibbeted in the following fashion: –

> Affrighted with the shadow of their rage,
> They broke the mirror of the times, the Stage;
> The Stage against them still maintained the war,
> When they debauched the Pulpit and the Bar.

"Pretty times, forsooth, of which one of that breed could be the mirror," whispered the little man at Ralph's elbow.

The play forthwith proceeded, and proved to be the attempt of a gentleman of fashion to compromise the honor of a lady of the Court whom he had mistaken for a courtesan. The audience laughed at every indelicate artifice of the libertine, and screamed when the demure maiden let fall certain remarks which bore a double significance. Finally, when the lady declared her interest in a cage of birds, and the gentleman drew from his pocket a purse of guineas, and, shaking them before her face, asked if those were the dicky-birds she wished for, the enjoyment of the audience passed all bounds of ordinary expression. The men in lace and linen lay back in their seats to give vent to loud guffaws, and the women flirted their fans coquettishly before their eyes, or used them to tap the heads of their male companions in mild and roguish remonstrance.

"Pity they didn't debauch the stage as well as the pulpit and bar, if this is its condition inviolate," whispered the little man again.

The intervals between the acts were occupied by part of the audience in drinking from the bottles which they carried strapped about their waists, and in singing snatches of songs. One broad-mouthed roysterer on the ground proposed the King's health, and supported the toast by a ballad in which "Great Charles, like Jehovah," was described as merciful and generous to the foes that would unking him and the vipers that would sting him. The chorus to this loyal lyric was sung by the "groundlings" with heartiness and unanimity: –

> Let none fear a fever,
> But take it off thus, boys;
> Let the King live forever,
> 'Tis no matter for us, boys.

Ralph found the atmosphere stifling in this place, which was grown noisome now to wellnigh every sense. He forced his way out through the swaying bodies and swinging arms of the occupants of the pit. As he did so he was conscious, though he did not turn his head, that close behind him, in the opening which he made in the crowd, his inevitable "Shadow" pursued him.

The air breathed free and fresh outside. Ralph walked from St. Leonard's Gate by a back lane to the Dam Side. The river as well as the old town was illuminated. Every boat bore lamps to the masthead. Lamps, too, of many colors, hung downwards from the bridge, and were reflected in their completed circle in the waters beneath them.

The night was growing apace, and the streets were thronged with people, some laughing, some singing, some wrangling, and some fighting. Every tavern and coffee-house, as Ralph went by, sent out into the night its babel of voices. Loyal Lancasterians were within, doing honor to the royal message of that day by observing the spirit while violating the letter of it.

Ralph had walked up the Dam Side near to that point at which the Covel Cross lies to the left, when a couple of drunken men came reeling out of a tavern in front of him. Their dress denoted their profession and rank. They were lieutenants of the regiment which had been newly quartered at the castle. Both were drunk. One was capering about in a hopeless effort to dance; the other was trolling out a stave of the ballad that was just then being sung at the corner of every street: –

> The blood that he lost, as I suppose
> (Fa la la la),
> Caused fire to rise in Oliver's nose
> (Fa la la la).
> This ruling nose did bear such a sway,
> It cast such a heat and shining ray,
> That England scarce knew night from day
> (Fa la la la).

The singer who thus described Cromwell and his shame was interrupted by a sudden attack of thirst, and forthwith applied the unfailing antidote contained in a leathern bottle which he held in one hand.

Ralph stepped off the pavement to allow the singer the latitude his condition required, when that person's companion pirouetted into his breast, and went backwards with a smart rebound.

"What's this, stopping the way of a gentleman?" hiccuped the man, bringing himself up with ludicrous effort to his full height, and suspending his capering for the better support of his soldierly dignity.

Then, stepping closer to Ralph, and peering into his face, he cried, "Why, it's the man of mystery, as the sergeant calls him. Here, I say, sir," continued the drunken officer, drawing with difficulty the sword that had dangled and clanked at his side; "you've got to tell us who you are. Quick, what's your name?"

The man was flourishing his sword with as much apparent knowledge of how to use it as if it had been a marlin-spike. Ralph pushed it aside with a stout stick that he carried, and was passing on, when the singing soldier came up and said, "Never mind his name; but whether he be Presbyter Jack or Quaker George, he must drink to the health of the King. Here," he cried, filling a drinking-cup from the bottle in his hand, "drink to King Charles and his glory!"

Ralph took the cup, and, pretending to raise it to his lips, cast its contents by a quick gesture over his shoulder, where the liquor fell full in the face of the Shadow, who had at that moment crept up behind him. The soldiers were too drunk to perceive what he had done, and permitted him to go by without further molestation. As he walked on he heard from behind another stave of the ballad, which told how –

> This Oliver was of Huntingdon
> (Fa la la la),
> Born he was a brewer's son
> (Fa la la la),
> He soon forsook the dray and sling,
> And counted the brewhouse a petty thing
> Unto the stately throne of a king
> (Fa la la la).

"What did the great man himself say?" asked the Shadow, stepping up to Ralph's side. "He said, 'I would rather have a plain, russet-coated captain who knows what he fights for, and loves what he knows, than what you call a gentleman.' And he was right, eh?"

"God knows," said Ralph, and turned aside.

He had stopped to look into the middle of a small crowd that had gathered about the corner of the Bridge Lane. A blind fiddler sat on a stool there and played sprightly airs. His hearers consisted chiefly of men and boys. But among them was one young girl in bright ribbons, who was clearly an outcast of the streets. Despite her gay costume, she had a wistful look in her dark eyes, as of one who was on the point of breaking into tears.

The dance tunes suddenly came to an end, and were followed by the long and solemn sweeps of a simple old hymn such as had been known in many an English home for many an age. Gradually the music rose and fell, and then gently, and before any were aware, a sweet, low, girlish voice took up the burden and sang the words. It was the girl of the streets who sang. Was it the memory of some village home that these chords had awakened? Was it the vision of her younger and purer days that came back to her amid the gayeties of this night – of the hamlet, the church, the choir, and of herself singing there?

The hymn melted the hearts of many that stood around, and tears now stood in the singer's downcast eyes.

At that hour of that night, in the solitary homestead far north, among the hills, what was Rotha's travail of soul?

Ralph dropped his head, and felt something surging in his throat.

At the same instant a thick-lipped man with cruel eyes crushed through the people to where the girl stood, and, taking her roughly by the shoulder, pushed her away.

"Hand thy gab," he said, between clinched teeth; "what's *thy* business singing hymns in t'streets? Get along home to bed; that's more in thy style, I reckon."

The girl was stealing away covered with shame, when Ralph parted the people that divided him from the man, and, coming in front of him, laid one hand on his throat. Gasping for breath, the fellow would have struggled to free himself, but Ralph held him like a vise.

"This is not the first time we have met; take care it shall be the last."

So saying, Ralph flung the man from him, and he fell like an infant at his feet.

Gathering himself up with a look compounded equally of surprise and hatred, the man said, "Nay, nay; do you think it'll be the last? don't you fear it!"

Then he slunk out of the crowd, and it was observed that when he had gained the opposite side of the street, the little, pale-faced elderly person who had been known as Ralph's Shadow, had joined him.

"Is it our man?"

"The same, for sure."

"Then it must be done the day. We've delayed too long already."

CHAPTER XXVIII

After Word Comes Weird

I

When Ralph lay down in his bed that night in a coffee-house in China Lane, there was no conviction more strongly impressed upon his mind than that it was his instant duty to leave Lancaster. It was obvious that he was watched, and that his presence in the old town had excited suspicion. The man who had pestered him for many days with his unwelcome society was clearly in league with the other man who had insulted the girl. The latter rascal he knew of old for a declared and bitter enemy. Probably the pair were only waiting for authority, perhaps merely for the verification of some surmise, before securing the aid of the constable to apprehend him. He must leave Lancaster, and at once.

Ralph rose from his bed and dressed himself afresh. He strapped his broad pack across his back, called his hostess, and paid his score. "Must the gentleman start away at midnight?" Yes; a sudden call compelled him. "Should she brew him a pot of hot ale? – the nights were chill in winter." Not to-night; he must leave without delay.

When Ralph walked through the streets of Lancaster that cold midnight, it was with no certainty as to his destination. It was to be anywhere, anywhere in this race for life. Any haven that promised solitude was to be his city of refuge.

The streets were quiet now, and even the roystering tipplers had gone off to their homes. For Ralph there was no home – only this wild hunt from place to place, with no safety and rest.

His heavy tread and the echo of his footfall were at length all that broke the stillness of the streets.

He walked southwards, and when he reached the turnpike he stood for a moment and turned his eyes towards the north. The fires that had been kindled were smouldering away, but even yet a red gleam lay across the square towers of the castle on the hill.

The old town was now asleep. Thousands of souls lay slumbering there.

Ralph thought of those who slept in a home he knew, far, far north of this town and those towers. What was his crime that he was banished from them – perhaps forever? What was his crime before God or man? His mother, his brother, Rotha –

Ralph struck his breast and turned about. No, it would not bear to be thought about. *That* dream, at least, was gone. Rotha was happy in his brother's love, and as for himself – as for him – it was his destiny, and he must bear it!

Yet what was life worth now that he should struggle like this to preserve it?

Ralph returned to his old conviction – God's hand was on him. The idea, morbid as it might be, brought him solace this time. Once more he stopped, and turned his eyes afresh towards the north and the fifty miles of darkness that lay between him and those he loved.

It was at that very moment of desolation that Rotha heard the neigh of a horse as she leaned out of her open window.

II

"Aye, poor man, about Martinmas the Crown seized his freehold and all his goods and chattels."

"It will be sad news for him when he hears that his old mother and the wife and children were turned into the road."

"Well, well, I will say, treason or none, that John Rushton was as good a subject as the loudest bagpipes of them all."

Ralph was sitting at breakfast in a wayside inn when two Lancashire yeomen entered and began to converse in these terms: "Aye, aye, and the leaven of Puritanism is not to be crushed out by such measures. But it's flat dishonesty, and nothing less. What did the proclamation of '59 mean if it didn't promise pardon to every man that fought for the Parliament, save such as were named as regicides?"

"Tut, man, it came to nought; the King returned without conditions; and the men who fought against him are reckoned as guilty as those that cut off his father's head." "But the people will never uphold it. The little leaven remains, and one day it will leaven the lump."

"Tut, the people are all fools – except such as are knaves. See how they're given up to drunkenness and vain pleasures. Hypocrisy and libertinism are safe for a few years' reign. England is *Merry* England, as they say, and she'll be merry at any cost."

"Poor John, it will be a sad blow to him!"

Ralph had been an eager listener to the conversation between the yeomen, who were clearly old Whigs and Parliamentarians.

"Pardon me, gentlemen," he interrupted, "do you speak of John Rushton of Aberleigh?"

"We do. As good a gentleman as lived in Lancashire."

"That's true, but where was he when this disaster befell his household?"

"God knows; he had fled from judgment and was outlawed."

"And the Crown confiscated his estate, you say, and turned his family into the road? What was the indictment – some trumpery subterfuge for treason?"

"Like enough; but the indictment counts for nothing in these days; it's the verdict that is everything, and that's settled beforehand."

"True, true."

"Did you know my neighbor John?"

"I did; we were comrades years ago."

With these words, Ralph rose from his unfinished breakfast and walked out of the house.

What mischief of the same sort might even now be brewing at Wythburn in his absence? Should he return? That would be useless, and worse than useless. What could he do?

The daring impulse suddenly possessed him to go on to London, secure audience of the King himself, and plead for amnesty. Yes, that was all that remained to him to do, and it should be done. His petition might be spurned; his person might be seized, and he might be handed over to judgment; but what of that? He was certain to be captured sooner or later, and this sorry race for liberty and for life would be over at length.

III

The same day Ralph Ray, still travelling on foot, had approached the town of Preston. It was Sunday morning, but he perceived that smoke like a black cloud overhung the houses and crept far up the steeples and towers. Presently a tumultuous rabble came howling and hooting out of the town. At the head of them, and apparently pursued by them, was a man half clad, who turned about at every few yards, and, raising his arm, predicted woe and desolation to the people he was leaving. He was a Quaker preacher, and his presence in Preston was the occasion of this disturbance.

"Oh, Preston," he cried, "as the waters run when the floodgates are up, so doth the visitation of God's love pass away from thee, oh, Preston!"

"Get along with thee; thou righteous Crister," said one of the crowd, lifting a stick above his head. "Get along, or ye'll have Gervas Bennett aback of ye again."

"I shall never cease to cry aloud against deceit and vanities," shrieked the preacher above the tumult. "You do profess a Sabbath, and dress yourselves in fine apparel, and your women go with stretched necks."

"Tush, tush! Beat him, stone him!"

"Surely the serpent will bite without enchantment," the preacher replied, "and a babbler is no better. The lips of a fool will swallow up himself."

The church bells were beginning to ring in the town, and the sound came across the fields and was heard even above the mocking laughter of the crowd.

"You have your steeple-houses, too," cried the preacher, "and the bells of your gospel markets are even now a-ringing where your priests and professors are selling their wares. But God dwells not in temples made with hands. Oh, men of Preston, did I not prophesy that fire, and famine, and plagues, and slaughter would come upon ye unless ye came to the light with which Christ hath enlightened all men? And have ye not the plague of the East at your doors already?"

"And who brought it, who brought it?" screamed more than one voice from the crowd. "Who brought the plague to us from the East? Beat him, beat him!" The mob, with many uplifted hands, swayed about the preacher. "Your cities will be laid waste, the houses without man, and the land be utterly desolate. And what will ye do, oh men of Preston, in the day of visitation, and in the desolation which shall come from far?"

The rabble had rushed past by this time, still hooting and howling at the wild, fiery-eyed enthusiast at their head.

Ralph walked on to the town and speedily discovered the cause of the black cloud which overhung it. An epidemic of an alarming nature had broken out in various quarters, and fears were entertained that it was none other than a great pestilence which had been brought to England from the East.

Indescribably eerie was the look of Preston that Sunday morning. Men and boys were bearing torches through the streets to disinfect them, and it was the smoke from these torches that hung like a cloud above the town. Through the thick yellow atmosphere the shapes of people passing to and fro in the thoroughfares stood out large and black.

IV

Ralph had travelled thus far in the fixed determination of pushing on to London, seeking audience of the King himself, and pleading for an amnesty. But the resolution which had never failed him before began now to waver. Surely there was more than his political offences involved in the long series of disasters that had befallen his household? He reflected that every link in that chain of evil seemed to be coupled to the gyves that hung about his own wrists. Wilson's life in Wythburn – his death – Sim's troubles – Rotha's sorrow – even his father's fearful end, and the more fearful accident at the funeral – then his mother's illness, nigh to death – how nigh to death by this time God alone could tell him here – all, all, with this last misery of his own banishment, seemed somehow to centre in himself. Yes, yes, sin and its wages must be in this thing; but what sin, what sin? What was the crime that cast its shadow over his life?

"As the waters run when the flood-gates are up," said the preacher, "so doth the visitation of God's love pass away from thee."

Of what use, then, would be the amnesty of the King? Mockery of mockeries! In a case like this only the Great King Himself could proclaim a pardon. Ralph put his hands over his eyes as the vision came back to him of a riderless horse flying with its dread burden across the fells. No sepulture! It was the old Hebrew curse – the punishment of the unpardonable sin.

He thought again of his stricken mother in the old home, and then of the love which had gone from him like a dream of the night. Heaven had willed it that where the heart of man yearned for love, somewhere in the world there was a woman's heart yearning to respond. But the curse came to some here and some there – the curse of an unrequitable passion.

The church bells were still ringing over the darkened town.

Rotha was happy in her love; Heaven be with her and bless her! As for himself, it was a part of the curse that lay on him that her face should haunt his dreams, that her voice should come to him in his sleep, and that "Rotha, Rotha," should rise in sobs to his lips in the weary watches of the night.

Yes, it must be as he had thought – God's hand was on him. Destiny had to work its own way. Why should he raise his feeble hands to prevent it? The end would be the end, whenever and wherever it might come. Why, then, should he stir?

Ralph had determined to go no farther. He would stay in Preston over the night, and set out again for the north at daybreak. Was it despair that possessed him? Even if so, he was stronger than before. Hope had gone, and fear went with it.

Take heart, Ralph Ray, most unselfish and long-suffering of men. God's hand is indeed upon you, but God Himself is at your right hand!

V

That day Ralph walked through the streets with a calmer mind. Towards nightfall he stepped into a tavern and secured a bed. Then he went into the parlor of the house and sat among the people gathered there, and chatted pleasantly on the topics of the hour.

The governing spirit of the company was a little man who wore a suit of braided black which seemed to indicate that he belonged to one of the clerkly professions. He was addressed by the others as Lawyer Lampitt, and was asked if he would be busy at the court house on the following morning. "Yes," he answered, with an air of consequence, "there's the Quaker preacher to be tried for creating a disturbance."

"Was he taken, then?" asked one.

"He's quiet enough now in the old tower," said the lawyer, stretching himself comfortably before the fire.

"I should have thought his tormentors were fitter occupants of his cell," said Ralph.

"Perhaps so, young man; I express no opinion."

"There was scarce a man among them whose face would not have hanged him," continued Ralph.

"There again I offer no opinion," said the lawyer, "but I'll tell you an old theory of mine. It is that a murderer and a hero are all but the same man."

The company laughed. They were accustomed to these triumphs of logic, and relished them. Every man braced himself up in his seat.

"Why, how's that, lawyer?" said a townsman who sat tailor-fashion on a bench; he would hardly have been surprised if the lawyer had proved beyond question that he swam swanlike among the Isles of Greece.

"I'll tell you a story," said the gentleman addressed. "There was an ancient family in Yorkshire, and the lord of the house was of a very splenetive temper. One day in a fit of jealousy he killed his wife, and put to death all of his children who were at home by throwing them over the battlements of his castle. He had one remaining child, and it was an infant, and was nursed at a farmhouse a mile away. He had set out for the farm with an intent to destroy his only remaining child, when a storm of thunder and lightning came on, and he stopped."

"Thought it was a warning, I should say," interrupted a listener.

"It awakened the compunctions of conscience, and he desisted from his purpose."

"Well?"

"What do you think he did next?"

"Cannot guess – drowned himself?"

"No, and this proves what I say, that a murderer and a hero are all but one. He surrendered himself to justice, and stood mute at the bar, and, in order to secure his estates to his surviving child, he had the resolution to die under the dreadful punishment of *peine forte*."

"What is that, lawyer?"

"Death by iron weights laid on the bare body until the life is crushed out of it."

"Dreadful! And did he secure his estates to his child by suffering such a death?"

"He did. He stood mute at the bar, and let judgment go against him without trial. It is all in black and white. The Crown cannot confiscate a man's estate until he is tried and condemned."

"What of an outlaw?" asked Ralph somewhat eagerly.

"A man's flight is equal to a plea of guilty."

"I had a comrade once," said Ralph with some tremor of voice; "he fled from judgment and was outlawed, and his poor children were turned into the road. Could he have kept his lands for his family by delivering his body to that death you speak of?"

"He could. The law stands so to this day."

"Think you, in any sudden case, a man could do as much *now?*"

"He *could*," answered the lawyer; "but where's the man who *would?* Only one who must die in any chance, and then none but a murderer, I should say."

"I don't know – I don't know that," said Ralph, rising with ill-concealed agitation, and stalking out of the room, without the curtest leave-taking.

VI

On Tuesday, Ralph was walking through Kendal on his northward journey. The day was young. Ralph meant to take a meal at the old coaching house, the Woodman, in Kirkland, by the river Kent, and then push on till nightfall.

The horn of the incoming coach fell on his ear, and the coach itself – the Carlisle coach, laden with passengers from back to front – swept into the courtyard of the inn at the moment he entered it afoot.

There was a little commotion there. A group of the serving folk, the maids in their caps, the ostlers bareheaded, and some occasional stable people were gathered near the taproom door. The driver of the coach got off his box and crushed into the middle of this company. His passengers paused in their descent from the top to look over the heads of those who were on the ground.

"Drunk, surely," said one of these to another; "that proclamation was not unnecessary."

"Some poor straggler, sir; picked him up insensible and fetched him along," said one of the ostlers.

Ralph walked past the group to the threshold of the inn.

"Loosen his neckcloth! – here, take my brandy," said a passenger.

"Came from the North, seemingly, sir. Looks weak from want and a long journey."

"From the North?" asked the coachman; "I'll give him a seat in the coach to-night and take him home."

Ralph stepped back and looked over some of the people.

A man was lying on the ground, his head in a woman's lap.

It was Simeon Stagg.

CHAPTER XXIX

Robbie's Quest Begun

When Robbie Anderson left Wythburn, his principal and immediate purpose was to overtake Simeon Stagg. It was of less consequence that he should trace and discover Ralph Ray. Clearly it had been Ralph's object on leaving home to keep out of reach of the authorities who were in pursuit of him. But there was no saying what course a man such as he might take in order to insure the safety of the people who were dear to him, and to whom he was dear. The family at Shoulthwaite Moss had been threatened with eviction. The ransom was Ralph's liberty. Sim had been sent to say so. But a graver issue lay close behind. This shadow of a great crime lay over Ralph's life. If Robbie could overtake Sim before Sim had time to overtake Ralph, he might prevent a terrible catastrophe. Even so fearless a man as Ralph was would surely hesitate if he knew, though but on hearsay, that perhaps a horrible accusation awaited him at Carlisle.

That accusation might be false – it must be false. Robbie believed he could swear that it was a lie if he stood before the Throne of Grace. But of what avail was the innocence of the accused in days when an indictment was equal to a conviction!

Sim was an old man, or at least he was past his best. He was a frail creature, unable to travel fast. There was little doubt in the mind of the lusty young dalesman as he took his "lang stroke o' the ground" that before many hours had gone by Sim would be overtaken and brought back.

It was Sunday morning when little Liza Branthwaite ferreted Robbie out of the Red Lion, and it was no later than noon of the same day when Robbie began his journey. During the first few miles he could discover no trace of Sim. This troubled him a little, until he reflected that it was late at night when Sim started away, and that consequently the tailor would pass the little wayside villages unobserved. After nine or ten miles had been covered, Robbie met with persons who had encountered Sim. The accounts given of him were as painful as they were in harmony with his character. Sim had shrunk from the salutations of those who knew him, and avoided with equal timidity the gaze of those by whom he was not known. The suspicion of being everywhere suspected was with the poor outcast abroad as well as at home.

Quickly as the darkness fell in on that Sunday in mid-winter, Robbie had travelled many miles before the necessity occurred to him of seeking lodgings for the night. He had intended to reach the little town of Winander that day, and he had done so. It was late, however, and after a frugal supper, Robbie went off to bed.

Early next day, Monday, the young dalesman set about inquiries among the townspeople as to whether a man answering to the description which he gave of Sim had been seen to pass through the town. Many persons declared that they had seen such a one the day before, and some insisted that he was still in Winander. An old fellow in a smock, who, being obviously beyond all active labor, employed his time and energies in the passive occupation of watching everybody from the corner of a street, and in chatting with as many as had conversation to spend on his superannuated garrulity, affirmed very positively that he had talked with Sim as recently as an hour ago.

Right or wrong, this was evidence of Sim's whereabouts which Robbie felt that he could not ignore. He must at least test its truthfulness by walking through the streets and inquiring further. It would be idle to travel on until this clew had been cleared up.

And so Robbie spent almost the whole day in what proved to be a fruitless search. It was apparent that if Sim had been in Winander he had left it on Sunday. Robbie reflected with vexation that it was now the evening of Monday, and that he was farther behind the man of whom he was in pursuit than he had been at starting from Wythburn.

In no very amiable mood Robbie set out afresh just as darkness was coming on, and followed the road as far as the village of Staveley. Here there was nothing more hopeful to do at a late hour on Monday night than to seek for a bed and sleep. On Tuesday morning Robbie lost no time in making inquiries, but he wasted several hours in ascertaining particulars that were at all reliable and satisfactory. No one appeared to have seen such a man as Sim, either to-day, yesterday, or on Sunday.

Robbie was perplexed. He was in doubt if it might not be his best course to turn back, when a happy inspiration occurred to him.

What had the people said of Sim's shyness and timidity? Why, it was as clear as noonday that the poor little man would try to avoid the villages by making a circuit of the fields about them.

With this conviction, Robbie set out again, intending to make no pause in his next stage until he had reached Kendal. Upon approaching the villages he looked about for the footpaths that might be expected to describe short arcs around them; and, following one of these, he passed a cottage that stood at a corner of a lane. He had made many fruitless inquiries hitherto, and had received replies that had been worse than valueless; but he could not resist the temptation to ask at this house.

Walking round the cottage to where the door opened on the front farthest from the lane, Robbie entered the open porch. His unfamiliar footstep brought from an inner room an old woman with a brown and wrinkled face, who curtsied, and, speaking in a meek voice, asked, or seemed to ask, his pleasure.

"Your pardon, mistress," said Robbie, "but mayhap you've seen a little man with gray hair and a long beard going by?"

"Do you say a laal man?" asked the old woman.

"Ey, wrinkled and wizzent a bit?" said Robbie.

"Yes," said the woman.

Robbie was uncertain as to what the affirmation implied. Taking it to be a sort of request for a more definite description, he continued, –

"A blate and fearsome sort of a fellow, you know."

"Yes," repeated the woman, and then there was a pause.

Robbie, getting impatient of the delay, was turning on his heel with scant civility, when the old woman said, "Are you seeking him for aught that is good?"

"Why, ey, mother," said Robbie, regaining his former position and his accustomed geniality in an instant. "Do you know his name?" she asked.

"Sim – that's to say Sim Stagg. Don't you fear me, mother; I'm a friend to Sim, take my word."

"You're a good-like sort of a lad, I think," said the old woman; "Sim was here ower the night last night."

"Where is he now?" said Robbie.

"He left me this morning at t' edge o' t' daylight. He axed for t' coach to Lancaster, and I telt him it started frae the Woodman, in Kirklands, and so he went off there."

"Kirklands; where's Kirklands?"

"In Kendal, near the church."

It turned out that the good old woman had known Sim many years before, when they were neighbors in a street of a big town. She had been with Sim's wife in her last illness, and had cared for his little daughter when the child's mother died.

Robbie did not know when the coach might leave Kendal for Lancaster; Sim was several hours in front of them, and therefore he took a hasty leave. The old woman, who lived a solitary life in the cottage, looked after the young man with eyes which seemed to say that, in spite of the instinct which prompted her to confide in Robbie, she half regretted what she had done.

CHAPTER XXX

A Race Against Life

No sooner had Ralph discovered that the straggler from the North who lay insensible in the yard of the inn at Kendal was Simeon Stagg than he pushed through the crowd, and lifting the thin and wasted figure in his arms, ordered a servant to show him to a room within.

There in a little while sensibility returned to Sim, who was suffering from nothing more serious than exhaustion and the excitement by which it had been in part occasioned.

When in the first moment of consciousness he opened his eyes and met the eyes of Ralph, who was bending above him, he exhibited no sign of surprise. With a gesture indicative of irritation he brushed his long and bony hand over his face, as though trying to shut out a vision that had more than once before haunted and tormented him. But when he realized the reality of the presence of the man whom he had followed over many weary miles, whose face had followed him in his dreams, – when it was borne in upon his scattered sense that Ralph Ray was actually here at his side, holding his hand and speaking to him in the deep tones which he knew so well, – then the poor worn wayfarer could no longer control the emotion that surged upwards from his heart.

It was a wild, disjointed, inconsequential tale which Sim thereupon told, which he had come all this way to tell, and which now revealed its full import to the eager listener in spite of the narrator's eagerness rather than by means of it. Amid spasms of feeling, however, the story came at length to an end; and gathering up the threads of it for himself, and arranging them in what seemed to him their natural sequence, Ralph understood all that it was essential to understand of his own position and the peril of those who were dear to him. That he was to be outlawed, and that his estate was to be confiscated; that his mother, who still lived, was, with his brother and Rotha, to be turned into the road, – this injustice was only too imminent.

"In a fortnight – was it so?" he asked. "In a fortnight they were to be back? A fortnight from what day?"

"Saturday," said Sim; "that's to say, a week come Saturday next."

"And this is Tuesday; ten full days between," said Ralph, walking with drooping head across the room; "I must leave immediately for the North. Heigh!" opening a window, and hailing the ostler who at the moment went past, "when does your next coach start for the North?"

"At nine o'clock, sir."

"Nine to-night? So late? Have you nothing before – no wagon – nothing?"

"Nothing before, sir; 'cept – leastways – no, nothing before. Ye see, it waits for the coach from Lancaster, and takes on its passengers."

"John, John," cried the landlady, who had overheard the conversation from a neighboring window, "mayhap the gentleman would like to take a pair of horses a stage or two an he's in a hurry."

"Have you a horse that can cover thirty miles to-day?" said Ralph.

"That we have, yer honor, and mair ner ya horse."

"Where will the coach be at six to-morrow?"

"At Penrith, I reckon," said the ostler, lifting his cap, and scratching his head with the air of one who was a good deal uncertain alike of his arithmetic and his geography.

"How long do they reckon the whole journey?"

"Twelve hours, I've heeard – that's if nothing hinders; weather, nor the like."

"Get your horse ready at once, my lad, and then take me to your landlady."

"You'll not leave me behind, Ralph," said Sim when Ralph had shut back the casement.

"You're very weak, old friend; it will be best for you to sleep here to-day, and take to-night's Carlisle coach as far back as Mardale. It will be early morning when the coach gets there, and at daybreak you can walk over the Stye Pass to Shoulthwaite."

"I dare not, I dare not; no, no, don't leave me here." Sim's importunity was irresistible, and Ralph yielded more out of pity than by persuasion. A second horse was ordered, and in less than half an hour the travellers, fortified by a meal, were riding side by side on the high road from Kendal to the North.

Sim was not yet so far recovered from his exhaustion but that the exertion of riding – at any time a serious undertaking to him – was quick in producing symptoms of collapse. But he held on to his purpose of accompanying Ralph on his northward journey with a tenacity which was unshaken either by his companion's glances of solicitude or yet by the broad mouthed merriment of the rustics, who obviously found it amusing to watch the contortions of an ill-graced, weak, and spiritless rider, and to fire off at him as he passed the sallies of an elephantine humor.

When the pair started away from Kendal, Sim had clearly no thought but that their destination was to be Wythburn. It was therefore with some surprise and no little concern that he observed that Ralph took the road to the right which led to Penrith and the northeast, when they arrived at that angle of the highway outside the town where two turnpikes met, and one went off to Wythburn and the Northwest.

"I should have reckoned that the nighest way home was through Staveley," Sim said with hesitation.

"We can turn to the left at Mardale," said Ralph, and pushed on without further explanation. "Do you say that mother has never once spoken?" he asked, drawing up at one moment to give Sim a little breathing space.

"Never once, Ralph – mute as the grave, she is – poor body."

"And Rotha – Rotha – "

"Yes, the lass is with her, she is."

"God bless her in this world and the next!"

Then the two pushed on again, with a silence between them that was more touching than speech. They rode long and fast this spell, and when they drew up once more, Ralph turned in his saddle and saw that the ruins that stood at the top of the Kendal Scar were already far behind them.

"It's a right good thing that you've given up your solitary life on the fells, Sim. It wilt cheer me a deal, old friend, to think you'll always live with the folks at Shoulthwaite." Ralph spoke as if he himself had never to return. Sim felt this before Ralph had realized the implication of his words.

"It's hard for a hermit to be a good man," continued Ralph; "he begins with being miserable and ends with being selfish and superstitious, and perhaps mad. Have you never marked it?"

"Maybe so, Ralph; maybe so. It's like it's because the world's bitter cruel that so many are buryin' theirsels afore they're dead."

"Then it's because they expect too much of the world," said Ralph. "We should take the world on easier terms. Fallible humanity must have its weaknesses and poor human life its disasters, and where these are mighty and inevitable, what folly is greater than to fly from them or to truckle to them, to make terms with them? Our duty is simply to endure them, to endure them – that's it, old friend."

There was no answer that Sim could make to this. Ralph was speaking to the companion who rode by his side; but in fact he seemed to be addressing himself.

"And to see a man buy a reprieve from Death!" he continued. "Never do that – never? Did you ever think of it, Sim, that what happens is always the best?"

"It scarce looks like it, Ralph; that it don't."

"Then it's because you don't look long enough. In the end, it is *always* the best that happens. Truth and the right are the last on the field; it always has been so, and always will be; it only needs that you should wait to the close of the battle to see *that*."

There would have been a sublime solemnity in these rude words of a rude man of action if Sim had divined that they were in fact the meditations of one who believed himself to be already under the shadow of his death.

The horses broke again into a canter, and it was long before the reins of the riders brought them to another pause. The day was bitterly cold, and, notwithstanding the exertion of riding, Sim's teeth chattered sometimes as with ague, and his fingers were numb and stiff. It was an hour before noon when the travellers left Kendal, and now they had ridden for two hours. The brighter clouds of the morning had disappeared, and a dull, leaden sky was overhead. Gradually the heavy atmosphere seemed to close about them, yet a cutting wind blew smartly from the east.

"A snowstorm is coming, Sim. Look yonder; how thick it hangs over the Gray Crag sheer ahead! We must push on, or we'll be overtaken."

"How long will it be coming?" asked Sim.

"Five hours full, perhaps longer," said Ralph; "we may reach Penrith before that time."

"Penrith!"

Sim's tone was one of equal surprise and fear.

Ralph gave him a quick glance; then reaching over the neck of his horse to stroke its long mane, he said, with the manner of one who makes too palpable an effort to change the subject of conversation: "Isn't this mare something like old Betsy? I couldn't but mark how like she was to our old mare that is lost when the ostler brought her into the yard this morning."

Sim made no reply.

"Poor Betsy!" said Ralph, and dropped his head on to his breast.

Another long canter. When the riders drew up again it was to take a steadier view of some objects in the distance which had simultaneously awakened their curiosity.

"There seem to be many of them," said Ralph; and, shielding his ear from the wind, he added, "do you catch their voices?"

"Are they quarrelling? – is it a riot?" Sim asked.

"Quick, and let us see."

In a few moments they had reached a little wayside village.

There they found children screaming and women wringing their hands. In the high road lay articles of furniture, huddled together, thrown in heaps one on another, and broken into fragments in the fall. A sergeant and company of musketeers were even then in the midst of this pitiful work of devastation, turning the people out of their little thatched cottages and flinging their poor sticks of property out after them. Everywhere were tumult and ruin. Old people were lying on the cold earth by the wayside. They had been born in these houses; they had looked to die in these homes; but houses and homes were to be theirs no more. Amidst the wreck strode the gaunt figure of a factor, directing and encouraging, and firing off meantime a volley of revolting oaths.

"What's the name of this place?" asked Ralph of a man who stood, with fury in his eyes, watching the destruction of his home.

"Hollowbank," answered the man between his teeth.

Ralph remembered that here had lived a well-known Royalist, whom the Parliament had dispossessed of his estates. The people of this valley had been ardent Parliamentarians during the long campaign. Could it be that his lordship had been repossessed of his property, and was taking this means of revenging himself upon his tenantry for resisting the cause he had fought for?

An old man lay by the hedge looking down to the ground with eyes that told only of despair. A little fair-haired boy, with fear in his innocent face, was clinging to his grandfather's cloak and crying piteously.

"Get off with you and begone!" cried the factor, rapping out another volley.

"Is it Hollowbank you call this place?" said Ralph, looking the fellow in the face. "Hellbank would be a fitter name."

The man answered nothing, but his eyes glared angrily as Ralph put spur to his horse and rode on.

"God in heaven!" cried Ralph when Sim had come up by his side, "to think that work like this goes on in God's sight!"

"Yet you say the best happens," said Sim.

"It does; it does; God knows it does, for all that," insisted Ralph. "But to think of these poor souls thrown out into the road like cattle. Cattle? To cattle they would be merciful! – thrown out into the road to lie and die and rot!"

"Have they been outlawed – these men?" said Sim.

"Damnation!" cried Ralph, as though at Sim's ignorant word a new and terrible thought had flashed upon his mind and wounded him like a dagger.

Then they rode long in silence.

Away they went, mile after mile, without rest and without pause, through dales and over uplands, past meres and across rivers, and still with the gathering blackness overhead.

What force of doom was spurring them on in this race against Life? It was the depth of a Cumbrian winter, and the days were short. Clearly they would never reach Penrith to-night. The delay at Hollowbank and the shortened twilight before a coming snowstorm must curtail their journey. They agreed to put up for the night at the inn at Askham.

As they approached that house of entertainment they observed that the coach which had left Carlisle that morning was in the act of drawing up at the door. It waited only while three or four passengers alighted, and then drove on and passed them in its journey south.

Five hours hence it would pass the northward coach from Kendal.

When Ralph and Sim dismounted at the Fox and Hounds, at Askham, the landlord came hastily to the door. He was a brawny dalesman, of perhaps thirty. He was approaching the travellers with the customary salutations of a host, when, checking himself, and coming to Ralph, he said in a low tone, "I ask pardon, sir, but is your name Ray? – Captain – hush!" he whispered; and then, becoming suddenly mute, without waiting for a reply to his questions, he handed the horses to a man who came up at the moment, and beckoned Ralph and Sim to follow him, not through the front of the house, but towards the yard that led to the back.

"Don't you know me?" he said as soon as he had conveyed them, as if by stealth, into a little room detached from the rest of the house.

"Surely it's Brown? And how are you, my lad?"

"Gayly; and you seem gayly yourself, and not much altered since the great days at Dunbar – only a bit lustier, mayhap, and with something more of beard. I'll never forget the days I served under you!"

"That's well, Brown; but why did you bring us round here?" said Ralph.

"Hush!" whispered the landlord. "I've a pack of the worst bloodhounds from Carlisle just come. They're this minute down by the coach. I know the waistrels. They've been here before to-day. They'd know you to a certainty, and woe's me if once the gommarels come abreast of you. It's like I'd never forgive myself if my old captain came by any ill luck in my house."

"How long will they stay?" "Until morning, it's like."

"How far is it to the next inn?"

"Three miles to Clifton."

"We shall sleep till daybreak to-morrow, Brown, on the settles you have here. And now, my lad, bloodhounds or none on our trail, bring us something to eat."

CHAPTER XXXI

Robbie, Speed On

Upon reaching the Woodman at Kendal, Robbie found little reason to doubt that Sim had been there and had gone. A lively young chambermaid, who replied to his questions, told him the story of Sim's temporary illness and subsequent departure with another man.

"What like of a man was he, lass – him as took off the little fellow?" asked Robbie.

"A very personable sort; maybe as fine a breed as you'd see here and there one," replied the girl.

"Six foot high haply, and square up on his legs?" asked Robbie, throwing back his body into an upright posture as a supplementary and explanatory gesture.

"Ey, as big as Bully Ned and as straight as Robin the Devil," said the girl.

Robbie was in ignorance of the physical proportions of these local worthies, but he was nevertheless in little doubt as to the identity of his man. It was clear that Sim and Ralph had met on this spot only a few hours ago, and had gone off together.

"What o'clock might it be when they left?" said Robbie.

"Nigh to noon – maybe eleven or so."

It was now two, and Ralph and Sim, riding good horses, must be many miles away. Robbie's vexation was overpowering when he thought of the hours that he had wasted at Winander and of the old gossip at the street corner who had prompted him to the fruitless search.

"The feckless old ninny," he thought in his mute indignation; "when an old man comes to be an old woman it's nothing but right that he should die, and have himself done with."

Robbie was unable to hire a horse in order to set off in pursuit of his friends; nor were his wits so far distraught by the difficulties tormenting them that he was unable to perceive that, even if he could afford to ride, his chance would be inconsiderable of overtaking two men who had already three hours' start of him.

He went into the taproom to consult the driver of the Carlisle coach, who was taking a glass before going to bed – his hours of work being in the night and his hours of rest being in the day. That authority recommended, with the utmost positiveness of advice, that Robbie should take a seat in his coach when he left for the North that night.

"But you don't start till nine o'clock, they tell me?" said Robbie.

"Well, man, what of that?" replied the driver; "yon two men will have to sleep to-night, I reckon; and they'll put up to a sartenty somewhear, and that's how we'll come abreast on 'em. It's no use tearan like a crazy thing."

The driver had no misgivings; his conjecture seemed reasonable, and whether his plan were feasible or not, it was the only one available. So Robbie had to make a virtue of a necessity, as happens to many a man of more resource.

He was perhaps in his secret heart the better reconciled to a few hours' delay in his present quarters, because he fancied that the little chambermaid had exhibited some sly symptoms of partiality for his society in the few passages of conversation which he had exchanged with her.

She was a bright, pert young thing, with just that dash of freedom in her manners which usually comes of the pursuit of her public calling; and it is only fair to Robbie's modesty to say that he had not deceived himself very grossly in his estimate of the interest he had suddenly excited in her eyes. It was probably a grievous dereliction of duty to think of a love encounter, however blameless, at a juncture like this – not to speak of the gravity of the offence of forgetting the absent Liza. But Robbie was undergoing a forced interlude in the march; the lady who dominated his affections was unhappily too far away to appease them, and he was not the sort of young fellow who could resist the assault of a pair of coquettish black eyes.

Returning from the taproom to announce his intention of waiting for the coach, Robbie was invited to the fire in the kitchen, – a privilege for which the extreme coldness of the day was understood to account. Here he lit a pipe, and discoursed on the route that would probably be pursued by his friends.

It was obvious that Ralph and Sim had not taken the direct road home to Wythburn, for if they had done so he must have met them as he came from Staveley. There was the bare possibility that he had missed them by going round the fields to the old woman's cottage; but this seemed unlikely.

"Are you quite sure it's an *old man* you're after?" said the girl, with a dig of emphasis that was meant to insinuate a doubt of Robbie's eagerness to take so much trouble in running after anything less enticing than one of another sex who might not be old.

Robbie protested on his honor that *he* was never known to run after young women, – a statement which did not appear to find a very ready acceptance. The girl was coming and going from the kitchen in the discharge of her duties, and on one of her journeys she brought a parchment map in her hand, saying: "Here's a paper that Jim, the driver, told me to show you. It gives all the roads atween Kendal and Carlisle. So you may see for yourself whether your friends could get round about to Wy'bern."

Robbie spread out the map on the kitchen table, and at once proceeded, with the help of the chambermaid, to trace out the roads that were open to Ralph and Sim to take. It was a labyrinthine web, that map, and it taxed the utmost ingenuity of both Robbie and his little acquaintance to make head or tail of it.

"Here you are," cried Robbie, with the air of a man making a valuable discovery, "here's the milestones – one, two, three – them's milestones, thou knows."

"Tut, you goose; that's only the scale," said the girl; "see what's printed, 'Scale of miles.'"

"Oh, ey, lass," said Robbie, not feeling sure what "scale" might mean, but too shrewd to betray his ignorance a second time in the presence of this learned chambermaid.

The riddle, nevertheless, defied solution. However much they pored over the map, it was still a maze of lines.

"It's as widderful as poor old Sim's face," said Robbie.

Robbie and the chambermaid put their heads together in more senses than one. The map was most inconveniently small. Two folks could not consult it at the same time without coming into really uncomfortable proximity.

"There you are," said Robbie, reaching over, pipe in hand, to where the girl was intent on some minute point.

Suddenly there was a cloud of smoke over the map. It also enveloped the students of geography. Then, somehow, there was a sly smack of lips.

"And there *you* are," said the girl, with a roguish laugh, as she brought Robbie a great whang over the ear and shot away.

Jim, the driver, came into the kitchen at that moment on his way to bed, and unravelled the mystery of the map by showing that it was possible for Robbie's friends to go off the Carlisle road towards Gaskarth and Wythburn at the village of Askham.

Robbie was satisfied with this explanation, and did his best under the circumstances to rest content until nine o'clock with the harbor into which he had drifted. He succeeded more completely, perhaps, in this endeavor than might be expected, when the peril of his friends and his allegiance to Liza Branthwaite is taken into account.

But when nine o'clock had come and gone, and still the coach stood in the yard of the inn, Robbie's sense of duty overcame his appetite for what he would have called a "spoag." It was usual for the Carlisle coach to await the coach from Lancaster, and it was because the latter had not yet arrived at Kendal that the former was unable to depart from it. Robbie's impatience waxed considerably during the half-hour thence ensuing; but when ten o'clock had struck, and still no definite movement was made, his indignation became boisterous.

There were to be four inside passengers, all women; and cold as the night might prove, Robbie's seat must be outside. The protestations of all five passengers were at length too loud, and their importunity was too earnest, to admit of longer delay. So the driver put in his horses and took his seat on the box.

This had scarcely been done when the horn of the Lancaster coach was heard in the distance, and some further waiting ensued.

"Let's hope you'll have no traffic out of, it when it does come," said Robbie with a dash of spite. A few minutes afterwards the late coach drove into the yard and discharged its travellers.

Two of these, who were going forward to Carlisle, climbed the ladder and took seats behind Robbie. It was too dark to see who or what they were except that they were men, that they were wrapped in long cloaks, and wore caps that fitted close to their heads and cheeks, being tied over their beards and beneath their chins.

The much-maligned Jim now gave a smart whip to his horses, and in a moment more the coach was on the road.

The night was dark and bitterly cold, and once outside the town the glimmer of the lamps which the coach carried was all the light the passengers had for miles.

A slight headache from which Robbie had suffered at intervals since the ducking of his head in the river at Wythburn had now quite disappeared, but a curious numbness, added to a degree of stupefaction, began to take its place. As the coach jogged along on its weary journey, not even the bracing surroundings of Robbie's present elevated and exposed position had the effect of keeping him actively awake. He dozed in short snatches and awoke with slight shudders, feeling alternately hot and cold.

In one of his intervals of wakefulness he heard fragments of a conversation which was being sustained by the strangers behind him. Robbie had neither activity nor curiosity to waste on their talk, but he could not avoid listening.

"He would have been the best agent in the King's service to a certainty," said one. "He's the 'cutest man *I* ever tackled. It's parlish odd how he baffles us."

The speaker was clearly a Cumbrian.

"Shaf!" replied his companion, in a kind of whisper, "he's a pauchtie clot-heed. I'll have him at Haribee in a crack."

The second speaker was as clearly a Scot who was struggling against the danger there might be of his speech bewraying him.

"Well, you're pretty smart on 'im. I never could rightly make aught of thy hate of 'im."

"Tut, man, live and learn. Let me have him in Wilfrey Lawson's hands, and ye'll see what for I hate the proud-stomached taistrel."

"Well," said the Cumbrian, in a tone indicative of more resignation than he had previously exhibited, "I've no more cause to love 'im than yourself. You saw 'im knock me down in the streets of Lancaster."

"May ye hang him up for it, Bailiff Scroope," replied the Scot. "May ye hang him up for it on the top of Haribee!"

Robbie understood enough of this conversation to realize the character and pursuit of his travelling companions; but the details and tone of the dialogue were not of an interest sufficiently engrossing to keep him awake. He dozed afresh, and in the unconsciousness of a fitful sleep he passed a good many miles of his dreary night ride.

A sudden glare in his eyes awoke him at one moment. They were passing the village of Hollowbank. Fires were lit on the road, and dark figures were crouching around them. Robbie was too drowsy to ask the meaning of these sights, and he soon slept once more.

When he awoke again, he thought he caught the echo of the word "Wythburn" as having been spoken behind him; but whether this were more than a delusion of the ear, such as sometimes comes at the moment of awakening, he could not be sure until (now fully awake) he distinctly heard the Cumbrian use the name of Ralph Ray.

Robbie's curiosity was instantly aroused, and in the effort to shake off the weight of his drowsiness he made a backward movement of the head, which was perceived by the strangers. He was conscious that one of the men had risen, and was leaning over to the driver to ask who he himself might be, and where he was going.

"A country lad of some sort," said Jim. "I know nought, no mair."

"I thought maybe he were a friend," said the stranger, with questionable veracity.

The conversation thereupon proceeded with unrestrained vigor.

"It baffles me, his going to Carlisle. As I say, he's a 'cute sort. What's his game in this hunt?"

"Shaf! he's bagged himself, stump and rump."

"I don't mind how soon we've done with this trapesing here and there. Which will be the 'dictment, think ye?"

"Small doubt which." "Murder, eh? Can you manage it, Wilfrey and yourself?"

"Leave that to the pair of us."

The perspiration was standing in beads on every inch of Robbie's body. He was struggling with an almost overpowering temptation to test the strength of his muscles at pitching certain weighty "bodies" off the top of that coach, in order to relieve it of some of the physical burden and a good deal of the moral iniquity under which it seemed to him just then to groan.

Snow began now to fall, and the driver gave the whip to his horses in order to reach a village which was not far away.

"We'll be bound to put up for the night," he said; "this snowstorm will soon stop us."

The two strangers were apparently much concerned at the necessity, and used every available argument to induce the driver to continue his journey.

Robbie could not bring himself to a conclusion as to whether it would be best for his purpose that the coach should stop, and so keep back the vagabonds who were sitting behind him, or go on, and so help him to overtake Ralph. The driver in due course settled the problem very decisively by drawing up at the inn of the hamlet of Mardale and proceeding to take his horses off the chains.

"There be some folk as have mercy neither on man nor beast," he said in reply to a protest from the strangers.

Jim's sentiment was more apposite than he thought.

The two men grumbled their way into the inn. Robbie remained outside and gave the driver a hand with the horses.

"Where's Haribee?" he asked.

"In Carlisle," said the driver.

"What place is it?" asked Robbie.

"Haribee? – why, the place of execution."

When left alone outside in the snow, Robbie began to reflect on the position of affairs. It was past midnight. The two strangers, who were obviously in pursuit of Ralph, would stay in this house at least until morning. Ralph himself was probably asleep at this moment, some ten miles or thereabouts farther up the road.

It was bitterly cold. Robbie's hands and face were numbed. The flakes of snow fell thicker and faster than before.

Robbie perceived that there was only one chance that would make it worth while to have come on this journey: the chance that he could overtake Ralph before the coach and its passengers could overtake him.

To do this he must walk the whole night through, let it rain or snow or freeze.

He could and he would do it!

Bravely, Robbie! A greater issue than you know of hangs on your journey. On! on! on!

CHAPTER XXXII

What the Snow Gave Up

The agitation of the landlord of the inn at Askham, who was an old Parliamentarian, on discovering the captain under whom he had served in the person of Ralph Ray, threatened of itself to betray him. With infinite perturbation he came and went, and set before Ralph and Sim such plain fare as his house could furnish after the more luxurious appetites of the Royalist visitors had been satisfied.

The room into which the travellers had been smuggled was a wing of the old house, open to the whitewashed rafters, and with the customary broad hearth. Armor hung about the walls – a sword here, a cutlass there, and over the rannel-tree a coat of chain steel. It was clearly the living-room of the landlord's family, and was jealously guarded from the more public part of the inn. But when the door was open into the passage that communicated with the rest of the house, the loud voices of the Royalists could be heard in laughter or dispute.

When the family vacated this room for the convenience of Ralph and Sim, they left behind at the fireside, sitting on a stool, a little boy of three or four, who was clearly the son of the landlord. Ralph sat down, and took the little fellow between his knees. The child had big blue eyes and thin curls of yellow hair. The baby lips answered to his smile, and the baby tongue prattled in his ear with the easy familiarity which children extend only to those natures that hold the talisman of child-love.

"And what is *your* name, my little man?" said Ralph.

"Darling," answered the child, looking up frankly into Ralph's face.

"Good. And anything else?"

"Ees, Villie."

"Do they not say you are like your mother, Willie?" said Ralph, brushing the fair curls from the boy's forehead. "Me mammy's darling," said the little one, with innocent eyes and a pretty curve of the little mouth.

"Surely. And what will you be when you grow up, my sunny boy?"

"A man."

"Ah! and a wit, eh? But what will you be at your work – a farmer?"

"Me be a soldier." The little face grew bright at the prospect.

"Not that, sweetheart. If you have luck like most of us, perhaps you'll have enough fighting in your life without making it your trade to fight. But you don't understand me yet, Willie, darling?"

The little one's father entered the room at this moment, and the opening of the door brought the sound of jumbled voices from a distant apartment. The noisy party of Royalists apparently belonged to the number of those who hold that a man's manners in an inn may properly be the reverse of what they are expected to be at home. The louder such roysterers talk, the more they rap out oaths, the oftener they bellow for the waiters and slap them on the back, the better they think they are welcome in a house of public entertainment.

Amidst the tumult that came from a remote part of the inn a door was heard to open, and a voice was distinguishable above the rest calling lustily for the landlord.

"I must go off to them," said that worthy. "They expect me to stand host as well as landlord, and sit with them at their drinking."

When the door closed again, Sim lifted the boy on to his knee, and looked at him with eyes full of tenderness. The little fellow returned his gaze with a bewildered expression that seemed to ask a hundred silent questions of poor Sim's wrinkled cheeks and long, gray, straggling hair.

"I mind me when my own lass was no bigger nor this," said Sim.

Ralph did not answer, but turned his head aside and listened.

"She was her mammy's darling, too, she was."

Sim's voice was thick in his throat.

"And mine as well," he added. "We used to say to her, laughing and teasing like, 'Who will ye marry, Rotie?' – we called her Rotie then, – 'who will ye marry, Rotie, when ye grow up to be a big, big woman?' 'My father,' she would say, and throw her little arms about my neck and kiss me."

Sim raised his hard fingers to his forehead to cover his eyes.

Ralph still sat silent, his head aside, looking into the fire.

"That's many and many a year agone; leastways, so it seems. My wife was living then. We were married in Gaskarth, but work was bad, and we packed up and went to live for a while in a great city, leagues and leagues to the south. And there my poor girl, Josephine – I called her Josie for short, and because it was more kind and close like – there my poor girl fell ill and died. Her face got paler day by day, but she kept a brave heart – she was just such like as Rotha that way – and she tended the house till the last, she did."

A louder burst of merriment than usual came from the distant room. The fellows were singing a snatch together.

"Do you know, Rotha called her mother, Josie, too. I checked her, I did; but my poor girl she said, said she, 'Never mind; the little one has been hearkening to yourself.' You'd have cried, I think, if you'd been with us the day she died. I was sitting at work, and she called out that she felt faint; so I jumped up and held her in my arms and sent our little Rotha for a neighbor. But it was too late. My poor darling was gone in a minute, and when the wee thing came running back to us, with red cheeks, she looked frightened, and cried, 'Josie! Josie!' 'My poor Rotie, my poor little lost Rotie,' I said, 'our dear Josie, she is in heaven!' Then the little one cried, 'No, no, no'; and wept, and wept till – till – I wept with her."

The door of the distant apartment must have been again thrown open, for a robustious fellow could be heard to sing a stave of a drinking song. The words came clearly in the silence that preceded a general outburst of chorus: –

> "Then to the Duke fill,
> Fill up the glass;
> The son of our martyr, beloved of the King."

"We buried her there," continued Sim; "ay, we buried her in the town;

and, with the crowds and the noise above her, there sleeps my brave Josie, and I shall see her face no more."

Ralph rose up, and walked to the door by which he and Sim had entered from the yard of the inn. He opened it and stood for a moment on the threshold. The snow was falling in thick flakes. Already it covered the ground and lay heavy on the roofs of the outhouses and on the boughs of the leafless trees. A great calm was on the earth and in the air.

Robbie speed on! Lose not an hour now, for an hour lost may be a life's loss.

Ralph was turning back into the room, and bolting the outer door, when the landlord entered hurriedly from the passage. He was excited.

"Is it not – captain, tell me – is it not Wy'bern – your father's home – Wy'bern, on Bracken Mere?"

"It *was* my father's home – why?"

"Then the bloodhounds *are* on your trail!"

The perspiration was standing in beads on Brown's forehead.

"They talk of nothing to each other but of a game that's coming on at Wy'bern, and what they'll do for some one that they never name. If they'd but let wit who he is I'd – I'd know them."

"Landlord, landlord!" cried a man whose uncertain footsteps could be heard in the passage, – "landlord, bring your two guests to us – bring them for a glass."

The fellow was making his way to the room into which Ralph and Sim had been hustled. The landlord slid out of it through the smallest aperture between the door and its frame that could discharge a man of his sturdy physique. When the door closed behind him he could be heard to protest against any intention of disturbing his visitors. The two gentlemen had made a long journey, travelling two nights and two days at a stretch; so they'd gone off to bed and were snoring hard by this time; the landlord could stake his solemn honor upon it.

The tipsy Royalist seemed content with the apology for non-appearance, and returned to his companions bellowing, –

"Let Tories guard the King;
Let Whigs in halters swing."

Ralph walked uneasily across the room. Could it be that these men were already on their way to Wythburn to carry out the processes of the law with respect to himself and his family?

In another minute the landlord returned.

"It's as certain as the Lord's above us," he whispered. "They wanted to get to you to have you drink the King's health with them, and when I swore you were asleep they ax't if you had no horses with you. I said you had one horse. 'One horse among two,' they said, with a great goasteren laugh; 'why, then, they're Jock and his mither.' 'One horse,' I said, 'or maybe two.' 'We must have 'em,' they said; 'we take possession on 'em in the King's service. We've got to cross the fells to Wy'bern in the morning.'"

"What are they, Brown?"

"Musketeers, three of 'em, and ya sour fellow that limps of a leg; they call him Constable David."

"Let them have the horses. It will save trouble to you."

Then turning to Sim, Ralph added, "We must be stirring betimes to-morrow, old friend; the daybreak must see us on the road. The snow will be thick in the morning, and perhaps the horses would have hindered us. Everything is for the best."

The landlord lifted his curly-headed son (now fast asleep) from Sim's knee, and left the room.

Sim's excitement was plainly visible, and even Ralph could not conceal his own agitation. Was he to be too late to do what it had been in his mind to do?

"Did you say Saturday week next? It is Tuesday to-day," said Ralph.

"A week come Saturday – that was what Rotha told me."

"It's strange – very strange!"

Ralph satisfied himself at length that the men in the adjoining, room were but going off to Wythburn nine days in advance in order to be ready to carry into effect the intended confiscation immediately their instructions should reach them. The real evils by which Ralph was surrounded were too numerous to allow of his wasting much apprehension on possible ones.

The din of the drinkers subsided at length, and toper after toper was helped to his bed.

Then blankets were brought into Ralph and Sim, and rough shakedowns were made for them on the broad settles. Sim lay down and fell asleep. Ralph walked to and fro for hours.

The quiet night was far worn towards morning when Brown, the landlord, tapped at the door and entered.

"Not a wink will come to me," he said, and sat down before the smouldering fire.

Ralph continued his perambulation to and fro, to and fro. He thought again of what had occurred, and of what must soon occur to him and his – of Wilson's death – his father's death – the flight of the horse on the fells – all, all, centring somehow in himself. There must be sin involved, though he knew not how – sin and its penalty. It was more and more clear that God's hand was on him – on *him*. Every act of his own hand turned to evil, and those whom he would bless were cursed. And this cruel scheme of evil – this fate – could it not be broken? Was there no propitiation? Yes, there was; there must be. That thing which he was minded to do would be expiation in the sight of Heaven. God would accept it for an atonement – yes; and there was soft balm like a river of morning air in the thought.

Sim slept on, and Brown crouched over the fire, with his head in his hands and his elbows on his knees. There was not a motion within the house or without; the world lay still and white like death.

Yes, it must be so; it must be that his life was to be the ransom.

And it should be paid! Then the clouds would rise and the sun appear.

"Fate that impedes, make way, make way! Mother, Rotha, Willy, wait, wait! I come, I come."

Ralph's face brightened with the ecstasy of reflection. Was it frenzy in which his morbid idea had ended? If so, it was the frenzy of a self-sacrifice that was sublimity itself.

At one moment Brown stirred in his seat and held his head aside, as though listening for some sound in the far distance.

"Did you hear it?" he asked, in a whisper that had an accent of fear.

"Hear what?" asked Ralph.

"The neigh of the horse," said Brown. "I heard nothing" replied Ralph, and walked to the window, and listened. "What horse?" he asked, turning about.

"Nay, none of us knows rightly. It's a horse that flies ower the fell o' nights, and whinnies and whinnies."

"One of the superstitions of your dale, – an old wife's tale, I suppose. Has it been heard for years?"

"No, nor for weeks neither."

Brown resumed his position in front of the fire, and the hours rolled on.

When the first glimmer of gray appeared in the east, Sim was awakened, and Ralph and he, after eating a hurried breakfast, started away on foot.

Where is Robbie now? A life hangs on the fortunes of this very hour!

"Tell them the horses came from the Woodman at Kendal," said Ralph as he parted from his old comrade. "You've done better than save our lives, Brown, God bless you!"

"That's a deal more nor my wages, captain," said the honest fellow.

The snow that had fallen during the night lay several inches deep on the roads, and the hills were white as far up as the eye could trace them. The dawn came slowly. The gray bars were long in stretching over the sky, and longer in making way for the first glint of mingled yellow and pink. But the sunrise came at length. The rosy glaives floated upwards over a lake of light, and the broad continents of cloud fell apart. Another day had breathed through another night.

Ralph and Sim walked long in silence. The snow was glistening like a million diamonds over the breast of a mountain, and the upright crags, on which it could not rest, were glittering like shields of steel.

"How beautiful the world is!" said Ralph.

"Ey, but it *is* that, after all," said Sim.

"After all," repeated Ralph.

They had risen to the summit of a little hill, and they could see as they began to descend on the other side that the snow lay in a deep drift at the bottom.

At the same moment they caught sight of some curious object lying in the distance.

"What thing is that, half covered with the snow?" asked Sim.

"I cannot say. We'll soon see."

Ralph spoke with panting breath.

"Why, it's a horse!" said Sim.

"Left out on such a night, too," said Ralph.

His face quivered with emotion. When he spoke again his voice was husky and his face livid.

"Sim, what is that on its back?"

"Surely it's a pack, the black thing across it," said Sim.

Ralph caught his breath and stopped. Then he ran forward.

"Great God!" he cried, "Betsy! It is Betsy, with the coffin."

CHAPTER XXXIII

Sepulture at Last

Truly, it was Betsy, the mare which they had lost on that fearful day at the Stye Head Pass. Her dread burden, the coffin containing the body of Angus Ray, was still strapped to her back. None had come nigh to her, or this must have been removed. She looked worn and tired as she rose now to her feet amid the snow. The old creature was docile enough this morning, and when Ralph patted her head, she seemed to know the hand that touched her.

She had crossed a range of mountains, and lived, no doubt, on the thin grass of the fells. She must have famished quickly had the snow fallen before.

Ralph was profoundly agitated. Never before had Sim seen him betray such deep emotion. If the horse with its burden had been a supernatural presence, the effect of its appearance on Ralph had not been greater. At first clutching the bridle, he looked like a man who was puzzled to decide whether, after all, this thing that had occurred were not rather a spectre that had wandered out of his dreams than a tangible reality, a blessed and gracious reality, a mercy for which he ought there and then to fling himself in gratitude on the ground, even though the snow drifted over him forever and made that act his last. Then the tears that tenderer moments could not bring stood in his enraptured eyes. Those breathless instants were as the mirror of what seemed to be fifty years of fear and hope.

Ralph determined that no power on earth should remove his hand from the bridle until his father had at length been buried. The parish of Askham must have its church and churchyard, and Angus Ray should be buried there. They had not yet passed by the church – it must be still in front of them – and with the horse and its burden by their side the friends walked on.

When Ralph found voice to speak, he said, "Wednesday – then it is three weeks to-day since we lost her, and for three weeks my father has waited sepulture!"

Presently they came within sight of a rude chapel that stood at the meeting of two roads. A finger-post was at the angle, with arms pointing in three directions. The chapel was a low whitewashed Gothic building, with a little belfry in which there hung no bell. At its rear was a house with broken gablets and round dormers stuck deep into the thatch. A burial ground lay in front of both edifices, and looked dreary and chilling now, with the snow covering its many mounds and dripping from the warm wood of its rude old crosses.

"This will be the minister's house," said Ralph.

They drew up in front and knocked at the door of a deep porch. An old man opened it and looked closely at his visitors through sharp, watchful eyes. He wore a close jerkin of thick blue homespun, and his broad-topped boots were strapped round his short pantaloons.

"Does the priest live here?" said Ralph, from the road, where he held the mare's head.

"No priest lives here," said the old man, somewhat curtly.

"Does the minister?"

"No, nor a minister."

The changes of ecclesiastical administration had been so frequent of late that it was impossible to say what formula was now in the ascendent. Ralph understood the old man's laconic answers to imply a remonstrance, and he tried again.

"Do you preach in this church?"

"*I* preach? No; I practise."

It transpired after much wordy fencing, which was at least as irritating as amusing to a man in Ralph's present temper, that there was no minister now in possession of the benefice, and that the church had for some months been closed, the spiritual welfare of the parishioners being consequently in a state of temporary suspension. The old man who replied to Ralph's interrogations proved to be the parish clerk, and whether his duties were also suspended – whether the parishioners did not die, and did not require to be buried – during the period in which the parish was deprived of a parson, was a question of more consequence to Ralph than the cause of the religious bankruptcy which the old man described.

Ralph explained in a few words the occasion of his visit, and begged the clerk to dig a grave at once.

"I fear it will scarce conform to the articles," the clerk said with a grave shake of his old head; "I'm sore afraid I'll suffer a penalty if it's known."

Ralph passed some coins into the old man's hand with as little ostentation as possible; whereupon the clerk, much mollified, continued, –

"But it's not for me to deny to any Christian a Christian burial – that is to say, as much of it as stands in no need of the book. Sir, I'll be with you in a crack. Go round, sir, to the gate."

Ralph and his companion did as they were bidden, and in a few minutes the old clerk came hurrying towards them from a door at the back of his house that looked into the churchyard.

He had a spade over his shoulder and a great key in his hand.

Putting the key into a huge padlock, he turned back its rusty bolt, and the gate swung stiff on its hinges, which were thick with moss.

Then Ralph, still holding the mare's head, walked into the churchyard with Sim behind him.

"Here's a spot which has never been used," said the old man, pointing to a patch close at hand where long stalks of yarrow crept up through the snow. "It's fresh mould, sir, and on the bright days the sun shines on it."

"Let it be here," said Ralph.

The clerk immediately cleared away the snow, marked out his ground with the edge of the spade, and began his work.

Ralph and Sim, with Betsy, stood a pace or two apart. It was still early morning, and none came near the little company gathered there.

Now and again the old man paused in his work to catch his breath or to wipe the perspiration from his brow. His communicativeness at such moments of intermission would have been almost equal to his reticence at an earlier stage, but Ralph was in no humor to encourage his garrulity, and Sim stood speechless, with something like terror in his eyes. "Yes, we've had no minister since Michaelmas; that, you know, was when the new Act came In," said the clerk.

"What Act?" Ralph asked.

"Why, sir, you never mean that you don't know about the Act of Uniformity?"

"That's what I do mean, my friend," said Ralph.

"Don't know the Act of Uniformity! Have you heard of the Five Mile Bill?"

"No."

"Nor the Test Bill that the Bishop wants to get afoot?"

"No."

"Deary me, deary me," said the clerk, with undisguised horror at Ralph's ignorance of the projected ecclesiastical enactments of his King and country. Then, with a twinkle in the corner of his upward eye as he held his head aside, the old man said, —

"Perhaps your honor has been away in foreign parts?"

Ralph had to decline this respectable cover for his want of familiarity with matters which were obviously vital concerns, and perhaps the subjects of daily conversation, with his interlocutor.

The clerk had resumed his labors. When he paused again it was in order to enlighten Ralph's ignorance on these solemn topics.

"You see, sir, the old 'piscopacy is back again, and the John Presbyters that joined it are snug in their churches, but the Presbyters that would not join it are turned out of their livings. There — that's the Act of Uniformity."

"The Act of Non-Conformity, I should say," replied Ralph.

"Well, the Jack Presbyters are not to be allowed within five miles of a market town – that's the new Five Mile Bill. And they are not to be made schoolmasters or tutors, or to hold public offices, unless they take the sacrament of the Church – and that's what the Bishop calls his Test Act; but he'll scarce get it this many a long year, say I – no, not he."

The clerk had offered his lucid exposition with the air of one who could afford to be modestly sensible of the superiority of his knowledge.

"And when he does get it he'll want an Act more, so far as I can see," said Ralph, "and that's a Burial Act – an Act to bury the Presbyters alive. They'd be full as well buried, I think.".

A shrewd glance from the old man's quick eyes showed that at that moment he had arrived at one of three conclusions – that Ralph himself was a Presbyter or a Roundhead, or both.

"Our minister was a Presbyter," he observed aloud, "and when the Act came in he left his benefice."

But Ralph was not minded to pursue the subject.

The grave was now ready; it had required to be long and wide, but not deep.

The snow was beginning to fall again.

"Hard work on a morning like this," said the clerk, coughing as he threw aside his spade. "This is the sort of early morning that makes an old man like me catch his breath. And I haven't always been parish clerk and dug graves. I was schoolmaster till Michaelmas."

It was time to commit to the grave the burden which had passed three long weeks on the back of the mare. Not until this moment did Ralph's hand once relax its firm grip of Betsy's bridle. Loosing it now, he applied himself to the straps and ropes that bound the coffin. When all was made clear, he prepared to lift the body to the ground. It was large and heavy, and required the hands of Sim and the clerk as well.

By their united efforts the coffin was raised off the horse's back and lowered. The three men were in the act of doing this, when Betsy, suddenly freed from the burden which she had carried, pranced aside, looked startled, plunged through the gate, and made off down the road.

"Let her go," said Ralph, and turned his attention once more to what now lay on the ground.

Then Angus Ray was lowered into his last home, and the flakes of snow fell over him like a white and silent pall.

Ralph stood aside while the old man threw back the earth. It fell from the spade in hollow thuds.

Sim crouched beside a stone, and looked on with frightened eyes.

The sods were replaced; there was a mound the more in the little churchyard of Askham, and that was the end. The clerk shouldered his spade and prepared to lock the gate.

It was then they were aware that there came from over their heads a sound like the murmuring of a brook under the leaves of June; like the breaking of deep waters at a weir; like the rolling of foam-capped wavelets against an echoing rock. Look up! Every leafless bough of yonder lofty elder-tree is thick with birds. Listen! A moment, and their song has ceased; they have risen on the wing; they are gone like a cloud Of black rain through the white feathery air. Then silence everywhere.

Was it God's sign and symbol – God's message to the soul of this stricken man? God's truce?

Who shall say it was not!

"A load is lifted off my heart," said Ralph. He was thinking of the terrible night he had spent on the fells. And indeed there was the light of another look in his face. His father had sepulture. God had shown him this mercy as a sign that what he purposed to do ought to be done. Such was Ralph's reading of the accidental finding of the horse.

They bade good morning to the old man and left him. Then they walked to the angle of the roads where the guidepost stood. The arms were covered with the snow, and Ralph climbed on to the stone wall behind and brushed their letters clear.

"To Kendal." That pointed in the direction from whence they came.

"To Gaskarth."

"That's our road," said Sim.

"No," said Ralph; "*this* is it – 'To Penrith and Carlisle.'"

What chance remained now to Robbie?

CHAPTER XXXIV

Fate that Impedes, Fall Back

A few minutes after the coach arrived at Mardale, Robbie was toiling along in the darkness over an unfamiliar road. That tiresome old headache was coming back to him, and he lifted a handful of snow now and again to cool his aching forehead.

It was a weary, weary tramp, such as only young, strong limbs, and a stout heart could have sustained. Villages were passed, but they lay as quiet as the people that slumbered in them. Five hours had gone by before Robbie encountered a living soul.

As daylight dawned the snow ceased to fall, and when Robbie had reached Askham the late sun had risen. He was now beginning to feel the need of food, and stepping into a cottage he asked an old daleswoman who lived there if he might trouble her in the way of trade to make him some breakfast. The good soul took compassion on the young man's weary face, and said he was welcome to such as she had. When Robbie had eaten a bowl of porridge and milk, the fatigue of his journey quite overcame him. Even while answering his humble hostess's questions in broken sentences he fell asleep in his chair. Out of pity the old woman allowed him to sleep on. "The lad's fair done out," she said, glancing at his haggard face. It was later than noon when he awoke.

Alas! what then was lost forever! What was gone beyond recall!

Starting up in annoyance at the waste of time, he set off afresh, and, calling at the inn as he passed by, he learned to his great vexation that if he had come on there when, at sunrise, he went into the cottage a hundred yards away, he must have been within easy reach of Sim and Ralph. The coach, nevertheless, had not yet got to this stage, and that fact partially reconciled Robbie to the delay.

He had little doubt which path to take when he reached the angle of the roads at the corner of the churchyard. If Ralph had taken the road leading to Gaskarth he might be safe, but if he had taken the road leading to Carlisle he must be in danger. Therefore Robbie determined to follow the latter.

He made no further inquiries until he had walked through the market town of Penrith, and had come out on the turnpike to the north of it. Then he asked the passers-by who seemed to come some distance if they had encountered two such men as he was in search of. In this way he learned many particulars of the toilsome journey that was being made by his friends. Sim's strength had failed him, and Ralph had wished to leave him at a lodging on the road while he himself pushed forward to Carlisle. But Sim had prayed to be taken on, and eventually a countryman going to the Carlisle market, and with space for one only on his cart, had offered to give Sim a lift. Of this tender the friends had thankfully availed themselves.

It was only too clear from every detail which Robbie gleaned that Ralph was straining every muscle to reach Carlisle. What terrible destiny could it be that was thus compelling him to fly, perhaps to his death!

Mile after mile Robbie plodded along the weary road. He was ill, though he had scarcely realized that fact. He took many a rest.

Daylight faded, and once more the night came on, but still the brave young dalesman held to his purpose. The snow had become crisp and easier to the foot, but the way was long and the wayfarer was sick at heart.

Morning came at last, and when the mists had risen above the meadows, Robbie saw before him, nigh at hand, the ancient city of Carlisle. A presentiment that he came too late took the joy out of the long-expected sight.

Was the sky gloomy? Did a storm threaten? Were the murmuring rivers and the roaring ghylls telling to Robbie's ear the hopeless tale that lay cold and silent at his heart? No!

The sun arose and sparkled over the white landscape. It thawed the stiff boughs of the trees, and the snow dropped from them in gracious drops like dew. All nature seemed glad – cruelly, mockingly, insensately glad – lightsome, jubilant. The birds forsook their frost-bound nests, and sang cheerily in the clear morning air. One little linnet – so very little – perched on a delicate silver birch, and poured its full soul out of its liquid throat.

Robbie toiled painfully along with a feeble step, and with nerveless despondency on every feature of his face – his coat flying open to his woollen shirt; one of his hands thrust with his pipe into his belt; the other hand dragging after him a heavy staff; his cap pushed back from his hot forehead.

When he walked listlessly into Carlisle it was through the Botcher-gate on the south. The clock of the cathedral was striking ten. Robbie passed along the streets scarcely knowing his own errand or destination. Without seeking for it he came upon the old Town Hall. Numbers of people were congregated in the Market Place outside, and crowds were hurrying up from the adjacent streets. Robbie had only once been in Carlisle before, but he felt convinced that these must be unaccustomed occurrences. He asked a townsman standing near him what the tumult meant. The man could tell him nothing. Then he asked another and another spectator of the scene in which there appeared to be nothing to see, but all seemed as ignorant as himself. Nevertheless there was an increasing commotion.

An old stone cross, raised high on steps, stood in the Market Place, and Robbie walked up to it and leaned against it. Then he was conscious that word had gone through the crowd that a famous culprit had surrendered. According to some authorities the culprit was a thief, according to others a murderer; some said that he was a forger, and some said a traitor, and some that he was another of the regicides, and would be sent on to London.

On one point only was there any kind of agreement, and that was that the culprit had voluntarily surrendered to a warrant issued for his arrest.

The commotion reached its climax when the doors of the old hall were seen to open and a company of soldiers and civilians passed out.

It was a guard for the prisoner, who was being taken to the common gaol to await his trial.

A dull, aching, oppressive pain lay at Robbie's heart. He climbed on to the cross and looked over the people's heads at the little company.

The prisoner was Ralph Ray. With a firm step, with upright and steadfast gaze, he walked between two soldiers; and close at his heels, with downcast eyes, Simeon Stagg toiled along.

Robbie's quest was at an end.

CHAPTER XXXV

Robbie's Quest Ended

It was all over now. The weary chase was done, and Robbie Anderson came late. Ralph had surrendered, and a sadder possibility than Robbie guessed at, a more terrible catastrophe than Rotha Stagg or Willy Ray had feared or looked for, lay in the sequel now to be unfolded.

The soldiers and their prisoner had gone; the crowd had gone with them, and Robbie stood alone in the Market Place. From his station on the steps of the cross he turned and looked after the motley company. They took the way down English Street.

How hot and tired his forehead felt! It had ached before, but now it burned like fire. Robbie pressed it hard against the cold stone of the cross. Then he walked aimlessly away. He had nowhere to go; he had nothing to do; and hour after hour he rambled through the narrow streets of the old town. The snow still hung in heavy flakes from the overhanging eaves and porches of the houses, and toppled at intervals in thick clots on to the streets. The causeways were swept dry.

Up and down, through Blackfriars Street, past the gaol that stood on the ruins of the monastery, along Abbey Street, and past the cathedral, across Head Lane, and into the Market Place again; then along the banks of the Caldew, and over the western wall that looked across the hills that stretched into the south; round Shaddon-gate to the bridge that lay under the shadow of the castle, and up to the river Eden and the wide Scotch-gate to the north. On and on, he knew not where, he cared not wherefore; on and on, till his weary limbs were sinking beneath him, until the long lines of houses, with their whitened timbers standing out from their walls, and their pediments and the windows that were dormered into their roofs seemed to reel about him and dance in fantastic figures before his eyes.

The incident of that morning had created an impression among the townspeople. There was a curious absence of unanimity as to the crime with which the prisoner would stand charged; but Robbie noticed that everybody agreed that it was something terrible, and that nobody seemed to suffer much in good humor by reason of the fate that hung over a fellow-creature. "Very shocking, very. Come, John, let's have a glass together!"

Robbie had turned into a byway that bore the name of King's Arms Lane. He paused without purpose or thought before a narrow recess in which a quaint old house stood back from the street. With its low flat windows deeply recessed into the stone, its curious heads carved long ago into bosses that were now ruined by frost and rain, it might have been a wing of the old abbey that had wandered somehow away. A little man, far in years, pottered about in front, brushing the snow and cleaning the windows.

"Yon man is just in time for the 'sizes," said a young fellow as he swung by with another, who was pointing to the house and muttering something that was inaudible to Robbie.

"What place is this?" said Robbie, when they had gone, stepping up to the gate and addressing the old man within.

"The judges' lodgings surely," replied the caretaker, lifting his eyes from his shovel with a look of surprise at the question.

"And the 'sizes, when are they on?"

"Next week; that's when they begin."

The ancient custodian was evidently not of a communicative temperament, and Robbie, who was in no humor for gossip, turned away.

It was of little use to remain longer. All was over. The worst had come to the worst. He might as well turn towards home. But how hot his forehead felt! Could it have been that ducking his head in the river at Wythburn had caused it to burn like a furnace?

Robbie thought of Sim. Why had he not met him in his long ramble through the town? They might have gone home together.

At the corner of Botcher-gate and English Street there stood two shops, and as Robbie passed them the shopkeepers were engaged in an animated conversation on the event of the morning. "I saw him go by with the little daft man; yes, I did. I was just taking down my shutters, as it might be so," said one of the two men, imitating the piece of industry in question.

"Deary me! What o'clock might that be?" asked the other.

"Well, as I say, I was just taking down my shutters, as it might be so," imitating the gesture again. "I'd not sanded my floor, nor yet swept out my shop; so it might have been eight, and it might have been short of eight, and maybe it was somewhere between the three quarters and the hour – that's as *I* reckon it."

"Deary me! deary me!" responded the other shopkeeper, whose blood was obviously curdling at the bare recital of these harrowing details.

Robbie walked on. Eight o'clock! Then he had been but two hours late – two poor little hours!

Robbie reflected with vexation and bitterness on the many hours which must have been wasted or ill spent since he left Wythburn on Sunday. He begrudged the time that he had given to rest and sleep.

Well, well, it was all over now; and out of Carlisle, through the Botchergate, and down the road up which he came, Robbie turned with weary feet. The snow was thawing fast, and the meadows on every side lay green in the sunshine. How full of grace they were! How cruel in her very gladness Nature still seemed to be!

Never for an instant did Robbie lose the sense of a great calamity hanging above him, but a sort of stupefaction was creeping over him nevertheless. He busied himself with reflections on every minor feature of the road. Had he marked this beech before, or that oak? Had he seen this gate on his way into Carlisle, or passed through that bar? A boy on the road was driving a herd of sheep before him. One drift of the sheep was marked with a red cross, and the other drift with a black patch. Robbie counted the two drifts of sheep one by one, and wondered whose they were and where they were going.

Then he sat down to rest, and let his forehead drop on to the grass to cool it. When he rose again the road seemed to swim around him. A farm servant in a smock was leading two horses, and as he passed he bade the wayfarer, "Good afternoon." Robbie went on without seeming to hear, but when the man had got beyond the sound of his voice he turned as if by sudden impulse, and, waving his hand with a gesture of cordiality, he returned the salutation.

Then he sat down once more and held his head between his hands. It was beating furiously, and his body, too, from head to foot, was changing rapidly from hot to cold. At length the consciousness took possession of him that he was ill. "I doubt I'm badly," he thought, and tried to realize his position. Presently he attempted to rise and call back the countryman with the horses. Lifting himself on one trembling knee, he waved a feeble arm spasmodically in the air, and called and called again. The voice startled him; it seemed not to be his own. His strength was spent. He sank back and remembered no more.

The man in the smock was gone, but another countryman was coming down the road at that moment from the direction of Carlisle. This was no other than little blink-eyed Reuben Thwaite. He was sitting muffled up in his farm wagon and singing merry snatches to keep the cold out of his lungs. Reuben had been at Carlisle over night with sundry hanks of thread, which he had sold to the linen weavers. He had found a good market by coming so far, and he was returning to Wythburn in high feckle. When he came (as he would have said) "ebbn fornenst" Robbie lying at the roadside, he jumped down from his seat. "What poor lad's this? Why, what! What say! What!" holding himself back to grasp the situation, "Robbie Anderson!"

Then a knowing smile overspread Reuben's wrinkled features as he stooped to pat and push the prostrate man, in an effort to arouse him to consciousness.

"Tut, Robbie, lad; Robbie, ma lad! This wark will nivver do, Robbie! Brocken loose agen, aye! Come, Robbie, up, lad!"

Robbie lay insensible to all Reuben's appeals, whether of the nature of banter or half-serious menace.

"Weel, weel, the lad *has* had a fair cargo intil him this voyage, anyway."

There was obviously no likelihood of awakening Robbie, so with a world of difficulty, with infinite puffing and fuming and perspiring, and the help of a passing laborer, Reuben contrived to get the young fellow lifted bodily into his cart. Lying there at full length, a number of the empty thread sacks were thrown over the insensible man, and then Reuben mounted to his seat and drove off.

"Poor old Martha Anderson!" muttered Reuben to himself. "It's weel she's gone, poor body! It wad nigh have brocken her heart – and it's my belief 'at it did."

They had not gone far before Reuben himself, with the inconsistency of more pretentious moralists, felt an impulse to indulge in that benign beverage of which he had just deplored the effects. Drawing up with this object at a public house that stood on the road, he called for a glass of hot spirits. He was in the act of taking it from the hands of the landlord, when a stage-coach drove up, and the coachman and two of the outside passengers ordered glasses of brandy.

"From Carlisle, eh?" said one of the latter, eyeing Reuben from where he sat and speaking with an accent which the little dalesman knew to be "foreign to these parts."

Reuben assented with a satisfied nod and a screwing up of one cheek into a wrinkle about the eyes. He was thinking of the good luck of his visit.

"What's the news there?" asked the other passenger, with an accent which the little dalesman was equally certain was not foreign to these parts.

"Threed's up a gay penny!" said Reuben.

"Any news at the Castle the day?"

"The Castle? No – that's to say, yes. I did hear 'at a man had given hissel' up, but I know nowt aboot it."

"Do you know his name?"

"No."

"Be quick in front, my gude man; let's be off; we've lost time enough with the snow already."

The coachman had mounted to his box, and was wrapping a sheepskin about his knees.

"What's that you have there?" he said to Reuben.

"Him? Why, that's Robbie Anderson, poor fellow. One o' them lads, thoo knows, that have no mair nor one enemy in all the world, and that's theirselves."

"Out for a spoag, eh?"

"Come, get along, man, and let's have no more botherment," cried one of the impatient passengers.

Two or three miles farther down the road Reuben was holding in his horse, in order to cross a river, when he thought that, in the comparative silence of his springless wagon, he heard Robbie speaking behind him.

"It's donky weather, this," Robbie was saying.

"Ey, wet and sladderish," said Reuben, in an insinuating tone, "baith inside and out, baith under foot and ower head."

"It was north of the bridge," Robbie whispered.

"What were – Carlisle?" asked Reuben in his most facetious vein.

"It blows a bit on the Stye Head to-day, Ralph. The way's ower narrow. I can never chain the young horse. Steady, Betsy; steady, lass; steady – "

"Why, the lad's ram'lin'," said Reuben to himself.

"It was fifty strides north of the bridge," Robbie whispered again; and then lifting his voice he cried, "She's gone; she's gone."

"He's ram'lin' for sure."

The truth now dawned on Reuben that on the present occasion at least Robbie was not drunk, but sick. With the illogical perversity of some healthy people, he thought to rally the ailing man out of his ailment, whatever it might be; so he expended all the facetiousness of which he was master on Robbie's unconscious figure.

Reuben's well-meant efforts were of no avail. Robbie alternately whispered, "It was north of the bridge," and chuckled, "Ah, ah! there's Garth, Garth – but I downed him, the dummel head!"

The little dalesman relinquished as hopeless all further attempt at rational converse, and gave himself the solemn assurance, conveyed to his acute intelligence by many grave shakes of the head, that "summat *was* ailin' the lad, after all."

Then they drove for hours in silence. It was dark when they passed through Threlkeld, and turned into the Vale of Wanthwaite on their near approach to Wythburn.

"I scarce know rightly where Robbie bides, now old Martha's dead," thought Reuben; "I'll just slip up the lonnin to Shoulth'et and ask."

CHAPTER XXXVI

Rotha's Confession

And to be wroth with one we love
Doth work like madness in the brain.

Coleridge.

When Reuben Thwaite formed this resolution he was less than a mile from Shoulthwaite. In the house on the Moss, Rotha was then sitting alone, save for the silent presence of the unconscious Mrs. Ray. The day's work was done. It had been market day, and Willy Ray had not returned from Gaskarth. The old house was quiet within, and not a breath of wind was stirring without. There was no sound except the crackling of the dry boughs on the fire and the hollow drip of the melting snow.

By the chair from which Mrs. Ray gazed vacantly and steadily Rotha sat with a book in her hand. She tried to read, but the words lost their meaning. Involuntarily her eyes wandered from the open page. At length the old volume, with its leathern covers clasped together with their great brass clasp, dropped quietly into the girl's lap.

At that moment there was a sound of footsteps in the courtyard. Getting up with an anxious face, Rotha walked to the window and drew the blind partly aside.

It was Matthew Branthwaite.

"How fend ye, lass?" he said on opening the door; "rubbin' on all reet? The roads are varra drewvy after the snow," he added, stamping the clods from his boots. Then looking about, "Hesn't our Liza been here to-neet?"

"Not yet," Rotha answered.

"Whearaway is t' lass? I thought she was for slipping off to Shoulth'et. But then she's olas gitten her best bib and tucker on nowadays."

"She'll be here soon, no doubt," said Rotha, giving Matthew his accustomed chair facing Mrs. Ray.

"She's a rare brattlecan to chatter is our Liza. I telt her she was ower keen to come away with all the ins and oots aboot the constables coming to Wy'bern yesterday. She had it pat, same as if she'd seen it in prent. That were bad news, and the laal hizzy ran bull-neck to gi'e it oot."

"She meant no harm, Matthew."

"But why duddent she mean some good and run bull-neck to-neet to bring ye the bettermer news?"

"Better news, Matthew? What is it?" asked Rotha eagerly, but with more apprehension than pleasure in her tone.

"Why, that the constables hev gone," said Matthew.

"Gone!"

"Gone! Another of the same sort came to-day to leet them, and away they've gone together."

Matthew clearly expected an outburst of delight at his intelligence. "What dusta say to that, lass?" he added between the puffs of a pipe that he was lighting from a candle. Then, raising his eyes and looking up at Rotha, he said, "Why, what's this? What ails thee? Ey! What's wrang?"

"Gone, you say?" said Rotha. "I fear that is the worst news of all, Matthew."

But now there was the rattle of a wagon on the lonnin. A moment later the door was thrown open, and Liza Branthwaite stood in the porch with Reuben Thwaite behind her.

"Here's Robbie Anderson back home in Reuben's cart," said Liza, catching her breath.

"Fetch him in," said Matthew. "Is he grown shy o' t'yance?"

"That's mair nor my share, Mattha," said Reuben. "The lad's dylt out – fair beat, I tell thee; I picked him up frae the brae side."

"He can scarce move hand or foot," cried Liza. "Come, quick!"

Rotha was out at the wagon in a moment.

"He's ill: he's unconscious," she said. "Where did you find him?"

"A couple of mile or so outside Carlisle," answered Reuben.

Rotha staggered, and must have fallen but for Matthew, who at the moment came up behind her.

"I'll tell thee what it is, lass," said the old man, "thoo'rt like to be bad thysel', and varra bad, too. Go thy ways back to the fire."

"Summat ails Robbie, no doubt about it," said Reuben.

"Of course summat *ails* him," said Mattha, with an insinuating emphasis on the word. "He nivver were an artistic drunkard, weren't Bobbie."

"He's been ram'lin' and ram'lin' all the way home," continued Reuben. "He's telt ower and ower agen of summat 'at were fifty yards north of the bridge."

"We must take him home," said Liza, who came hurrying from the house with a blanket over her arm. "Here, cover him with this, Rotha can spare it."

In a minute more Robbie's insensible form was wrapped round and round.

"Give him room to breathe," said Mattha; "I declare ye're playing at pund-o'-mair-weight with the lad!" he added as Rotha came up with a sheepskin and a shawl.

"The night is cold, and he has all but three miles to ride yet!" said the girl.

"He lodges with 'Becca Rudd; let's be off," said Liza, clambering into the cart by the step at the shaft. "Come up, father; quick!"

"What, Bobbie, Bobbie, but this is bad wark, bad wark," said Mattha, when seated in the wagon. "Hod thy tail in the watter, lad, and there's hope for thee yit."

With this figurative expression Mattha settled himself for the drive. Rotha turned to Reuben Thwaite.

"At Carlisle, did you hear anything – meet anybody?" she asked.

"Baith," said Reuben, with a twinkle which was lost in the darkness.

"I mean from Wythburn. Did you meet anybody from – did you see Ralph or my father?"

"Nowther."

"Nor hear of them?"

"No – wait – deary me, deary me, now 'at I mind it – I nivver thought of it afore – I heeard 'at a man had been had up at the Toon Hall and taken to the gaol. It cannot be 'at the man were – no, no – I'm ram'lin' mysel sure-ly."

"Ralph; it was Ralph!" said Rotha, trembling visibly. "Be quick. Good night!" "Ralph at Carlisle!" said Mattha. "Weel, weel; after word comes weird. That's why the constables are gone, and that's why Robbie's come. Weel, weel! Up with thee, Reuben, and let us try the legs of this auld dobbin of thine."

How Rotha got back into the house that night she never knew. She could not remember to have heard the rattle of the springless cart as it was being driven off. All was for the moment a blank waste.

When she recovered consciousness she was sitting by the side of Mrs. Ray, with her arms about the neck of the invalid and her head on the unconscious breast. The soulless eyes looked with a meaningless stare at the girl's troubled face.

The agony of suspense was over, and the worst had happened. What now remained to her to say to Willy? He knew nothing of what she had done. Sim's absence had been too familiar an occurrence to excite suspicion, and Robbie Anderson had not been missed. What should she say?

This was the night of Thursday. During the long hours of the weary days since Sunday, Rotha had conjured up again and again a scene overflowing with delight, in which she should tell Willy everything. This was to be when her father or Robbie or both returned, and the crown of her success was upon her. But what now was the word to say?

The noise of wheels approaching startled the girl out of her troubled dream. Willy was coming home. In another minute he was in the house.

"Rotha, Rotha," he cried excitedly, "I've great news, great news."

"What news?" asked Rotha, not daring to look up.

"Great news," repeated Willy.

Lifting her eyes furtively to his face, Rotha saw that, like his voice, it was brimming over with delight.

"The bloodhounds are gone," he said, and, throwing off his cloak and leggings, he embraced the girl and kissed her and laughed the laugh of a happy man. Then he hurried out to see to his horse.

What was Rotha to do? What was she to say? This mistake of Willy's made her position not less than terrible. How was she to tell him that his joyousness was misplaced? If he had come to her with a sad face she might then have told him all – yes, all the cruel truth! If he had come to her with reproaches on his tongue, how easily she might have unburdened her heavy heart! But this laughter and these kisses worked like madness in her brain.

The minutes flew like thought, and Willy was back in the house.

"I thought they dare not do it. You'll remember I told them so. Ah! ah! they find I was in the right."

Willy was too much excited with his own reading of this latest incident to sit in one seat for two minutes together. He walked up and down the room, laughing sometimes, and sometimes pausing to pat his mother's head.

It was fortunate for Rotha that she had to busy herself with the preparations for Willy's supper, and that this duty rendered less urgent the necessity for immediate response to his remarks. Willy, on his part, was in no mood at present to indulge in niceties of observation, and

Rotha's perturbation passed for some time unnoticed.

"Ralph will be back with us soon, let us hope," he said. "There's no doubt but we do miss him, do we not?"

"Yes," Rotha answered, leaning as much as possible over the fire that she was mending.

The tone of the reply made an impression on Willy. In a moment more he appeared to realize that there, had throughout been something unusual in the girl's demeanor.

"Not well, Rotha?" he asked in a subdued tone. It had flashed across his mind that perhaps her father was once more in some way the cause of her trouble.

"Oh, very well!" she answered, throwing up her head with a little touch of forced gayety.

"Why, there are tears in your eyes, girl. No? Oh, but there are!" They are tears of joy, he thought. She loves Ralph as a brother. "*I* laugh when I'm happy, Rotha; it seems that *you* cry."

"Do I?" she answered, and wondered if the merciful Father above would ever, ever, ever let this bitter hour pass by.

"No, it's worry, Rotha, that's it; you're not well, that's the truth."

Willy would have been satisfied to let the explanation resolve itself into this, but Rotha broke silence, saying, "What if it were *not* good news – "

The words were choking her, and she stopped.

"Not good news – what news?" asked Willy, half muttering the girl's words in a bewildered way.

"The news that the constables have gone."

"Gone! What is it? What do you mean, Rotha?"

"What if the constables have gone," said the girl, struggling with her emotion, "only because – what if they have gone – because – because

Ralph is taken."

"Taken! Where? What are you thinking of?"

"And what if Ralph is to be charged, not with treason – no, but with – with murder? Oh, Willy!" the girl cried in her distress, throwing away all disguise, "it is true, true; it is true."

Willy sat down stupefied. With a wild and rigid look, he stared at Rotha as they sat face to face, eye to eye. He said nothing. A sense of horror mastered him.

"And this is not all," continued Rotha, the tears rolling down her cheeks. "What would you say of the person who did it – of the person who put Ralph in the way of this – this death?" cried the girl, now burying her face in her hands.

Willy's lips were livid. They moved as if in speech, but the words would not come.

"What would I say?" he said at length, bitterly and scornfully, as he rose from his seat with rigid limbs. "I would say – " He stopped; his teeth were clinched. He drew one hand impatiently across his face. The idea that Simeon Stagg must have been the informer had at that moment got possession of his mind. "Never ask me what I would *say*," he cried.

"Willy, dear Willy," sobbed Rotha, throwing her arms about him, "that person – "

The sobs were stifling her, but she would not spare herself.

"That person was MYSELF!"

"You!" cried Willy, breaking from her embrace. "And the murder?" he asked hoarsely, "whose murder?"

"James Wilson's."

"Let me go – let me go, I say."

"Another word." Rotha stepped into the doorway. Willy threw her hastily aside and hurried out.

CHAPTER XXXVII

Which Indictment

Under the rude old Town Hall at Carlisle there was a shop which was kept by a dealer in second-hand books. The floor within was paved, and the place was lighted at night by two lamps, which swung from the beams of the ceilings. At one end a line of shelves served to separate from the more public part of the shop a little closet of a room, having a fire, and containing in the way of furniture a table, two or three chairs, and a stuffed settle.

In this closet, within a week of the events just narrated, a man of sinister aspect, whom we have met more than once already in other scenes, sat before a fire.

"Not come down yet, Pengelly?" said, this man to the bookseller, a tottering creature in a long gown and velvet skull cap.

"Not yet."

"Will he ever come? It's all a fool's errand, too, I'll swear it is."

Then twisting his shoulders as though shivering, he added, –

"Bitter cold, this shop of yours."

"Warmer than Doomsdale, eh?" replied the bookseller with a grin as he busied himself dusting his shelves.

The other chuckled. He took a stick that lay on the hearth and broke the fire into a sharp blaze. The exercise was an agreeable one. It was accompanied by agreeable reflections, too.

"I hear a foot on the stair." A man entered the shop.

"No use, none," said the new-comer. "It's wasted labor talking to Master Wilfrey."

The tone was one of vexation.

"Did ye tell him what I heard about Justice Hide and his carryings on at Newcastle?"

"Ey, and I told 'im he'd never bring it off with Hide on the bench."

"And what did the chiel say to it?"

"'Tut,' he said, says he, 'Millet is wi' 'im on the circuit, and he'll see the law's safe on treason.'"

"So he will not touch the other indictment?"

"'It's no use,' says he, 'the man's sure to fall for treason,' he says, 'and it's all botherment trying to force me to indict 'im for murder.'"

"Force him! Ha! ha! that's good, that is; force him, eh?"

The speaker renewed his attentions to the fire.

"He'll be beaten," he added, – "he'll be beaten, will Master Wilfrey. With Hide oh the bench there'll be no conviction for treason. And then the capital charge will go to the wall, and Ray will get away scot free."

"It baffles me yet aboot Ray, his giving himself up."

"Shaf, man! Will ye never see through the trick? It was to stand for treason and claim the pardon, or be fined, or take a year in Doomsdale, and escape the gallows. He's a cunning taistrel. He'll do aught to save his life."

"You're wrong there; I cannot but say you're wrong there. I know the man, and as I've told you there's nothing in the world he dare not do. Why, would you credit it, I saw 'im one day – "

"Tut, haud yer tongue. Ye'd see him tremble one day if this sheriff of yours were not flayt by his own shadow. Ye'd see him on Haribee; aye, and maybe ye *will* see him there yet, sheriff or no sheriff."

This was said with a bitterness indicative of fierce and deadly hatred.

Shifting uneasily under the close gaze of his companion, the other said, –

"What for do you look at me like that? I've no occasion to love him, have I?"

"Nor I, nor I," said the first speaker, his face distorted with evil passions; "and you shall spit on his grave yet, Master Scroope, that you shall; and dance on it till it does yer soul good; you shall, you shall, sheriff or none."

Just then a flourish of trumpets fell on the ear. Conversation was interrupted while the men, with the bookseller, stepped to the door. Numbers of townspeople were crowding into the Market Place. Immediately afterwards there came at a swift pace through Scotch Street a gayly bedecked carriage, with outriders in gold lace and a trumpeter riding in front.

"The judges – going through to King's Arms Lane," observed the bookseller.

"What o'clock do the 'sizes start, Mr. Pengelly?" asked a loiterer outside.

"Ten in the morning, that's when the grand jury sit," the bookseller answered.

CHAPTER XXXVIII

Peine Forte Et Dure

The court was densely packed at ten next morning. Every yard of available space was thronged with people. The crown court lay on the west of the Town Hall. It was a large square chamber without galleries. Rude oak, hewn with the axe straight from the tree, formed the rafters and principals of the roofs. The windows were small, and cast a feeble light. A long table like a block of granite, covered with a faded green cloth and having huge carved legs, stood at one end of the court, and stretched almost from side to side. On a dais over this table sat the two judges in high-backed chairs, deeply carved and black. There was a stout rail at one end of the table, and behind it were steps leading to a chamber below. This was the bar, and an officer of the court stood at one side of it. Exactly opposite it were three rows of seats on graduated levels. This was the jury box. Ranged in front of the table were the counsel for the King, the clerk of the court, and two or three lawyers. An ancient oak chest, ribbed with iron and secured by several massive padlocks, stood on the table.

The day was cold. A close mist that had come from the mountains hovered over the court and crept into every crevice, chilling and dank.

There was much preliminary business to go through, and the people who thronged the court watched it with ill-concealed impatience. True bills were found for this offence and that: assaults, batteries, larcenies.

Amid a general hush the crier called for Ralph Ray.

Ralph stepped up quietly, and laid one hand on the rail in front of him. The hand was chained. He looked round. There was not a touch either of pride or modesty in his steady gaze. He met without emotion the sea of faces upturned to his own face. Near the door at the end of the court stood the man who had been known in Lancaster as Ralph's shadow. Their eyes met, but there was no expression of surprise in either face. Close at hand was the burlier ruffian who had insulted the girl that sang in the streets. In the body of the court there was another familiar face. It was Willy Ray's, and on meeting his brother's eyes for an instant Ralph turned his own quickly away. Beneath the bar, with downcast eyes, sat Simeon Stagg.

The clerk of the court was reading a commission authorizing the court to hear and determine treasons, and while this formality was proceeding Ralph was taking note of his judges. One of them was a stout, rubicund person advanced in years. Ralph at once recognized him as a lawyer who had submitted to the Parliament six years before. The other judge was a man of austere countenance, and quite unknown to Ralph. It was the former of the two judges who had the principal management of the case. The latter sat with a paper before his face. The document sometimes concealed his eyes and sometimes dropped below his mouth.

"Gentlemen," said the judge, beginning his charge, "you are the grand inquest for the body of this county, and you have now before you a prisoner charged with treason. Treason, gentlemen, has two aspects: there is treason of the wicked imagination, and there is treason apparent: the former poisons the heart, the latter breaks forth in action."

The judge drew his robes about him, and was about to continue, when the paper suddenly dropped from the face of the other occupant of the bench.

"Your pardon, brother Millet," he interrupted, and pointed towards Ralph's arms. "When a prisoner comes to the bar his irons ought to be taken off. Have you anything to object against these irons being struck away?"

"Nothing, brother Hide," replied the judge rather testily. "Keeper, knock off the prisoner's irons."

The official appealed to looked abashed, and replied that the necessary instruments were not at hand.

"They are of no account, my lord," said Ralph.

"They must be removed."

When the delay attending this process was over and the handcuffs fell to the ground, the paper rose once more in front of the face of Justice Hide, and Justice Millet continued his charge. He defined the nature and crime of treason with elaboration and circumlocution. He quoted the ancient statute wherein the people, speaking of themselves, say that they recognize no superior under God but only the King's grace. "I do no speak my own words," he said, "but the words of the law, and I urge this the more lest any persons should draw dangerous inferences to shadow their traitorous acts. Gentlemen, the King is the vicegerent of God, and has no superior. If any man shall shroud himself under any pretended authority, you must know that this is not an excuse, but the height of aggravation."

Once more the judge paused, drew his robes about him, and turned sharply to the jury to observe the effect of his words; then to his brother on the bench, for the light of his countenance. The paper was covering the eyes of Justice Hide.

"But now, gentlemen, to come from the general to the particular. It is treason to levy war against the King's person, and to levy war against the King's authority is treason too. It follows, therefore, that all acts which were done to the keeping of the King out of the exercise of his kingly office were treason. If persons assembled themselves in a warlike manner to do any of these acts, that was treason. Remember but this, and I have done."

A murmur of assent and approbation passed over the court when the judge ceased to speak. Perhaps a close observer might have marked an expression of dissatisfaction on the face of the other judge as often as the document held in front of it permitted the eyes and mouth to be seen. He shifted restlessly from side to side while the charge was being delivered, and at the close of it he called somewhat impatiently for the indictment.

The clerk was proceeding to give the names of the witnesses, when Ralph asked to be permitted to see the indictment. With a smile, the clerk handed him a copy in Latin. Ralph glanced at it, threw it back to the table, and asked for a translation.

"Let the indictment be read aloud and in English," said Justice Hide.

It was then read, and purported that, together with others, Ralph Ray, not having the fear of God before his eyes, and being instigated by the devil, had traitorously and feloniously, contrary to his due allegiance and bounden duty, conspired against the King's authority on sundry occasions and in divers places.

There was a strained attitude of attention while the indictment was being read, and a dead stillness when the prisoner was called upon to plead.

"How sayest thou, Ralph Ray? Art thou guilty of that treason whereof thou standest indicted and for which thou hast been arraigned, or not guilty?"

Ralph did not reply at once. He looked calmly around. Then, in a firm voice, without a trace of emotion, he said, –

"I claim exemption under the Act of Oblivion."

There was a murmur of inquiry.

"That will avail you nothing," replied the judge who had delivered the charge. "The Act does not apply to your case. You must plead Guilty or Not Guilty."

"Have I no right to the benefit of the Act of Oblivion?"

The clerk rose again.

"Are you Guilty or Not Guilty?"

"Have I liberty to move exceptions to the indictment?"

"You shall have the liberty that any subject can have," replied Justice Millet. "You have heard the indictment read, and you must plead, Guilty or Not Guilty."

The paper had again gone up before the face of Justice Hide.

"I stand at this bar," said Ralph quietly, "charged with conspiring against the King's authority. The time of the alleged treason is specified. I move this exception to the indictment, that the King of England was *dead* at the period named."

There was some shuffling in the court. The paper had dropped below the eyes.

"You trouble the court with these damnable excursions," cried Justice Millet, with no attempt to conceal his anger. "By the law of England the King never dies. Your plea must be direct, – 'Guilty,' or 'Not Guilty.' No man standing in your position at the bar must make any other answer to the indictment."

"Shall I be heard, my lord?"

"You shall, sir, but only on your trial."

"I urge a point of law, and I ask for counsel," said Ralph; "I can pay."
"You seem to be versed in proceedings of law, young man," replied the
judge, with an undisguised sneer.

The paper dropped below the mouth.

"Mr. Ray," said Justice Hide, in a friendly tone, "the course is that you
should plead."

"I stand charged, my lord, with no crime. How, then, shall I plead?"

"Mr. Ray," said the judge again, "I am sorry to interrupt you. I hold that
a man in your position should have every leniency shown to him. But
these discourses are contrary to all proceedings of this nature. Will you
plead?"

"He *must* plead, brother; there is no *will you?*" rejoined the other
occupant of the bench.

The paper went up over the eyes once more. There was some laughter
among the men before the table.

"He thinks it cheap to defy the court," said counsel for the King.

"Brother Millet," said Justice Hide, "when a prisoner at the bar would
plead anything in formality, counsel should be allowed."

"Oh, certainly, certainly," replied the judge, recovering his suavity.
Then turning to Ralph, he said, –

"What is the point of law you urge?"

"What I am accused of doing," replied Ralph, "was done under the
command of the Parliament, when the Parliament was the supreme
power."

"Silence, sir," cried Justice Millet. "The Parliament was made up of a
pack of usurpers with a low mechanic fellow at their head. Gentlemen,"

turning with a gracious smile to the jury, "you will remember what I said."

"The Parliament was appointed by the people," replied Ralph quietly, "and recognized by foreign princes."

"It was only a third part of the constitution."

"It did not live in a corner. The sound of it went out among many nations."

Ralph still spoke calmly. The spectators held their breath.

"Do you know where you are, sir?" cried the judge, now grown scarlet with anger. "You are in the court of his Majesty the King. Would you have the boldness here, before the faces of the servants of that gracious Prince, to justify your crimes by claiming for them the authority of usurpers?" "I am but charged," replied Ralph, "with putting my hand to that plough which all men were then compelled to follow. I am but accused of fidelity to that cause which some of my prosecutors, as I see, did themselves at first submit to, and afterwards betray."

At this there were loud murmurs in the court. The paper had fallen from the face of Justice Hide. His brother justice was livid with rage.

"What fellow is this?" said the latter judge, with obvious uneasiness. "A dalesman from the mountains, did you say?"

"Dalesman or not, my lord, a cunning and dangerous man," replied counsel.

"I see already that he is one who is ready to say anything to save his miserable life."

"Brother Millet," interrupted the other judge, "you have rightly observed that this is a court of his Gracious Majesty. Let us conduct it as such."

There was a rustle of gowns before the table and some whispering in the court.

"Mr. Ray, you have heard the indictment. It charges you as a false traitor against his Most Gracious Majesty, your supreme and natural lord. The course is for you to plead Guilty or Not Guilty."

"Have I no right to the General Pardon?" asked Ralph.

Justice Millet, recovering from some temporary discomfiture, interposed, –

"The proclamation of pardon was issued before his Majesty came into possession."

"And my crime – was not that committed before the King came into possession? Are the King's promises less sacred than the people's laws?"

Again some murmuring in the court.

"Brother Hide, is the court to be troubled longer with these idle disputations?"

"I ask for counsel," said Ralph.

"This," replied Justice Hide, "is not a matter in which counsel can be assigned. If your crime be treason, it cannot be justified; if it be justifiable, it is not treason. The law provides that *we* shall be your counsel, and, as such, I advise that you do not ask exemption under the Act of Oblivion, for that is equal to a confession." "I do not confess," said Ralph.

"You must plead Guilty or Not Guilty. There is no third course. Are you Guilty or Not Guilty?"

There was a stillness like that of the chamber of death in the court as this was spoken.

Ralph paused, lifted his head, and looked calmly about him. Every eye was fixed on his face. That face was as firm as a rock. Two eyes near the door were gleaming with the light of fiendish triumph. Ralph returned his gaze to the judges. Still the silence was unbroken. It seemed to hang in the air.

"Guilty or Not Guilty?"

There was no reply.

"Does the prisoner refuse to plead?" asked Justice Hide. Still there was no reply. Not a whisper in the court; not the shuffle of a foot. The judge's voice fell slowly on the ear, –

"Ralph Ray, we would not have you deceive yourself. If you do not plead, it will be the same with you as if you had confessed."

"Am I at liberty to stand mute?"

"Assuredly not," Justice Millet burst out, pulling his robes about him.

"Your pardon, brother; it is the law that the prisoner may stand mute if he choose."

Then turning to Ralph, –

"But why?"

"To save from forfeiture my lands, sheep, goods, and chattels, and those of my mother and brother, falsely stated to be mine."

Justice Millet gave an eager glance at Justice Hide.

"It is the law," said the latter, apparently replying to an unuttered question. "The estate of an offender cannot be seized to the King's use before conviction. My Lord Coke is very clear on that point. It is the law; we must yield to it."

"God forefend else!" replied Justice Millet in his meekest tone.

"Ralph Ray," continued the judge, "let us be sure that you know what you do. If you stand mute a terrible punishment awaits you."

Justice Millet interposed, –

"I repeat that the prisoner *must* plead. In the ancient law of *peine forte et dure* an exception is expressly made of all cases of regicide."

"The indictment does not specify regicide as the prisoner's treason."

Justice Millet hid his discomfiture in an ostentatious perusal of a copy of the indictment.

"But do not deceive yourself," continued the judge, turning again towards the prisoner. "Do you know the penalty of standing mute? Do you know that to save your estates to your family by refusing to plead, you must suffer a terrible death, – a death without judgment, a death too shocking perhaps for so much as bare contemplation? Do you know this?"

The dense throng in the court seemed not to breathe at that awful moment. Every one waited for the reply. It came slowly and deliberately, –

"I know it."

The paper dropped from the judge's hand, and fluttered to the floor. In the court there was a half-uttered murmur of amazement. A man stood there to surrender his life, with all that was near and dear to it. Not dogged, trapped, made desperate by fate, but cheerfully and of his own free will.

Wonder and awe fell on that firmament of faces. Brave fellows there found the heart swell and the pulse beat quick as they saw that men – plain, rude men, Englishmen, kinsmen – might still do nobly. Cowards shrank closer together.

And, in the midst of all, the man who stood to die wore the serenest look to be seen there. Not an eye but was upturned to his placid face.

The judge's voice broke the silence, –

"And was it with this knowledge and this view that you surrendered?"

Ralph folded his arms across his breast and bowed.

The silence could be borne no longer. The murmurs of the spectators broke into a wild tumult of cheers, like the tossing of many waters; like the roar and lash of mighty winds that rise and swell, then ebb and surge again.

The usher of the court had not yet suppressed the applause, when it was observed that a disturbance of another kind had arisen near the door. A young woman with a baby in her arms was crushing her way in past the javelin man stationed there, and was craning her neck to catch sight of the prisoner above the dense throng that occupied every inch of the floor.

"Let me have but a glance at him – one glance – for the dear God's sake let me but see him – only once – only for a moment."

The judge called for silence, and the officer was hurrying the woman away when Ralph turned his face full towards the door.

"I see him now," said the woman. "He's not my husband. No," she added, "but I've seen him before somewhere."

"Where, my good woman? Where have you seen him before the day?"

This was whispered in her ear by a man who had struggled his way to her side.

"Does he come from beyond Gaskarth?" she asked.

"Why, why?"

"This commotion ill befits the gravity of a trial of such grave concernment," said one of the judges in an austere tone.

In another moment the woman and her eager interlocutor had left the court together.

There was then a brief consultation between the occupants of the bench.

"The pardon is binding," said one; "if it were otherwise it were the hardest case that could be for half the people of England."

"Yet the King came back without conditions," replied the other.

There was a general bustle in the court. The crier proclaimed silence.

"The prisoner stands remanded for one week."

Then Ralph was removed from the bar.

CHAPTER XXXIX

The Fiery Hand

They drove Robbie Anderson that night to the house of the old woman with whom he lodged, but their errand was an idle one. Reuben Thwaite jumped from the cart and rapped at the door. Old 'Becca Rudd opened it, held a candle over her head, and peered into the darkness. When she heard what sick guest they had brought her, she trembled from head to foot, and cried to them not to shorten the life of a poor old soul whose days were numbered.

"Nay, nay; take him away, take him away," she said.

"Art daft, or what dusta mean?" said Mattha from his seat in the cart.

"Nay, but have mercy on me, have mercy on me," cried 'Becca beseechingly.

"Weel, weel," said Mattha, "they do say as theer's no fools like auld fools. Why, the lad's ram'lin'. Canst hear? – ram'lin'. Wadst hev us keck him intil the dike to die like ony dog?"

"Take him away, take him away," cried 'Becca, retiring inwards, her importunity becoming every moment louder and more vehement.

"I reckon ye wad be a better stepmother to yon brocken-backt bitch of yours an it had the mange?" said Mattha.

"Nay, but the plague – the plague. Ye've heard what the new preachers are telling about the plague. Robbie's got it, Robbie's got the plague; I'm sure of it, sure."

'Becca set down the candle to wring her hands.

"So thoo's sure of it, ista?" said Mattha. "Weel, I'll tell thee what *I*'s sure on, and that is that thoo art yan o' them folks as waddant part with the reek off their kail. Ye'r nobbut an auld blatherskite, 'Becca, as preaches mair charity in a day ner ye'r ready to stand by in a twelvemonth. Come, Reuben, whip up yer dobbin. Let's away to my own house. I'd hev to be as poor as a kirk louse afore I'd turn my back on a motherless lad as is nigh to death's door."

"Don't say that, father," whimpered Liza.

"Nay, Mattha, nay, man," cried 'Becca, "it's nought of that. It's my life that's in danger."

"Shaf! that 'at is nowt is nivver in danger. Whear's the plague as wad think it worth while to bodder wid a skinflint like thee? Good neet, 'Becca, good neet, and 'od white te, lass, God requite thee!"

So they drove to Matthew Branthwaite's cottage, and installed the sick man in the disused workroom, where the loom had stood silent for nearly ten years.

A rough shakedown was improvised, a log fire was speedily kindled, and in half an hour Mrs. Branthwaite was sitting at Robbie's bedside bathing his hot forehead with cloths damped in vinegar. The little woman – timid and nervous in quieter times – was beginning to show some mettle now.

"Robbie has the fever, the brain fever," she said. She was right. The old wife's diagnosis was as swift as thought. Next day they sent for the doctor from Gaskarth. He came; looked wise and solemn; asked three questions in six syllables apiece, and paused between them. Then he felt the sick man's pulse. He might almost have heard the tick of it. Louder was the noise of the beating heart. Still not a word. In the dread stillness out came the lance, and Robbie was bled. Then sundry hums and ahs, but no syllable of counsel or cheer.

"Is there any danger?" asked little Liza in a fretful tone. She was standing with head averted from the bowl which was in her mother's hands, with nervous fingers and palpitating breast.

The wise man replied in two guarded words.

Robbie had appeared to be conscious before the operation of the lance. He was wandering again. He would soon be wildly delirious.

The great man took up his hat and his fee together. His silence at least had been golden.

"Didsta iver see sic a dumb daft boggle?" said Mattha as the doctor disappeared. "It cannot even speak when it's spoken to."

The medical ghost never again haunted that particular ghost-walk.

Robbie lay four days insensible, and Mrs. Branthwaite was thenceforward his sole physician and nurse. On the afternoon of the third day of Robbie's illness – it was Sunday – Rotha Stagg left her own peculiar invalid in the care of one of the farm women and walked over to Mattha's house.

Willy Ray had not returned from Carlisle. He had exchanged scarcely six words with her since the interview previously recorded. Rotha had not come to Shoulthwaite for Willy's satisfaction. Neither would she leave it for his displeasure.

When the girl reached the weaver's cottage and entered the sick-room, Mattha himself was sitting at the fireside, with a pipe, puffing the smoke up the chimney. Mrs. Branthwaite was bathing the sick man's head, from which the hair had been cut away. Liza was persuading herself that she was busy sewing at a new gown. The needle stuck and stopped twenty times a minute. Robbie was delirious.

"Robbie, Robbie, do you know who has come to see you?" said Liza, bending over him.

"Ey, mother, ey, here I am, home at last," muttered Robbie.

"He's ram'lin' agen," said Mattha from the chimney corner.

"Bless your old heart, mammy, but I'll mend my management. I will, that I will. It's true *this* time, mammy, ey, it is. No, no; try me again just *once*, mammy!"

"He's forever running on that, poor lad," whispered Mattha. "I reckon it's been a sair point with him sin' he put auld Martha intil t' grund."

"Don't greet, mammy; don't greet."

Poor Liza found the gown wanted close attention at that moment. It went near enough to her eyes.

"I say it was fifty strides to the north of the bridge! Swear it? Ey, swear it!" cried Robbie at a fuller pitch of his weakened voice.

"He's olas running on that, too," whispered Mattha to Rotha. "Dusta mind 'at laal Reuben said the same?"

In a soft and pleading tone Robbie mumbled on, –

"Don't greet, mammy, or ye'll kill me sure enough. Killing *you?* Ey, it's true it's true; but I'll mend my management – I *will*." There were sobs in Robbie's voice, but no tears in his bloodshot eyes.

"There, there, Robbie," whispered Mrs. Branthwaite soothingly in his ear; "rest thee still, Robbie, rest thee still."

It was a pitiful scene. The remorse of the poor, worn, wayward, tender-hearted lad seemed to rend the soul in his unconscious body.

"If he could but sleep!" said Mrs. Branthwaite; "but he cannot."

Liza got up and went out.

Robbie struggled to raise himself on one elbow. His face, red as a furnace, was turned aside as though in the act of listening for some noise far away. Then in a thick whisper he said, –

"Fifty strides north of the bridge. No dreaming about it – north, I say, north."

Robbie sank back exhausted, and Rotha prepared to leave.

"It were that ducking of his heed did it, sure enough," said Mattha, "that and the drink together. I mind Bobbie's father – just sic like, just sic like! Poor auld Martha, she *hed* a sad bout of it, she hed, what with father and son. And baith good at the bottom, too, baith, poor lads."

A graver result than any that Mattha dreamt of hung at this moment on Robbie's insensibility, and when consciousness returned the catastrophe had fallen.

CHAPTER XL

Garth and the Quakers

As Rotha left the weaver's cottage she found Liza in the porch.

"I'm just laughing at the new preachers," she said huskily. She was turning her head aside slyly to brush the tears from her eyes into a shawl which was over her head.

"There they are by the Lion. It's wrong to laugh, but they are real funny, aye!"

The artifice was too palpable to escape Rotha's observation. Without a word she put her arms about Liza and kissed her. Then the lurking tears gushed out openly, and the girl wept on her breast. They parted in silence, and Rotha walked towards a little company gathered under the glow of a red sun on the highway, and almost in front of the village inn. They were the "new preachers" of whom Liza had spoken. The same that had, according to Robbie's landlady, foretold the plague. They were three men, and they stood in the middle of a ring of men, women, and children. One of them, tall and gaunt, with long gray hair and wild eyes, was speaking at the full pitch of his voice. Another was emphasizing his words with loud hallelujahs. Then the third dropped down on his knees in the road, and prayed with earnestness in a voice that rang along the village street – silent to-day, save for him – and echoed back and back. Before the prayer had quite ended a hymn was begun in a jaunting measure, with a chorus that danced to a spirit of joyfulness.

Then came another exhortation. It was heavy with gloomy prediction. The world was full of oppression, and envy, and drunkenness, and vain pleasures. Men had forsaken the light that should enlighten all men. They were full of deceit and vanities. They put their trust in priests and professors who were but empty hollow casks. "Yet the Lord is at hand," cried the preacher, "to thrash the mountains, and beat them to dust."

Another hymn followed, more jubilant than before. One by one the people around caught the contagion of excitement. There were old men there with haggard faces that told of the long hard fight with the world in which they were of the multitude of the vanquished; old women, too, jaded and tired, and ready to slip into oblivion, their long day's duty done; mothers with babes in their arms and young children nestling close at their sides; rollicking boys and girls as well, with all the struggle of life in front of them.

The simple Quaker hymn told of a great home of rest far away, yet very near.

The tumult had attracted the frequenters of the Red Lion, and some of these had stepped out on to the causeway. Two or three of them were already drunk. Among them was Garth, the blacksmith. He laughed frantically, and shrieked and crowed at every address and every hymn. When the preachers shouted "Hallelujah," he shouted "Hallelujah" also; shouted again and again, in season and out of season; shouted until he was hoarse, and the perspiration poured down his crimsoning face. His tipsy companions at first assisted him with noisy cheers. When one of the men in the ring lifted up his voice in the ardor of prayer, Garth yelled out yet louder to ask if he thought God Almighty was deaf.

The people began to tremble at the blacksmith's blasphemies. The tipsiest of his fellows slunk away from his side.

The preacher spoke at one moment of the numbers of their following.

"You carry a bottle of liquor somewhere," cried Garth; "that's why they follow you."

Wearied out by such a shrieking storm of discord, one of the three Quakers – a little man with quick eyes and nervous lips – made his way through the crowd to where the blacksmith stood at the outskirts of it. Garth propped his back against the wall of the inn and laughed hysterically at the preacher's remonstrance: "Woe to thee and such as thee when God's love passes away from thee."

Garth replied with a mocking blasphemy too terrible for record. He repeated it, shouted it, screamed it.

In sheer horror the Quaker dropped on his knees in front of the blacksmith and muttered a prayer that was almost inaudible: –

"God grant that the seven devils, yea seven times seven, may come out of him!"

Then Garth was silent for a moment.

"I knew such a one as thou art five years ago," said the Quaker; "and where thinkest thou he died?"

"Where?" said Garth, with a drunken hiccup.

"But he was a saved man at last – saved by the light with which Christ enlightened all men – saved – "

"Where?" repeated Garth, with a hideous imprecation.

"On the gallows – he had killed his own father – he was – "

"Curse you! Curse you on earth and in hell!"

The people who had crowded round held their hands to their ears to shut out the fearful blasphemies. Garth, sobered somewhat by rage which was no longer assumed but real, pushed them aside and strode down the lane.

Rotha turned away from the crowd and walked towards Shoulthwaite. Before her, at fifty paces, the blacksmith tramped doggedly on, with head towards the ground. Drunk, mad, devilish as at this moment he might be, Rotha felt an impulse to overtake him. She knew not what power prompted her, or what idea or what hope. Never before had she felt an instinct drawing her to this man. Yet she wished to speak with him now. Would she had done so! Would she had done so – not for his sake or yet for hers – but now, even now, while the impieties were hot on his burning lips!

Rotha ran a step or two and stopped. Garth shambled sullenly on. He never lifted his eyes to the sky.

When he reached his home he threw himself on the skemmel drawn up to the hearth. He was sober now. His mother had been taking her Sunday afternoon's sleep on the settle, which stood at one side of the kitchen. His noisy entrance awoke her. He broke the peat with the peat-stick and kicked it into the fire.

"What's come ower thee?" said Mrs. Garth, opening her eyes and yawning.

"What's come over you more like?" growled Joe.

"What now?"

"Do you sell your own flesh and blood?" said Joe. "Sell? What's thy mare's nest now, thou weathercock? One wouldn't think that butter wad melt in thy mouth sometimes, and then agen – "

"I'm none so daft as daftly dealt with, mother," interrupted the blacksmith.

"I've telt thee afore thou'rt yan of the wise asses. What do you mean by *sell?*"

"I reckon *you* know when strangers in the street can tell me."

The blacksmith coiled himself up in his gloomy reserve and stared into the fire.

"Oh, thou's heard 'at yon man's in Doomsdale, eh?"

Joe grunted something that was inarticulate.

"I mean to hear the trial," continued Mrs. Garth, with a purr of satisfaction.

"Maybe you wouldn't like to see me in his place, mother? Oh, no; certainly not."

"Thou great bledderen fool," cried Mrs. Garth, getting on to her feet and lifting her voice to a threatening pitch; "whearaway hast been?"

Joe growled again, and crept closer over the fire, his mother's brawny figure towering above him.

CHAPTER XLI

A Horse's Neigh

A bleared winter sun was sinking down through a scarf of mist. Rotha was walking hurriedly down the lonnin that led from the house on the Moss. Laddie, the collie, had attached himself to her since Ralph's departure, and now he was running by her side.

She was on her way to Fornside, but on no errand of which she was conscious. Willy Ray had not yet returned. Her father had not come back from his long journey. Where was Willy? Where was her father? What kept them away? And what of Ralph – standing as he did, in the jaws of that Death into which her own hands had thrust him! Would hope ever again be possible? These questions Rotha had asked herself a hundred times, and through the responseless hours of the long days and longer nights of more than a week she had lived on somehow, somehow, somehow.

The anxiety was burning her heart away; it would be burnt as dry as ashes soon. And she had been born a woman – a weak woman – a thing meant to sit at home with her foot on the treadle of her poor little wheel, while dear lives were risked and lost elsewhere.

Rotha was a changed being. She was no longer the heartsome lassie who had taken captive the stoical fancy of old Angus. Tutored by suffering, she had become a resolute woman. Goaded by something akin to despair, she was now more dangerous than resolute.

She was to do strange things soon. Even her sunny and girlish ingenuousness was to desert her. She was to become as cunning as dauntless. Do you doubt it? Put yourself in her place. Think of what she had done, and why she had done it; think of what came of it, and may yet come of it. Then look into your own heart; or, better far, look into the heart of another – you will be quicker to detect the truth and the falsehood that lies *there*.

Then listen to what the next six days will bring forth.

The cottage at Fornside has never been occupied since the tailor abandoned it. Hardly in Wythburn was there any one so poor as to covet such shelter for a home. It was a single-storied house with its back to the road. Its porch was entered from five or six steps that led downwards from a little garden. It had three small rooms, with low ceilings and paved floors. In the summer the fuchsia flecked its front with white and red. In these winter days the dark ivy was all that grew about it.

Lonely, cheerless, and now proscribed by the fears and superstitions of the villagers, it stood as gaunt as a solitary pine on the mountain head that has been blasted and charred by the lightning.

When Rotha reached it she hesitated as if uncertain whether to go in or go back. She stood at the little wicket, while the dog bounded into the garden. In another moment Laddie had run into the house itself.

How was this? She had locked the door. The key had been hidden as usual in the place known only to her father and herself. Rotha hurried down, and pushed her hand deep into the thatch covering the porch. The key was gone. The door stood open.

And now, besides the pat of the dog's feet, she heard noises from within.

Rotha put her hand to her heart. Could it be that her father had come home? Was he here, here?

The girl stepped into the kitchen. Then a loud clash, as of a closing chest, came from an inner room. In an instant there was the rustle of a dress, and Mrs. Garth and Rotha were face to face in that dim twilight.

The recoil of emotion was too much for the girl. She stood silent. The woman looked at her for an instant with something more like a frightened expression than had yet been seen on her hard face.

Then she brushed past her and away.

"Stop!" cried Rotha, recovering herself.

The woman was gone, and the girl did not pursue her.

Rotha went into the room which Mrs. Garth had come from. It was Wilson's room. There was his trunk still, which none had claimed. The trunk – the hasty closing of its lid had been the noise she heard! But it had always been heavily locked. With feverish fingers Rotha clutched at the great padlock that hung from the front of the trunk. It had a bunch of keys suspended from it. They were strange to her. Whose keys were they?

The trunk was not locked; the lid had merely been shut down. Rotha raised it with trembling hands. Inside were clothes of various kinds, but these had been thrust hurriedly aside, and beneath them were papers – many papers – scattered loosely at the bottom. What were they?

It was growing dark. Rotha remembered that there was no candle in the house, and no lamp that had oil. She thrust her hand down to snatch up the papers, meaning to carry them away. She touched the dead man's clothes, and shrank back affrighted. The lid fell heavily again.

The girl began to quiver in every limb.

Who could say that the spirits of the dead did not haunt the scenes of their lives and deaths? Gracious heaven! she was in Wilson's room!

Rotha tottered her way out in the gathering gloom, clutching at the door as she went. Back in the porch again, she felt for the key to the outer door. It was in the lock. She should carry it with her this time. Then she remembered the keys in the trunk. She must carry them away also. She never asked herself why. What power of good or evil was prompting the girl?

Calling the dog, she went boldly into the house again, and once more into the dead man's room. She fixed the padlock, turned the key, drew it out of its wards, and put the bunch of keys in her pocket. In two minutes more she was on the high road, walking back to Shoulthwaite.

There was something in her heart that told her that to-day's event was big with issues. And, truly, an angel of light had led her to that dark house.

The sun was gone. A vapory mist was preceding the night. The dead day lay clammy on her hands and cheeks.

When she reached the Fornside road, her eyes turned towards the smithy. There it was, and a bright red glow from the fire, white at its hissing heart, lit up the air about it. Rotha could hear the thick breathing of the bellows and the thin tinkle of the anvil. Save for these all was silent. What was the secret of the woman who lived there? That it concerned her father, Ralph, herself, and all people dear to her, was as clear as day to Rotha. The girl then resolved that, come what should or could, that secret should be torn from the woman's heart.

The moon was struggling feebly through a ridge of cloud, lighting the sky at moments like a revolving lamp at sea. On the road home Rotha passed two young people who were tripping along and laughing as they went.

"Good night, Rotha," said the young dalesman.

"Good night, dear," said his sweetheart.

Rotha returned the salutations.

"Fine lass that," said the young fellow in a whisper.

"Do you think so? She's too moapy for me," replied his companion. "I hate moapy folks."

After this slight interruption the two resumed the sport of their good spirits.

The moon had cleared the clouds now.

It was to be just such a night – save for the frost and wind – as that fateful one on which Ralph and Rotha walked together from the Red Lion. How happy that night had seemed to her then to be – happy, at least, until the end! She had even sung under the moonlight. But her songs had been truer than she knew – terribly, horribly true.

> One lonely foot sounds on the keep,
> And that's the warder's tread.

Step by step Rotha retraced every incident of that night's walk; every word of Ralph's and every tone.

He had told her that her father was innocent, and that he knew it was so.

He had asked her if she did not love her father, and she had said,

"Better than all the world."

Had that been true, quite *true?* Rotha stopped and plucked at a bough in the fence.

When she had asked him the cause of his sadness, when she had hinted that perhaps he was keeping something behind which might yet take all the joy out of the glad news that he gave her – what, then, had he said? He had told her there was nothing to come that need mar her happiness or disturb her love. Had that also been true, *quite* true? No, no, no, neither had been true; but the falsehood had been hers.

She loved her father, yes; but not, no, not better than all the world. And what had come after had marred her happiness and disturbed her love. Where lay her love – where?

Rotha stopped again, and as though to catch her breath. Nature within her seemed at war with itself. It was struggling to tear away a mask that hid its own face. That mask must soon be plucked aside.

Rotha thought of her betrothal to Willy, and then a cold chill passed over her.

She walked on until she came under the shadow of the trees beneath which Angus Ray had met his death. There she paused and looked down. She could almost conjure up the hour of the finding of the body.

At that moment the dog was snuffling at the very spot. Here it was that she herself had slipped; here that Ralph had caught her in his arms; here, again, that he had drawn her forward; here that they had heard noises from the court beyond.

Stop – what noise was *that!* It was the whinny of a horse! They had heard that too. Her dream of the past and the present reality were jumbling themselves together.

Again? No, no; that was the neigh – the real neigh – of a horse. Rotha hastened forward. The dog had run on. A minute later Laddie was barking furiously. Rotha reached the courtyard.

There stood the old mare, exactly as before!

Was it a dream? Had she gone mad? Rotha ran and caught the bridle.

Yes, yes! It was a reality. It was Betsy!

There was no coffin on her back; the straps that had bound it now dangled to the ground.

But it was the mare herself, and no dream.

Yes, Betsy had come home.

CHAPTER XLII

The Fatal Witness

Long before the hour appointed for the resumption of the trial of Ralph Ray, a great crowd filled the Market Place at Carlisle, and lined the steps of the old Town Hall, to await the opening of the doors. As the clock in the cupola was striking ten, three men inside the building walked along the corridor to unbar the public entrance.

"I half regret it," said one; "you have forced me into it. I should never have touched it but for you."

"Tut, man," whispered another, "you saw how it was going. With yon man on the bench and yon other crafty waistrel at the bar, the chance was wellnigh gone. What hope was there of a conviction?"

"None, none; never make any more botherment about it, Master Lawson," said the third.

"The little tailor is safe. He can do no harm as a witness."

"I'm none so sure of that," rejoined the first speaker.

The door was thrown open and the three men stepped aside to allow the crush to pass them. One of the first to enter was Mrs. Garth. The uncanny old crone cast a quick glance about her as she came in with the rest, hooded close against the cold. Her eyes fell on one of the three men who stood apart. For a moment she fixed her gaze steadfastly upon him, and then the press from behind swept her forward. But in that moment she had exchanged a swift and unmistakable glance of recognition. The man's face twitched slightly. He looked relieved when the woman had passed on.

Dense as had been the throng that filled the court on the earlier hearing, the throng was now even yet more dense. The benches usually provided for the public had been removed, and spectators stood on every inch of the floor. Some crept up to the windows, and climbed on to the window boards. One or two daring souls clambered over the shoulders of their fellows to the principals of the roof, and sat perched across them. The old court house was paved and walled with people.

From the entrance at the western end the occupants of the seats before the table filed in one by one. The first to come was the sheriff, Wilfrey Lawson. With papers in hand, he stationed himself immediately under the jurors' box and facing the bar. Then came the clerk of the court, who was making an ostentatious display of familiarity with counsel for the King, who walked half a pace behind him.

The judges took their seats. As they entered, the gentleman of the rubicund complexion was chatting in a facetious vein with his brother judge, who, however, relaxed but little of the settled austerity of his countenance under the fire of many jests.

Silence was commanded, and Ralph Ray was ordered to the bar. He had scarcely taken his place there when the name of Simeon Stagg was also called. For an instant Ralph looked amazed. The sheriff observed his astonishment and smiled. The next moment Sim was by his side. His face was haggard; his long gray-and-black hair hung over his temples. He was led in. He clutched feverishly at the rail in front. He had not yet lifted his eyes. After a moment he raised them, and met the eyes of Ralph turned towards him. Then he shuffled and sidled up to Ralph's elbow. The people stretched their necks to see the unexpected prisoner.

After many preliminary formalities it was announced that the grand jury had found a true bill for murder against the two prisoners.

The indictment was read. It charged Ralph Ray and Simeon Stagg with having murdered with malice aforethought James Wilson, agent to the King's counsel.

The prisoners were told to plead. Ralph answered promptly and in a clear tone, "Not Guilty." Sim hesitated, looked confused, stammered, lifted his eyes as if inquiringly to Ralph's face, then muttered indistinctly, "Not Guilty."

The judges exchanged glances. The clerk, with a sneer on his lip, mumbled something to counsel. The spectators turned with a slight bustle among themselves. Their pleas had gone against the prisoners – at least against Ralph.

When the men at the bar were asked how they would be tried, Ralph turned to the bench and said he had been kept close prisoner for seven days, none having access to him. Was he to be called to trial, not knowing the charge against him until he was ordered to the bar?

No attention was paid to his complaint, and the jury was empanelled. Then counsel rose, and with the customary circumlocution opened the case against the prisoners. In the first place, he undertook to indicate the motive and occasion of the horrid, vile, and barbarous crime which had been committed, and which, he declared, scarce anything in the annals of justice could parallel; then, he would set forth the circumstances under which the act was perpetrated; and, finally, he proposed to show what grounds existed for inferring that the prisoners were guilty thereof.

He told the court that the deceased James Wilson, as became him according to the duty of his secret office, had been a very zealous person. In his legal capacity he had sought and obtained a warrant for the arrest of the prisoner Ray. That warrant had never been served. Why? The dead body of Wilson had been found at daybreak in a lonely road not far from the homes of both prisoners. The warrant was not on the body. It had been missing to that day. His contention would be that the prisoners had obtained knowledge of the warrant; that they had waylaid the deceased agent in a place and at a time most convenient for the execution of their murderous design. With the cunning of clever criminals, they had faced the subsequent coroner's inquiry. One of them, being the less artful, had naturally come under suspicion. The other, a cunning and dangerous man, had even taken an active share in defending his confederate. But being pursued by a guilty conscience, they dared not stay at the scene of their crime, and both had fled from their homes. All this would be justified by strong and undeniable circumstances.

Counsel resumed his seat amid the heavy breathings and inaudible mutterings of the throng behind him. He was proceeding to call his witnesses, when Ralph asked to be heard.

"Is it the fact that I surrendered of my own free will and choice?"

"It is." "Is it assumed that I was prompted to that step also by a guilty conscience?"

Counsel realized that he was placed on the horns of a dilemma. Ignoring Ralph, he said, –

"My lords, the younger prisoner *did* surrender. He surrendered to a warrant charging him with conspiring to subvert the King's authority. He threw himself on the mercy of his Sovereign, and claimed the benefit of the pardon. And why? To save himself from indictment on the capital charge; at the price, peradventure, of a fine or a year's imprisonment to save himself from the gallows. Thus he tried to hoodwink the law; but, my lords," – and counsel lifted himself to his utmost height, – "the law is not to be hoodwinked."

"God forfend else!" echoed Justice Millet, shifting in his seat and nodding his head with portentous gravity.

"I was loath to interrupt you," said Justice Hide, speaking calmly and for the first time, "or I should have pointed out wherein your statement did not correspond with the facts of the prisoner Ray's conduct as I know it. Let us without delay hear the witnesses."

The first witness called was a woman thinly and poorly clad, who came to the box with tears in her eyes, and gave the name of Margaret Rushton. Ralph recognized her as the young person who had occasioned a momentary disturbance near the door towards the close of the previous trial. Sim recognized her also, but his recollection dated farther back.

She described herself as the wife of a man who had been outlawed, and whose estates had been sequestered. She had been living the life of a vagrant woman.

"Was your husband named John Rushton?" asked Ralph.

"Yes," she replied meekly, and all but inaudibly.

"John Rushton of Aberleigh!"

"The same."

"Did you ever hear him speak of an old comrade – Ralph Ray?"

"Yes, yes," answered the witness, lifting her hands to her face and sobbing aloud.

"The prisoner wastes the time of the court. Let us proceed."

Ralph saw the situation at a glance. The woman's evidence – whatever it might be – was to be forced from her. "Have you seen these prisoners before?"

"Yes, one of them."

"Perhaps both?"

"Yes, perhaps both."

"Pray tell my lords and the jury what you know concerning them."

The woman tried to speak and stopped, tried again and stopped.

Counsel, coming to her relief, said, –

"It was in Wythburn you saw them; when was that?"

"I passed through it with my two children at Martinmas," the witness began falteringly.

"Tell my lords and the jury what happened then."

"I had passed by the village, and had come to a cottage that stood at the angle of two roads. The morning was cold, and my poor babies were crying. Then it came on to rain. So I knocked at the cottage, and an old man opened the door."

"Do you see the old man in this court?"

"Yes – there," pointing to where Sim stood in the dock with downcast eyes.

There was a pause.

"Come, good woman, let my lords and the jury hear what further you know of this matter. You went into the cottage!"

"He said I might warm the children at the fire; their little limbs were as cold as stone."

"Well, well?"

"He seemed half crazed, I thought; but he was very kind to me and my little ones. He gave them some warm milk, and said we might stay till the weather cleared. It did not clear all day. Towards nightfall the old man's daughter came home. She was a dear fine girl, God bless her!"

The silence of the court was only disturbed by a stifled groan from the bar, where Sim still stood with downcast eyes. Ralph gazed through a blinding mist at the rafters overhead.

"She nursed the little ones, and gave them oaten cake and barley bread. The good people were poor themselves; I could see they were. It rained heavier than ever, so the young woman made a bed for us in a little room, and we slept in the cottage until morning."

"Was anything said concerning the room you slept in?" "They said it was their lodger's room; but he was away, and would not return until the night following."

"Next day you took the road towards the North?"

"Yes, towards Carlisle. They told me that if my husband were ever taken he would be brought to Carlisle. That was why I wished to get here. But I had scarce walked a mile – I had a baby at the breast and a little boy who could just toddle beside me – I had scarce walked a mile before the boy became ill, and could not walk. I first thought to go back to the cottage, but I was too weak to carry both children. So I sat with my little ones by the roadside."

The witness paused again. Ralph was listening with intense eagerness. He was leaning over the rail before him to catch every syllable. When the woman had regained some composure he said quietly, –

"There is a bridge thereabouts that spans a river. Which side of the bridge were you then?"

"The Carlisle side; that is to say, the north."

The voice of counsel interrupted a further inquiry.

"Pray tell my lords and the jury what else you know, good woman."

"We should have perished of cold where we sat, but looking up I saw that there was a barn in a field close by. It was open to the front, but it seemed to be sheltered on three sides, and had some hay in it. So I made my way to it through a gate, and carried the children."

"What happened while you were there? – quick, woman, let us get to the wicked fact itself."

"We stayed there all day, and when the night came on I covered the little ones in the hay, and they cried themselves to sleep."

The tears were standing in the woman's eyes. The eyes of others were wet.

"Yes, yes, but what *occurred?*" said counsel, to whom the weeping of outcast babes was obviously less than an occurrence.

"*I* could not sleep," said the woman hoarsely; and lifting her voice to a defiant pitch, she said, "Would that the dear God had let me sleep that night of all nights of my life!"

"Come, good woman," said counsel more soothingly, "what next?"

"I listened to the footsteps that went by on the road, and so the weary hours trailed on. At last they had ceased to come and go. It was then that I heard a horse's canter far away to the north."

The witness was speaking in a voice so low as to be scarcely audible to the people, who stood on tiptoe and held their breath to hear.

"My little boy cried in his sleep. Then all was quiet again."

Sim shuddered perceptibly. He felt his flesh creep.

"The thought came to me that perhaps the man on the horse could give me something to do the boy good. If he came from a distance, he would surely carry brandy. So I labored out of the barn and trudged through the grass to the hedge. Then I heard footsteps on the road. They were coming towards me."

"Was it dark?"

"Yes, but not very dark. I could see the hedge across the way. The man on foot and the man on the horse came together near where I stood."

"How near – twenty paces?"

"Less. I was about to call, when I heard the man on foot speak to the other, who was riding past him."

"You saw both men clearly?"

"No," replied the woman firmly; "not clearly. I saw the one on the road. He was a little man, and he limped in his walk."

In the stillness of the court Ralph could almost hear the woman breathe.

"They were quarrelling, the two men; you heard what they said?" said counsel, breaking silence.

"It's not true," cried the witness, in a hurried manner, "*I* heard nothing."

"This is no suborned witness, my lords," said counsel in a cold voice, and with a freezing smile. "Well, woman?"

"The tall man leapt off his horse, and there was a struggle. The little man was swearing. There was a heavy fall, and all was quiet once more."

As she spoke the woman recoiled to the back of the box, and covered her face in her hands.

"What manner of man was the taller one?" "He had a strong face with big features and large eyes. I saw him indistinctly."

"Do you see him now?".

"I cannot swear; but – but I think I do."

"Is the prisoner who stands to the left the man you saw that night?"

"The voice is the same, the face is similar, and he wears the same habit – a long dark coat lined with light flannel."

"Is that all you know of the matter?"

"I knew that a crime had been committed in my sight. I felt that a dead body lay close beside me. I was about to turn away, when I heard a third man come up and speak to the man on the horse."

"You knew the voice?"

"It was the cottager who had given us shelter. I ran back to the barn, snatched up my two children in their sleep, and fled away across the fields – I know not where."

Justice Hide asked the witness why she had not spoken of this before; three months had elapsed since then.

She replied that she had meant to do so, but it came into her mind that perhaps the cottager was somehow concerned in the crime, and she remembered how good he and his daughter had been to her.

"How had she come to make the disclosures now?"

The witness explained that when she crushed her way into the court a week ago it was with the idea that the prisoner might be her husband. He was not her husband, but when she saw his face she remembered that she had seen him before. A man in the body of the court had followed her out and asked her questions.

"Who was the man?" asked the judge, turning to the sheriff.

The gentleman addressed pointed to a man near at hand, who rose at this reference, with a smile of mingled pride and cunning, as though he felt honored by this public disclosure of his astuteness. He was a small man with a wrinkled face, and a sinister cast in one of his eyes, which lay deep under shaggy brows. We have met him before.

The judge looked steadily at him as he rose in his place. After a minute or two he turned again to look at him. Then he made some note on a paper in his hand.

The witness looked jaded and worn with the excitement. During her examination Sim had never for an instant upraised his eyes from the ground. The eagerness with which Ralph had watched her was written in every muscle of his face. When liberty was given him to question her, he asked in a soft and tender voice if she knew what time of the night it might be when she had seen what she had described.

Between nine and ten o'clock as near as she could say, perhaps fully ten.

Was she sure which side of the bridge she was on – north or south?

"Sure; it was north of the bridge."

Ralph asked if the records of the coroner's inquiry were at hand. They were not. Could he have them examined? It was needless. But why?

"Because," said Ralph, "it was sworn before the coroner that the body was found to the south of the bridge – fifty yards to the south of it."

The point was treated with contempt and some derisive laughter. When Ralph pressed it, there was humming and hissing in the court.

"We must not expect that we can have exact and positive proof," said Justice Millet; "we would come as near as we can to circumstances by which a fact of this dark nature can be proved. It is easy for a witness to be mistaken on such a point."

The young woman Margaret Rushton was being dismissed.

"One word," said Justice Hide. "You say you have heard your husband speak of the prisoner Ray; how has he spoken of him?"

"How? – as the bravest gentleman in all England!" said the woman eagerly.

Sim lifted his head, and clutched the rail. "God – it's true, it's true!" he cried hysterically, in a voice that ran through the court.

"My lords," said counsel, "you have heard the truth wrung from a reluctant witness, but you have not heard all the circumstances of this horrid fact. The next witness will prove the motive of the crime."

A burly Cumbrian came into the box, and gave the name of Thomas Scroope. He was an agent to the King's counsel. Ralph glanced at him. He was the man who insulted the girl in Lancaster.

He said he remembered the defendant Ray as a captain in the trained bands of the late Parliament. Ray was always proud and arrogant. He had supplanted the captain whose captaincy he afterwards held.

"When was that?"

"About seven years agone," rejoined the witness; adding in an undertone, and as though chuckling to himself, "he's paid dear enough for that sin' then."

Ralph interrupted.

"Who was the man I supplanted, as you say – the man who has made me pay dear for it, as you think?"

No answer.

"Who?"

"No matter that," grumbled the witness. His facetiousness was gone.

There was some slight stir beneath the jurors' box.

"Tell the court the name of the man you mean."

Counsel objected to the time of the court being wasted with such questions.

Justice Hide overruled the objection.

Amid much sensation, the witness gave the name of the sheriff of Cumberland, Wilfrey Lawson.

Continuing his evidence in a defiant manner, the witness said he remembered the deceased agent, James Wilson. He saw him last the day before his death. It was in Carlisle they met. Wilson showed witness a warrant with which he was charged for Ray's arrest, and told him that Ray had often threatened him in years past, and that he believed he meant to take his life. Wilson had said that he intended to be beforehand, for the warrant was a sure preventive. He also said that the Rays were an evil family; the father was a hard, ungrateful brute, who had ill repaid him for six years' labor. The mother was best; but then she was only a poor simple fool. The worst of the gang was this Ralph, who in the days of the Parliament had more than once threatened to deliver him – Wilson – to the sheriff – the other so-called sheriff, not the present good gentleman.

Ralph asked the witness three questions.

"Have we ever met before?"

"Ey, but we'll never meet again, I reckon," said the man, with a knowing wink.

"Did you serve under me in the army of the Parliament?"

"Nowt o' t' sort," with a growl.

"Were you captured by the King's soldiers, and branded with a hot iron, as a spy of their own who was suspected of betraying them?"

"It's a' a lie. I were never brandet."

"Pull up the right sleeves of your jerkin and sark."

The witness refused.

Justice Hide called on the keeper to do so.

The witness resisted, but the sleeves were drawn up to the armpit. The flesh showed three clear marks as of an iron band.

The man was hurried away, amid hissing in the court.

The next witness was the constable, Jonathan Briscoe. He described being sent after Wilson early on the day following that agent's departure from Carlisle. His errand was to bring back the prisoner. He arrived at Wythburn in time to be present at the inquest. The prisoner Stagg was then brought up and discharged.

Ralph asked if it was legal to accuse a man a second time of the same offence.

Justice Millet ruled that the discharge of a coroner (even though he were a resident justice as well) was no acquittal.

The witness remembered how at the inquiry the defendant Ray had defended his accomplice. He had argued that it was absurd to suppose that a man of Stagg's strength could have killed Wilson by a fall. Only a more powerful man could have done so.

"Had you any doubt as to who that more powerful man might be?"

"None, not I. I knew that the man whose game it was to have the warrant was the likest man to have grabbed it. It warn't on the body. There was not a scrap of evidence against Ray, or I should have taken him then and there."

"You tried to take him afterwards, and failed."

"That's true enough. The man has the muscles of an ox."

The next two witnesses were a laborer from Wythburn, who spoke again to passing Sim on the road on the night of the murder, and meeting Wilson a mile farther north, and Sim's landlord, who repeated his former evidence.

There was a stir in the court as counsel announced his last witness. A woman among the spectators was muttering something that was inaudible except to the few around her. The woman was Mrs. Garth. Willy Ray stood near her, but could not catch her words.

The witness stepped into the box. There was no expression of surprise on Ralph's face when he saw who stood there to give evidence against him. It was the man who had been known in Lancaster as his "Shadow"; the same that had (with an earlier witness) been Robbie Anderson's companion in his night journey on the coach; the same that passed Robbie as he lay unconscious in Reuben Thwaite's wagon; the same that had sat in the bookseller's snug a week ago; the same that Mrs. Garth had recognized in the corridor that morning; the same that Justice Hide had narrowly scrutinized when he rose in the court to claim the honor of ferreting the facts out of the woman Rushton.

He gave the name of Mark Wilson.

"Your name again?" said Justice Hide, glancing at a paper in his hand.

"Mark Wilson."

Justice Hide beckoned the sheriff and whispered something. The sheriff crushed his way into an inner room.

"The deceased James Wilson was your brother?"

"He was."

"Tell my lords and the jury what you know of this matter."

"My brother was a zealous agent of our gracious King," said the witness, speaking in a tone of great humility. "He even left his home – his wife and family – in the King's good cause."

At this moment Sim was overtaken by faintness. He staggered, and would have fallen. Ralph held him up, and appealed to the judges for a seat and some water to be given to his friend. The request was granted, and the examination continued.

The witness was on the point of being dismissed when the sheriff re-entered, and, making his way to the bench, handed a book to Justice Hide. At the same instant Sim's attention seemed to be arrested to the most feverish alertness. Jumping up from the seat on which Ralph had placed him, he cried out in a thin shrill voice, calling on the witness to remain. There was breathless silence in the court.

"You say that your brother," cried Sim, – "God in heaven, what a monster he was! – you say that he left his wife and family. Tell us, did he ever go back to them?"

"No."

"Did you ever hear of money that your brother's wife came into after he'd deserted her – that was what he did, your lordships, deserted her and her poor babby – did you ever hear of it?"

"What if I did?" replied the witness, who was apparently too much taken by surprise to fabricate a politic falsehood.

"Did you know that the waistrel tried to get hands on the money for himself?"

Sim was screaming out his questions, the sweat standing in round drops on his brow. The judges seemed too much amazed to remonstrate.

"Tell us, quick. Did he try to get hands on it?"

"Perhaps; what then?"

"And did he get it?"

"No."

"And why not – why not?"

The anger of the witness threw him off his guard.

"Because a cursed scoundrel stepped in and threatened to hang him if he touched the woman's money."

"Aye, aye! and who was that cursed scoundrel?"

No answer.

"Who, quick, who?"

"That man there!" pointing to Ralph.

Loud murmurs came from the people in the court. In the midst of them a woman was creating a commotion. She insisted on going out. She cried aloud that she would faint. It was Mrs. Garth again. The sheriff leaned over the table to ask if these questions concerned the inquiry, but Sim gave no time for protest. He never paused to think if his inquiries had any bearing on the issue.

"And now tell the court your name."

"I have told it."

"Your *true* name, and your brother's."

Justice Hide looked steadily at the witness. He held an open book in his hand.

"Your *true* name," he said, repeating Sim's inquiry.

"Mark Garth!" mumbled the witness. The judge appeared to expect that reply.

"And your brother's?"

"Wilson Garth."

"Remove the perjurer in charge."

Sim sank back exhausted, and looked about him as one who had been newly awakened from a dream.

The feeling among the spectators, as also among the jurors, wavered between sympathy for the accused and certainty of the truth of the accusation, when the sheriff was seen to step uneasily forward and hand a paper to counsel. Glancing hastily at the document, the lawyer rose with a smile of secure triumph and said that, circumstantial as the evidence on all essential points had hitherto been, he was now in a position to render it conclusive.

Then handing the paper to Ralph, he asked him to say if he had ever seen it before. Ralph was overcome; gasping as if for breath, he raised one hand involuntarily to his breast.

"Tell the court how you came by the instrument in your hand."

There was no reply. Ralph had turned to Sim, and was looking into his face with what appeared to be equal pity and contrition.

The paper was worn, and had clearly been much and long folded. It was charred at one corner as if at some moment it had narrowly escaped the flames.

"My lords," said counsel, "this is the very warrant which the deceased Wilson carried from Carlisle for the arrest of the prisoner who now holds it; this is the very warrant which has been missing since the night of the murder of Wilson; and where, think you, my lords, it was found? It was found – you have heard how foolish be the wise – look now how childishly a cunning man can sometimes act, how blundering are clever rogues! – it was found this morning on the defendant Ray's person while he slept, in an inner breast pocket, which was stitched up, and seemed to have been rarely used."

"That is direct proof," said Justice Millet, with a glance at his brother on the bench. "After this there can be no doubt in any mind."

"Peradventure the prisoner can explain how he came by the document," said Justice Hide.

"Have you anything to say as to how you became possessed of it?"

"Nothing."

"Will you offer the court no explanation?"

"None."

"Would the answer criminate you?"

No reply.

For Ralph the anguish of years was concentrated in that moment. He might say where he was on the night of the murder, but then he had Sim only for witness. He thought of Robbie Anderson – why was he not here? But no, Robbie was better away; he could only clear him of this guilt by involving his father. And what evidence would avail against the tangible witness of the warrant? He had preserved that document with some vague hope of serving Sim, but here it was the serpent in the breast of both.

"This old man," he said, – his altered tone startled the listeners, – "this old man," he said, pointing to Sim at his side, "is as innocent of the crime as the purest soul that stands before the White Throne."

"And what of yourself?"

"As for me, as for me," he added, struggling with the emotion that surged in his voice, "in the sight of Him that searcheth all hearts I have acquittal. I have sought it long and with tears of Him before whom we are all as chaff."

"Away with him, the blasphemer!" cried Justice Millet. "Know where you are, sir. This is an assembly of Christians. Dare you call God to acquit you of your barbarous crimes?"

The people in the court took up the judge's word and broke out into a tempest of irrepressible groans. They were the very people who had cheered a week ago.

Sim cowered in a corner of the box, with his lank fingers in his long hair.

Ralph looked calmly on. He was not to be shaken now. There was one way in which he could quell that clamor and turn it into a tumult of applause, but that way should not be taken. He could extricate himself by criminating his dead father, but that he should never do. And had he not come to die? Was not this the atonement he had meant to make? It was right, it was right, and it was best. But what of Sim; must he be the cause of Sim's death also? "This poor old man," he repeated, when the popular clamor had subsided, "he is innocent."

Sim would have risen, but Ralph guessed his purpose and kept him to his seat. At the same moment Willy Ray among the people was seen struggling towards the witness-bar. Ralph guessed his purpose and checked him, too, with a look. Willy stood as one petrified. He saw only one of two men for the murderer – Ralph or his father.

"Let us go together," whispered Sim; and in another moment the judge (Justice Millet) was summing up. He was brief; the evidence of the woman Rushton and of the recovered warrant proved everything. The case was as clear as noonday. The jurors need not leave the box.

Without retiring, the jury found a verdict of guilty against both prisoners.

The crier made proclamation of silence, and the awful sentence of death was pronounced.

It was remarked that Justice Hide muttered something about a "writ of error," and that when he rose from the bench he motioned the sheriff to follow him.

CHAPTER XLIII

Love Known at Last

Early next morning Willy Ray arrived at Shoulthwaite, splashed from head to foot, worn and torn. He had ridden hard from Carlisle, but not so fast but that two unwelcome visitors were less than half an hour's ride behind him.

"Home again," he said, in a dejected tone, throwing down his whip as he entered the kitchen, "yet *home* no longer."

Rotha struggled to speak. "Ralph, where is he? Is he on the way?" These questions were on her lips, but a great gulp was in her throat, and not a word would come.

"Ralph's a dead man," said Willy with affected deliberation, pushing off his long boots.

Rotha fell back apace. Willy glanced up at her.

"As good as dead," he added, perceiving that she had taken his words too literally. "Ah, well, it's over now, it's over; and if you had a hand in it, girl, may God forgive you!"

Willy said this with the air of a man who reconciles himself to an injury, and is persuading his conscience that he pardons it. "Could you not give me something to eat?" he asked, after a pause.

"Is that all you have to say to me?" said Rotha, in a voice as husky as the raven's.

Willie glanced at her again. He felt a passing pang of remorse.

"I had forgotten, Rotha; your father, he is in the same case with Ralph."

Then he told her all; told her in a simple way, such as he believed would appeal to what he thought her simple nature; told her of the two trials and final conviction, and counselled her to bear her trouble with as stout a heart as might be.

"It will be ended in a week," he said, in closing his narrative; "and then, Heaven knows what next." Rotha stood speechless by the chair of the unconscious invalid, with a face more pale than ashes, and fingers clinched in front of her.

"It comes as a shock to you, Rotha, for you seemed somehow to love your poor father."

Still the girl was silent. Then Willy's sympathies, which had for two minutes been as unselfish as short-sighted, began to revolve afresh about his own sorrows.

"I can scarce blame you for what you did," he said; "no, I can scarce blame you, when I think of it. He was not your brother, as he was mine. You could know nothing of a brother's love; no, you could know nothing of that."

"What *is* the love of a brother?" said Rotha.

Willy started at the unfamiliar voice.

"What would be the love of a world of brothers to such a love as *mine?*"

Then stepping with great glassy eyes to where Willy sat, the girl clutched him nervously and said, "I loved him."

Willy looked up with wonder in his face.

"Yes, I! You talk *your* love; it is but a drop to the ocean I bear him. It is but a grain to the desert of love in my heart that shall never, never blossom."

"Rotha!" cried Willy, in amazement.

"Your love! Why look you, under the wing of death – now that I may never hope to win him – I tell you that I love Ralph."

"Rotha!" repeated Willy, rising to his feet.

"Yes, and shall love him when the grass is over him, or me, or both!"

"Love him?"

"To the last drop of my blood, to the last hour of my life, until Death's cold hand lies chill on this heart, until we stand together where God is, and all is love for ever and ever, I tell you I love him, and shall love him, as God Himself is my witness."

The girl glowed with passion. Her face quivered with emotion, and her upturned eyes were not more full of inspiration than of tears.

Willy sank back into his seat with a feeling akin to awe.

"Let it be so, Rotha," he said a moment later; "but Ralph is doomed. Your love is barren; it comes too late. Remember what you once said, that death comes to all." "But there is something higher than death and stronger," cried Rotha, "or heaven itself is a lie and God a mockery. No, they shall not die, for they are innocent."

"Innocence is a poor shield from death. It was either father or Ralph," replied Willy, "and for myself I care not which."

Then at a calmer moment he repeated to her afresh the evidence of the young woman Rushton, whom she and her father had housed at Fornside.

"You are sure she said 'fifty yards to the *north* of the bridge'?" interrupted Rotha.

"Sure," said Willy; "Ralph raised a question on the point, but they flung it aside with contempt."

"Robbie Anderson," thought Rotha. "What does Robbie know of this that he was forever saying the same in his delirium? Something he *must* know. I shall run over to him at once."

But just then the two officers of the sheriff's court arrived again at Shoulthwaite, and signified by various forms of freedom and familiarity that it was a part of their purpose to settle there until such time as judgment should have taken its course, and left them the duty of appropriating the estate of a felon in the name of the crown.

"Come, young mistress, lead us up to our room, and mind you see smartly to that breakfast. Alack-a-day; we're as hungry as hawks."

"You come to do hawks' business, sir," said Rotha, "in spoiling another's nest."

"Ha! ha! ha! happy conceit, forsooth! But there's no need to glare at us like that, my sharp-witted wench. Come, lead on, but go slowly, there. This leg of mine has never mended, bating the scar, since yonder unlucky big brother of yours tumbled me on the mountains."

"He's not my brother."

"Sweetheart, then, ey? Why, these passages are as dark as the grave."

"I wish they were as silent, and as deep too, for those who enter them."

"Ay, what, Jonathan? Grave, silent, deep – but then you would be buried with us, my pretty lassie."

"And what of that? Here's your room, sirs. Peradventure it will serve until you take every room." "Remember the breakfast," cried the little man, after Rotha's retreating figure. "We're as hungry as – as – "

"Hold your tongue, and come in, David. Brush the mud from your pantaloons, and leave the girl to herself."

"The brazen young noddle," muttered David.

It was less than an hour later when Rotha, having got through her immediate duties, was hastening with all speed to Mattha Brander's cottage. In her hand, tightly grasped beneath her cloak, was a bunch of keys, and on her lips were the words of the woman's evidence and of Robbie's delirium. "It was fifty yards to the north of the bridge."

This was her sole clew. What could she make of it?

CHAPTER XLIV

The Clew Discovered

An hour before Rotha left Shoulthwaite, Robbie Anderson was lying on a settle before the fire in the old weaver's kitchen. Mattha himself and his wife were abroad, but Liza had generously and courageously undertaken the task of attending to the needs of the convalescent.

"Where's all my hair gone?" asked Robbie, with a puzzled expression. He was rubbing his close-cropped head.

Liza laughed roguishly.

"Maybe it's fifty yards north of the bridge," she said, with her head aside.

Robbie looked at her with blank amazement.

"Why, who told you that, Liza?" he said.

"Told me what?"

"Ey? *That!*" repeated Robbie, no more explicit.

"Foolish boy! Didn't you tell us yourself fifty times?"

"So I did. Did I though? What am I saying? When did I tell you?"

Robbie's eyes were staring out of his head. His face, not too ruddy at first, was now as pale as ashes.

Liza began to whimper.

"Why do you look like that?" she said.

"Look? Oh, ey, ey! I'm a ruffian, that's what I am. Never mind, lass."

Robbie's eyes regained their accustomed expression, and his features, which had been drawn down, returned to their natural proportions.

Liza's face underwent a corresponding change.

"Robbie, have you 'downed' him – that Garth?"

"Ey?"

The glaring eyes were coming back. Liza, frightened again, began once more to whimper prettily.

"I didn't mean to flayte you, Liza," Robbie said coaxingly. "You're a fair coax when you want something," said Liza, trying to disengage herself from the grasp of Robbie's arm about her waist. He might be an invalid, Liza thought, but he was wonderfully strong, and he was holding her shockingly tight. What *was* the good of struggling?

Robbie snatched a kiss.

"Oh you – oh you – oh! oh! If I had known that you were so wicked – oh!"

"Forgive me, forgive me, forgive me, or I will never let you go, never," cried Robbie.

"Never?" Liza felt that she *must* forgive this tyrant.

"Well, if you'll loosen this arm I'll – I'll *try*."

"Liza, how much do you love me?" inquired Robbie.

"Did you speak to me?"

"Oh, no, to crusty old 'Becca down the road. How much do you love me?"

Robbie's passion was curiously mathematical.

"Me? How much? About as much as you might put in your eye."

Robbie pretended to look deeply depressed. He dropped his head, but kept, nevertheless, an artful look out of the corner of the eye which was alleged to be the measure of his sweetheart's affection.

Thinking herself no longer under the fire of Robbie's glances, Liza's affectation of stern disdain melted into a look of tenderness.

Robbie jerked his head up sharply. The little woman was caught. She revenged herself by assuming a haughty coldness. But it was of no use. Robbie laughed and crowed and bantered.

At this juncture Mattha Branth'et came into the cottage.

The weaver was obviously in a state of profound agitation. He had just had a "fratch" with the Quaker preachers on the subject of election.

"I rub't 'm t' wrang way o' t' hair," said the old man, "when I axt 'em what for they were going aboot preaching if it were all settled aforehand who was to be damned and who was to be saved. 'Ye'r a child of the devil,' says one. 'Mebbee so,' says I, 'and I dunnet know if the devil iver had any other relations; but if so, mebbee yersel's his awn cousin.'"

It was hard on Matthew that, after upholding Quakerism for years against the sneers of the Reverend Nicholas Stevens, he should be thus disowned and discredited by the brotherhood itself.

"Tut! theer's six o' tean an' hofe a duzzen of t' tudder," said the old sage, dismissing the rival theologians from his mind forever.

"Oh, Robbie, lad," said Matthew, as if by a sudden thought, "John Jackson met Willy Ray coming frae Carlisle, and what think ye hes happent?"

"Nay, what?" said Robbie, turning pale again.

"Ralph Ray and Sim Stagg are condemned to death for t' murder of auld Wilson."

Robbie leapt to his feet.

"The devil!"

"Come, dunnet ye tak on like the Quakers," said Matthew.

Robbie had caught up his coat and hat.

"Why, where are you going?" said Liza.

"Going? Aye? Going?"

"Yes, where? You're too weak to go anywhere. You'll have another fever."

A light wagon was running on the road outside. Reuben Thwaite was driving.

Robbie rushed to the door, and hailed him.

"Going off with thread again, Reuben?"

"That's reets on't," answered the little man.

"Let me in with you?"

And Robbie climbed into the cart.

Mattha got up and went out in the road.

The two men had hardly got clear away when Rotha entered the cottage all but breathless.

"Robbie, where is he?"

"Gone, just gone, not above two minutes," replied Liza, still whimpering.

"Where?"

"I scarce know – to Penrith, I think. There was no keeping him back. When father came in and told him what had happened at Carlisle, he flung away and would not be hindered. He has gone off in Reuben's wagon."

"Which way?"

"They took the low road."

"Then I've missed them," said Rotha, sinking into a chair in a listless attitude.

"And he's as weak as water, and he'll take another fever, as I told him, and ramble on same as – "

"Liza," interrupted Rotha, "did you ever tell him – in play I mean – did you ever repeat anything he had said when he was unconscious?"

"Not that about his mammy?"

"No, no; but anything else?"

"I mind I told him what he said over and over again about his fratch with that Garth."

"Nothing else?"

"Why, yes, now I think on't. I mind, too, that I told him he was always running on it that something was fifty yards north of the bridge, and he could swear it, swear it in hea – "

"What did he say to *that?*" asked Rotha eagerly.

"Say! he said nothing, but he glowered at me till I thought sure he was off again."

"Is that all?"

"All what, Rotha?"

"They said in evidence that Ralph – it was a lie, remember – they said that Wilson was killed fifty yards to the north of the bridge. Now his body was found as far to the south of it. Robbie knows something. I hoped to learn what he knows; but oh, everything is against me – everything, everything."

Rising hastily, she added, "Perhaps Robbie has gone to Carlisle. I must be off, Liza."

In another moment she was hurrying up the road.

Taking the high path, the girl came upon the Quaker preachers, surrounded by a knot of villagers. To avoid them she turned up an unfrequented angle of the road. There, in the recess of a gate, unseen by the worshippers, but commanding a view of them, and within hearing of all that was sung and said, stood Garth, the blacksmith. He wore his leathern apron thrown over one shoulder. This was the hour of mid-day rest. He had not caught the sound of Rotha's light footstep as she came up beside him. He was leaning over the gate and listening intently. There was more intelligence and also more tenderness in his face than Rotha had observed before.

She paused, and seemed prompted to a nearer approach, but for the moment she held back. The worshippers began to sing a simple Quaker hymn. It spoke of pardon and peace: –

> Though your sins be red as scarlet,
> He shall wash them white as wool.

Garth seemed to be touched. His hard face softened; his lips parted, and his eyes began to swim.

When the singing ceased, he repeated the refrain beneath his breath. "What if one could but think it?" he muttered, and dropped his head into his hands.

Rotha stepped up and tapped his shoulder.

"Mr. Garth," she said.

He started, and then struggled to hide his discomposure. There was only one way in which a man of his temperament and resource could hope to do it – he snarled.

"What do you want with me?"

"It was a beautiful hymn," said Rotha, ignoring his question.

"Do you think so?" he growled, and turned his head away.

"What if one could but think it?" she said, as if speaking as much to herself as to him.

Garth faced about, and looked at her with a scowl.

The girl's eyes were as meek as an angel's.

"It's what I was thinking mysel', that is," he mumbled after a pause; then added aloud with an access of irritation, "Think what?"

"That there is pardon for us all, no matter what our sins – pardon and peace."

"Humph!"

"It is beautiful; religion is very beautiful, Mr. Garth."

The blacksmith forced a short laugh.

"You'd best go and hire yourself to the Quakers. They would welcome a woman preacher, no doubt"

She would have bartered away years of her life at this instant for one glimpse of what was going on in that man's heart. If she had found corruption there, sin and crime, she would have thanked God for it as for manna from above. Rotha clutched the keys beneath her cloak and subdued her anger.

"You scarce seem yourself to-day, Mr. Garth," she said.

"All the better," he replied, with a mocking laugh. "I've heard that they say my own sel' is a bad sel'."

The words were hardly off his lips when he turned again sharply and faced Rotha with an inquiring look. He had reminded himself of a common piece of his mother's counsel; but in the first flash of recollection it had almost appeared to him that the words had been Rotha's, not his.

The girl's face was as tender as a Madonna's.

"Maybe I *am* a little bit out of sorts to-day; maybe so. I've felt daizt this last week end; I have, somehow."

Rotha left him a minute afterwards. Continuing her journey, she drew the bunch of keys from under her cloak and examined them.

They were the same that she had found attached to Wilson's trunk on the night of her own and Mrs. Garth's visit to the deserted cottage at

Fornside. There were perhaps twenty keys in all, but two only bore any signs of recent or frequent use. One of these was marked with a cross scratched roughly on the flat of the ring. The other had a piece of white tape wrapped about the shaft. The rest of the keys were worn red with thick encrustation of rust. And now, by the power of love, this girl with the face of an angel in its sweetness and simplicity – this girl, usually as tremulous as a linnet – was about to do what a callous man might shrink from.

She followed the pack-horse road beyond the lonnin that turned up to Shoulthwaite, and stopped at the gate of the cottage that stood by the smithy near the bridge. Without wavering for an instant, without the quivering of a single muscle, she opened the gate and walked up to the door.

"Mrs. Garth," she called.

A young girl came out. She was a neighbor's daughter.

"Why, she's away, Rotha, Mistress Garth is," said the little lassie.

"Away, Bessy?" said Rotha, entering the house and seating herself. "Do you know where she's gone?"

"Nay, that I don't; but she told mother she'd be away three or four days."

"So you're minding house for her," said Rotha vacantly, her eyes meantime busily traversing the kitchen; they came back to the little housekeeper's face in a twinkling.

"Deary me, what a pretty ribbon that is in your hair, Bessy. Do you know it makes you quite smart. But it wants just a little bow like this – there, there."

The guileless child blushed and smiled, and sidled slyly up to where she could catch a sidelong glance at herself in a scratched mirror that hung against the wall.

"Tut, Bessy, you should go and kneel on the river bank just below, and look at yourself in the still water. Go, lass, and come back and tell me what you think now."

The little maiden's vanity prompted her to go, but her pride urged her to remain, lest Rotha should think her too vain. Pride conquered, and Bessy hung down her pretty head and smiled. Rotha turned wearily about and said, "I'm very thirsty, and I can't bear that well water of Mrs. Garth's."

"Why, she's not got a well, Rotha."

"Hasn't she? Now, do you know, I thought she had, but it must be 'Becca Rudd's well I'm thinking of."

Bessy stepped outside for a moment, and came back with a basin of water in her hand.

"What sort of water is this, Bessy – river water?" said Rotha languidly, with eyes riveted on an oak chest that stood at one side of the kitchen.

"Oh, no; spring water," said the little one, with many protestations of her shaking head.

"Now, do you know, Bessy – you'll think it strange, won't you? – do you know, I never care for spring water."

"I'll get you a cup of milk," said Bessy.

"No, no; it's river water *I* like. Just slip away and get me a cup of it, there's a fine lass, and I'll show you how to tie the ribbon for yourself."

The little one tripped off. Vanity reminded her that she could kill two birds with one stone. Instantly she had gone Rotha rose to her feet and drew out the keys. Taking the one with the tape on it, she stepped to the oak chest and tried it on the padlock that hung in front of it. No; that was not the lock it fitted. There was a corner cupboard that hung above the chest. But, no; neither had the cupboard the lock which fitted the key in Rotha's hand.

There was a bedroom leading out of the kitchen. Rotha entered it and looked around. A linen trunk, a bed, and a chair were all that it contained. She went upstairs. There were two bedrooms there, but no chest, box, cabinet, cupboard, not anything having a lock which a key like this might fit.

Bessy would be back soon. Rotha returned to the kitchen. She went again into the adjoining bedroom. Yes, under the bed was a trunk, a massive plated trunk. She tried to move it, but it would not stir. She went down on her knees to examine it. It had two padlocks, but neither suited the key. Back to the kitchen, she sat down half bewildered and looked around.

At that instant the little one came in, with a dimple in her rosy cheeks and a cup of water in her hand.

Rotha took the water and tried to drink.

She was defeated once more. She put the keys into her pocket. Was she ever to be one step nearer the heart of this mystery?

She rose wearily and walked out, forgetting to show the trick of the bow to the little housekeeper who stood with a rueful pout in the middle of the floor.

There was one thing left to do; with this other key, the key marked with a cross, she could open Wilson's trunk in her father's cottage, look at the papers, and perhaps discover wherein lay their interest for Mrs. Garth. But first she must examine the two places in the road referred to in the evidence at the trial.

In order to do this at once, Rotha turned towards Smeathwaite when she left the blacksmith's cottage, and walked to the bridge.

The river ran in a low bed, and was crossed by the road at a sharp angle. Hence the bridge lay almost out of sight of persons walking towards it.

Fifty yards to the north of it was the spot where the woman Rushton said she saw the murder. Fifty yards to the south of it was the spot where the body was picked up next morning.

Rotha had reached the bridge, and was turning the angle of the road, when she drew hastily back. Stepping behind a bush for further concealment, she waited. Some one was approaching. It was Mrs. Garth. The woman walked on until she came to within fifty paces of where Rotha stood. Then she stopped. The girl observed her movements, herself unseen.

Mrs. Garth looked about her to the north and south of the road and across the fields on either hand. Then she stepped into the dike and prodded the ground for some yards and kicked the stones that lay there.

Rotha's breath came and went like a tempest.

Mrs. Garth stooped to look closely at a huge stone that lay by the highway. Then she picked up a smaller stone and seemed to rub it on the larger one, as if she wished to remove a scratch or stain.

Rotha was sure now.

Mrs. Garth stood on the very spot where the crime was said to have been committed. This woman, then, and her son were at the heart of the mystery. It was even as she had thought.

Rotha could hear the beat of her own heart. She plunged from behind the bush one step into the road. Then she drew back.

The day was cold but dry, and Mrs. Garth heard the step in front of her. She came walking on with apparent unconcern. Rotha thought of her father and Ralph condemned to die as innocent men.

The truth that would set them free lay with seething dregs of falsehood at the bottom of this woman's heart. It should come up; it should come up.

When Mrs. Garth had reached the bridge Rotha stepped out and confronted her. The woman gave a little start and then a short forced titter.

"Deary me, lass, ye mak a ghost of yersel', coming and going sa sudden."

"And you make ghosts of other people." Then, without a moment's warning, Rotha looked close into her eyes and said, "Who killed James Wilson? Tell me quick, quick."

Mrs. Garth flinched, and for the instant looked confused.

"Tell me, woman, tell me; who killed him *there* – there where you've been beating the ground to conceal the remaining traces of a struggle?"

"Go off and ask thy father," said Mrs. Garth, recovering herself; and then she added, with a sneer, "but mind thou'rt quick, or he'll never tell thee in this world." "Nor will you tell me in the next. Woman, woman!" cried Rotha in another tone, "woman, have you any bowels? You have no heart, I know; but can you stand by and be the death of two men who have never, never done you wrong?"

Rotha clutched Mrs. Garth's dress in the agony of her appeal.

"You have a son, too. Think of him standing where they stand, an innocent man."

Rotha had dropped to her knees in the road, still clinging to Mrs. Garth's dress.

"What's all this to me, girl? Let go yer hod, do you hear? Will ye let go? What wad I know about Wilson – nowt."

"It's a lie," cried Rotha, starting to her feet. "What were you doing in his room at Fornside?"

"Tush, maybe I was only seeking that fine father of thine. Let go your hod, do you hear? Let go, or I'll – I'll – "

Rotha had dropped the woman's dress and grasped her shoulders. In another instant the slight pale-faced girl had pulled this brawny woman to her knees. They were close to the parapet of the bridge, and it was but a few inches high.

"As sure as God's in heaven," cried Rotha with panting breath and flaming eyes, "I'll fling you into this river if you utter that lie again. Woman, give me the truth! Cast away these falsehoods, that would blast the souls of the damned in hell."

"Get off. Wilta not? Nay, then, but I'll mak thee, and quick."

The struggle was short. The girl was flung aside into the road.

Mrs. Garth rose from her knees with a bitter smile on her lips. "I mak na doubt 'at thou wouldn't be ower keen to try the same agen," she said, going off. "Go thy ways to Doomsdale, my lass, and ax yer next batch of questions there. I've just coom't frae it mysel', do you know?"

Late the same evening, as the weary sun went down behind the smithy, Rotha hastened from the cottage at Fornside back to the house on the Moss at Shoulthwaite. She had a bundle of papers beneath her cloak, and the light of hope in her face.

The clew was found.

CHAPTER XLV

The Condemned in Doomsdale

When Ralph, accompanied by Sim, arrived at Carlisle and surrendered himself to the high sheriff, Wilfrey Lawson, he was at once taken before the magistrates, and, after a brief examination, was ordered to wait his trial at the forthcoming assizes. He was then committed to the common gaol, which stood in the ruins of the old convent of Black Friars. The cell he occupied was shared by two other prisoners – a man and a woman. It was a room of small dimensions, down a small flight of steps from the courtyard, noisome to the only two senses to which it appealed – gloomy and cold. It was entered from a passage in an outer cell, and the doors to both were narrow, without so much as the ventilation of an eye-hole, strongly bound with iron, and double locked. The floor was the bare earth, and there was no furniture except such as the prisoners themselves provided. A little window near to the ceiling admitted all the light and air and discharged all the foul vapor that found entrance and egress.

The prisoners boarded themselves. For an impost of 7s per week, an under gaoler undertook to provide food for Ralph and to lend him a mattress. His companions in this wretched plight were a miserable pair who were suspected of a barbarous and unnatural murder. They had been paramours, and their victim had been the woman's husband. Once and again they had been before the judges, and though none doubted their guilt, they had been sent back to await more conclusive or more circumstantial evidence. Whatever might hitherto have been the ardor of their guilty passion, their confinement together in this foul cell had resulted in a mutual loathing. Within the narrow limits of these walls neither seemed able to support the barest contact with the other. They glared at each other in the dim light with ghoul-like eyes, and at night they lay down at opposite sides of the floor on bundles of straw for beds. This straw, having served them in their poverty for weeks and even months, had fermented and become filthy and damp.

Such was the place and such the society in which Ralph spent the seven days between the day on which he surrendered and that on which he was indicted for treason.

The little window looked out into the streets, and once or twice daily Simeon Stagg, who discovered the locality of Ralph's confinement,

329

came and exchanged some words of what were meant for solace with his friend. It was small comfort Ralph found in the daily sight of the poor fellow's sorrowful face; but perhaps Ralph's own brighter countenance and cheerier tone did something for the comforter himself.

Though the two unhappy felons were made free of the spacious courtyard for an hour every day, the like privilege was not granted to Ralph, who was kept close prisoner, and, except on the morning of his trial, was even denied water for washing and cleansing.

When he was first to appear before the judges of assize, this prisoner of state, who had voluntarily surrendered himself, after many unsuccessful efforts at capturing him, was bound hand and foot. On the hearing of his case being adjourned, he was taken back to the cell which he had previously shared; but whether he felt that the unhappy company was more than he could any longer support, or whether the foul atmosphere of the stinking room seemed the more noisome from the comparative respite of a crowded court, he determined to endure the place no longer. He asked to be permitted to write to the governor of the city. The request was not granted. Then, hailing Sim from the street, he procured by his assistance a bundle of straw and a candle. The straw, clean and sweet, he exchanged with his fellow-prisoners for that which had served them for beds. Then, gathering the rotten stuff into a heap in the middle of the floor, he put a light to it and stirred it into a fire. This was done partly to clear the foul atmosphere, which was so heavy and dank as to gather into beads of moisture on the walls, and partly to awaken the sluggish interest of the head gaoler, whose rooms, as Ralph had learned, were situated immediately above this cell. The former part of the artifice failed (the filthy straw engendered as much stench as it dissipated), but the latter part of it succeeded effectually. The smoke found its way where the reeking vapor which was natural to the cell could not penetrate.

Ralph was removed forthwith to the outer room. But for the improvement in his lodgings he was punished indirectly. Poor Sim had dislocated a bar of the window in pushing the straw into Ralph's hands, and for this offence he was apprehended and charged with prison breaking. Four days later the paltry subterfuge was abandoned, as we know, for a more serious indictment. Ralph's new abode was brighter and warmer than the old one, and had no other occupant. Here he passed the second week of his confinement. The stone walls of this cell had a melancholy interest. They were carved over nearly every available inch with figures of men, birds, and animals, cut, no doubt, by the former prisoners to beguile the weary hours.

In these quarters life was at least tolerable; but tenancy of so habitable a place was not long to be Ralph's portion.

When the trial for murder had ended in condemnation, Ralph and Sim were removed from the bar, not to the common gaol from whence they came, but to the castle, and were there committed to a pestilential dungeon under the keep. This dungeon was known as Doomsdale. It was indeed a "seminary of every vice and of every disease." Many a lean and yellow culprit, it was said, had carried up from its reeking floor into the court an atmosphere of pestilence which avenged him on his accusers. Some affirmed that none who ever entered it came out and lived. The access to it was down a long flight of winding stairs, and through a cleft hewn out of the bare rock on which the castle stood. It was wet with the waters that oozed out of countless fissures and came up from the floor and stood there in pools of mire that were ankle deep.

Ralph was scarcely the man tamely to endure a horrible den like this. Once again he demanded to see the governor, but was denied that justice.

As a prisoner condemned to die, he, with Sim, was allowed to attend service daily in the chapel of the castle. The first morning of his imprisonment in this place he availed himself of the privilege. Crossing the castle green towards the chapel, he attempted to approach the governor's quarters, but the guard interposed. Throughout the service he was watchful of any opportunity that might arise, but none appeared. At the close he was being taken back to Doomsdale, side by side with his companion, when he saw the chaplain, in his surplice, crossing the green to his rooms. Then, at a sudden impulse, Ralph pushed aside the guard, and, tapping the clergyman on the shoulder, called on him to stop and listen.

"We are condemned men," he said; "and if the law takes its course, in six days we are to die; but in less time than that we will be dead already if they keep us in that hell on earth."

The chaplain stared at Ralph's face with a look compounded equally of amazement and fear.

"Take him away," he cried nervously to the guard, who had now

331

regained possession of their prisoner.

"You are a minister of the Gospel," said Ralph.

"Your servant," said the clergyman, with mock humility.

"My servant, indeed!" said Ralph; "my servant before God, yet beware of hypocrisy. You are a Christian minister, and you read in your Bible of the man who was cast into a lion's den, and of the three men who were thrown into the fiery furnace. But what den of lions was ever so deadly as this, where no fire would burn in the pestilential air?"

"He is mad," cried the chaplain, sidling off; "look at his eyes." The guard were making futile efforts to hurry Ralph away, but he shouted again, in a voice that echoed through the court, –

"You are a Christian minister, and your Master sent his disciples over all the earth without purse or scrip, but you lie here in luxury, while we die there in disease. Look to it, man, look to it! A reckoning day is at hand as sure as the same God is over us all!"

"The man is mad and murderous!" cried the affrighted chaplain. "Take him away."

Not waiting for his order to be executed, the spick-and-span wearer of the unsoiled surplice disappeared into one of the side rooms of the court.

This extraordinary scene might have resulted in a yet more rigorous treatment of the prisoners, but it produced the opposite effect. Within the same hour Ralph and Sim were removed from Doomsdale and imprisoned in a room high up in the Donjon tower.

Their new abode was in every way more tolerable than the old one. It had no fire, and it enjoyed the questionable benefit of being constantly filled with nearly all the smoke of every fire beneath it. The dense clouds escaped in part through a hole in the wall where a stone had been disturbed. This aperture also served the less desirable purpose of admitting the rain and the wind.

Here the days were passed. They were few and short. Doomsdale itself could not have made them long.

With his long streaky hair hanging wild about his temples, Sim sat hour after hour on a low bench beneath the window, crying at intervals that God would not let them die.

CHAPTER XLVI

The Skein Unravelled

It was Thursday when they were condemned, and the sentence was to be carried into effect on the Thursday following. Saturday, Sunday, and Monday passed by without any event of consequence. On Tuesday the under gaoler opened the door of their prison, and the sheriff entered. Ralph stepped out face to face with him. Sim crept closer into the shadow.

"The King's warrant has arrived," he said abruptly.

"And is this all you come to tell us?" said Ralph, no less curtly.

"Ray, there is no love between you and me, and we need dissemble none."

"And no hate – at least on my part," Ralph added.

"I had good earnest of your affections," answered the sheriff with a sneer; "five years' imprisonment." Then waving his hand with a gesture indicative of impatience, he continued, "Let that be as it may. I come to talk of other matters."

Resting on a bench, he added, –

"When the trial closed on Thursday, Justice Hide, who showed you more favor than seemed to some persons of credit to be meet and seemly, beckoned me to the antechamber. There he explained that the evidence against you being mainly circumstantial, the sentence might perchance, by the leniency of the King, be commuted to one of imprisonment for life."

A cold smile passed over Ralph's face.

"But this great mercy – whereof I would counsel you to cherish no certain hope – would depend upon your being able and willing to render an account of how you came by the document – the warrant for your own arrest – which was found upon your person. Furnish a credible story of how you came to be possessed, of that instrument, and it may occur – I say it *may* occur – that by our Sovereign's grace and favor this sentence of death can yet be put aside."

Sim had risen to his feet in obvious excitement.

Ralph calmly shook his head.

"I neither will nor can," he said emphatically.

Sim sank back into his seat.

A look of surprise in the sheriff's face quickly gave way to a look of content and satisfaction.

"We know each other of old, and I say there is no love between us," he observed, "but it is by no doing of mine that you are here. Nevertheless, your response to this merciful tender shows but too plainly how well you merit your position."

"It took you five days to bring it – this merciful tender, as you term it," said Ralph.

"The King is now at Newcastle, and there at this moment is also Justice Hide, in whom, had you been an innocent man, you must have found an earnest sponsor. I bid you good day."

The sheriff rose, and, bowing to the prisoner with a ridiculous affectation of mingled deference and superiority, he stepped to the door.

"Stop," said Ralph: "you say we know each other of old. That is false! To this hour you have never known, nor do you know now, why I stand here condemned to die, and doomed by a harder fate to take the life of this innocent old man. You have never known me: no, nor yourself neither – never! But you shall know both before you leave this room. Sit down."

"I have no time to waste in idle disputation," said the sheriff testily; but he sat down, nevertheless, at his prisoner's bidding, as meekly as if the positions had been reversed.

"That scar across your brow." said Ralph, "you have carried since the day I have now to speak of."

"You know it well," said the sheriff bitterly. "You have cause to know it."

"I have," Ralph answered.

After a pause, in which he was catching the thread of a story half forgotten, he continued: "You said I supplanted you in your captaincy. Pehaps so; perhaps not. God will judge between us. You went over to the Royalist camp, and you were among the garrison that had reduced this very castle. The troops of the Parliament came up one day and summoned you to surrender. The only answer your general gave us was to order the tunnel guns to fire on the white flag. It went down. We lay entrenched about you for six days. Then you sent out a dispatch assuring us that your garrison was well prepared for a siege, and that nothing would prevail with you to open your gates. That was a lie!"

"Well?"

"Your general lied; the man who carried your general's dispatch was a liar too, but he told the truth for a bribe."

"Ah! then the saints were not above warming the palm?"

"He assured our commander we might expect a mutiny in your city if we continued before it one day longer; that your castle was garrisoned only by a handful of horse, and two raw, undisciplined regiments of militia; that even from these desertions occurred hourly, and that some of your companies were left with only a score of men. This was at night, and we were under an order to break up next morning. That order was countermanded. Your messenger was sent back the richer by twenty pounds."

"How does this concern me?" asked the sheriff.

"You shall hear. I had been on the outposts that night, and, returning to the camp, I surprised two men robbing, beating, and, as I thought, murdering a third. One of the vagabonds escaped undetected, but with a blow from the butt of my musket which he will carry to his grave. The other I thrashed on the spot. He was the bailiff Scroope, whom you put up to witness against me. Their victim was the messenger from the castle, and he was James Wilson, otherwise Wilson Garth. You know this? No? Then listen. Rumor of his treachery, and of the price he had been paid for it, had already been bruited abroad, and the two scoundrels had gone out to waylay and rob him. He was lamed in the struggle and faint from loss of blood. I took him back and bound up his wound. He limped to the end of his life."

"Still I fail to see how this touches myself," interrupted the sheriff.

"Really? I shall show you. Next morning, under cover of a thick fog, we besieged the city. We got beneath your guns and against your gates before we were seen. Then a company of horse came out to us. *You* were there. You remember it? Yes? At one moment we came within four yards. I saw you struck down and reel out of the saddle. 'This man,' I thought, 'believes in his heart that I did him a grievous wrong. I shall now do him a signal service, though he never hear of it until the Judgment Day.' I dismounted, lifted you up, bound a kerchief about your head, and was about to replace you on your horse. At that instant a musket-shot struck the poor beast, and it fell dead. At the same instant one of our own men fell, and his riderless horse was prancing away. I caught it, threw you on to its back, turned his head towards the castle, and drove it hard among your troops. Do you know what happened next?"

"Happened next – " repeated the sheriff mechanically, with astonishment written on every feature of his face.

"No, you were insensible," continued Ralph. "At that luckless moment the drum beat to arms in a regiment of foot behind us. The horse knew the call and answered it. Wheeling about, it carried you into the heart of our own camp. There you were known, tried as a deserter, and imprisoned. Perhaps it was natural that you should set down your ill fortune to me."

The sheriff's eyes were riveted on Ralph's face, and for a time he seemed incapable of speech.

"Is this truth?" he asked at length.

"God's truth," Ralph answered.

"The kerchief – what color was it?"

"Yellow."

"Any name or mark on it? I have it to this day."

"None – wait; there was a rose pricked out in worsted on one corner."

The sheriff got up, with lips compressed and wide eyes. He made for the door, and pulled at it with wasted violence. It was opened from the other side by the under gaoler, and the sheriff rushed out.

Without turning to the right or left, he went direct to the common gaol. There, in the cell which Ralph had occupied between the first trial and the second one, Mark Garth, the perjurer, lay imprisoned.

"You hell-hound," cried the sheriff, grasping him by the hair and dragging him into the middle of the floor. "I have found out your devilish treachery," he said, speaking between gusts of breath. "Did you not tell me that it was Ray who struck me this blow – this" (beating with his palm the scar on his brow)? "It was a lie – a damned lie!"

"It was," said the man, glaring back, with eyes afire with fury.

"And did you not say it was Ray who carried me into their camp – an insensible prisoner?"

"That was a lie also," the man gasped, never struggling to release himself from the grip that held him on the floor.

"And did you not set me on to compass the death of this man, but for whom I should now myself be dead?"

"You speak with marvellous accuracy, Master Lawson," returned the perjurer.

The sheriff looked down at him for a moment, and then flung him away.

"Man, man! do you know what you have done?" he cried in an altered tone. "You have charged my soul with your loathsome crime."

The perjurer curled his lip.

"It was *I* who gave you that blow," he said, with a cruel smile, pointing with his thin finger at the sheriff's forehead. It was false.

"You devil!" cried the sheriff, "and you have killed the man who saved your brother's life, and consorted with one of two who would have been his murderers."

"I was myself the second," said the man, with fiendish calmness. It was the truth. "I carry the proof of it here," he added, touching a place at the back of his head where the hair, being shorn away, disclosed a deep mark.

The sheriff staggered back with frenzied eyes and dilated nostrils. His breast heaved; he seemed unable to catch his breath.

The man looked at him with a mocking smile struggling over clinched teeth. As if a reptile had crossed his path, Wilfrey Lawson turned about and passed out without another word.

He returned to the castle and ascended the Donjon tower.

"Tell me how you became possessed of the warrant," he said. "Tell me, I beg of you, for my soul's sake as well as for your life's sake."

Ralph shook his head.

"It is not even yet too late. I shall take horse instantly for Newcastle."

Sim had crept up, and, standing behind Ralph, was plucking at his jerkin.

Ralph turned about and looked wistfully into the old man's face. For an instant his purpose wavered.

"For the love of God," cried the sheriff, "for your own life's sake, for this poor man's sake, by all that is near and dear to both, I charge you, if you are an innocent man, give me the means to prove you such."

But again Ralph shook his head.

"Then you are resolved to die?"

"Yes! But for my old friend here – save him if you will and can."

"You will give me no word as to the warrant?"

"None."

"Then all is over."

But going at once to the stables in the courtyard, he called to a stableman, –

"Saddle a horse and bring it round to my quarters in half an hour."

In less time than that Wilfrey Lawson was riding hard towards Newcastle.

CHAPTER XLVII

The Black Camel at the Gate

Next morning after Rotha's struggle with Mrs. Garth at the bridge, the rumor passed through Wythburn that the plague was in the district. Since the advent of the new preachers the people had seen the dreaded scourge dangling from the sleeve of every stranger who came from the fearsome world without. They had watched for the fatal symptoms: they had waited for them: they had invited them. Every breeze seemed to be freighted with the plague wind; every harmless ailment seemed to be the epidemic itself.

Not faith in the will of God, not belief in destiny, not fortitude or fatalism, not unselfishness or devil-may-care indifference, had saved the people from the haunting dread of being mown down by the unseen and insidious foe.

And now in very truth the plague seemed to have reached their doors. It was at the cottage by the smithy. Rumor said that Mrs. Garth had brought it with her from Carlisle, but it was her son who was stricken down.

The blacksmith had returned home soon after Rotha had left him. His mother was there, and she talked to him of what she had heard of the plague. This was in order to divert his attention from the subject that she knew to be uppermost in his thoughts – the trial, and what had come of it. She succeeded but too well.

Garth listened in silence, and then slunk off doggedly to the smithy.

"I'm scarce well enough for work to-day," he said, coming back in half an hour.

His mother drew the settle to the fire, and fixed the cushions that he might lie and rest.

But no rest was to be his. He went back to the anvil and worked till the perspiration dripped from his forehead. Then he returned to the house.

"My mouth is parched to-day, somehow," he said; "did you say a parched mouth was a sign?"

"Shaf, lad! thou'rt hot wi' thy wark."

Garth went back once more to the smithy, and, writhing under the torture of suspense, he worked until the very clothes he wore were moist to the surface. Then he went into the house again.

"How my brain throbs!" he said; "surely you said the throbbing brain was a sign, mother; and my brain *does* throb."

"Tut, tut! it's nobbut some maggot thou's gitten intil it."

"My pulse, too, it gallops, mother. You said the galloping pulse was a sign. Don't say you did not. I'm sure of it, I'm sure of it; and *my* pulse gallops. I could bear the parched mouth and the throbbing brain if this pulse did not run so fast."

"Get away wi' thee, thou dummel-heed. What fagot has got hold on thy fancy now?"

There was only the swollen gland wanted to make the dread symptoms complete.

Garth went back to the anvil once more. His eyes rolled in his head. They grew as red as the iron that he was welding. He swore at the boy who helped him, and struck him fiercely. He shouted frantically, and flung away the hammer at every third blow. The boy slunk off, and went home affrighted. At a sudden impulse, Garth tore away the shirt from his breast, and thrust his left hand beneath his right arm. With that the suspense was ended. A mood of the deepest sadness and dejection supervened. Shuddering in every limb beneath all his perspiration, the blacksmith returned for the last time to the house.

"I wouldn't mind the parched mouth and the throbbing brain; no, nor the galloping pulse, mother; but oh, mother, mother, the gland, it's swelled; ey, ey, it's swelled. I'm doomed, I'm doomed. No use saying no. I'm a dead man, that's the truth, that's the truth, mother."

And then the disease, whether plague or other fever, passed its fiery hand over the throbbing brain of the blacksmith, and he was put to bed raving.

Little Betsy, like the boy in the smithy, stole away to her own home with ghastly stories of the blacksmith's illness and delirium.

At first the neighbors came to inquire, prompted partly by curiosity, but mainly by fear. Mrs. Garth shut the door, and refused to open it to any comers.

To enforce seclusion was not long a necessity. Desertion was soon the portion of the Garths, mother and son. More swift than a bad name passed the terrible conviction among the people at Wythburn that at last, at long last, the plague, the plague itself, was in their midst.

The smithy cottage stood by the bridge, and to reach the market town by the road it was necessary to pass it within five yards. Pitiful, indeed, were the artifices to escape contagion resorted to by some who professed the largest faith in the will of God. They condemned themselves to imprisonment within their own houses, or abandoned their visits to Gaskarth, or made a circuit of a mile across the breast of a hill, in order to avoid coming within range of the proscribed dwelling.

After three days of rumor and surmise, there was not a soul in the district would go within fifty yards of the house that was believed to hold the pestilence. No doctor approached it, for none had been summoned. The people who brought provisions left them in the road outside, and hailed the inmates. Mrs. Garth sat alone with her stricken son, and if there had been eyes to see her there in her solitude and desolation, perhaps the woman who seemed hard as flint to the world was softening in her sorrow. When the delirium passed away, and Garth lay conscious, but still feverish, his mother was bewailing their desertion.

"None come nigh to us, Joey, none come nigh. That's what the worth of neighbors is, my lad. They'd leave us to die, both on us; they'd leave us alone to die, and none wad come nigh."

"Alone, mother! Did you say alone?" asked Garth.

"We're not alone, mother. Some one *has* come nigh to us."

Mrs. Garth looked up amazed, and half turned in her seat to glance watchfully around.

"Mother," said Garth, "did you ever pray?"

"Hod thy tongue, lad, hod thy tongue," said Mrs. Garth, with a whimper.

"Did you ever pray, mother?" repeated Garth, his red eyes aflame, and his voice cracking in his throat. "Whisht, Joey, whisht!"

"Mother, we've not lived over well, you and I; but maybe God would forgive us, after all."

"Hod thy tongue, my lad; do, now, do."

Mrs. Garth fumbled with the bedclothes, and tucked them about the sufferer.

Her son turned his face full upon hers, and their eyes met.

"Dunnet look at me like that," she said, trying to escape his gaze. "What's comin' ower thee, my lad, that thou looks so, and talks so?"

"What's coming over me, mother? Shall I tell thee? It's Death that's coming over me; that's what it is, mother – Death!"

"Dunnet say that, Joey."

The old woman threw her apron over her head and sobbed.

Garth looked at her, with never a tear in his wide eyes.

"Mother," said the poor fellow again in his weak, cracked voice, – "mother, did you ever pray?"

Mrs. Garth uncovered her head. Her furrowed face was wet. She rocked herself and moaned.

"Ey, lad, I mind that I did when I was a wee bit of a girl. I had rosy cheeks then, and my own auld mother wad kiss me then. Ey, it's true. We went to church on a Sunday mornin' and all the bells ringin'. Ey, I mind that, but it's a wa', wa' off, my lad, it's a wa', wa' off."

The day was gaunt and dreary. Toward nightfall the wind arose, and sometimes its dismal wail seemed to run around the house. The river, too, now swollen and turbulent, that flowed beneath the neighboring bridge, added its voice of lamentation as it wandered on and on to the ocean far away.

In the blacksmith's cottage another wanderer was journeying yet faster to a more distant ocean. The darkness closed in. Garth was tossing on his bed. His mother was rocking herself at his side. All else was still.

Then a step was heard on the shingle without, and a knock came to the door. The blacksmith struggled to lift his head and listen. Mrs. Garth paused in her rocking and ceased to moan.

"Who ever is it?" whispered Garth.

"Let them stay where they are, whoever it be," his mother mumbled, never shifting from her seat. The knock came again.

"Nay, mother, nay; it is too late to – "

He had said no more when the latch was lifted, and Rotha Stagg walked into the room.

"I've come to help to nurse you, if you please," she said, addressing the sick man.

Garth looked steadily at her for a moment, every feature quivering. Shame, fear, horror – any sentiment but welcome – was written on his face. Then he straggled to twist his poor helpless body away; his head, at least, he turned from her to the wall.

"It wad look better of folk if they'd wait till they're axt," muttered Mrs. Garth, with downcast eyes.

Rotha unpinned the shawls that had wrapped her from the cold, and threw them over a chair. She stirred the fire and made it burn brightly; there was no other light in the room. The counterpane, which had been dragged away in the restlessness of the sufferer, she spread afresh. Reaching over the bed, she raised the sick man's head tenderly on her arm while she beat out his pillow. Never once did he lift his eyes to hers.

Mrs. Garth still rocked herself in her seat. "Folks should wait till they're wanted," she mumbled again; but the words broke down into a stifled sob.

345

Rotha lit a candle that stood at hand, went to the cupboard in the corner of the adjoining kitchen, and took out a jar of barley; then to the hearth and took up a saucepan. In two minutes she was boiling something on the fire.

Mrs. Garth was following every movement with watchful eyes.

Presently the girl came to the bedside again with a basin in her hand.

"Take a little of this, Mr. Garth," she said. "Your mouth is parched."

"How did you know that?" he muttered, lifting his eyes at last.

She made no reply, but held her cool hand to his burning forehead. He motioned to her to draw it away. She did so.

"It's not safe – it's not safe for you, girl," he said in his thin whisper, his breath coming and going between every word.

She smiled, put back her hand and brushed the dank hair from his moist brow.

Mrs. Garth got up from her seat by the bedside and hobbled to the fire. There she sat on a low stool, and threw her apron over her head.

Again raising the blacksmith from his pillow, Rotha put a spoonful of barley-water to his withered lips. He was more docile than a child now, and let her have her will.

For a moment he looked at her with melancholy eyes, and then, shifting his gaze, he said, –

"You had troubles enow of your own, Rotha, without coming to share ours – mother's and mine."

"Yes," she answered, and a shadow crossed the cheerful face.

"Will they banish him?" he said with quick-coming breath. "Mother says so; will they banish him from the country?"

"Yes, perhaps; but it will be to another and a better country," said Rotha, and dropped her head.

Garth glanced inquiringly into her face. His mother shifted on her stool.

"How, how?" he said, nervously clutching at the bedclothes.

"Why do you bother him, girl?" said Mrs. Garth, turning about. "Rest thee, my lad, rest thee still."

"Mother," said Garth, drawing back his head, but never shifting the determination of his gaze from Rotha's face, "what does she mean?"

"Haud thy tongue, Joey."

"What does she mean, mother?"

"Whisht! Never heed folks that meddle afore they're axt."

Mrs. Garth spoke peevishly, rose from her seat, and walked between Rotha and the bed.

Garth's wide eyes were still riveted on the girl's face.

"Never mind that she's not asked," he said; "but what does she mean, mother? What lie is it that she comes to tell us!"

"No lie, Mr. Garth," said Rotha, with tearful eyes. "Ralph and father are condemned to die, and they are innocent."

"Tush! get away wi' thee!" mumbled Mrs. Garth, brushing the girl aside with her elbow. The blacksmith glared at her, and seemed to gasp for breath.

"It *is* a lie; mother, tell her it *is* a lie."

"God knows it is not," cried Rotha passionately.

"Say I believed it," said Garth, rising convulsively on one elbow, with a ghastly stare; "say I believed that the idiots had condemned them to death for a crime they never committed – never; say I believed it – but it's a lie, that's what it is. Girl, girl, how can you come with a lie on your lips to a poor dying man? Cruel! cruel! Have you no pity, none, for a wretched dying man?"

The tears rolled down Rotha's cheeks. Mrs. Garth returned to her stool, and rocked herself and moaned.

The blacksmith glared from one to the other, the sweat standing in heavy beads on his forehead.

Then an awful scream burst from his lips. His face was horribly distorted.

"It is true," he cried, and fell back and rolled on the bed.

All that night the fiery hand lay on the blacksmith's brain, and he tossed in a wild delirium.

The wind's wail ran round the house, and the voice of that brother wanderer, the river beneath the bridge crept over the silence when the sufferer lay quiet and the wind was still.

No candle was now lighted, but the fire on the hearth burnt bright. Mrs. Garth sat before it, hardly once glancing up.

Again and again her son cried to her with the yearning cry of a little child. At such times the old woman would shrink within herself, and moan and cower over the fire, and smoke a little black pipe.

Hour after hour the blacksmith rolled in his bed in a madness too terrible to record. The memory of his blasphemies seemed to come back upon him in his raving, and add fresh agony to his despair.

A naked soul stood face to face with the last reality, battling meantime, with an unseen foe. There was to be no jugglery now.

Oh! that awful night, that void night, that night of the wind's wail and the dismal moan of the wandering river, and the frequent cry of a poor, miserable, desolate, despairing, naked soul! Had its black wings settled forever over all the earth?

No. The dawn came at last. Its faint streak of light crept lazily in at the curtainless window.

Then Garth raised himself in his bed.

"Give me paper – paper and a pen – quick, quick!" he cried.

"What would you write, Joe?" said Rotha.

"I want to write to him – to Ralph – Ralph Ray," he said, in a voice quite unlike his own.

Rotha ran to the chest in the kitchen and opened it. In a side shelf pens were there and paper too. She came back, and put them before the sick man.

But he was unconscious of what she had done.

She looked into his face. His eyes seemed not to see.

"The paper and pen!" he cried again, yet more eagerly.

She put the quill into his hand and spread the paper before him.

"What writing is this," he cried, pointing to the white sheet; "this writing in red?"

"Where?"

"Here – everywhere."

The pen dropped from his nerveless fingers.

"To think they will take a dying man!" he said. "You would scarce think they would have the heart, these people. You would scarce think it, would you?" he said, lifting his poor glassy eyes to Rotha's face.

"Perhaps they don't know," she answered soothingly, and tried to replace him on his pillow.

"That's true," he muttered; "perhaps they don't know how ill I am."

At that instant he caught sight of his mother's ill-shapen figure cowering over the fire. Clutching Rotha's arm with one hand, he pointed at his mother with the other, and said, with an access of strength, –

"I've found her out; I've found her out."

Then he laughed till it seemed to Rotha that the blood stood still in her heart.

When the full flood of daylight streamed into the little room, Garth had sunk into a deep sleep.

CHAPTER XLVIII

"Out, Out, Brief Candle"

As the clock struck eight Rotha drew her shawls about her shoulders and hurried up the road.

At the turning of the lonnin to Shoulthwaite she met Willy Ray. "I was coming to meet you," he said, approaching.

"Come no closer," said Rotha, thrusting out the palm of one hand; "you know where I've been – there, that is near enough."

"Nonsense, Rotha!" said Willy, stepping up to her and putting a hand on her arm. There was confidence in the touch.

"To-morrow is the day," Willy added, in an altered tone. "I am leaving for Carlisle at noon – that is, in four hours."

"Could you not wait four hours longer?" said Rotha.

"I could if you wish it; but why?"

"I don't know – that is, I can't say – but wait until four o'clock, I beg of you."

The girl spoke with deep earnestness.

"I shall wait," said Willy, after a pause.

"And you'll meet me at the bridge by the smithy?" said Rotha.

Willy nodded assent.

"At four precisely," he said.

"This is all I came to ask. I must go back."

"Rotha, a word: what is your interest in these Garths? Does it concern your father and Ralph?"

"I'll tell you at the bridge," said Rotha, sidling off.

"Every one is aghast at your going," he said.

"I have better reasons than any one knows of," she replied.

"And better faith, and a nobler heart," he added feelingly as he turned his head away.

Garth was still asleep when she got back to the cottage. A feeble gleam of winter sunshine came languidly through the little window. It fell across the bed and lit up the blue eyelids and discolored lips of the troubled sleeper.

The fire had smouldered out. Only a charred bough and a damp clod of peat lay black among the gray ashes on the hearth.

As Rotha re-entered Mrs. Garth got up from the stool on which she had sat the long night through. There was a strange look on her face. During the heavy hours she had revolved within herself a dark problem which to her was unsolvable, and the puzzle was still printed on her face. Drawing the girl aside, she said in a grating whisper, –

"Tell me, do ye think it's reet what the lad says?"

"About Ralph and father?" asked Rotha.

"Tush! about hissel'. Do ye think he'll die?"

Rotha dropped her head.

"Tell me: do ye think so?"

Rotha was still silent. Mrs. Garth looked searchingly into her face, and in answer to the unuttered reply, she whispered vehemently, –

"It's a lie. He'll be back at his anvil to-morrow. Why do you come wi' yer pale face to me? Crying? What's it for? tell me!"

And the old woman shook the girl roughly by the shoulders.

Rotha made no response. The puzzled expression on Mrs. Garth's face deepened at that instant, but as she turned aside she muttered again, with every accent of determination, –

"He'll be back at his anvil to-morrow, that he will."

The blacksmith awoke as serene as a child. When he looked at Rotha his hard, drawn face softened to the poor semblance of a smile. Then a shadow crossed it, and once more he turned his head to the wall.

And now to Rotha the hours went by with flying feet. Every hour of them was as precious to her as her heart's blood. How few were the hours of morning! The thing which above all she came here to do was not being done. A dull dead misery seemed to sit cold on her soul.

Rotha tended the sufferer with anxious care, and when the fitful sleep slid over him, she sat motionless with folded hands, and gazed through the window. All was still, sombre, chill, and dreary. The wind had slackened; the river ran smoother. In a field across the valley a woman was picking potatoes. No other human creature was visible.

Thus the hours wore on. At one moment Garth awoke with a troubled look, and glanced watchfully around. His mother was sitting in her accustomed seat, apparently asleep. He clutched at Rotha's gown, and made a motion to her to come closer. She did so, a poor breath of hope fluttering in her breast. But just then Mrs. Garth shifted in her seat, and faced about towards them. The blacksmith drew back his hand, and dropped his half-lifted head.

Towards noon Mrs. Garth got up and left the bedroom. Her son had appeared to be asleep but he was alert to every movement. Again he plucked Rotha's gown, and essayed to speak. But Mrs. Garth returned in a moment, and not a word was said.

Rotha's spirits flagged. It was as though she were crawling hour after hour towards a gleam of hope that fled farther and farther away.

The darkness was gathering in, yet nothing was done. Then the clock struck four, and Rotha drew on her shawl once more, and walked to the bridge.

Willy was there, a saddled horse by his side.

"You look jaded and out of heart, Rotha," he said.

"Can you stay four hours longer?" she asked.

"Until eight o'clock? It will make the night ride cold and long," he answered.

"True, but you can stay until eight, can you not?"

"You know why I go. God knows it is not to be present at that last scene of all: that will be soon after daybreak."

"You want to see him again. Yes; but stay until eight o'clock. I would not make an idle request, Willy. No, not at a solemn hour like this."

"I shall stay," he said.

The girl's grief-worn face left no doubt in his mind of her purpose. They parted.

When Rotha re-entered the sick-room a candle was burning on a table by the bedside. Mrs. Garth still crouched before the fire. The blacksmith was awake. As he lifted his eyes to Rotha's face, the girl saw that they wore the same watchful and troubled expression as before.

"Shall I read to you, Mr. Garth?" she asked, taking down from a shelf near the rafters a big leather-bound book. It was a Bible, dust-covered and with rusty clasps, which had lain untouched for years.

"Rotha," said Garth, "read to me where it tells of sins that are as scarlet being washed whiter nor wool."

The girl found the place. She read aloud in the rich, soft voice that was like the sigh of the wind through the long grass. The words might have brought solace to another man. The girl's voice might have rested on the ear as a cool hand rests on a throbbing brow. But neither words nor voice brought peace to Garth. His soul seemed to heave like a sea lashed by a storm.

At length he reached out a feeble hand and touched the hand of the girl.

"I have a sin that is red as scarlet," he said. But before he could say more, his mother had roused herself and turned to him with what Rotha perceived to be a look of warning.

354

It was plainly evident that but for Mrs. Garth, the blacksmith would make that confession which she wished above all else to hear.

Then Rotha read again. She read of the prodigal son, and of Him who would not condemn the woman that was a sinner. It was a solemn and terrible moment. The fathomless depths of the girl's voice, breaking once and again to a low wail, then rising to a piercing cry, went with the words themselves like an arrow to the heart of the dying man. Still no peace came to him. Chill was the inmost chamber of his soul; no fire was kindled there. His face was veiled in a troubled seriousness, when, at a pause in the reading, he said, –

"There can be no rest for me, Rotha, till I tell you something that lies like iron at my heart."

"Whisht thee, lad; whisht thee and sleep. Thou'rt safe to be well to-morrow," said Mrs. Garth in a peevish whimper.

"Mother, mother," cried Garth aloud in a piteous tone of appeal and remonstrance, "when, when will you see me as I am?"

"Tush, lad! thou'rt mending fast. Thou'rt safe to be at thy fire to-morrow."

"Ey, mother," replied the blacksmith, lifting himself feebly and glaring at her now with a fierce light in his eyes, – "eh, mother, but it will be the everlasting fire if I'm to die with this black sin heavy on my soul."

In spite of her self-deception, the woman's mind had long been busy with its own secret agony, and at these words from her son the rigid wrinkles of her face relaxed, and she turned her head once more aside.

Rotha felt that the moment had at length arrived. She must speak now or never. The one hope for two innocent men who were to die as soon as the world woke again to daylight lay in this moment.

"Mr. Garth," she began falteringly, "if a sin lies heavy on your soul, it is better to tell God of it and cast yourself on the mercy of our Heavenly Father."

Gathering strength, the girl continued: "And if it is a dark secret that touches others than yourself – if others may suffer, or are suffering, from it even now – if this is so, I pray of you, as you hope for that

Divine mercy, confess it now, confess it before it is too late – fling it forth from your stifled heart – do not bury its dead body there, and leave it to be revealed only at that judgment when every human deed, be it never so secret, shall be stripped naked before the Lord, that retribution may be measured out for ever and ever."

Rotha had risen to her feet, and was leaning over the bed with one hand in an attitude of acutest pain, convulsively clutching the hand of the blacksmith.

"Oh, I implore you," she continued, "speak out what is in your heart for your own sake, as well as the sake of others. Do not lose these precious moments. Be true! be true at last! at last! Then let it be with you as God shall order. Do not carry this sin to the eternal judgment. Blessed, a thousand times blessed, will be the outpouring of a contrite heart. God will hear it."

Garth looked into the girl's inspired face.

"I don't see my way clearly," he said. "I'm same as a man that gropes nigh midway through yon passage underground at Legberthwaite. The light behind me grows dimmer, dimmer, dimmer, and not yet comes the gleam of the light in front. I'm not at the darkest; no, I'm not."

"A guest is knocking at your heart, Mr. Garth. Will you open to him?" Then, in another tone, she added: "To-morrow at daybreak two men will die in Carlisle – my father and Ralph Ray – and they are innocent!"

"Ey, it's true," said the blacksmith, breaking down at length.

Then struggling once more to lift himself in bed, he cried, "Mother, tell her *I* did it, and not Ralph. Tell them all that it was I myself who did it. Tell them I was driven to it, as God is my judge."

The old woman jumped up, and, putting her face close to her son's, she whispered, –

"Thou madman! What wadsta say?"

"Mother, dear mother, my mother," he cried, "think of what you would do; think of me standing, as I must soon stand – very soon – before God's face with this black crime on my soul. Let me cast it off from me forever. Do not tempt me to hide it! Rotha, pray with her; pray that she will not let me stand before God thus miserably burthened, thus red as scarlet with a foul, foul sin!"

Garth's breath was coming and going like a tempest. It was a terrible moment. Rotha flung herself on her knees. She had not been used to pray, but the words gushed from her.

"Dear Father in heaven," she prayed, "soften the hearts of all of us here in this solemn hour. Let us remember our everlasting souls. Let us not barter them for the poor comforts of this brief life. Father, thou readest all hearts. No secret so secret, none so closely hidden from all men's eyes, but Thou seest it and canst touch it with a finger of fire. Help us here to reveal our sins to Thee. If we have sinned deeply, forgive us in Thy heavenly mercy; in Thy infinite goodness grant us peace. Let Thy angel hover over us even now, even now, now."

And the angel of the Lord was indeed with them in that little cottage among the desolate hills.

Rotha rose up and turned to Garth.

"Under the shadow of death," she said, "tell me, I implore you, how and when you committed the crime for which father and Ralph are condemned to die to-morrow."

Mrs. Garth had returned once more to her seat. The blacksmith's strength was failing him. His agitation had nigh exhausted him. Tears were now in his eyes, and when he spoke in a feeble whisper, a sob was in his throat.

"He was my father," he said, "God forgive me – Wilson was my father – and he left us to starve, mother and me; and when he came back to us here we thought Ralph Ray had brought him to rob us of the little that we had." "God forgive me, too," said Mrs. Garth, "but that was wrong."

"Wrong?" inquired the blacksmith.

"Ey, it came out at the trial," muttered his mother.

Garth seemed overcome by a fresh flood of feeling. Rotha lifted a basin of barley-water to his lips.

"Yes, yes; but how was it done – how?"

"He did not die where they threw him – Ralph – Angus – whoever it was – he got up some while after and staggered to this house – he said Ray had thrown him and he was hurt – Ray, that was all. He wanted to come in and rest, but I flung the door in his face and he fell. Then he got up, and shrieked out something – it was something against myself; he called me a bastard, that's the fact. Then it was as if a hand behind me pushed me on. I opened the door and struck him. I didn't know that I had a hammer in my hand, but I had. He fell dead."

"Well, well, what next?"

"Nothing – yes – late the same night I carried him back to where I thought he had come from – and that's all!"

The little strength Garth had left was wellnigh spent.

"Would you sign a paper saying this?" asked Rotha, bending over him.

"Ey, if there would be any good in it."

"It might save the lives of father and Ralph; but your mother would need to witness it."

"She will do that for me," said Garth feebly. "It will be the last thing I'll ask of her. She will go herself and witness it."

"Ey, ey," sobbed the broken woman, who rocked herself before the fire.

Rotha took the pen and paper, and wrote, in a hand that betrayed her emotion, –

"This is to say that I, Joseph Garth, being near my end, yet knowing well the nature of my act, do confess to having committed the crime of killing the man known as James Wilson, for whose death Ralph Ray and Simeon Stagg stand condemned."

"Can you sign it now, Joe?" asked Rotha, as tenderly as eagerly.

Garth nodded assent. He was lifted to a sitting position. Rotha spread the paper before him, and then supported him from behind with her arms.

He took the pen in his graspless hand, and essayed to write. Oh, the agony of that effort! How every futile stroke of that pen went to the girl's heart like a stab of remorse! The name was signed at length, and in some sorry fashion. The dying man was restored to his pillow.

Peace came to him there and then.

The clock struck eight.

Rotha hurried out of the house and down the road to the bridge. The moon had just broken over a ridge of black cloud. It was bitterly cold.

Willy Ray stood with his horse at the appointed place.

"How agitated you are, Rotha; you tremble like an aspen," he said. "And where are your shawls?"

"Look at this paper," she said. "You can scarce see to read it here; but it is a confession. It states that it was poor Joe Garth who committed the murder for which father and Ralph are condemned to die at daybreak."

"At last! Thank God!" exclaimed Willy.

"Take it – put it in your breast – keep it safe as you value your eternal soul – ride to Carlisle as fast as your horse will carry you, and place it instantly before the sheriff."

"Is it signed?"

"Yes."

"And witnessed?"

"The witness will follow in person – a few hours – a very few – and she will be with you there."

"Rotha, God has put it into your heart to do this thing, and He has given you more than the strength of a strong man!"

"In how many hours might one ride to Carlisle at the fastest – in the night and in a cart?" asked the girl eagerly.

"Five, perhaps, if one knew every inch of the way."

"Then, before you set out, drive round to Armboth, and ask Mr. Jackson to bring his wagon across to this bridge at midnight. Let him not say 'No' as he hopes for his salvation! And now, good bye again, and God speed you on your journey!"

Willy carried a cloak over his arm. He was throwing it across Rotha's unprotected shoulders.

"No, no," she said, "you need it yourself. I shall be back in a minute."

And she was gone almost before he was aware.

Willy was turning away when he heard a step behind. It was the Reverend Nicholas Stevens, lantern in hand, lighting himself home from a coming-of-age celebration at Smeathwaite. As he approached, Willy stepped up to him.

"Stop," cried the parson, "was she who parted from you but now the daughter of the man Simeon Stagg?"

"The same," Willy answered.

"And she comes from the home of the infected blacksmith?"

"She is there again, even now," said Willy. "I thought you might wish to take the solace of religion to a dying man – Garth is dying."

"Back – away – do not touch me – let me pass," whispered the parson in an accent of dread, shrinking meantime from the murderous stab of the cloak which Willy carried over his arm.

Rotha was in the cottage once again almost before she had been missed.

Joe was dozing fitfully. His mother was sighing and whimpering in turns. Her wrinkled face, no longer rigid, was a distressing spectacle. When Rotha came close to her she whispered, –

"The lad was wrang, but I dare not have telt 'im so. Yon man were none of a father to Joe, though he were my husband, mair's the pity."

Then getting up, glancing nervously at her son, lifting a knife from the table, creeping to the side of the bed and ripping a hole in the ticking, she drew out a soiled and crumpled paper.

"Look you, lass, I took this frae the man's trunk when he lodged wi' yer father and yersel' at Fornside."

It was a copy of the register of Joe's birth, showing that he was the son of a father unknown.

"I knew he must have it. He always threatened that he'd get it. He wad have made mischief wi' it somehow."

Mrs. Garth spoke in whispers, but her voice broke her son's restless sleep. Garth was sinking fast, but he looked quieter when his eyes opened again. "I think God has forgiven me my great crime," he said calmly, "for the sake of the merciful Saviour, who would not condemn the woman that was a sinner."

Then he crooned over the Quaker hymn, –

> Though your sins be red as scarlet,
> He shall wash them white as wool.

Infinitely touching was it to hear his poor, feeble, broken voice spend its last strength so.

"Sing to me, Rotha," he said, pausing for breath.

"Yes, Joe. What shall I sing?"

"Sing 'O Lord, my God,'" he answered. And then, over the murmuring voice of the river, above the low wail of the rising wind, the girl's sweet, solemn voice, deep with tenderness and tears, sang the simple old hymn, –

> O Lord, my God,
> A broken heart
> Is all my part:
> Spare not Thy rod,
> That I may prove
> Therein Thy love.

"Ey, ey," repeated Garth, "a broken heart is *all* my part."

Very tremulous was the voice of the singer as she sang, –

> O Lord, my God,
> Or ere I die,
> And silent lie
> Beneath the sod,
> Do Thou make whole
> This bruisèd soul.

"This bruised soul," murmured the blacksmith.

Rotha had stopped, and buried her face in her hands.

"There's another verse, Rotha; there's another verse."

But the singer could sing no more. Then the dying man himself sang in his feeble voice, and with panting breath, –

> Dear Lord, my God –
> Weary and worn,
> Bleeding and torn –
> Spare now Thy rod.
> Sorely distressed –
> Lord, give me rest.

There was a bright light in his eyes. And surely victory was his at last. The burden was cast off forever. "Lord, give me rest," he murmured again, and the tongue that uttered the prayer spoke no more.

Rotha took his hand. His pulse sank – slower, slower, slower. His end was like the going out of a lamp – down, down, down – then a fitful flicker – and then –

Death, the merciful mediator; Death, the Just Judge; Death, the righter of the wronged; Death was here – here!

Mrs. Garth's grief was uncontrollable. The hard woman was as nerveless as a baby now. Yet it was not at first that she would accept the evidence of her senses. Reaching over the bed, she half raised the body in her arms.

"Why, he's dead, my boy he's dead!" she cried. "Tell me he's not dead, though he lies sa still."

Rotha drew her away, and, stooping, she kissed the cold wasted whitened lips.

At midnight a covered cart drove up to the cottage by the smithy. John Jackson was on the seat outside. Rotha and Mrs. Garth got into it. Then they started away.

As they crossed the bridge and turned the angle of the road that shut out the sight of the darkened house they had left, the two women turned their heads towards it and their hearts sank within them as they thought of him whom they left behind. Then they wept together.

CHAPTER XLIX

Peace, Peace, and Rest

In Carlisle the time of the end was drawing near. Throughout the death-day of the blacksmith at Wythburn the two men who were to die for his crime on the morrow sat together in their cell in the Donjon tower.

Ralph was as calm as before, and yet more cheerful. The time of atonement was at hand. The ransom was about to be paid. To break the hard fate of a life, of many lives, he had come to die, and death was here!

Bent and feeble, white as his smock, and with staring eyes, Sim continued to protest that God would not let them die at this time and in this place.

"If He does," he said, "then it is not true what they have told us, that God watches over all!"

"What is that you are saying, old friend?" returned Ralph. "Death comes to every one. The black camel kneels at the gate of all. If it came to some here and some there, then it would be awful indeed."

"But to die before our time is terrible, it is," said Sim.

"Before our time – what time?" said Ralph. "To-day or to-morrow – who shall say which is your time or mine?"

"Aye, but to die like this!" said Sim, and rocked himself in his seat.

"And is it not true that a short death is the sovereign good hap of life?"

"The shame of it – the shame of it," Sim muttered.

"That touches us not at all," said Ralph. "Only the guilty can feel the shame of a shameful death. No, no; death is kindest. And yet, and yet, old friend, I half repent me of my resolve. The fatal warrant, which has been the principal witness against us, was preserved in the sole hope that one day it might serve you in good stead. For your sake, and yours only, would to God that I might say where I came by it and when!"

"No, no, no," cried Sim, with a sudden access of resolution; "I *am* the guilty man after all, and it is but justice that *I* should die. But that *you* should die also – you that are as innocent as the babe unborn – God will never look down on it, I tell you. God will never witness it; never, never!"

At that moment the organ of the chapel of the castle burst on the ear. It was playing for afternoon service. Then the voices of the choir came, droned and drowsed and blurred, across the green and through the thick walls of the tower. The sacred harmonies swept up to them in their cell as the intoned Litanies sweep down a long cathedral aisle to those who stand under the sky at its porch. Deep, rich, full, pure, and solemn. The voice of peace, peace, and rest.

The two men shut their eyes and listened.

In that world on which they had turned their backs men were struggling, men were fighting, men's souls were being torn by passion. In that world to which their faces were set no haunting, hurrying footsteps ever fell; no soul was yet vexed by fierce fire, no dross of budded hope was yet laid low. All was rest and peace.

The gaoler knocked. A visitor was here to see Ralph. He had secured the permission of the under sheriff to see him for half an hour alone.

Sim rose, and prepared to follow the gaoler.

"No," said Ralph, motioning him back; "it is too late for secrets to come between you and me. He must stay," he added, turning to the gaoler.

A moment later Robbie Anderson entered. He was deeply moved.

"I was ill and insensible at the time of the trial," he said.

Then he told the long story of his fruitless quest.

"My evidence might have saved you," he said. "Is it yet too late?"

"Yes, it is too late," said Ralph.

"I think I could say where the warrant came from."

"Robbie, remember the vow you took never to speak of this matter again."

At mention of the warrant, Sim had once more crept up eagerly. Ralph saw that the hope of escape still clung to him. Would that muddy imperfection remain with him to the last?

"Robbie, if you ever had any feeling for me as a friend and comrade, let this thing lie forever undiscovered in your mind."

Unable to speak, the young dalesman bent his head.

"As for Sim, it wounds me to the soul. But for myself, what have I now to live for? Nothing. I tried to save the land to my mother and brother. How is she?"

"Something better, as I heard."

"Poor mother! And – Rotha – is she – "

"She is well."

"Thank God! Perhaps when these sad events are long gone by, and have faded away into a dim memory, perhaps then she will be happy in my brother's love."

"Willy?" said Robbie, with look and accent of surprise.

Then there was a pause.

"She has been an angel," said Robbie feelingly.

"Better than that – she has been a woman; God bless and keep her!" said Ralph.

Robbie glanced into Ralph's face; tears stood in his eyes.

Sim sat and moaned.

"My poor little Rotie," he mumbled. "My poor little lost Rotie!"

The days of her childhood had flowed back to him. She was a child once more in his memory.

"Robbie," said Ralph, "since we have been here one strange passage has befallen me, and I believe it is real and not the effect of a disturbed fancy."

"What is it, Ralph?" said Robbie.

"The first night after we were shut up in this place, I thought in the darkness, being fully awake, that one opened the door. I turned my head, thinking it must be the gaoler. But when I looked it was Rotha. She had a sweet smile on her dear face. It was a smile of hope and cheer. Last night, again, I was awakened by Sim crying in his sleep – the strange, shrill, tearless night-cry that freezes the blood of the listener. Then I lay an hour awake. Again I thought that one opened the door. I looked to see Rotha. It was she. I believe she was sent to us in the spirit as a messenger of peace and hope – hope of that better world which we are soon to reach."

The gaoler knocked. Robbie's time had expired. "How short these last moments seem!" said Ralph; "yet an eternity of last moments would be brief. Farewell, my lad! God bless you!"

The dalesmen shook hands. Their eyes were averted.

Robbie took his leave with many tears.

Then rose again the voices of the unseen choir within the chapel. The organ pealed out in loud flute tones that mounted like a lark, higher, higher, higher, winging its way in the clear morning air. It was the chant of a returning angel scaling heaven. Then came the long sweeps of a more solem harmony. Peace, peace! And rest! And rest!

CHAPTER L

Next Morning

Next morning at daybreak the hammering of the carpenters had ceased in the Market Place, and their lamps, that burned dim in their sockets, like lights across a misty sea, were one by one put out. Draped in black, the ghastly thing that they had built during the night stood between the turrets of the guard-house.

Already the townspeople were awake. People were hurrying to and fro. Many were entering the houses that looked on to the market. They were eager to secure their points of vantage from which to view that morning's spectacle.

The light came slowly. It was a frosty morning. At seven o'clock a thin vapor hung in the air and waved to and fro like a veil. It blurred the face of the houses, softened their sharp outlines, and seemed at some moments to carry them away into the distance. The sun rose soft and white as an autumn moon behind a scarf of cloud.

At half past seven the Market Place was thronged. On every inch of the ground, on every balcony, in every window, over every portico, along the roofs of the houses north, south, east, and west, clinging to the chimney-stacks, hanging high up on the pyramidical turrets of the guard-house itself, astride the arms of the old cross, peering from between the battlements of the cathedral tower and the musket lancets of the castle, were crowded, huddled, piled, the spectators of that morning's tragedy.

What a motley throng! Some in yellow and red, some in black; men, women, and children lifted shoulder-high. Some with pale faces and bloodshot eyes, some with rubicund complexion and laughing lips, some bantering as if at a fair, some on the ground hailing their fellows on the roofs. What a spectacle were they in themselves!

There at the northeast of the Market Place, between Scotch Street amid English Street, were half a hundred men and boys in blouses, seated on the overhanging roof of the wooden shambles. They were shouting sorry jests at half a dozen hoydenish women who looked out of the windows of a building raised on pillars over a well, known as Carnaby's Folly.

On the roof of the guard-house stood five or six soldiers in red coats. One fellow, with a pipe between his lips, leaned over the parapet to kiss his hand to a little romping serving-wench who giggled at him from behind a curtain in a house opposite. There was an open carriage in the very heart of that throng below. Seated within it was a stately gentleman with a gray peaked beard, and dressed in black velvet cloak and doublet, having lace collar and ruffles; and side by side with him was a delicate young maiden muffled to the throat in fur. The morning was bitterly cold, but even this frail flower of humanity had been drawn forth by the business that was now at hand. Where is she now, and what?

A spectacle indeed, and for the eye of the mind a spectacle no less various than for the bodily organ.

Bosoms seared and foul and sick with uncleanliness. Hearts bound in the fetters of crime. Hot passions broken loose. Discord rampant. Some that smote the breast nightly in the anguish of remorse. Some that knew not where to hide from the eye of conscience the secret sin that corroded the soul.

Lonely, utterly lonely, in this dense throng were some that shuddered and laughed by turns.

There were blameless men and women, too, drawn by curiosity and by another and stronger magnet that they knew of. How would the condemned meet their end? Would it be with craven timidity or with the intrepidity of heroes, or again with the insensibility of brutes? Death was at hand – the inexorable, the all-powerful. How could mortal man encounter it face to face? This was the great problem then; it is the great problem now.

Two men were to be executed at eight that morning. Again and again the people turned to look at the clock. It hung by the side of the dial in the cupola of the old Town Hall. How slowly moved its tardy figures! God forgive them, there were those in that crowd who would have helped forward, if they could, its passionless pulse. And a few minutes more or fewer in this world or the next, of what account were they in the great audit of men who were doomed to die?

In a room of the guard-house the condemned sat together. They had been brought from the castle in the night.

"We shall fight our last battle to-day," said Ralph. "The enemy will take our camp, but, God willing, we shall have the victory. Never lower the flag. Cheer up! Keep a brave heart! A few swift minutes more, and all will be well!"

Sim was crouching at a fire, wringing his lean hands or clutching his long gray hair.

"Ralph, it shall never be! God will never see it done!"

"Put away the thought," replied Ralph. "God has brought us here."

Sim jumped to his feet and cried, "Then I will never witness it – never!"

Ralph put his hand gently but firmly on Sim's arm and drew him back to his seat.

The sound of singing came from without, mingled with laughter and jeers.

"Hark!" cried Sim, "hearken to them again; nay, hark!"

Sim put his head aside and listened. Then, leaping up, he shouted yet more wildly than before, "No, no! never, never!"

Ralph took him once more by the arm, and the poor worn creature sank into his seat with a low wail.

There was commotion in the corridors and chief chamber of the guard-house.

"Where is the sheriff?" was the question asked on every hand.

Willy Ray was there, and had been for hours closeted with the sheriff's assistant.

"Here is the confession duly signed," he said for the fiftieth time, as he walked nervously to and fro.

"No use, none. Without the King's pardon or reprieve, the thing must be done."

"But the witnesses will be with us within the hour. Put it back but one little hour and they must be here."

"Impossible. We hold the King's warrant, and must obey it to the letter."

"God in heaven! Do you not see yourself, do you not think that if this thing is done, two innocent men will die?"

"It is not for me to think. My part is to act."

"Where is your chief? Can you go on without him?"

"We can and must."

The clock in the Market Place registered ten minutes to eight. A pale-faced man in the crowd started a hymn.

"Stop his mouth," cried a voice from the roof of the shambles, "the Quaker rascal!" And the men in blouses started a catch. But the singing continued; others joined in it, and soon it swelled to a long wave of song and flowed over that human sea.

But the clock was striking, and before its last bell had ceased to ring, between the lines of the hymn, a window of the guard-house was thrown open and a number of men stepped out.

In a moment the vast concourse was hushed to the stillness of death.

"Where is Wilfrey Lawson?" whispered one.

The sheriff was not there. The under sheriff and a burly fellow in black were standing side by side.

Among those who were near to the scaffold on the ground in front of it was one we know. Robbie Anderson had tramped the Market Place the long night through. He had not been able to tear himself from the spot. His eye was the first to catch sight of two men who came behind the chaplain. One of these walked with a firm step, a broad-breasted man, with an upturned face. Supported on his arm the other staggered along, his head on his breast, his hair whiter, and his step feebler than of old. Necks were craned forward to catch a glimpse of them.

"This is terrible," Sim whispered.

"Only a minute more, and it will be over," answered Ralph.

Sim burst into tears that shook his whole frame.

"Bravely, old friend," Ralph said, melted himself, despite his words of cheer. "One minute, and we shall meet again. Bravely, then, and fear not."

Sim was struggling to regain composure. He succeeded. His tears were gone, but a wild look came into his face. Ralph dreaded this more than tears.

"Be quiet, Sim," he whispered; "be still, and say no word."

The under sheriff approached Ralph.

"Have you any statement to make?" he said.

"None."

"Nor you?" said the officer, turning to Ralph's companion.

Sim was trying to overcome his emotion.

"He has nothing to say," said Ralph quietly. Then he whispered again in Sim's ear, "Bravely."

Removing his arm from Sim's convulsive grasp, he threw off his long coat. At that moment the bleared sun lit up his lifted face. There was a hush of awe.

Then, with a frantic gesture, Sim sprang forward, and seizing the arm of the under sheriff, he cried hysterically, –

"Ay, but I *have* something to say. He is innocent – take me back and let me prove it – he is innocent – it's true – it's true – I say it's true – let me prove it."

With a face charged with sorrow, Ralph walked to Sim and said, "One moment more and we had clasped hands in heaven."

But now there was a movement at the back. The sheriff himself was seen stepping from the window to the scaffold. He was followed by Willy Ray and John Jackson. Two women stood together behind, Rotha and Mrs. Garth.

Willy came forward and fell on his brother's neck.

"God has had mercy upon us," he cried, amid a flood of tears.

Ralph looked amazed. The sheriff said something to him which he did not hear. The words were inaudible to the crowd, but the quick sympathy of the great heart of the people caught the unheard message.

"A reprieve! a reprieve!" shouted fifty voices.

A woman fainted at the window behind. It was Rotha.

The two men were led off with staring eyes. They walked like men in a dream.

Saved! saved! saved!

Then there went up a mighty shout. It was one vast voice, more loud than the blast on the mountains, more deep than the roar of the sea!

CHAPTER LI

Six Months After

It was the height of a Cumbrian summer. Bracken Mere was as smooth as a sheet of glass. The hills were green, gray, and purple to the summits, and their clear outlines stood out against the sky. The sky itself would have been cloudless but for one long scarf of plaited white which wore away across a lake of blue. The ghyll fell like a furled flag. The thin river under the clustering leaves sang beneath its breath. The sun was hot and the air was drowsed by the hum of insects.

And full of happy people was the meadow between the old house on the Moss and the pack-horse road in front of it. It was the day of the Wythburn sports, and this year it was being celebrated at Shoulthwaite. Tents had been pitched here and there in out-of-the-way corners of the field, and Mrs. Branthwaite, with her meek face, was appointed chief mistress and dispenser of the hospitality of the Shoulthwaite household.

"This is not taty-and-point," said her husband, with a twinkle in his eyes and a sensation of liquidity about the lips as he came up to survey the outspread tables.

Mattha Branthwaite was once more resplendent in those Chapel-Sunday garments with which, in the perversity of the old weaver's unorthodox heart, that auspicious day was not often honored. Mrs. Ray had been carried out in her chair by her stalwart sons. Her dear old face looked more mellow and peaceful than before. Folks said the paralysis was passing away. Mattha himself, who never at any time took a melancholy view of his old neighbor's seizure, stands by her chair to-day and fires off his sapient saws at her with the certainty that she appreciates every saw of them.

"The dame's to the fore yit," he says, "and lang will be."

At Mrs. Ray's feet her son Willy lies on the grass in a blue jerkin and broad-brimmed black hat with a plume. Willy's face is of the type on which trouble tells. Behind him, and leaning on the gate that leads from the court to the meadow, is Ralph, in a loose jacket with deep collar and a straw hat. He looks years younger than when we saw him last. He is just now laughing heartily at a batch of the schoolmaster's scholars who are casting lots close at hand. One bullet-headed little fellow has picked up a couple of pebbles, and after putting them through some unseen and mysterious manoeuvres behind him, is holding them out in his two little fists, saying, –

> Neevy, neevy nack,
> Whether hand will ta tack –
> T' topmer or t' lowmer?

"What hantle of gibberish is that?" says Monsey Laman himself.

"*I* is to tumble the poppenoddles," cries the bullet-headed gentleman. And presently the rustic young gamester is tossing somersets for a penny.

In the middle of the meadow, and encircled by a little crowd of excited male spectators, two men are trying a fall at wrestling. Stripped to the waist, they are treating each other to somewhat demonstrative embraces.

At a few yards' distance another little circle, of more symmetrical outlines, and comprising both sexes, are standing with linked hands. A shame-faced young maiden is carrying a little cushion around her companions. They are playing the "cushion game."

At one corner of the field there is a thicket overgrown with wild roses, white and red. Robbie Anderson, who has just escaped from a rebellious gang of lads who have been climbing on his shoulders and clinging to his legs, is trying to persuade Liza Branthwaite that there is something curious and wonderful lying hidden within this flowery ambush.

"It's terrible nice," he says, rather indefinitely. "Come, lass, come and see."

Liza refuses plump.

The truth is that Liza has a shrewd suspicion that the penalty of acquiescence would be a kiss. Now, she has no particular aversion to that kind of commerce, but since Robbie is so eager, she has resolved, like a true woman, that his appetite shall be whetted by a temporary disappointment.

"Not I," she says, with arms akimbo and a rippling laugh of knowing mockery. Presently her sprightly little feet are tripping away.

Still encircled by half a score of dogs, Robbie returns to the middle of the meadow, where the wrestlers have given way to some who are preparing for a race up the fell. Robbie throws off his coat and cap, and straps a belt about his waist.

"Why, what's this?" inquires Liza, coming up at the moment, with mischief in her eyes, and bantering her sweetheart with roguish jeers. "*You* going to run! Why, you are only a bit of a boy, you know. How can *you* expect to win?"

"Just you wait and see, little lass," says Robbie, with undisturbed good humor.

"You'll slidder all the way down the fell, sure enough," saves Liza.

"All right; just you get a cabbish-skrunt poultice ready for my broken shins," says Robbie.

"I would scarce venture if I were you," continues Liza, to the vast amusement of the bystanders. "Wait till you're a man, Robbie."

The competitors – there are six of them – are now stationed; the signal is given, and away they go.

The fell is High Seat, and it is steep and rugged. The first to round the "man" at the summit and reach the meadow again wins the prize.

Over stones, across streams, tearing through thickets, through belts of trees – look how they go! Now they are lost to the sight of the spectators below; now they are seen, and now they are hidden; now three of the six emerge near the top.

The excitement in the field is at full pitch. Liza is beside herself with anxiety.

"It's Robbie – no, yes – no – egg him on, do; te-lick; te-smack."

One man has rounded the summit, and two others follow him neck-and-neck. They are coming down, jumping, leaping, flying. They're here, here, and it is – yes, it *is* Robbie that leads!

"Well done! Splendid! Twelve minutes! Well done! Weel, weel, I oles do say 'at ye hev a lang stroke o' the grund, Robbie," says Mattha.

"And what do *you* say?" says Robbie, panting, and pulling on his coat as he turns to Liza, who is trying to look absent and unconcerned.

"Ay! Did you speak to me? I say that perhaps you didn't go round the 'man' at all. You were always a bit of a cheat, you know."

"Then here goes for cheating you." Robbie had caught Liza about the waist, and was drawing her to that rose-covered thicket. She found he was holding her tight. He was monstrously strong. What ever *was* the good of trying to get away?

Two elderly women were amused spectators of Liza's ineffectual struggles.

"I suppose you know they are to be wedded," said one.

"I suppose so," rejoined the other; "and I hear that Ralph is to let a bit of land to Robbie; he has given him a horse, I'm told."

Matthew Branthwaite had returned to his station by Mrs. Ray's chair.

"Whear's Rotha?" says the old weaver.

"She said she would come and bring her father," said Willy from the grass, where he still lay at his mother's feet.

"It was bad manishment, my lad, to let the lass gang off agen with Sim to yon Fornside."

Mattha is speaking with an insinuating smile.

"Could ye not keep her here? Out upon tha for a good to nowt."

Willy makes no reply to the weaver's banter.

At that moment Rotha and her father are seen to enter the meadow by a gate at the lower end.

Ralph steps forward and welcomes the new-comers.

Sim has aged fast these last six months, but he is brighter looking and more composed. The dalespeople have tried hard to make up to him for their former injustice. He receives their conciliatory attentions with a somewhat too palpable effort at cordiality, but he is only less timid than before.

Ralph leads Rotha to a vacant chair near to where his mother sits.

"A blithe heart maks a blooming look," says Mattha to the girl. Rotha's face deserves the compliment. To-day it looks as fresh as it is always beautiful. But there is something in it now that we have never before observed. The long dark lashes half hide and half reveal a tenderer light than has hitherto stolen into those deep brown eyes. The general expression of the girl's face is not of laughter nor yet of tears, but of that indescribable something that lies between these two, when, after a world of sadness, the heart is glad – the sunshine of an April day.

"This seems like the sunny side of the hedge at last, Rotha," says Ralph, standing by her side, twirling his straw hat on one hand.

There is some bustle in their vicinity. The schoolmaster, who prides himself on having the fleetest foot in the district, has undertaken to catch a rabbit. Trial of speed is made, and he succeeds in two hundred yards.

"Theer's none to match the laal limber Frenchman," says Mattha, "for catching owte frae a rabbit to a slap ower the lug at auld Nicky Stevens's."

"Ha! ha! ha!" laughs Reuben Thwaite, rather boisterously, as he comes up in time to hear the weaver's conceit.

"There's one thing I never caught yet, Master Reuben," says Monsey.

"And what is it?" says the little blink-eyed dalesman.

"A ghost on a lime-and-mould heap!"

"Ha! ha! ha! He's got a lad's heart the laal man has," says Mattha, with the manner of a man who is conscious that he is making an original observation.

And now the sun declines between the Noddle Fell and Bleaberry. The sports are over, but not yet is the day's pleasure done. When darkness has fallen over meadow and mountain the kitchen of the house on the Moss is alive with bright faces. The young women of Wythburn have brought their spinning-wheels, and they sit together and make some pretence to spin. The young men are outside. The old folks are in another room with Mrs. Ray.

Presently a pebble is heard to crack against the window pane.

"What ever can it be?" says one of the maidens with an air of profound amazement.

One venturesome damsel goes to the door "Why, it's a young man!" she says, with overpowering astonishment.

The unexpected creature enters the kitchen, followed by a longish line of similar apparitions. They seat themselves on the table, on the skemmels, on the stools between the spinners – anywhere, everywhere.

What sport ensues! what story-telling! what laughing! what singing!

Ralph comes downstairs, and is hailed with welcomes on all hands. He is called upon for a song. Yes, he can sing. He always sang in the old days. He must sing now.

"I'll sing you something I heard in Lancaster," he says.

"What about – the Lancashire witches?"

"Who writ it – little Monsey?"

"No, but a bigger man than Monsey," said Ralph with a smile.

"He *would* be a mite if he were no bigger than the schoolmaster," put in that lady of majestic stature, Liza Branthwaite.

Then Ralph sang in his deep baritone, "Fear no more the heat o' the sun."

And the click of the spinning-wheels seemed to keep time to the slow measure of the fine old song.

Laddie, the collie, was there. He lay at Ralph's feet with a solemn face. He was clearly thinking out the grave problems attaching to the place of dogs on this universe.

"Didn't I hear my name awhile ago?" said a voice from behind the door. The head of the speaker emerged presently. It was Monsey Laman. He had been banished with the "old folks."

"Come your ways in, schoolmaster," cried Robbie Anderson. "Who says 'yes' to a bout of play-acting?"

As a good many said "Yes," an armchair was forthwith placed at one corner of the kitchen with its back to the audience. Monsey mounted it. Robbie went out of doors, and, presently re-entering with a countenance of most woeful solemnity, approached the chair, bent on one knee, and began to speak, –

> Oh wad I were a glove upo' yon hand
> 'At I med kiss yon feàce.

A loud burst of laughter rewarded this attempt on the life of the tragic muse. But when the schoolmaster, perched aloft, affecting a peuking voice (a strangely unnecessary artistic effort), said, –

"Art thou not Romeo and a Montague?" and the alleged Romeo on his knees replied, "Nowther, sweet lass, if owther thoo offend," the laughter in the auditorium reached the point of frantic screams. The actors, like wise artists, were obviously indifferent to any question of the kind of impression produced, and went at their task with conscientious ardor.

The little schoolmaster smiled serenely, enchantingly, bewitchingly. Robbie panted and gasped, and sighed and moaned.

"Did you ever see a man in such a case?" said Liza, wiping away the hysterical tears of merriment that coursed down her cheeks.

"Wait a bit," said Robbie, rather stepping out of his character.

It was a part of the "business" of this tragedy, as Robbie had seen it performed in Carlisle, that Romeo should cast a nosegay up into the balcony to Juliet. Robbie had provided himself with the "property" in question, and, pending the moment at which it was necessary to use it, he had deposited it on the floor behind him. But in the fervor of impersonation, he had not observed that Liza had crept up and stolen it away.

"Where's them flowers?" cried Romeo, scarcely *sotto voce*.

When the nosegay was yielded up to the lover on his knees, it was found to be about three times as big as Juliet's head.

The play came to an abrupt conclusion; the spinning-wheels were pushed aside, a fiddle was brought out, and then followed a dance.

"Iverything has a stopping spot but time," said Mattha Branthwaite, coming in, his hat and cloak on.

The night was spent. The party must break up.

The girls drew on their bonnets and shawls, and the young men shouldered the wheels.

A large company were to sail up the mere to the city in the row-boat, and Rotha, Ralph, and Willy walked with them to Water's Head. Sim remained with Mrs. Ray.

What a night it was! The moon was shining at the full from a sky of deep blue that was studded with stars. Not a breath of wind was stirring. The slow beat of the water on the shingle came to the ear over the light lap against the boat. The mere stretched miles away. It seemed to be as still as a white feather on the face of the dead, and to be alive with light. Where the swift but silent current was cut asunder by a rock, the phosphorescent gleams sent up sheets of brightness. The boat, which rolled slowly, half-afloat and half-ashore, was bordered by a fringe of silver. When at one moment a gentle breeze lifted the water into ripples, countless stars floated, down a white waterway from yonder argent moon. Not a house on the banks of the mere; not a sign of life; only the low plash of wavelets on the pebbles. Hark! What cry was that coming clear and shrill? It was the curlew. And when the night bird was gone she left a silence deeper than before.

The citizens, lads and lasses, old men and dames, got into the boat. Robbie Anderson and three other young fellows took the oars.

"We'll row ourselves up in a twinkling," said Liza, as Ralph and Willy pushed the keel off the shingle.

"Hark ye the lass!" cried Mattha. "We hounds slew the hare, quo' the terrier to the cur."

The sage has fired off the last rustic proverb that we shall ever hear from his garrulous old lips.

When they were fairly afloat, and rowing hard up the stream, the girls started a song.

The three who stood together at the Water's Head listened long to the dying voices.

A step on the path broke their trance. It was a lone woman, bent and feeble. She went by them without a word.

The brothers exchanged a look.

"Poor Joe," said Rotha, almost in a whisper.

But the girl's cup of joy could bear this memory. She knew her love at last.

Willy stepped between Rotha and Ralph. He was deeply moved. He was about to yield up the dream of his life. He tried to speak, and stopped. He tried again, and stopped once more. Then he took Rotha's hand and put it into Ralph's, and turned away in silence.

And now these two, long knit together, soul to soul, parted by sorrow, purified by affliction, ennobled by suffering, stand in this white moonlight hand in hand.

Hereafter the past is dead to them, and yet lives. What was sown in sorrow is raised in joy; what was sown in affliction is raised in peace; what was sown in suffering is raised in love.

And thus the tired old world wags on, and true it is to-day as yesterday that WHOM GOD'S HAND RESTS ON HAS GOD AT HIS RIGHT HAND.

THE END.

Lightning Source UK Ltd.
Milton Keynes UK
08 June 2010

9 788132 048718